Forbidden HERO

REDLEG SECURITY

JACKIE WALKER

Editor: Mindy Root
Proofreading by: VB Proofreads
Cover Design: Kate Decided to Design

Disclaimer: The following book is a work of fiction. Names, characters, places, and events included are either the product of the author's imagination or are used fictitiously for entertainment purposes only. Any resemblance to actual people or entities is purely coincidental.

For content/trigger warnings, please visit www.authorjackiewalker.com or scan this QR Code:

❀ Created with Vellum

To everyone who has their own little monsters inside them. Rage monsters, horny monsters, awkward monsters, sad monsters, silly monsters, or sarcastic monsters.
Go crazy. Embrace that shit.

Prologue

SAWYER

I'm insanely attracted to women surrounded in drama like they were dipped in an egg wash and dredged in dramatic breadcrumbs.

Always have been. It's my curse. That's the bad news.

The good news?

I think I was born with some type of drama sonar because I can find that shit anywhere.

Bonus points: women deep-fried in drama tend to be hot as hell and adventurous in bed.

So as for my attraction to women — like all things in my life — I've learned to take the good with the bad.

Considering my relationship history, it makes perfect sense that I'm staring at my best friend's little sister — who's in the middle of a personal crisis — like she's a Little Debbie snack cake, and I'm fresh off a seven-day juice cleanse.

"Get all your stuff, Sammy. You're not coming back here," I tell her.

She shifts back on her heels, dragging a hand through her hair, which is damp from a recent shower and smells way too fucking good.

And I know it does because she attacked me with a huge hug when she saw me standing at her door a few minutes ago, and I couldn't help but sniff her. It wasn't pervy. It just happened. I was merely minding my business, and her scent wafted into my nose uninvited. What did you want me to do... not breathe? I'd die.

I'm rolling my eyes at you so hard right now for wishing death upon me so early in my story.

She eyes the dingy motel room I found her in. "Right. That makes sense."

Scurrying to the closet, she pulls out a duffel bag and starts tossing in her belongings. She's moving quickly and muttering to herself as she works.

I'm trying to avoid checking out her ass. Of course, I'm failing. And failing spectacularly. But someone wiser than me once said it's the thought that counts.

So stop having thoughts about her ass, asshole.

Stepping out of the room, I give the parking lot another quick scan for danger. All clear.

My toe taps with impatience.

Well, it's either that or the six coffees I've had so far today.

Nah. I'm sure it's just the impatience.

Besides, I need at least seven cups of coffee for patience. Yep. All signs point to a classic case of non-caffeine related impatience.

"We should get going. Need any help?"

She pauses and meets my eyes. "No, I don't have much. I had to leave in a hurry."

"When did you get down to Florida?"

After zipping the bag closed, she pulls the strap over her shoulder. "Uh... um. I don't know. A few weeks ago."

Her vague answer sparks a twinge of rage. "You don't know when you got here?"

She puts a hand on her hip and eyes me down. "Not exactly. Excuse the fuck out of me for not marking it on my calendar or having the date engraved on my watch."

She still has that same sassy mouth I remember. My junk twitches.

I try to shake off my inappropriate thoughts about what I'd like to do to her mouth. And once again, I fail miserably.

Stop it, dick. She's Leo's sister. You can't do anything to her mouth.

She brushes past me. "Cocky ass. I'd like to see you escape from that psychopath."

I tamp down the rage her words incite by asking another question as we head to my Redleg Security SUV. "Where have you been all these years?"

"Salida, Colorado. It's a small town a few hours south of Denver."

After taking her duffel from her shoulder, I open the passenger door to usher her inside. As she enters, I notice a scar on her forearm that makes my stomach turn.

If I had made a move on her when I first met her like I wanted to, she might not have ended up with that abusive asshole, and things would be different now. She wouldn't have had to escape him under the cover of night. Her beautiful skin wouldn't be marred like that.

And I'd know how she tastes.

But I can't change the past. It's best to move forward.

"On the way, you can tell me how and why you faked your death." More to myself, I mutter, "Crushing my best friend's heart in the process."

Sammy tilts her head and cuts a stern glare at me. She probably objects to my judgmental tone. But I can't help the way I feel. It's frustrating as hell that I'm as attracted to her now as I was when I last saw her years ago. More importantly, I'm fucking pissed at her for hurting Leo the way she did.

And for hurting me.

She snaps her seatbelt. "It's a long story." Her gaze is downcast, like she's afraid to meet my eyes.

I close her door and check over my shoulder, looking around the parking lot one last time before circling the car to enter.

We're a few minutes into our twenty-minute drive to headquarters when I break the tense silence, trying for lightheartedness. "Five bucks says your brother will shit a solid gold brick when he sees you."

"Leo." She sighs. "How is he?"

My head rolls from side to side, shrugging off the tension. "Umm... he's had good days and bad days since you... uh... died or left or whatever the fuck you want to call it. But these past several days have been interesting."

"Interesting? Like how?"

"He fell for a girl he was guarding several months ago. Her name is Sue O'Malley. Sweet gal from a big Irish family. But it didn't work out. Not sure why since he won't talk about it — even with me. I only know he took it hard and has had a rough time letting her go or moving on."

Her head tilts in my direction as she crosses one leg over the other. I muster all my strength to avoid looking at her svelte thighs.

Eyes on the road, asshole.

"Poor Leo. That really sucks. But how does that relate to what's going on these last few days? And why didn't he come to get me? I was expecting him to show up any day."

"He doesn't know you're alive yet. At the beginning of last week, he got a text from an unknown number threatening Sue — saying they would take her away from Leo and accused him of stealing from them. So he rushed to her side to save her and took her away to his cabin."

"Leo has a cabin?"

There is so much she's out of the loop on. I suppose that makes sense, given she's been presumed dead for more than three years.

Damn. I still can't believe she's alive after all this time.

"Yeah, he owns a house here in Clearwater and has a small cabin by the Ocala National Forest. But that's not important right now."

She puts her head down and fidgets with her hands in her lap. "Sorry. Go on."

The way she's folding in on herself twists my gut. That's not the Sammy I once knew.

With a thickness in my voice at the thought of what she may have suffered these last years, I force a playful vibe. "Anyhoo, he got the threat, took her away, and now they're all lovey-dovey in the cabin while his Redleg family tries to find the fucker who's threatening them. And that's where you come in... you and your fucking boyfriend." I want to spit. Even thinking about him makes me sick.

"And you think it's Craig."

His name puts an acrid taste in my mouth. From the edge of my gaze, I notice her hand raise to protectively cup her throat. My knuckles flash white as I wrap them tighter around the wheel to stop myself from reaching out to comfort her.

"When we get to headquarters, Big Al can show you all the texts, and we'll see what you think. But ever since I figured out you were alive and in town, all signs point to Craig."

"I knew he'd come for me. He'll never let me go." Her voice cracks. "That's why I was hiding out at the damn motel instead of running to my family. I wanted to keep them safe." She sighs and hangs her head. "Dammit. I'll never be free."

The urge to soothe her is more than I can stand. Reaching over, I take both her hands in one of mine to stop them from wringing. A surge of heat travels from her skin to mine and shoots straight to my chest, giving me a jolt. With a quick glance, our eyes meet. Hers widen as her breath catches.

My heart strums loudly in my chest.

Shifting my eyes quickly back to the road, I clear my throat before speaking. "Sammy, listen to me. It's going to be okay. You're safe now. Redleg's got you. *I've* got you. And that asshole's not going to lay another fucking finger on you. I promise. You never have to go back to him. Ever."

She squeezes my hand before breaking free of my hold. "Thank you, Sawyer." After clearing the emotion from her voice, she asks, "What is Redleg?"

I put my hand back on the wheel and heave a sigh. "That's the name of the company we work for. Big Al founded it a few years back. A few other guys from our old Ranger unit are part of the Redleg Security family, along with your brother and me. We provide personal protection and security services. Usually, it's rich assholes and celebrities, but we get the occasional case like yours."

"What do you mean, *like mine*?"

A smile creases my lips, and I try to inject some of my patented charm. "A case where it'll be our fucking pleasure to stop the asshole responsible and save the damsel in distress."

Her spine stiffens, and she crosses her arms. "I'm not a damsel in distress. I can take care of myself."

With a flirty wink, I reply, "Good. 'Cause I'm not attracted to weak women."

Narrowing her eyes at me, she shakes her head almost imperceptibly. "Are you seriously flirting with me right now?"

"I flirt with most beautiful women. Why should you be any different?"

Her blush and quiet chuckle go straight to my dick.

Fuck. I'm in trouble.

"Well, for one, my brother would hang you by your entrails if you tried anything with me. That's assuming he even wants anything to do with me once he finds out what I've done."

"He will. Don't worry about that. This is Lionheart we're talking about. He's got the biggest heart of anyone I know."

"Let's hope so."

"Although he is pretty damn protective of the women he loves. And I do prefer to keep my entrails on the inside."

"And two, because I'm married." Her words are the softest whisper.

But my answer comes out loud as fuck. "*Married?* You *married* that cocksucker? Are you fucking kidding me right now?"

As soon as the words are out of my mouth, I wish I could shove them back in. She flinches and cowers toward the door to the SUV with her shoulders rolled in protectively.

Fuck me and my stupid mouth. I scared her.

This woman just escaped an abusive *husband*, and here I am, raising my voice at her.

Good job, asshole.

"Sorry, Sammy. I didn't mean to yell. I'm just a little shocked that you married that ass clown."

She forces her shoulders to roll back like she's manually infusing the strength into her spine. "It's fine. Sorry. It's just Craig... he yelled a lot."

Mirroring her quiet volume, I say, "Sammy, I'm really sorry. If you married him, I'm sure you had your reasons. I'm not here to judge you. I'm only here to take you to Redleg Headquarters and keep you safe until you reunite with your family."

And after that? I have no fucking idea.

"Sometimes, I have no clue why I married him. Why I left Maine with him and went along with his stupid fake suicide plan. Hell, I don't even remember why I dated him in the first place."

She rests her forehead in her palm. My grip on the wheel tightens once more to keep myself in check. I want to comfort her so damn badly.

I'm usually the fun-loving, good-time guy who doesn't take much of anything seriously. But something about Samantha Mason has always made me a little mushy.

Except my dick.

Sammy makes that thing as hard as steel.

Fucking Superman in my pants the first time I saw her.

Wait a minute. That sounds horrible. I didn't actually have a superhero in my pants.

Then again, my dick is pretty fucking spectacular, so maybe that is what I mean.

Oh, fuck it. Never mind. I'm way off-topic now.

To see if I can lighten her spirits, I try out my fake New York mobster accent on her. "Fuggedaboudit, kid. It ain't nothin'." I snap a few times in quick succession. "Piece of deep-dish pie. We're gonna take that fucker out. Badabing, badaboom. Eh?"

Her answering giggle brings a smile to my face. We finish the next two minutes of the drive in comfortable silence.

When we pull into the parking lot of headquarters, her eyes widen. "Big Al runs this place? It's huge."

"That's what she said," I quip.

She covers her laugh with her hand while shaking her head. I feel like Hercules for cracking her up like that. *Dammit.* This woman is already crawling right back under my skin. Returning to where she implanted herself a decade ago.

When I open her door and offer her my hand, she hesitates briefly before taking it. When she finally does, our eyes meet as she slips out of the vehicle. We stand there, toe to toe and face to face, for a full three seconds. Just staring at each other like we've been smacked with a stupid stick. A whiff of her shampoo hits me, and I force myself to drop her hand.

Shaking it off, I pull away from her. "Welcome to Redleg. Let's get you inside so we can crack the case and bring your brother and his new woman back home."

Her shoulders rise and fall with a deep breath. "Let's do it, Sawyer."

The naughtiest of images flash through my mind. Her, naked on my bed, getting intimately acquainted with the superhero in my pants.

I try to hold the words back, but I can't. I wasn't built that way. "That's also what she said."

She busts out laughing, big and bright as a double rainbow. Her hand lands on my chest as we laugh together in the parking lot.

I can't be certain, but it feels like my whole damn world just tilted on its axis. My head is spinning, my cock is pulsing with need, and my heart is beating out the opening to ABBA's "Take a Chance on Me."

What is happening right now?

All I know is that the very beautiful and extremely off-limits Sammy fucking Mason is back in my life.

And I'm not sure if it will be a good thing or a bad thing. But one thing is for sure... it will be *something*.

A few hours later

Sammy

"Sammy, grab the wheel," Sawyer grunts.

My trembling hand shoots over to grip the steering wheel. The SUV swerves, but I manage to keep us on the road.

Barely.

Thankfully, there was no oncoming traffic, or else it might have been a different story.

Craig was driving, but he's either unconscious or dead, thanks to

Sawyer's handiwork. If I'm being honest, I'd prefer the latter. And maybe that makes me as big a monster as Craig.

My other hand moves to the emergency brake. "Should I pull the brake?"

"No. We'll skid out. Sammy, listen very carefully. With your free hand, unbuckle your seatbelt, then lean over and unbuckle Craig's seatbelt."

The vehicle swerves while I follow his instructions, but I straighten it immediately. Sawyer's tone is so calm and cool, like he didn't just ninja attack my abuser into submission in a matter of two seconds flat. I half expected to see some nunchucks flying or those metal throwing star things piercing the windshield.

He was *that* damn stealthy.

And it all happened so fast. One moment, Craig was bitching at me for making him chase me all the way to Florida. The next, he was out like a light, and Sawyer was giving me instructions.

"Okay. Got it. What now?"

"Very good, Sammy. Now I'm going to pull him out of the driver's seat before we crash. When I do, you're going to slide behind the wheel and take over. Got it?"

I nod silently, feeling too stunned to speak.

Hell, I'm still processing everything that's happened tonight. A few hours ago, I was hiding out at a motel in Clearwater, trying to figure out my next move to stay one step ahead of my abusive husband. Then Sawyer was at my door — someone I haven't seen in years — telling me we need to leave and go help my brother.

Just a few minutes ago, we found Craig attacking Leo, his girlfriend, and another bodyguard at Leo's cabin in the woods. Craig had come after them to get to me. He always promised he'd find me if I ever left, and in a way, I guess he did.

But I wasn't alone this time. I had Sawyer and his Redleg team.

Now that Craig isn't a direct threat, my thoughts go back to the scene at the cabin. I hope they're all okay. I'll never forgive myself if someone is seriously hurt or worse because of me. Leo and his girlfriend looked okay — a little banged up — but the other guy was bleeding badly from a gunshot wound.

A shiver rolls down my spine when I think of all the blood everywhere. I still don't have any idea how I managed to keep my composure and follow the plan to lure Craig away. I told him we'd go back home, and everything would be as it was before. And he foolishly believed me.

Like a hidden hero, Sawyer concealed himself in the back of the SUV, and when the moment was right, he attacked Craig from behind.

Sawyer counts down from three, shaking me from the replay running through my mind.

When he gets to one, he hefts Craig's body out of the driver's seat. I slide over as instructed. The SUV bumps along when I hit the shoulder of the road, but I quickly straighten it as soon as I'm fully in the driver's seat.

Grunts and heavy breaths come from the back seat, but I focus on the road.

I haven't driven a vehicle in over three years. Craig never let me go anywhere without him. The wheel feels foreign in my hands. I'm not sure how, but my heart rate spikes even faster than it was.

After calming myself with deep breathing, I realize I don't know where I'm supposed to be driving to.

"What do I do now? Should I pull over? Turn around? Find a police station?"

"Can you turn around and take us back to the cabin?"

Nodding, I mash my foot down on the brakes and prepare for a U-turn. I must hit the brakes too hard because we jerk to a rough stop. That's when the adrenaline rush hits me. My eyes go hazy with tears, and I'm shaking too much to drive safely, so I shift into park. With my head on the wheel, all I can do is quiver, breathe, and cry.

I cry and cry.

Is my nightmare finally over? Can it be that easy?

Chancing a peek over my shoulder, I see Craig has regained consciousness, but only slightly.

Dammit. He's still alive.

So my nightmare *isn't* over.

Am I a bad person for wishing he were dead?

He's bleeding from the temple, his nose is crooked, and Sawyer has his hands bound and is working on his legs and knees.

Craig's eyes meet mine, and my heart stops. He's furious with me. The hatred and vitriol I see there are enough to make my gut wretch. I open the door and empty the contents of my stomach onto the side of the road.

From over my shoulder, I hear the car door slam and footsteps approaching. I can only assume it's Sawyer, unless Craig managed to overpower him silently while tied up.

Not likely.

Sawyer was extremely competent in his movements, and I feel safe with him.

Safe.

What an unusual feeling. It's one I haven't had much in my life before now.

A large palm runs up and down my spine as I suck in a deep breath.

Sawyer whispers softly over my shoulder, "It's okay, Sammy. Let it out. It's all over now. You're safe. You don't have to be scared again."

When the nausea subsides, I stand and wipe my face with my shirt sleeve.

Our eyes meet as he reaches up to graze my cheek with his thumb, wiping a tear away. He stays at my side, comforting me. Soothing me.

Eventually, he takes me in his arms, wrapping me up in his warmth.

Safe. All I feel is safe. After all this time.

His heat seeps through my clothes and pierces straight to my solar plexus.

To be held like this, with kindness and safety, is a powerful balm, creeping into the cracks of my soul.

I had no idea how much I missed the feel of a gentle, loving touch.

We stay like that for a long time. It could be seconds, minutes, or hours.

Time doesn't matter right now. Because for the first time in years, I feel safe.

Chapter One

40% CHANCE OF COFFEE SHOWERS

Two years later

Sammy

My jaw drops to my chest. "You're kidding, right? A smash house?"

Jaynie's dimples pop with playfulness as she waggles her brows. I don't see this side of her much. "I've heard it can be extremely therapeutic for trauma survivors. You've come a long way since our first session. Maybe smashing some stuff will help you deal with your residual anger."

I feel my eyes narrow with skepticism.

"What can it hurt, Sammy?"

My gaze searches the ceiling while I try to process my therapist's random advice. This woman is something else — in a good way.

When people think of therapy, they often imagine lying on a couch and talking about their childhood while someone takes precarious notes on a yellow legal pad and keeps asking, "And how does that make you feel?"

But that's not what therapy is like with Jaynie. Not even close.

This lady is a trip, and everything about her is unique.

She's older and often kicks back in a reclining chair with her feet up. She typically has a few pencils sticking out of her wild, curly hair; it gives her a mad scientist look that I find endearing. While she's quick with a joke, she also manages to be comforting and warm. In a way, she reminds me of a badass grandma. The kind who rides motorcycles on the weekends and throws back wine by the box full.

You know, like the classiest wine drinkers do. We do love a good *Cardboardeaux*.

In the year and a half I've been seeing her, she's had me do some crazy shit.

Let's see. She's had me jumping up and down in her office, waving my hands around like a sports fan gone wild. We went outside and screamed into the wind together like feral creatures. That was fun. I've written angry letters to both my father and Craig. She even let me mail one to Craig in jail.

Side note: I hope he rots there forever. That fuck nugget.

When my soon-to-be sister-in-law, Sue, recommended her therapist, I wasn't entirely sure it made sense. I assumed she specialized in anxiety, ADHD, or autism — all things Sue has. Whereas my issue is a little different.

I'm a rage monster.

In fact, sometimes I hear an actual angry voice inside me. Telling me to smash shit, get stabby, or throat punch someone. Is that weird?

Probably.

In the wake of fleeing my abusive relationship, a lot has happened. Initially, I cried a lot. Every day. It was primarily from the guilt I carried for hurting my family with my disappearing act. We've worked through that for the most part, though.

I was a little jumpy the first few months PC — post-Craig — and suffered from the occasional panic attack. Especially at night. That was all to be expected, given everything I'd been through.

But I healed. *Mostly.*

I filed for a divorce with a side order of the restraining variety — just in case he ever gets out of jail. Knowing him, it's entirely possible.

After moving in with my mother and reconnecting with my family, my anxiety is virtually non-existent. I sleep like a baby, and I don't drink to excess or do anything risky. I'm not sexually promiscuous — quite the opposite, actually, since the thought of being intimate with someone makes me feel a little queasy.

All in all, things are going fairly well for me.

Except for this motherfucking anger.

I wear it like a second skin.

Every time I think about what Craig took from me — what I *let* him take — my blood pressure spikes, my face turns red, and my fists clench like the Arthur's fist meme. They're practically aching to punch something.

I suppose that's why Jaynie is suggesting I go to this type of activity center. One where the whole point is breaking shit.

"I guess it can't hurt anything," I reply thoughtfully.

And really... what could it hurt? Assuming I have on protective gear, it's probably a safe activity.

Maybe it will be fun. I smile and nod. "Okay, I'll do it."

Jaynie claps her hands once. "Good! Who are you going to bring with you?"

"You don't want to come?"

She smiles warmly. "I think this is something you can do without me. My old busted back wouldn't like me slinging around an ax or a sledgehammer."

"Good point," I concede while thinking about who I could convince to come with me.

I know who I *want* to ask.

Sawyer.

But I really shouldn't spend any extra time with him. He's already taken up permanent residence in my dreams — sexy and otherwise.

As much as being intimate with someone nauseates me, something about Sawyer revs my hormonal engine.

Hanging out with him more than I already do is just tempting fate. I can't go there. Not now. Not with him. Among other reasons, my brother would have a coronary.

"Glad that's decided. Okay... moving on. When we last spoke, you were telling me about some work-related stress. Talk to me about that, and let's see what we can do to help you cope."

My eyes roll so hard at the thought of my stupid, crummy job that I'm lucky they don't get stuck facing backward.

Work? Gross.

Not a fun topic, but I guess it needs to happen. Not all our appointments are exercises in releasing pent-up anger. We do talk about my feelings, but even that doesn't go how I would have expected. She doesn't simply ask leading questions, hoping I'll draw my own conclusions. Jaynie helps me interpret my feelings, making insightful observations that make me think back on my life. Best of all, I end up feeling less like a victim and more like a survivor.

And dammit. That's what I want to be.

A survivor.

The long-lost member of Destiny's Child.

Hell, she's even taught me how to meditate. Surprisingly, I enjoy it and do it before bed each night. It seems to keep the nightmares at bay.

Maybe if I open up about my job stress, she can help me figure out how to handle it better. I can't keep breaking glasses in the dishwashing room when no one is looking. That's not an appropriate coping mechanism.

"Well, Jaynie. Work just plain old sucks. I still can't believe I'm thirty-two years old and waitressing. At a bar, no less. It's pathetic." My volume rises the more I talk. "It's bad enough I still live with my mother, but cocktail waitressing? It's miles away from where I thought I'd be in my career by this age. And the customers. *Ugh*. Don't get me started on the handsy freaking customers." My fist pounds into my thighs a few times. "If I get ass-grabbed one more time, I'm going to use that move Leo showed me to break a fucker's wrist."

"I see you're getting worked up. Let's take a calming breath before we continue."

Shit. See what I mean?

Total fucking rage monster.

Jaynie leads me through guided breathing, and it helps calm me down.

"Now that you're calm, I want to circle back to the inappropriate harassment in the workplace. Customers should *not* be grabbing you like that. Have you talked to your manager about it?"

"Of course, but it doesn't help. He can't possibly kick out every customer who gets a little too familiar after a few cocktails. It's a bar, and don't forget, I work for tips."

Jaynie's lips press into a hard line, showcasing her disapproval of my blasé response. "Sammy, there is no advice I can give you to make you like this job. And given the way you're being treated, I highly recommend you find something else. Plus, like we've discussed before, *you* must take the first step if you want your situation to change."

My lip quirks on one side. "By breaking a wrist or two?"

Her eyes narrow. "Deflect with humor all you want. That's fine for now. But I'm serious. You have employable skills, and there is no reason you can't get back to your career in software development. Or you can apply anywhere you won't be treated inappropriately."

My shoulders hunch forward, and my spine goes slack. "I don't want to work in software anymore, Jaynie. Too many memories. Bad ones. No corporate jobs for me. No thanks."

I met Craig when I worked for Banks Software — his father's company. Craig was an executive there, and I was promoted quickly. I didn't know it at the time, but he was trying to get close to me and then keep me under his thumb. The manipulation of Sammy Mason started before we were even dating.

And why am I thinking about myself in the third person? That's new.

My therapist eyes me cautiously with a hint of concern in her intelligent eyes. "And you're okay allowing Craig to continue controlling you?"

"Don't be ridiculous, Jaynie. He's in jail. He's not controlling me anymore. I'm free of him."

"Are you free, Sammy?" She pauses, letting her words permeate the room like a dog fart. "Or are you avoiding a viable career path because you don't want to be reminded of him? It seems like the latter to me."

Ouch.

Anger flares red hot inside me. Not because she's wrong, but because she's right on the money.

"I'm trying my best, Jaynie. It's not easy."

She leans forward, placing her elbows on her legs as she meets my eyes. Her face is warm, comforting, and understanding. "I know you are, Sammy. And you're doing incredibly well. But I'd be lying to you if I told you I agreed that you're finally free of his influence. I don't believe you are. Not yet."

An ache travels from my fists up through my arms due to the prolonged clenching. I force them open and stretch my fingers in all directions.

She's right. I haven't put Craig behind me yet. No matter how much I want to move on, and I swear, I do. He's always there — a ghost over my shoulder. I can hear his criticisms in everything I do, like a voice in the back of my mind.

After a moment of silence, I ask, "Will he ever *truly* be in my past?"

She nods encouragingly.

"I was finally starting to think I'd moved on, but you're right. I haven't. How will I know when I've finally succeeded in letting him go?"

She leans back, raising the footrest of her recliner. "When you no longer allow his memory to influence your decisions — good or bad. I'll keep encouraging you, and we'll keep working toward that goal. But only you will know when you're truly ready to move on. When you can follow your heart without thinking of him, when you can date or find someone to share your life with, and when you can look at your life and be happy with how far you've come — I think that's when you'll finally be free."

I can't hold back my eye roll. All that sounds impossible — an insurmountable task.

Jaynie lifts her coffee cup to her mouth, and I let my head fall back in defeat. She always loves to drop a whopper and let it sink in.

But this time, I don't need to think about it since I already know how right on the money she is. So I go for a joke. That's how I roll.

"With all due respect, I think I'd rather break a wrist or two."

A coughing sound comes from across the room as Jaynie does a spit-take with her coffee, coating my face and hair.

My dark humor comes with a cost. Smelling like coffee is what I'll have to pay today for being so damn funny.

Chapter Two

THE PRICE OF A PRANK

Sawyer

Rapping my fist on the doorjamb, I stick my head in Sue's office. She's at her computer, looking lost in thought. That's typical for her. She's a deep thinker, making her a great asset to Redleg.

"Knock, knock. Hey, neighbor. Can I borrow more of that double-sided tape?"

Sue levels me with an annoyed glare, but her lip quirks at the corners. "Why?"

Tilting my head to one side, I innocently throw my eyes to the ceiling, thread my hands together behind my back, and whistle, trying to feign innocence. "Nothing nefarious. I promise."

She reaches into her desk drawer to grab the tape. Before handing it to me, she looks at it closely, then back at me. "The fact that you said that means it's definitely nefarious. If I give you this tape, can you guarantee it will not come back to bite me?"

Looking like the picture of righteousness, I place my hand over my heart. "I'm insulted you think so little of me, Sue O'Malley. Shame on you. I'm merely helping with some office..." I trail off, searching for the word. "Renovations."

Her lips screw over to the side of her face, and one brow arches. "Renovations in a multimillion-dollar building using two-sided tape?"

The jig is up.

"Okay, *fine*. You outsmarted me. It's that time again. I need to hang another sign." I reach my hand out across her desk. "Tape, please?"

She places the roll in my hand while shaking her head at me. "How many of those did you buy?"

Her eyes fall back to her computer. She's not dismissing me, but also not engaging me either. I've gotten used to this behavior from her. At first, she seemed a little standoffish, but that's just Sue. She doesn't mean anything by it.

"A few," I answer.

"A few hundred, you mean." She makes a *psh* sound. "I've been working here part time for almost two years. And you've replaced the sign well over a hundred times. Did you buy them in bulk?"

"That's how you get the best deals. It's why those membership clubs like Sam's and Costco are still in business when every other store has been beaten out by Amazon. It's all about the power of bulk." I twirl the roll of tape around my fingers. "Plus, I knew Tomer would keep throwing the signs in the trash, but he'd never do anything else about it, thinking he could outlast me. He just didn't realize how committed I am to my art."

"Art? You mean pranks."

"You say potato. I say french fries."

"That's not how the expression goes." She rolls her eyes. "Why do you keep up this prank? It was funny at first, but now... meh."

"Someone's gotta be the shit disturber, Sue. It's my cross to bear." Using a fake French accent, I add, "I prank. Therefore, I am."

She heaves a weary sigh and places her forehead in her hands. It's a common reaction from people who don't get my humor. "When Leo and Big Al asked me to come work here, I didn't think I'd be babysitting. Yet here I am."

I cover my snicker with my hand. "It's all in good fun, Sue."

"It's like being with my siblings. But without my mom's good cooking."

Sue comes from a big Irish family, and she's one of seven siblings.

And as a former foster child, am I jealous?

Maybe a little.

"Yeah, but you still love us. You know you do."

"I love *one* of you. The rest of you are questionable."

"Speaking of Leo, where is the big guy?" I ask, referring to my best friend, who's also Sue's main squeeze.

She glances at her watch. "Should be getting back any minute, actually. He just put his clients on a flight back to Bahrain."

An uncharacteristic smile paints her face.

I feel my eyes widen. "Why the smile?"

"We're taking a few days off to celebrate."

"We are?" My mouth falls open wide, and I lean forward like we're sharing girl time. Raising the pitch of my voice, I ask, "What are we celebrating, girlfriend?" I bat my eyelashes to better sell my shtick.

Her nose wrinkles. "Don't do that. In fact, never do that again. Speak normally to me."

One day... one sweet day, I'll get this girl to laugh at one of my voices or fake accents. I will not rest until that triumphant day. I know she has a sense of humor. She and Leo laugh and giggle all the time like middle schoolers. But for some reason, she doesn't appreciate my top-tier comedic stylings.

"Fine. I'll be boring, normal Sawyer. Now tell me what we're celebrating."

"You're not celebrating anything. Leo and I are."

"Ugh. Semantics," I groan. "What are you and Leo celebrating?"

"He didn't tell you?" Under her breath, she adds, "That's quite strange. I thought for sure he would have."

"We haven't talked much lately. He's been guarding the royal family from Bahrain, and I've been leading my own team for a change."

"Oh, really? Moving up in the world, huh?"

"If you came to staff briefings, you'd know this already. Why don't you come to those meetings?"

"Too many people. Ew." She shrivels up her face and shakes her shoulders dramatically.

I can't hold back my laugh. She said it so plainly and then added the full-body cringe. Comedy gold, and she doesn't even realize it.

"Why do you hate people so much, Sue? Everyone here loves you. You've helped us with so many cases already. You're part of the Redleg family."

And I genuinely mean that. Before she started consulting for us, we didn't have anyone who could profile the bad guys with a fraction of her accuracy. Sue's been studying psychology and criminology. Plus, she has a great mind for details. All things that make her a top-notch profiler for when we need insight into a perp's mind.

Not sure why she's so hard on herself.

"Do you honestly want to know why I don't go to staff meetings?" she asks.

"I really do."

She looks at the wall and closes her eyes. "A few years ago, I was a temp at a law firm. I had only been working in their file room for a few weeks. Things were going okay-ish up to that point. One fateful day, they invited me to a staff meeting. A few minutes before the meeting began, I walked in, and everyone was standing around, looking gloomy."

"And?"

With a heavy breath, her eyes pop open as she finishes her story in a rush. "Jokingly, I asked, 'who died?' Everyone looked at me like I had five heads and horns. Because someone had *actually* died. The meeting was to tell us that one of the partners had passed away."

A deep laugh bellows out of me.

"It's not funny, Sawyer. I never went back after that and begged my brother to hire me so I could work from home to avoid people."

The look of mortification on her face gives me secondhand embarrassment. I try to disguise my laugh as a cough but fail spectacularly.

At least she finds the attempt to hold in my laugh amusing, because she eventually joins me.

"And now you know why I'll never go to another staff meeting for as long as I shall live. So help me, St. Paddy."

My cheeks hurt from smiling so much.

After we recover from the residual hysterics, I direct her back to the question I asked. "All right then. With that out of the way, tell me what you and Leo are celebrating."

She holds up her left hand, wiggling her ring finger in front of a beaming smile. A sparkling diamond engagement ring rests on it.

"Holy shit. He finally did it, huh?"

She nods as her face grows beet red. "The other night."

How sweet.

"That's terrific. Congratulations."

I move in for a hug, but she awkwardly sticks out her hand for a shake instead. This girl. She cracks me up.

"Does Big Al know?" I ask after swatting her hand away playfully.

"I have no idea. I didn't tell him. Not sure if Leo did."

"Can I tell people?"

She looks genuinely baffled. "Do you think they'll care?"

"Are you kidding? You and Leo are part of the Redleg family. Of course they'll care."

"Fine with me if you tell people. I don't give a flip."

Smiling, I leave her office and head down to get another sign from my secret hiding place so I can put it up on Tomer's office door after he leaves.

As I walk through headquarters, I think about Leo and Sue's big news. I'm elated for my best friend. He's found his person. Good for him. For them both.

It would have been nice if he'd told me he was finally going to propose, but that's no big deal. I knew he was going to ask her someday. He's been biding his time for two years. He wanted to marry her as soon as they got back from Ocala after...

My throat gets tight.

After Sammy came back.

I wonder if she knows about the proposal already. I think I'll text her later and ask.

No, it's not just an excuse to contact her. And you can fuck off for even suggesting that.

Glancing down the hallway, I make sure it's clear in both directions before opening the janitor's closet. Using a ladder, I climb to the top shelf and grab the box hidden behind a case of glass cleaner. I retrieve another placard, slide it into my back pocket, and exit the way I came.

If Tomer ever found my stash of signs, it would be *game over*. Fortunately, he doesn't seem intent on looking. He's in the office far more than I am since he hates field work. If he wanted to find them, he would have done it by now.

When I get back to my office, I fire off a congratulations text to Leo and ask him to call me when he's free. I kill more time working on schedules for my team and answering emails.

I refill my coffee three times, but each time I check, Tomer is still in his office.

Fucking leave already, man.

My fingers tap on the desk while I wait. Big Al needs feedback on one of the guys I had on my team during the last job, so I send him a summary of strengths and weaknesses.

I'd like to have the door closed so I can play music on my Bose stereo system while I work, but I won't be able to hear when Tomer leaves. His office is a few doors down from mine, and I've got my ears open for his departure.

Even though most of us are guarding clients in the field the majority of the time, Big Al — or Boss, as we often call him — thinks it's important for each of us to have a place of our own. So all the senior team members have their own offices. The junior team members have cubicles. Everyone has a place to call their own. It sure as hell beats carrying around our shit in a rucksack. That's how it was in the service.

I don't miss those days one bit. I like high-quality personal items too much to live that way ever again. Some people might call me *bougie*.

And I'd agree with them.

About forty-five minutes later, Tomer leaves for the day.

Fucking finally, dude!

It's not like I have anyone to rush home to, but I also don't want to hang out at headquarters all damn night.

After shutting off my computer and hitting the lights, I take the borrowed tape and sign, then head to Tomer's office.

Instead of having his name placard on his door, only the wooden frame remains. Each time I put up a new sign, he takes it down a few days later.

Every damn time. Without fail.

And oddly enough, it never fucking gets old. Not for me, at least. Perhaps for him. Er... nah. I'm sure he's laughing. On the inside.

I'm snickering to myself as I place the sign on the wooden frame and tape it in place. The name placard reads *Chuck Nofunfuck*.

Yes, I'm always this mature. You can deal with it or get fucked. Respectfully.

And also, yes. I did have these signs made in bulk a few years ago, just like Sue surmised.

Back then, we had a job protecting a gal named Millie Amos from a psycho ex who was stalking her. Fun fact, she's now married to Sue's brother Nick. Anyway, during that gig, Tomer had to cover a few protection shifts since we had more clients than guards, given the size of the Amos family. He covered Millie a few times, and she couldn't remember his name. She called him *Chuck the no-fun-fuck*.

More comedy gold.

As soon as Millie told me about that, I had the signs ordered and delivered.

And thus, the gag was born.

Just shy of three years later, and it's still going strong.

Another great moment in comedic history, courtesy of yours truly.

Even though we don't call him Chuck anymore, I still do the door sign gag. If I stopped, he'd miss it. Everyone would.

And yes, I'll keep telling myself that.

On my way out of the office, I notice Sue's office light shining from under her closed door.

Odd.

She doesn't usually keep her door closed. It's super late for her to still be here. I better check on her. Leo would expect me to make sure his girl is safe.

As I approach her door, I hear strange tapping sounds coming from inside. I'm about to knock on the door when I hear a deep groan. A groan that sounds like my best friend getting his rocks off.

Not saying I know what that sounds like.

It's just an educated guess.

And now I hear Sue moaning, chanting his name.

Gross. Heebie jeebies. Gag. Deploy fingers to ears.

Shaking out my shoulders, I run down the hallway while humming nonsense. *La, la, la. I don't hear a thing. La, la, la. Not my best friend having office sex. La, la, la. Nothing to hear at all. Just complete silence in the office.*

I suppose this is what I get for staying late to put up another sign. I could always grow up and stop pulling childish pranks. I am thirty-six years old, after all.

Nah.

Fuck that. If I had to hear Leo and Sue banging in order to prank the no-fun-fuck, it's a price I'm willing to pay.

As I start my car and leave the parking lot, one thought keeps running through my head on replay. *I'm not at all jealous that my best friend has someone to bang. Someone to propose to. Someone to love.*

Good for him.

Good. For. Him.

Nope. Not at all jealous that all his dreams are coming true while I'm stuck in limbo. Hung up on a woman I can't have. One who probably doesn't even consider me a viable candidate for a relationship.

Totally not jealous.

Good. For. Him.

Fucking hell. I'm so damn jealous.

Chapter Three

FROM THE TEXTS OF SAMMY AND SAWYER

Sawyer: Hey. You busy?

Sammy: I was just thinking about you.
What's up?

Sawyer: Oh, you were, huh? Do go on and tell
me what you were thinking about. <gif of Jeff
Goldblum from Jurassic Park, leaning in and
looking interested>

Sammy: Not like that, you pervert.

Sawyer: Damn. <gif of a gamer looking angry
that reads: Goddammit'ing intensifies>

Sammy: LOL. I'd send a gif reply, but I can't
compete with your level of gif expertise.

Sawyer: Not many can, sadly.

Sammy: Why were you messaging me?

Sawyer: I wanted to know if you heard the big
news about your brother and Sue.

Sammy: Yes! Isn't it awesome? I was supposed to help him pull off the surprise, but he ended up asking her sooner than planned. It all worked out, though. She said yes. Exciting, huh?

Sawyer: Yep. Cool. No one told me it was coming, and he didn't ask for my help with the proposal or anything. But no big deal.

Sammy: Oh my gosh. Are you jealous?

Sawyer: Me? Jealous? No way. I think it's great. Wonderful even. I'm very happy for them. And I definitely didn't hear them having premarital relations in the office tonight before I left.

Sammy: <gif of woman gagging>

Sawyer: I'd be gagging too if I'd heard that. But since I didn't, everything is fine. Totally fine. <gif of dog sipping coffee while the room is on fire>

Sammy: Not sure how long it's going to take for you to get those sounds out of your mind. But I wish you all the best in your recovery.

Sawyer: Thanks, smart-ass. So what were you thinking about me for if not for "eyebrow wiggling reasons"?

Sammy: I was thinking of calling you to ask a favor.

Sawyer: The answer is yes. Unless, of course, a no is required.

Sammy: Is that from something? It sounds familiar.

Sawyer: Nope. I invented it. In fact, I invented all good phrases. It's definitely not from the animated movie "Madagascar" because as a grown man with no children, I'd have no reason to watch such a film.

Sammy: <gif of woman saying: You sound insane.>

Sawyer: Are you going to tell me what the favor is?

Sammy: I need someone to take me somewhere, and I was wondering if you'd be willing to do it.

Sawyer: Like to a hotel? Or Big Pete's House of Munch?

Sammy: Okay, that's definitely from something.

Sawyer: Invented that phrase too. It's definitely not from Family Guy.

Sammy: You can't see it, but I'm shaking my head at you.

Sawyer: Can't see it, but I can imagine it. And you look beautiful.

Sammy: ...

Sawyer: Where do I need to take you and when?

Chapter Four

WELL, SOMETHING IS RAGING. MIGHT BE THE HORMONES

Sammy

"Bye, Mom. My ride is here. I'll be back later."

Grabbing my purse, I head to the door with a slight bounce in my step, utterly giddy with anticipation. And that *always* seems to be the case when I'm about to see Sawyer.

The added bonus of unleashing some pent-up rage is the proverbial icing on the cake.

Get ready to smash some shit, yells my inner rage voice.

Aww, my little monster. She's always there, under the surface and ready to pounce.

Mom comes over to the doorway with her arms open for a hug. I lean in and give her a squeeze, relishing the hearty affection she's always so generous with.

Jaynie helped me figure out that touch is my love language. Going without *loving* human contact for so many years has been agony. I didn't realize how much I missed it until I was back around my family. Now, I never pass up an opportunity for a warm embrace.

Even if I am getting a touch aggravated at being treated like a child.

When we pull out of the hug, she asks, "Will you be back for dinner?"

"I have no idea. Probably. Maybe."

Decisions are hard.

Mom looks somewhat annoyed with my response. "Can you text me later and let me know?"

Don't get mad, Sammy. She thought you were dead for three years. Give her a break and let her treat you like a teenager for a while longer. Plus, you live in her house, so her rules apply.

"If I'm not home when you want to eat, just go ahead without me. I can always make a sandwich."

Despite my internal pep talk, my tone may have been a tad harsh, judging by her pursed lips and wide eyes. Guilt presses warmly against my sternum.

Fuck off, guilt. I've got enough emotions swirling today. I don't need your bullshit.

"Sorry, Ma. I just don't know how long this will take. I'll text you later." I press my lips against her cheek in apology.

"I just worry about you when I don't hear from you, dear. I don't mean to smother you."

"Can't spell smother without mother, huh?" I tease.

"Fine. I guess I deserve that, but at least I can own being the smother mother. I think I've earned it." She turns to head back to the kitchen and calls over her shoulder, "Have *fun* with Sawyer."

Was it just me, or was there something different in her tone when she said that? And how she emphasized the word *fun* like it meant something more. It was almost as if she was teasing or... gloating? But that doesn't make sense.

Shaking it off, I bound down the front porch stairs. When he sees me coming, Sawyer gets out and saunters around to my side of his SUV to open the door for me. Such a gentleman.

"Hey, gorgeous. Ready to rage?"

He flashes his dark eyes at me, and I ovulate. Right there on the spot. A full order of double ovary ovulation with a side of vagina clenching.

Easy, lady parts. He's just a friend.

Sawyer has the smolderiest eyes in the entire state of Florida. And that chiseled jaw is a lethal weapon that should be illegal in a minimum of four states.

Wiping the nonexistent drool off my chin, I try for a nonchalant reply. "Yep."

I'm as good with words as I am with making decisions today.

After I slide into the passenger seat, he closes the door behind me and smiles at me through the window. A dimple pops in his left cheek, and another egg pops into my left fallopian tube — giving another meaning to the phrase *what's poppin*?

Starting to think this was a mistake.

I should have asked Leo to drive me to smash some shit. I just didn't want to wait until he and Sue got back from their weekend getaway. For some reason, when Jaynie gives me an assignment during therapy, it's my mission to complete it before the next week's appointment. Time is running out, and I'll be working every other day between now and my next therapy session.

Since I'm still not comfortable driving myself and can't afford to buy a car anyhow, it was either ask a friend to take me or get a ride from a stranger with one of those rideshare apps. But given my past, trusting people isn't something I easily do. So asking Sawyer was my best option.

Besides, he meets the qualification of being a friend.

Just a friend. Honest.

Other than my family, I don't have many friends, aside from Sue — but she's only my friend because of Leo. And I didn't want to bring my mother with me when I unleashed the beast. I've been doing a good job of keeping my anger issues hidden from her. If she knew what was going on in my head most of the time, she'd be worried sick.

I've already done enough damage to her mental health. I won't add to it with this trivial shit.

As Sawyer slides behind the wheel and buckles his seatbelt, he asks, "Are you sure you want to do this?"

"Absolutely. My therapist suggested it."

"All right. Let's do it then."

A whiff of his aftershave hits me. Damn, he smells good.

Before putting the car in gear, he runs his big hands across his jean-covered thighs. The movement draws my attention, and I have to force myself not to stare.

While we're driving, he plays angry rock music. Our heads start nodding at the same part, in time with the song's bass riff. We probably look like Chris Kattan and Will Ferrell from *A Night at the Roxbury*. I don't know the artist, but it sounds pretty good. My love for music dried up a few years ago, though, along with a large part of my soul.

He bangs the steering wheel along with the beat. "I think this should get us in the mood."

"I don't need any help getting in the mood."

He opens his mouth to say something, but I wag my index finger at him and cut him off with a playful glare. "Don't you dare say *that's what she said.*"

His jaw falls to his chest, and he scoffs overdramatically. "I'll have you know that I wasn't going to say that."

He was most definitely going to say that.

Cocking my head to the side, I stare him down. He glances over at me a few times, fighting back a big grin.

I remain silent and wait for him to tell me what he was going to say. Knowing Sawyer, he won't be able to keep it in much longer.

Using a terrible British accent, he says, "'Tis what she proclaimed."

Chuckling, I say, "There it is. Close enough."

He's smiling wide again, and I'm relieved the cheek with the dimple is on the far side of his face. His rich-sounding laugh makes my nipples pebble. The dimple would have probably made me start panting and salivating like one of Pavlov's dogs at a bell factory.

Dammit. I *really* need to get laid.

Sorry to be crass about it, but I'm feeling some top-tier sexual frustration lately. At age thirty-two, I'm probably coming into my sexual prime, yet I'm as single as can be — with the exception of my battery powered boyfriend. Not that I'm interested in dating any time soon — if ever again. A one-night stand or three is probably the best I can hope for to ease this persistent ache.

But I haven't done it yet because I can't stand the thought of someone putting their hands on me in that way.

Will I ever be ready?

My electric boyfriend barely takes the edge off lately. The cravings are getting unbearable. I need a man's touch. The skin-to-skin contact. The sweeping caresses and the fingertips digging into my thighs. The heat of another person flush against me. The pressure of their weight on me or mine on them. The tingle of a man's chest hair against my breasts.

I need all of that. Repeatedly.

Sadly, I don't know if I'll be able to tolerate it without panicking. This dichotomy of feelings provides so much cognitive dissonance.

Yet if my reaction to being this close to Sawyer today is anything to go by, maybe I am ready.

My attraction to Sawyer would probably be more manageable if I had some relief.

Of course, I can't get that relief from him. I've had enough drama for one lifetime. Sleeping with him is a complication I don't need. I wouldn't want to screw up Leo's relationship with his best friend.

I'm not worth it.

Not that Sawyer would be interested in me. He's way out of my league — physically, financially, and emotionally. He probably has a whole harem of women begging for his attention.

I'm a mess, and he's got his life together.

He's hot as fuck with those rippling muscles, tanned skin, bright white teeth, and beaming smile, along with a jaw so sharp it could cut a block of cheese.

Sure, he flirts with me. But this is Sawyer we're talking about. He flirts with *all* women. Hell, I've even seen him flirt with men before. It was for a joke, but it still counts.

Speaking of jokes, he tells me a few more and makes pleasant chitchat the rest of the way to the smash house. I find myself laughing and smiling more on this twenty-minute drive than I do an entire week without him. He's freaking funny. And all the voices? My gosh. It's impossible not to smile in his presence. Sawyer's like a one-man variety show.

And so fucking hot. Did I mention he's hot?

He's so fucking hot, he's fuck hot to the third power.

Somehow, I manage to keep my thirsty thoughts to myself and avoid staring at the way his hands grip the steering wheel. I also pay zero attention to how delicious his corded forearms look when he takes a turn. Not to mention how I barely notice how his heather gray V-neck top pulls across his strong pecs or his bulging biceps test the stretch capacity of his shirt sleeves. I bet he could crack a walnut with his biceps.

Yep. Totally not noticing any of that.

Liar, liar, panties on fire.

Chapter Five

BLOW YOUR TOP

Sawyer

"Did you decide on a package yet?" the young kid working the register asks with a hint of boredom in his tone. He's wearing a red and white striped shirt, like the rest of the staff members.

"The *Full Gallagher* package, please," Sammy replies.

"Excellent choice. Forty-five minutes to smash as much as you can, including a watermelon. All gear included."

She pulls out her credit card and plunks it on the counter. Before he can grab it, I put my hand over the card and throw down my own instead while giving him Pacino's *Scarface* eye. You know that eye. It's the one that screams *don't fuck with me*.

"No way. I'm paying for this. It's for me." Her protests are adorable, but they're not going to work. I know how tight money is for her.

I turn to the kid. "Make it two. We can go in together, right?"

"Yes, sir."

I nod at him, then look over at Sammy. Her face is a touch red, and her lips are pressed into a hard line.

"That's not necessary, Sawyer," she hisses.

Yeah, she clearly needs to let out the rage. The sweet yet sassy girl I remember from years ago is gone, replaced by a ticking time bomb, ready to blow with the slightest provocation. I know an IED when I see one.

For me? The smash room will be a fun and entertaining way to pass the time. But for her? This will be therapeutic as fuck.

At least, I hope so.

"Sammy, did you honestly think I was going to come all the way down here and *not* smash shit? Are you kidding me? I've got rage too." I make a show of gritting my teeth and growling like a rabid beast.

She wrinkles her nose and glares at me as if she doesn't believe me.

The clerk gives us waivers to sign, then hands me a credit card slip. I scrawl my name on the line while Sammy seethes next to me. Her eyes burn a hole into the side of my head. How did such a sweet girl go from being perfectly amiable to a rage case in such a short amount of time?

Unbelievable.

"What's the deal with signatures, huh?" I ask her, trying to cut the tension.

"What?" She looks baffled, which is good. I'll take that over pissed off.

"Signatures. They're a weird phenomenon. I wonder who came up with the idea. Think about it for a second. If I print my name, it's not official enough for a purchase. But if I take my name and make it look like the visual equivalent of *yodel-ay-hee-hoo*, it's good enough to take to the bank. That's weird, right?"

Reluctantly, her angry mask falls, and a smile breaks free and dances across her cherry lips.

Victory.

Damn. I love her smile.

And her face. Her hair. How she fills out those jeans. The hint of cleavage peeking out of her shirt. The sound of her voice and her breathy laugh. Her jokes and sense of humor.

Even with her time bomb persona, she's still unbelievably attractive.

Fuck me. Why does she have to be Leo's sister?

If she were anyone else, I could make a move on her. I would have done so a thousand times over by now.

With a shake of her head, she fills her arms with the items the clerk stacked on the counter for us — gloves, large coveralls, rubber boots, chest protectors, face shields, and hard hats.

"Thank you, and I'll pay you back," she quietly tells me.

"Not necessary. It's my pleasure." I give her my most genuine smile. The one with zero sarcasm. I don't use it often, but I want her to know I'm serious about this and happy to be here with her.

Once we've gathered all the protective equipment from the counter, the clerk tells us, "Go ahead and get geared up, then wait over there by the lockers. You'll be going in next." He hands us a laminated piece of paper. "These are your music choices. You'll let your rage master know which playlist you want before going in. Thank you for choosing *Blow Your Top* for your smashing needs."

My lip quirks at his monotone delivery. "Rage master?"

He leans across the counter and lowers his voice. "Yeah, it's like a play on ringmaster for the circus theme. They make us say it."

Sammy throws her head back, chuckling. "Thank goodness they don't make me say stupid shit like that at my job. I'd never make it through half a shift before I had to smash shit." To herself, she softly adds, "Not that I usually make it that long without breaking shit anyway."

Interesting.

Does she mean that she's clumsy at her waitressing job, or is she breaking things in anger?

As we move toward the corner with the lockers and benches, I decide to let that question go unanswered for now. She's just started to lighten up again, and I don't want to tank the mood.

A few minutes later, we're all geared up in our protective equipment and waiting for our turn. A pleasant older woman with a warm smile comes out wearing a black top hat and black suspenders with some buttons pinned on them. One reads *Too Blessed to be Stressed*. She's got the same red and white uniform top as the other employees.

Boy, they really went all in on the circus theme.

"Hi. I'm Kammy, and I'll be your rage master today."

I bite my lower lip so I don't laugh in her sweet old face. She looks absolutely nothing like a rage *anything*. She's the anti-rage master. She might as well be wearing an apron and offering us milk and cookies. What is she doing working here? Shouldn't she be tending to the children who live in the shoe?

"Please select a weapon." Kammy motions to a rack on the wall displaying an assortment of sledgehammers, baseball bats, crowbars, and golf clubs.

"Ladies first," I say while motioning for Sammy to make her choice.

She curtsies and smiles. "Thank you, good sir."

My dick thumps at the back of my fly at her use of *sir*, but since I'm a grown-ass man and not a horny teenager, I stop it from turning into another weapon option for our smashing pleasure.

For now.

But if she grunts while we're smashing shit, I can't be sure I'll be able to stop my cock from shape-shifting into a weapon of mass destruction.

After Sammy opts for a heavy-duty sledgehammer that's almost as tall as she is, I go for the simple wooden baseball bat.

We give our music selection to Kammy, the non-rage master, and she goes over the rules and safety procedures with us. She tells us to save the watermelons for the end since it can get slippery once those explode.

A few minutes later, we're in a small wooden box of a room that's about fifteen by fifteen. Inside is an assortment of glass bottles, small electronics, and appliances like clock radios, microwaves, and old-fashioned printers. There are even a few small pieces of wooden furniture, along with two watermelons.

One of the walls has a target painted on it, presumably for us to throw things at. Another wall has a shelf with an assortment of paints we can use to graffiti the walls. The paint shelf and the walls are the only things we're not supposed to smash, but everything else is fair game.

"Have fun, kids," Kammy says as she closes the door.

A few seconds later, the clock on the wall starts counting down our forty-five minutes, and the room fills with Pink's "U+UR Hand," the first selection on the playlist Sammy picked. An older song, but lots of angst. Good for smashing.

I tighten my grip on the bat while deciding what to hit first. "I guess we can just sta —"

Sammy cuts me off with a loud roar as she rears back, drawing the sledgehammer over her shoulder, then smashing the ever-loving fuck out of a toaster, sending pieces flying in all directions.

"Yes! Unleash the beast!" Kammy's voice comes over the intercom.

With my eyes bugging out of my head — both at sweet little Kammy's unexpected rage and Sammy's instant smash — I quip, "In the words of the great Ace Ventura, *alllrighty then.*"

Sammy's laughter fills the small room, echoing louder than the music. She doubles over for a brief moment, heaving deep guffaws.

"Fuck. That felt good." She straightens herself and looks at me. "Your turn."

I choose my target while twirling the bat in my hand, à la Jasper from *Twilight* — yes, I'm cultured like that. I point the end of my bat at a lone beer bottle sitting on a table.

In a spot-on impersonation of the renowned Cubs announcer, I say, "Good afternoon, everybody. Harry Caray here. Are we ready for another great day of Cubs baseball? Sawyer steps up to the plate, and oh my goodness, he's calling his shot. Here's the pitch. And..." I shut up long enough to take a swing at the bottle. "He's done it. He's done it. Cubs win. Oh my God, the Cubs win."

Sammy's laughs mingle with my own, reverberating off the plywood walls and soaking into my soul, leaving me with a warm feeling all over my body. Trying not to read too much into that.

After the laughter fades, we take turns smashing things for a few minutes. She goes at it with more gusto than me. I try to keep the mood light by being my normal, charming, and hilarious self, which works for a while.

But about ten minutes of smashing later, something shifts. Her laughter fades, leaving only the pain-soaked screams. Not only has she unleashed the beast, she's thrown a saddle on it and is riding it around like a rodeo bull.

Something tells me to take a step back and give her some room. It seems like she's going through something, and I want to let her process whatever it is she needs to deal with. She needs this more than I do.

If her therapist suggested she visit this place, then she must think it'll help with her anger issues. I'm self-aware enough to know better than to make this about me.

My role was to keep her company and be her chauffeur. And like I always do, I'll make sure she stays safe, but I back away to give her the floor, so to speak.

"You need a break already?" she asks once she realizes I'm no longer alternating smashing with her. "I thought you Redleg guys had more stamina than that."

Oh, don't poke the flirty bear, Sammy. Or I'll unleash my beast on you.

"Trust me. My stamina is just fine, princess. I could show you if you'd like," I tease, then dial back the innuendo. "I'm just giving you some space to let your rage loose. Go ahead."

"This isn't a show, Sawyer. I'm not here for your entertainment," she sing-songs like the line in the Pink song from earlier.

"Why are you here?" I ask before I can stop myself. I don't know why I'm asking that, and I know enough about her past to understand why she might have some anger.

But something inside me wants to be more connected to her. To know her — inside and out.

She sets the sledgehammer down against the wall and puts her hands on her hips while avoiding my eyes. After a moment, she lifts the visor of her face shield and removes one of the gloves before swiping at her cheek.

A few tears have escaped her beautiful blue eyes. Eyes that look so much like my best friend's — reminding me to keep my distance.

I feel like shit that my innocuous question made her tear up. Perhaps all the anger she's getting out of her system has to leak from her eyes too.

"You okay?"

Without speaking, she nods, puts the glove back on, then flips down the plastic visor. Heaving a weary breath, she picks up the sledgehammer, ignoring both of my questions.

As she walks toward the coffee table covered with electronic devices, she flatly says, "I'm here to let out some anger in a safe environment where it's socially acceptable to break things without causing myself or others any needless harm." Her delivery makes it sound like she's reading from a brochure or reciting something her therapist told her.

Taking a step in her direction, I itch to force her to be honest with me about what she's dealing with. I can't help her move past this — whatever *this* is — if I don't know what's going on inside her mind. Deeper than the superficial shit.

As the need to soothe her bubbles to the surface, I try to tamp it down because anything I do to help her will only make my attachment to her more intense, and that's a road I can't venture down.

A battle to keep my emotional distance from Sammy wars with my desire to be everything she needs to return to the woman she once was.

You can't be what she needs, Sawyer.

But dammit, I still want to try.

I'm not entirely sure why her past trauma is causing her so much anger. Given what I know about both her rocky childhood and her time with her fuck nugget ex-husband, I'd have thought she'd be more depressed and anxiety-ridden rather than angry.

But what do I know?

The thought of all she's gone through is what causes me to halt my forward progress and retreat to the corner.

She's already had enough drama to deal with in her life.

If I get closer to her, it will be even harder to keep my lips and hands off her. Acting on this attraction isn't what she needs.

I'm not what she needs.

As she lines up her weapon with an old tape recorder, she speaks so softly I find myself leaning in to hear her over the blaring music — "Bad to the Bone," by George Thorogood.

"This is for taking me away from my family," she whispers before smashing the Walkman.

Ah, so she's going to start directing some of this anger to where it belongs — her ex, Craig. That's gotta be a good thing, right?

"This is for convincing me to fake my own death." She destroys two old vinyl records laying on the table.

Hopefully, it wasn't good music. That would be a shame.

"This is for making me feel like I'd be nothing without you," she whispers, then pounds her weapon into the coffee table, breaking the wood into jagged pieces.

"This is for taking away my autonomy." She smashes a blender to bits.

The deafening sound of the glass shattering makes me flinch.

"This is for every time you put your hands on me," she says — much louder this time — almost yelling. She follows it by destroying an old record player.

My pulse increases, and blood rushes through my veins as her words register.

I want to leave.

Now.

I don't want to hear what she's going to say next. She's only getting started, and I know her words are about to get much worse.

I won't leave her, but I also don't want to fucking hear those words. It'll hurt too much. Even if I have my suspicions about what she's endured, I don't want the confirmation. Ignorance is bliss.

I've already got enough guilt where Sammy is concerned. I'd rather not know he sexually assaulted her too.

"This is for every scar you gave me — inside and out." She sends a hubcap flying at the wall.

"This is for forcing yourself on me," she roars, then smashes a glass drink pitcher.

"I said no. Every time. Every. Fucking. Time," she bellows, smacking another glass bottle with each word.

Rage floods my system at her words, along with a shitload of the most profound sadness I've ever felt.

Rage for not killing that fucker when I had the chance.

And sadness for what she's suffered at his hands.

Those feelings swirl around inside me, mixing with a heavy dose of regret, until I find myself gripping the baseball bat again in preparation to smash something.

But right as I'm about to take a shot at an ugly puke-green lamp with my bat, she starts screaming at the top of her lungs — no words, just pained wails — drawing all my attention back to her.

All my anger and hurt are nothing compared to hers.

Nothing.

Repeatedly, she smashes an old sink — the pipes, faucet, and the porcelain basin. When it's shattered beyond recognition, she turns her sledgehammer on the plywood wall. She starts smashing the wall, over and over again. Her rage-filled screams get louder and louder until they hurt my ears.

"I hate you!" she shouts through her tears. "How could you do this to me? I fucking hate you. I hope you burn in hell. You monster. I hate you!"

My bat clatters to the floor. The desire to express my own anger is gone, replaced with a deep-seated need to soothe her. To ease her pain. To stop the swirling fury that's eating her alive.

I also need to stop her before she hurts herself or gets us thrown out of here. The sledgehammer has already pierced a hole in the plywood. We're allowed to throw things at the walls but not hit them directly.

The lights in the room flicker on and off twice in warning. Kammy's voice comes over the intercom. "No hitting the wall with the sledgehammer, please."

Sammy must hear it because she halts her wall assault. Unfortunately, it's not enough to stop her cathartic outburst. It doesn't even slow her down. Instead, she turns around and surveys the room for something else to smash. Her breathing is frantic, and her eyes are wild.

Once she has an old nineties-style stereo system in her sights, she marches over and lays into it with all her anger.

All her rage.

All her fury.

All her wrath.

All her devastating pain.

Again and again.

She continues yelling expletives as she pounds away. Each swing of the mallet feels like it's going straight into my gut. I can feel her pain so acutely in this moment.

It's agony.

Helpless to do anything, I can only watch. Nothing I could do would heal her pain. Nothing could take away her anger. I can't go back in time and stop her from being hurt in the first place.

If I could resolve any of these things for her, she'd be healed by now.

I'm impotent and powerless. All I can do is stand here and watch her break down. Wait for her to get all this ire out of her system. And then I'll be here to pick up the pieces.

With the next slam of her sledgehammer into the stereo, the head of the hammer breaks off.

Damn.

She doesn't realize it's broken, and she rears back with full force to swing again. Without the heavy head of the mallet to balance her swing, she's off balance, and when she pulls the wooden handle up, she falls backward.

She hits the ground with an *oomph*. I rush to her side, kneeling beside her.

"Sammy, are you hurt?"

Through shaky breaths, she says, "No. I'm okay."

She tries to sit up, but I put my hand on her shoulder, holding her in place flat on the floor. "Give it a second. Just breathe."

As she slams her eyes closed, the force of the movement expels more tears down her bright red cheeks, flushed from exertion and pain. She rests her helmet-clad head on the ground while I stay at her side, hand on her shoulder, squeezing it gently as if I can infuse solace into my touch.

Kammy opens the door and sticks her head in the room. "Everything okay?"

"Fine. We just need a minute," I answer.

She replies kindly, "It can be overwhelming sometimes. Take your time."

I hear the door close but keep my eyes squarely on Sammy's despondent face. It's the chin quiver that just about does me in.

I would give anything to ease her pain.

Anything.

After removing my safety gloves, I lift my face shield, then hers.

I run the back of my knuckles across her cheek, trying to provide some comfort. "Breathe, Sammy. Just breathe. I think we're about done here."

Her breathing slows, growing less strained, but she still won't meet my eyes.

"We didn't smash the watermelons yet," she says before breaking out in uncontrollable laughter.

And here I thought I'd be the one who had to tell a joke to break the tension.

Chapter Six

EMOTIONS. EMOTIONS EVERYWHERE

Sammy

Throwing my forearm over my eyes, I wipe my tears with my sleeve as I wait for these bizarre chuckles to cease.

But I'm not just trying to remove the moisture. I'm hiding myself from Sawyer. I can't meet his eyes. I'm terrified of what I'll see reflected back at me.

Shock?

Disgust?

Pity?

Fear?

Not that I'd be a danger to him, of course. He's a former Army Ranger and all-around badass. But perhaps he'd be scared of how damaged and insane I am.

If I stay here in the darkness provided by my arm and tightly closed eyelids, then I'll never need to know what he thinks of me now that he's had a look under the hood at all my mismatched parts and defective wiring.

"After you calm down, you can smash the watermelons before we go," he says. "Deal?"

Without uttering a word, I nod.

"Because you can't say you've gone full Gallagher unless you've smashed a watermelon," he adds.

I want to smile at him, and maybe I do. I'm not sure since I'm trying so hard to hold myself together right now.

He stays beside me on the floor, and I listen to the rhythmic sound of his breathing, drawing comfort from his presence. His thighs must be right near my midsection because the heat of his body is seeping in through these coveralls. Occasionally, his hand squeezes my upper arm like he's lending me strength — a metaphorical thread to stitch myself back together.

I wonder if he's as unsure about how to move on from this disastrous moment as I am. It's not like him to stay silent. In fact, I don't think I've ever been around Sawyer for this long without him cracking a joke.

Once my tears have dried and my breathing has returned to normal, I remove my arm from my face.

Concern.

That's what I see reflecting in his eyes. And I guess that makes sense, considering how much of a mess I am. As Leo's best friend, he probably feels some level of responsibility for me.

My mouth starts moving before my brain can filter the words to make me sound slightly less insane than I truly am. "I can't get up until you promise that you will take what happened here today to the grave. You saw nothing. I didn't have a total meltdown that culminated with me rage crying myself into a puddle of nothingness on the floor. I wasn't possessed by some Viking berserker hellbent on vengeance against small appliances."

The more I rant, the more his skin around his eyes and mouth crinkles into soft laugh lines. His smile is radiant.

"And I certainly didn't detonate like a Samsung phone in an airplane. You can't tell Leo or my mom about my mental collapse. Can you promise me that, please?"

His eyes flash with a hint of mischievousness. "What are you talking about? You did none of those things. I was just thinking to myself about how incredibly calm you've been all day. It was like you floated in and out of here on a cloud of Valium."

His sarcasm truly knows no bounds, but it gets a tension-breaking chuckle out of me.

"Excellent. Thank you."

When I reach my hand out, he takes it and pulls me up to a sitting position. His face sobers, which is unusual for him. Typically, he wears a mask of sarcasm and snark. I suspect he uses it to shield the real him from the world, and I understand that on so many levels.

We sit face to face for a few seconds with our outer thighs pressed together. No words, just a peaceful stillness — I wouldn't know what to say anyhow. This feels like an intimate moment where silence speaks louder than words.

And I have no idea what to make of that right now.

After witnessing my meltdown, I'd have guessed he'd be itching to drop me off at my house so he could get away from me faster than Usain Bolt in the 100-meter sprint.

Oddly enough, Sawyer doesn't seem like he's in a hurry to get rid of me. Nope.

In fact, he's inching closer.

He's slowly leaning his head toward mine, centimeter by centimeter and second by second. His focus bounces from my eyes to my lips as his breathing grows shallow. I find myself licking my lips and inclining my face toward his.

Right before our lips press together, a flicker of something passes over his face, and he abruptly pulls away.

Without warning, he stands brusquely and takes a step away from me. "Okay. Yeah. Umm. So is it watermelon smashing time?"

Blinking, I shake the haze from my field of vision.

What the hell just happened?

Unbidden, an image of a meme pops into my mind. It's the one with Woody and Buzz from *Toy Story* that says: *Emotions. Emotions everywhere.*

Yeah. Emotions.

That's all that was. I was simply overcome with all manner of feelings from my rage-filled emotional explosion. Some of my emotions must have splattered on Sawyer in the process, causing him to suffer from a momentary lapse in judgment, resulting in a temporary arousal flare.

There.

Perfect explanation.

"Yep. I'm ready to *calmly* smash a watermelon. Then we can go."

With a tight smile, he offers me his hand. Hesitantly, I take it, allowing him to pull me to a standing position. As soon as I'm upright, I drop my hand from his grasp and rub my palm down the front of my coveralls as if I can wipe off the intoxicating feel of his skin.

Does he have to be this hot? Smell this good? And have such smoldering eyes?

It's like he was created in a lab with the sole purpose of turning me on.

If he could dial back his hot factor by at least 36 percent, I wouldn't be three seconds from jumping his bones.

It'd probably be more like five seconds.

My eyes search the floor for the sledgehammer so I can smash the damn watermelon and get the hell out of this confined space with this man who makes me feel all kinds of things I shouldn't.

When I find it, my gut sinks. Oh yeah. I broke the damn thing.

"I wonder if they're going to charge me for the sledgehammer," I muse as I study the two pieces.

"Nah. Kammy's the one who told you to unleash the beast, so how can she fault you? Plus, I'm sure it happens all the time."

My skeptical eyes meet his sarcastic ones, and I can't help but roll them. "Sure. People break industrial-strength sledgehammers all the time."

He hands me the baseball bat, handle first. "Here. You can use this to annihilate that watermelon. Treat it like it owes you money and has been dodging your calls."

My lip quirks at his words. He's always so damn cheeky.

After taking the wooden bat, I lower my face shield and exhale deeply. As I stand there, eyeing the melon, Sawyer starts chanting. He's quiet at first, growing in volume as he goes. "Smash that melon. Smash that melon. Smash that melon."

Even if most of the rage seems to have left my body, I still want to see this fruit smashed to bits. Tightening my grip on the handle, I take a deep breath and obliterate it with all my strength. It takes three swats, but I finally get the damn thing to burst apart, right down the middle. Bits and pieces of the green rind and juicy red filling go in all directions. The scent of watermelon assaults me.

I hand the bat back to him so he can destroy his own watermelon. Right before he takes his shot, he bellows, "Get fucked, fruit!"

He smashes it on the first try.

I'm not sure who throws the first shot, but we spend a few minutes having a watermelon fight, tossing pieces at each other and laughing like loons, slipping and sliding over the floor. I feel lighter than I have in years.

There was something truly cleansing about this entire experience. And not only because of the havoc and destruction I caused but also because of the company I had. Letting loose with Sawyer and his effervescent personality was really... uplifting. And once again, I felt safe with him. Safe enough to drop my guard and let my feelings come to the surface. Despite the tears and the meltdown, I had a damn good time today.

I'll need to thank Jaynie for the *smashing* recommendation.

Ha ha ha. Sorry. I'll show myself out.

After we've exited the room, cleaned up, and removed all the protective gear, we head out to his car.

As he closes my door and walks to the driver's side, something catches my eye in the side mirror. Or *someone*, I should say.

I whip around to get a closer look.

Wait. Could it be?

No way. He has no reason to be here in Florida.

But... it *really* looks like him.

My heart stops.

Okay, it doesn't actually stop. *Don't be so literal. Nobody likes a smart-ass.*

But my heart is definitely doing *something* abnormal right now. As is my stomach, twisting and turning. And that little pulse point in my neck is flapping wildly and *shit!* Now my eye is twitching.

It can't be him.

But it's either him or his twin, and he doesn't have one — *thank fuck.* I cringe at the thought of two of those evil men roaming the earth. *Shudder.*

Contorting myself, I bring my knee onto the seat to angle my body for a better view. I track his path along the sidewalk as he moves away from us. Like the coward I always was in his presence, I stay hidden behind the headrest.

As he disappears down the street, the words he said the last time I saw him play out in my head.

The horrifying threat he made.

The memories assault me, making ice flood my veins.

"What's wrong?" Sawyer asks, startling me and making me jump.

Blinking rapidly, I steady myself with a calming breath. "Nothing. I'm fine."

Turning around quickly, I sink back into my seat and put on the seat-belt wordlessly.

"Sammy, what the hell? You look like you've seen a ghost."

Close. But more like the devil.

Shaking my head, I scrunch my nose and try to play it off. "I thought I saw someone from work. It's not him, though."

His head tips and lips purse in a pout. "You work with people you're scared of?"

I've shown Sawyer enough of my stellar personality for one day. I think we should move on before he has me thrown in a padded room.

"No, I'm fine. Let's just head home. I'm tired," I lie and force a smile I don't feel.

"You sure you're okay?"

I nod. "Yeppers."

When I meet his eyes, his expression practically screams: *Do I look like I fell off the turnip truck?*

Leaning over, I tap his leg twice and say, "Let's roll, chief."

Chief? Where the fuck did that come from?

The doubting and suddenly stoic stud beside me lets me have my lie. He starts the engine and turns on the radio — drowning out the uncomfortable silence.

Thank fuck.

As we drive home, his intoxicating presence makes me *nearly* forget the almost-sighting of the devil and the horrible memories that almost surfaced.

We chat amiably as we meander through the streets of Clearwater. He doesn't offer to take me out for dinner or drinks, and I don't suggest it either. I don't catch him gazing at my lips again, and his touch doesn't linger on my skin when he helps me out of the car. I don't let him walk me to the front door. One almost kiss today was enough.

But if I'm being honest... it's not him trying to kiss me goodbye that I'm afraid of.

Nope.

I'm more fearful that he won't try.

And damn it, I desperately want him to kiss me.

I'm so screwed.

Chapter Seven

MY TO-NOT-DO LIST

Sawyer

Drive away, Sawyer.

Do not slam on the brakes.

Do not stay in this driveway.

Do not jump out of your SUV, grab her before she gets inside the house, and kiss those lush pink lips.

Do not push her against the house and let her feel how hard she makes you.

Do not tell her you'll never hurt her and how you want to be her safe harbor.

Do not tell her that even though you know she's hurting, you'll wait a thousand years for her to be ready for you.

Do not tell her you'll protect and guard her heart so she never has to hurt like that again.

And whatever you do, do *not* tell her you're in love with her. Even if you are and have been since the first time you saw her over a decade ago.

Do not do any of those things.

Just. Drive. Away.

Chapter Eight

YOU KNOW YOU'RE MESSED UP WHEN YOU GET KICKED OUT OF CHURCH

Twelve years ago – Afghanistan

Sawyer

Sweat pours down my brow, stinging my eyes. I blink away the burn, wipe my brow with the back of my wrist, grit my teeth, and press on. For the umpteenth time, I wish we'd have gotten the fuck to the chopper before sunrise. It goes from fifty degrees to over a hundred in the span of a few hours in this hellhole. The sun here is brutal.

Big Al, our squad leader, holds up his fist, and we all freeze in place before instantly dropping down to make ourselves the smallest targets possible. My head pivots from side to side, looking for danger as the hairs on the back of my neck stand. We're on the outskirts of a tiny shit-stain of a village. Looks abandoned and ravaged by war. But looks can be deceiving.

"Boss, we need to take cover. I've got a bad feeling about this area," Lionheart whispers after five seconds of tense silence.

"You sense it too?" Big Al asks him while looking through his scope at the horizon line.

"Yeah, Boss."

Something is definitely wrong.

We were supposed to double-time it three more clicks to our exfil location. This mission to take out a Taliban HVT — high-value target — was completed with no casualties on our end, and we need to get the fuck out of here before that changes.

As my eyes meet those of my teammates, I can see we all have that same feeling.

The shit's about to go tits up.

"There. That building. Double-time — go!" Big Al points to the shell of a building that's seen better days.

We all tear off toward what's left of a small concrete structure, stealthily weaving through the uneven terrain, silent as gun-toting mice. Big Al and I take the rear to watch the team's six while Leo is on point. Wiggy's right on his tail, followed by Shep and Pierson.

Leo kicks open the door and enters with his rifle poised to fire. Like a perfectly choreographed ballet, he moves left to scan the room for hostiles. Shep splits to clear the right while Pierson and Wiggy trail them for backup, also alternating left then right. Big Al and I hang back to make sure no one comes up behind us from the street.

"Clear," Leo bellows.

"Clear," Shep echoes, signaling the structure is safe for us to enter.

"Head in," Big Al orders me.

Before I can turn to duck inside the building, gunshots pop and whoosh all around me. My shoulder is hit with enough force to slam my entire body against the building, knocking the breath out of me. A second later, a searing pain shoots from the area like I've been branded with a hot iron.

I've been hit.

Fuck, fuck, fuck.

My team returns fire from the structure. Pierson appears at my side to help Big Al drag me inside the shelter.

The whizzing sound of bullets travels through the early morning air. Return fire steadily decreases as our enemies are presumably taken out one by one. No fucking clue how many there were or if more are on the way. It could have been just a few random Afghans thinking we meant them harm. Or it could have been Taliban soldiers who've come to pay us back for taking out one of their leaders earlier this morning.

Who the fuck knows?

This could be our Alamo moment. And I might not live to see how it ends.

When the gunfire ceases, an eerie silence is all that remains, except for my pained, ragged breaths. My vision fades in and out as the pain rages in my shoulder.

Big Al starts barking out orders. "Lionheart, take the east window. Shep, guard the west. Pierson, take the south. Wiggy, with me."

Benjamin Wiggins, or Wiggy, as we call him, is our team's medic. Thank fuck it wasn't him who was hit. I might have a chance if he can patch me up enough so I can walk out of here.

Everyone rustles into position, three of them guarding our makeshift compound, while Boss and Wiggy go to work on me. I grunt and gnash my teeth, trying to hold it together.

"He's shot in the upper chest; the bullet missed his body armor by half an inch. Dammit," Boss says.

"That's a lot of blood, Boss," Wiggy says, digging through his pack. My eyes meet his, and he leans in. "We're going to take care of you, Sawyer. Don't you fucking worry."

"We need to check for an exit wound," Boss says.

Working in tandem, they roll me to my side. I hiss and let out a litany of cuss words that would make a sailor blush.

"Sorry, man. Hang tight. Almost done," Wiggy reassures me.

"Do you see one?" Boss asks.

Hands trail along the back of my shoulder. I'm so nauseous from the pain I can't fucking see straight. I have no idea who is touching me. My only thought is something along the lines of *fucking son of a bitch ball sack cock gobblers.*

"Found it. Through and through," Wiggy answers.

"Thank fuck," I groan.

"There's nowhere to put a tourniquet. We need to irrigate the wounds, pack them with clotting bandages, and apply pressure. I'll give him some morphine and start a line for fluids. That's all we can do until we get him back to base. He's gonna need a transfusion for the blood loss. Looks like the bullet missed his carotid. But it might have nicked his subclavian artery."

I must black out from the morphine or the pain because when I fade back in, Wiggy tells me they've got me bandaged up, and Big Al is applying pressure to my wound.

"How long are we camping out here like sitting fucking ducks, Boss?" Shep asks from somewhere behind me.

"Do you think you can march?" Big Al asks me.

"I can try."

He looks from Wiggy to me, then shakes his head.

"Why did you ask if you already knew the answer?" I wisecrack through clenched teeth. I'll never be too injured to joke. If I lose my sense of humor, then the terrorists win.

Big Al gives me a sad smile, then looks up. "Shep, with Sawyer down, I need you to check the perimeter for more hostiles."

My gut swirls with nausea, and I think it's because I'm worried for Shep more than the pain. Since I'm known for my stealth recon skills, it's usually my job to sneak around the compound to look for any combatants without being detected. I don't want my friend to get hit because I was dumb enough to get myself taken off the roster and let my team down.

"It'd be better for Shep to sneak out the back. Were there any doors on that side of the building, Lionheart?" I ask Leo, pointing my good hand to the side of the building he cleared earlier.

He nods to the door we all entered through. "Nope. Only this one."

Shit. If we didn't hit all the enemies in our little firefight, then Shep will be a big fucking target as soon as he opens the door.

I fade out again, and when I return to consciousness, Leo's in front of me.

"Shep make it back?" I ask.

"Yeah, man. He did. There are eight hostiles, maybe nine, armed with assault rifles. Fortunately, he didn't see any heavy artillery, so it's not likely they can blow up our little compound."

Let's hope.

I blink, and Wiggy is giving me another bag of IV fluids. Time is fuzzy. I must have lost gallons of blood.

A muffled voice comes from somewhere behind me. I'm too out of it to recognize it. "We aren't going to be walking out of here anytime soon. If we were six healthy, we could take them. But with a man down, we're screwed."

"I'll radio for an evac. Not sure if we'll get it or how long it will take them to get here. We'll need to be ready to defend our position while we wait. And if it takes too long, we'll have to go on the offense and figure out a way to fight with four. I'm not leaving Sawyer unprotected."

I should tell them to go on without me. Get the fuck out of here before it's too late.

Blinking, I force my eyes open and find Leo's concerned face right over mine. He looks like a wreck of emotion. As big and lethal as he is, Leo has a gentle and compassionate side. None of us are strangers to losing a team-mate in battle. It comes with the territory of being a soldier.

That doesn't mean they want me to go home in a fucking pine box.

I don't want my team to lose another man — not now. Not this soon after we lost Bowman.

My gut twists at the thought of our fallen brother and how he was taken out with a roadside bomb. So many good soldiers have been lost.

And for what?

The burning returns a little while later; the morphine must be wearing off. I try to rearrange my positioning, and Leo is right there, helping me attempt to get comfortable. He wipes at my sweaty forehead with a towel and applies pressure to my wounds.

Darkness takes over, and I'm out again.

When I wake next, the sunbeams have shifted across this fucking sweatbox of a hut. I scan the room and see the drained faces of my team-mates. Everyone sits still, conserving energy and trying not to let the wait drive them mad. Big Al paces in frustration while Wiggy and Leo sit with me.

Wiggy's feeling around my neck for my pulse as I fade out again.

Like a voice coming from the end of a tunnel, I hear, "His breathing has slowed in the last few minutes. It's growing dangerously shallow."

"Come on, man. Hang the fuck in there," Leo tells me as he taps my cheeks softly, rousing me.

"Just resting." My voice is barely a whisper.

Leo sounds as calm as can be. Like nothing is wrong. Just another day at the office.

"Did I ever tell you the story about when my sister got us banned from our church?" he asks.

I shake my head subtly.

Leo smiles warmly. "It was Easter weekend. Sammy was about ten years old, and I was probably fifteen. My mother was on one of her religious sprees, which is something she usually did whenever she'd kick my father out. He would never stay gone for long, unfortunately. But while he was away, she'd drag us kids to church a few times each week to pray for our family. Pray for my dad to beat his alcoholism. Pray that we'd all heal from his abuse. Pray for us to find our way in the world without him. Whatever. None of us kids much cared for it." Leo pauses, shaking his head at the memory.

He's been open with our team about the abuse he and his siblings suffered at his father's hands. He's talked about his family so much that it feels like I know them even more than I actually do. Hell, we've all shared our sob stories. Way too much downtime for us to not know pretty much everything there is to know about one another.

Plus, we have to trust each other with our lives. So confiding in each other about our past heartaches and emotional wounds is nothing in comparison.

"Anyway, we were at the church helping set up for a celebration picnic thing the day before Easter. Sammy didn't want to be there. Not one freaking bit. She'd been invited to go with her school friends to a big party and egg hunt at their house, but Mom wasn't having it. Sammy bitched and moaned and begged and whined her face off, but Mom didn't give a shit. We were spending Easter weekend together at church as a family, come hell or high water."

"Makes sense," I rasp.

I've always enjoyed the stories he tells about the time his family spent without his dickhead father around — about his sister, Sammy, in particular.

She's a troublemaker and a prankster, like me. Every story Leo tells about her — and there are plenty — makes me feel an even closer kinship to her.

I met her a few months ago when I went to Maine with Leo on leave. We'd just lost Bowman on an op, and none of us have been the same since. Our CO insisted we take some time to get our heads right.

Since I don't have a family of my own to spend time with, Leo insisted I go with him. The Mason family was warm and welcoming, which makes sense, considering Leo's disposition. He has to get that kindness from somewhere, and we all know it's not from his asshole father.

But Sammy was... intriguing. And freaking beautiful.

The mere thought of her makes my breath come deeper and my pulse stronger. I pull a huge wave of air into my lungs. My shoulder stings with the movement, but the pain and fresh oxygen invigorate me, as do Leo's words about Sammy.

Sammy.

I'll never forget how it felt when we finally met in person. It was like being hit in the chest with cupid's stupid arrow.

Now, whenever Leo talks about his family, I find myself clinging to any little detail he shares about her.

It's pathetic.

The deep timbre of Leo's voice shakes me from my wandering thoughts. "As adults, we know it's a perfectly reasonable expectation to have your family spend a holiday together. But when you're a shy ten-year-old and the cool kids finally invite you into their inner circle, you jump at the chance. Somehow Sammy got it in her head that if she pissed off Mom and made our time at church miserable enough, she'd be sent home. Then she could sneak out to go to her friend's house."

I cough a few times — not a good sign — but then I smile. "What did she do?"

Through muffled laughs, Leo says, "She came running out of the rectory yelling and carrying on that she was possessed. Her mouth was full of foam, and she was sputtering and spewing white bubbles everywhere."

He pauses to wipe the tears of laughter from his eyes, and his happiness makes my chest hurt less. I suppose that's why Leo picked this story. He wanted to give me something to focus on besides pain and a reason to hang in there a little longer.

It seems to be working.

"My hellion sister had put two Alka-Seltzer tablets in her mouth to make it foam like that."

Damn, that's a good one. Wish I'd have thought of it. My shoulders shake with silent laughter, even if the movement hurts like hell.

Once the guys have stopped snickering, Leo finishes by saying, "Yeah, so they asked us not to come back after that."

"Did she make it to the party?" Shep asks, bringing another smile to my face.

Leo shakes his head. "Hell no. She made it onto the prayer list of everyone in the church and got grounded for two weeks."

A few seconds later, Big Al's radio crackles with an incoming message. Next thing I know, another Ranger team is swooping in to help us get our asses out safely.

I'm on a gurney and rushed off to surgery as soon as our chopper touches down. The medic tells me he thinks I'm going to live to fight another day.

Before the anesthesia takes me under, the medic's words reverberate through my mind, but something about what he said was wrong.

I wasn't living to fight another day. Nope. I was living to see Sammy Mason again.

Chapter Nine

NOT YOUR ORDINARY EVENING

Present Day

Sammy

This sucks. My feet are killing me tonight, but not as much as my arms. When did baskets of fries become so heavy?

Good question, right?

And speaking of good questions, here's another one for you.

Who would have thought the day after smashing a ton of crap with a huge sledgehammer that's like twice my size, I'd have this much muscle soreness?

Not me. Because apparently, I'm an idiot.

How could I have been so stupid to go to Blow Your Top the day before I had to work a double shift? There's another good question.

Fuck my life.

And these dead-weight arms. Fuck them bitches too.

My arms feel like they weigh eighty-five pounds each, my shoulders need a rub, and if I have to carry one more tray of drinks tonight, I'm going to cry all the way to the table.

Hope you wanted salt in your margaritas, folks, because my tears are flowing, and I'm too weak to suck them back into my eye sockets.

At least I'm not screaming and wanting to throw shit tonight. Pretty sure it's because I wouldn't be able to lift my arms to throw an empty glass across the room. But hey... a win is a win, right? Look at me, focusing on the bright side.

High five to me. Jaynie would be so proud. Therapy gold star.

Maybe the point of the smash house is to make you so physically sore you don't have any energy left to expend on unhappiness or anger. If that's the case, then mission accomplished.

I wonder if Sawyer is sore today.

Probably not. He's built like a brick shit house. After dropping me off last night, he probably went home and did five thousand push-ups and an hour of wall squats. Maybe that's how he gets that dump truck ass.

His ass is a thing of beauty.

Then again, what part of him isn't?

"Order up, Sammy," Tony yells through the kitchen window, shaking me from my lustful thoughts.

"Coming," I holler back at my manager.

Tony's working in the back tonight since our expediter called in sick. On the bright side, since he'll be occupied in the kitchen, he likely won't notice if I slack off a little.

Oh my shitsickles. Did you hear that? I did it again. I focused on the silver lining.

Am I healed? A changed woman? Did eighteen months of therapy and one trip to the smash house finally reform me from my Hulk-tastic angry ways?

"Excuse me, miss. Can I get another beer?"

"Yeah, yeah. Keep your damn pants on," I bark back with a snarl.

Okay. False alarm. Evidently, I'm not *entirely* healed yet.

As I reach up to remove the basket of crab cakes from the window, I whimper quietly in pain. It's only two little breadcrumb-filled crab cakes — not an entire bushel of actual crabs. But my arms can't tell the difference.

My phone buzzes in my back pocket, momentarily distracting me from the pain.

After I drop the food off at the table and get the needy asshole another bottle of Bud Light, I check my phone. Despite the ache radiating over every inch of my body, a smile tugs at my lips.

It's him.

The man with the ass of steel and heart of gold. The man who does as many vocal impressions as he has rippling muscles. The man who makes my liver quiver. The man who makes me wet by merely existing.

The man I shouldn't be lusting over since he's my brother's best friend and way out of my league.

Sawyer: Hey, Sammy. Just checking in to see how you're feeling tonight.

Me: I'm sore AF but otherwise good. Are you sore?

Sawyer: Why the hell would I be sore? <gif of John C. Reilly as Dr. Steve Brule looking extremely confused and slightly panicked>

Me: I'm sore from slinging that damn sledgehammer around. But perhaps it was just another afternoon for you and all your rippling muscles.

Sawyer: You working tonight?

Me: Yep.

Sawyer: Maybe I'll see you later. Shep and I are looking for a place where the service is terrible, and the atmosphere is mediocre, but the beers are cold.

Me: <gif of Star Lord winding up his finger to flip a bird>

Sawyer: <winking emoji>

I smile as I slide my phone into my back pocket and get back to work. While I bus and wipe down two high-top tables near the front of the bar, I try my best not to dwell on the fact that he didn't flirt with me like he normally would.

In the past, any mention of his physical attractiveness would merit a smart-ass retort. And then we'd flirt a little before I shut him down. That's just how we are; it's like a routine or a bit we do. Typically, it would be something about him noticing that I've commented on his appearance and perhaps even chastising me for getting fresh, then he'd offer said body part for a closer inspection, and I'd tell him no. End scene. Fin.

But tonight, I mentioned his rippling muscles, and he just moved on to the next topic. That's not like him.

Oh well. I'm sure it's nothing. Maybe he's busy.

Besides, it's for the best that he doesn't flirt with me. I didn't bring a spare pair of panties with me to work.

Another hour goes by as I trudge through serving drinks and slinging wings, burgers, and an occasional she-crab soup. My mood alternates between *Jesus, take the wheel* and *I wish a heifer would* with an occasional foray into *namaste* territory.

Very bizarre.

As in... *I'm* feeling very bizarre. The night is fairly standard as far as working at the Sassy Parrot goes.

It's a greasy little bar and grill on Gulf Boulevard across from the beach. Since it's the busy season, the tips are decent, which is good because I want to pay Sawyer back for buying my Gallagher experience yesterday.

While I'm washing beer mugs at the triple sink sanitizer station, a door chime sounds. I can barely hear it over the din of the typical bar sounds — the jukebox, drunken conversations, and the hiss of the fryer coming from the kitchen. But I'm pretty sure it was the back door — likely a delivery person.

"Can you check the back, Sammy?" Tony asks me, confirming my suspicions.

With a nod, I dry my hands and make my way to the back door. I pop the emergency lock button and kick the door open, sticking my head around the corner to see who it is.

No one's there.

I step outside into the alleyway to look for the driver, and the door closes behind me. I look around, my head on a swivel, but the alley is clear. A chill creeps up my spine.

"Hello? Anyone there?" I call, but no one answers.

Shrugging it off, I turn to return to the bar. I grab the door to pull it open, but it's locked.

Damn.

I must not have clicked the little button on the door all the way.

Sweat prickles across my forehead, and my chest grows tight. My hand yanks and tugs on the door handle, rattling it around, but it won't budge. With twitchy muscles, my heart rate spikes as I make a fist and start pounding on the door. Hard.

Over and over again, I bang on the door, and all traces of my former arm pain have vanished. I bang and bang. At least eight or nine times. But it's so loud inside the bar, they'll never hear me.

"Somebody, let me in! I'm locked out here," I yell, an almost frantic sound to my voice.

Get a grip, girl. You're panicking for no reason. I repeat the phrase to myself a few times and force a few calming breaths.

As soon as my heart rate starts to slow, the sound of metal crashing to the ground comes from somewhere over my shoulder. The jarring sound causes me to jump clear off the ground, and my pulse skyrockets once more. I spin around, slamming my back against the door. It's dark out, but there are some lights in the alley. My hand goes to my chest as I struggle to catch my breath while trying to see where the threat is coming from.

From under a nearby dumpster, a dark four-legged creature scurries away.

Shit. It's just a raccoon.

Thank goodness.

I put my head down and force a few more deep breaths while chuckling out loud at my own stupidity and paranoia.

Once my common sense returns, I remember the doorbell. I ring it and wait impatiently for someone to come to my aid. Tony opens the door a few moments later with a pissed-off look on his face.

"Sorry, I locked myself out here," I explain.

"Where's the delivery?"

"No one was out here when I opened the door. I stepped out to look around, and that's when the door closed on me."

He looks at me skeptically, his brows furrowed and lips curled on one side. Why doesn't he believe me? Why would I lie about that?

Damn, I hate this place.

"Can you check the lock to make sure it's functioning properly?" I ask before heading back into the bar.

Tony closes the door behind me, then fusses with the lock.

I head into the restroom to splash water on my face. It helps me settle down enough that I can function, but I'm still on edge. And for the next half hour, I have the distinct feeling I'm being watched.

But that makes no sense.

The customers who were already in here before I got locked outside are still here. The regulars are still crowded around the bar, joking and laughing with each other and the bartender. Some college kids fill the booths along the back wall by the dart boards, just like before I had my raccoon-fueled jump scare. The creepy pervert guy is at the pool table, like always. And some tourists are scattered around the high-top tables.

Everything is fine. Completely normal.

So why do I feel like something is off?

I try to shake off the weirdness by focusing on completing my side work and keeping everyone's drinks filled.

After another forty minutes, two friendly faces walk into the bar, and my heart rate spikes for an entirely different reason.

Sawyer and his friend Shepherd have arrived, as promised.

It's a relief to see them tonight. And not just because they're both incredibly handsome, which they are. But it's because I feel safe with them. For some reason, I'm really craving safety tonight.

Desperately.

They sit down at an open high-top table on the far wall, and I head over with an extra spring in my step.

"Hi, there. My name is Sammy, and unfortunately, I'm out of sick leave and not independently wealthy. So I'll be your server this evening. Can I get you something to drink?"

After a deep chuckle, Shep says, "Sammy, you get more beautiful each time I see you." He wraps an arm around me in a friendly hug. When he pulls away, he gives me a flirty wink.

I roll my eyes, blowing him off entirely. He's almost as much of a flirt as Sawyer.

Speaking of Mr. Sex-on-a-stick, he's leveling a harsh as fuck glare at Shep across the table. That's weird. Sawyer is usually so jovial and playful, but he looks thoroughly pissed right now.

And he hasn't even said hi to me yet.

Rude.

Shep ignores him entirely and orders a Dos Equis accompanied by another flattering compliment.

"What about you, Sawyer?" I ask, tapping his foot with my sneaker-covered toes.

"Make it two," he says coldly without even meeting my eyes. He's still shooting daggers at Shep.

"You okay?" I ask him.

He finally shifts his gaze to me, and the hard lines on his face soften incrementally. "Everything is fine. Nice to see you." His eyes drop down to the table, effectively ending our interaction.

Nice to see me? What the hell?

Feeling a touch triggered by his out-of-character dismissive treatment, I spin on my heel to head to the bar. Why did he come here if he didn't want to see me? I didn't twist his arm. Hell, I didn't even ask him to come here. It's not like it's the only dive bar in town. It's not even one of the good ones with karaoke.

I grab two beers from the cooler, pop the caps with my opener, and swiftly drop them off at the table without another word.

As much as I'd love to figure out what his problem is, I don't have time.

I really don't want to figure it out. That was just sarcasm. Fuck him right now.

Three other groups of customers have just arrived. Sawyer and Shep are lucky they got here when they did because it looks like our late-night rush is beginning.

An attractive blond flits in a few minutes later and joins Sawyer and Shepherd. My hackles rise with something resembling jealousy until I look closer and realize who she is. It's Kri, another guard from Redleg.

Something tells me she and Shep have something going on. I've seen them together a few times, and the looks they give one another could melt the arctic.

As I approach the table to get her order, she waves and gives me a kind smile. "Hey, Sammy. How have you been?"

"All good, Kri. What are you drinking tonight?"

"Margarita on the rocks. Top shelf with salt. Make it two. I need to catch up."

"Two margaritas? My kind of girl. I knew I liked you," I tease and flash her a smile.

As I turn from Kri toward the bar, I notice Sawyer watching me with that same cold expression on his face. My smile fades, and my heart squeezes uncomfortably.

When I return with her drinks, I tap Sawyer on the arm and whisper, "Can I talk to you really quick?"

I'm going to get to the bottom of this. I didn't flee an abusive piece of shit like Craig to end up being anyone's punching bag ever again — emotional or physical.

Sawyer nods, and I bend my head toward the back of the bar. After rising smoothly, he follows me to the hallway leading to the restroom, where we'll have a smidgen of privacy.

"What?" he snaps.

Planting my feet firmly and with my hands on hips, I turn around and skewer him with a glare that I normally reserve for my handsy customers. "What the fuck is your problem tonight? Why are you treating me like shit?"

He heaves an exaggerated sigh, dragging a hand through his short hair. "I had a bad day. That's all."

"And you thought coming here and treating me like shit would make you feel better?"

He finally looks repentant, his eyes pinched and lips turned downward. My anger goes from a rolling boil to barely a simmer.

"Talk to me," I encourage gently, taking a step closer to him.

The Florida sun has nothing on the heat that comes off this man's skin. And I'd love to get that first-of-the-season sunburn right about now.

His haunting brown eyes pierce right into mine. He opens and closes his mouth a few times as he struggles for a comeback.

"Are you a guppy or something?" I tease, opening and closing my mouth twice to mimic him with a popping sound. I smile, trying to lighten the mood and bring my playful friend back to me.

"Talk to me," I repeat.

He remains silent, just staring into my eyes.

Not sure why, but I take one more step forward. We're toe to toe now, and my head is tilted backward so I can look up at his striking face.

Instinctively, my hand reaches out and lands on his chest. I'm so overcome by his masculine presence that the pain from lifting my arm doesn't even register.

"You're driving me insane," he fumes.

The tension rippling off him is unnerving, but I'm not scared.

Sawyer would never hurt me.

My lower lip curls under in a pout, and my head ticks back like he slapped me. "Me? What the hell did I do?" I realize I sound like an indulgent child, but I don't give a shit. I didn't do anything to him. Why is he mad at me?

"You didn't... it's just..." He trails off and runs his hand through his hair while I try to avoid noticing how his bicep and tricep muscles pop with the movement.

He looks pained with the tight set of his jaw and worry etched in the lines around his mouth and eyes. Something is very wrong with my friend tonight. Does he suddenly want nothing to do with me because of how things went at the smash place?

I don't want to lose our friendship. He means so much to me. I can't lose him. I'll do anything.

No longer feeling angry or defensive, I simply want to make him feel better. "Tell me what's going on, Sawyer. Tell me what I did wrong so I can fix it. Please, tell me."

Like it has a mind of its own, my hand flexes a little, giving his pectoral the slightest squeeze.

Fuck, it feels like warm granite under my palm.

Bringing his hand up, he encircles my wrist with his fingers, locking my hand in place on his chest. His flesh burns against mine, sending pulsing dots of electricity across my skin. His eyes dance from our hands to my face, landing on my lips. Fire burns behind his irises.

Pure wildfire.

Without warning, he leans forward and slams his mouth to mine.

I suffer a brief moment of frozen panic before my body takes control. My mind might not know what's happening or why, but my body doesn't give a shit.

His hands move eagerly yet tenderly up the sides of my neck and nestle into the hair at the back of my head as his lips caress mine like the softest petals.

Something snaps inside me, reminding me of a dam breaking open. A wealth of feelings rush to the surface — physical and emotional. I'm awash in desire, burning with need and succumbing to his gentle adoration.

His passionate, *loving* touch sets me off. I haven't been kissed like this in so long... if ever. And dammit, I want more.

I want his supple lips. I want the tentative strokes of his tongue. I want to be freely pressed up against him. My choice.

It's *my* choice.

And damn, if I'm only going to get this one chance to feel the rightness of Sawyer's kiss, I'm going to make it count. In another moment or two, my good sense will return, and I'll see this for the giant mistake it is.

But for now.

Now, I'm going to give myself to him willingly.

Chapter Ten

SNAPPED

Sawyer

I snapped.

That's the only explanation.

My brain broke.

It happened when Shep started flirting with her to get my goat. And he fucking got it, all right. The goat and the rest of the damn petting zoo.

Leo will surely understand. Things like this happen. Brains break all the time, and the next thing you know, you're kissing the fuck out of your best friend's sister in the back of a beachside dive bar.

She tastes like diet coke and smells like a beautiful mistake. Somehow, my hands are in her hair, and we're pressed against each other like magnets. Her hands are wrapped around my neck, pulling me down closer to her. *Finally.*

I've *always* wanted to be closer.

In fact, I've never been close enough to Samantha Mason.

Her lips feel like pillows under mine as they move in tandem. The hint of sweetness I get as I tentatively taste her for the first time will forever be branded in my mind as the most delicious flavor I've ever sampled.

I swipe at the seam of her lips, and she opens for me instinctively. Her warm, wet, velvet tongue strokes against mine in a delicious dance, twirling and teasing.

In all my thirty-six years, no one has ever felt so perfect wrapped tightly in my arms.

No one.

All my senses are overwhelmed by her. Her smell, her taste, the feel of her skin pressing against mine. Gone is the sound of the bar, replaced with breathy moans and the whooshing sound of my pulse throbbing through my veins.

Speaking of throbbing...

I don't think I've ever gotten fully erect in such a short period of time before. It was like going from zero to titanium baseball bat in two point three seconds flat.

Damn, what this woman does to me. *Fuck.*

She's exquisite.

Her delicate hands roam over my shoulders and lace into the hair at the nape of my neck, where she gives me a little tug. At the same time, she nips my lower lip, bringing a growl from deep inside me.

Pulling away, I catch a glimpse of her heavy-lidded eyes, then quickly dive back in for more.

More of her fire.

More of her desire.

More of her pain.

More of her beauty.

Just more of *her.*

When our lips finally break apart, I inhale deeply, dragging my mouth and nose over her cheek, jaw, and down her neck, where I draw in the coconut scent of her skin. I move my lips along the curve of her neck, listening to the euphoric whimpers I elicit from her heavenly mouth. Placing a few kisses along her pulse point, I allow my hands to journey down her shoulders, moving lower until they rest on the small of her back.

I'm about to nuzzle my way back up to her decadent lips when the sound of a throat being cleared causes my eyes to pop open. Some asshole walks by to use the restroom, effectively ending our passionate moment. All too soon, it's over.

Fucker.

Our ragged breaths echo off the hallway walls. Her hands move to my chest, giving me a gentle shove.

"What the hell was that?" she asks in a rush. Her voice is raspy with arousal, and her gaze is fixed on my chest.

I drag my hand across my face as I take another step back, trying to regain some composure to figure out how colossal this fuck-up may have been.

I can't speak.

I mean, I *should* speak. There are many, many things I need to say right now. Hundreds of things I could say.

But I can't.

This is a first for me. I've never been speechless before, but I'm physically incapable of talking.

I've wanted to kiss her for more than a decade. And damn, she was more than worth the wait.

Lips of an angel. Tongue of a goddess. Body of a temptress. Perfection in my arms.

I try to catch her gaze to assess how she's reacting, but her eyes have shifted to the floor.

My heart fractures into a million pieces when she says, "We can't do that again. That shouldn't have happened."

It hurts, but she's right. We can't do that again. It was reckless. Stupid.

Anyone could have walked around the corner and caught us. Word would undoubtedly get back to Leo, and he'd have my head on a spike — especially considering how protective he's been over her since she got back.

Plus, she's not ready for a relationship yet. Yesterday's emotional display at the smash place was evidence of that. And even if she were ready, I'd be no good for her. Never have been and never will be.

My words come out quietly, laced with my pain, confusion, and regret. Regret for so many reasons. "That was my fault. I'm sorry. I should probably go."

"No apologies. But yeah... you should go. I need to get back to work."

With that, she turns and rushes into the restroom, leaving me standing there like an idiot with an erection who just fucked up the closest thing he's ever had to a family.

Shit.

After counting to ten and getting my dick back under control, I make my way through the bar. I toss a twenty on the table and make my excuses.

"But I just got here," Kri pouts.

"Something has come up. I'll catch you tomorrow."

Shepherd narrows his eyes at me but remains silent. He'll probably grill me for details later, but I don't give a shit. I just need to go. Now.

As I drive home, I wonder if I'm ever going to be able to salvage my friendship with Leo. How can I face him after what I've done? Should I tell him? If I do, how will he react? Will I lose him?

Keeping it a secret doesn't seem like an option. The guilt will eat me alive. I've never kept secrets from him. Certainly nothing as important as this. I know how important Sammy is to him and how protective he is over her. As he should be... she was a fucking ghost for three years, for fuck's sake.

And what about Sammy?

How can I return to being just her friend after that kiss? Will she even want to see me again after that? The thought of losing her again feels like it's ripping a freaking hole in my chest.

When I get home, I toss my keys on the counter and head to my room, shrugging off my clothes as I go. I need to wash the day off. Wash my sins off. Wash her scent off me.

As I step into the warm spray, I let the water soothe my aching muscles, which are sore from smashing shit, even if I'll never admit it.

But more than that, I let the shower soothe away my heartache.

I finally had her in my arms. *Finally*. After so many years of wanting her. Missing her. Mourning her. Getting her back and then wanting her all over again.

And that kiss was epic perfection — everything I've ever wanted. As memories of her soft lips and warm body pressed against me return to the forefront of my mind, my cock hardens again.

I know I shouldn't have these thoughts about her, but I'm going to let myself have this one more time before I force myself to move on.

How many times has Leo referred to me as his brother? How many times has Mrs. Mason called me her third son? They've welcomed me into their family, and if that's the case... what does that make Sammy?

You shouldn't want to fuck your *sister* so hard there's an indention in your six-thousand-dollar mattress for days afterward. Yet here I am.

Even if she's not truly my sister, this still feels so wrong.

Shame fills me as I take my length in my hand and squeeze — my grip firm and rough like a punishment for my transgression.

I steadily stroke myself up and down while bringing forth the memory of her rosy, pillow-soft lips. The swell of her breasts pressed up against me. The scent of her coconut skin as I breathed her into my body. Her dainty moans, and the way she grabbed my hair, then nipped my lip.

My hand moves faster and harder around my engorged cock, squeezing and tugging on the angry purple head with each stroke as I relive each breath, each moment. My hips thrust forward into my brutal grip. I run my thumb over my slit and hiss out in pleasure.

With my left hand braced against the cool shower wall, I call out her name as I spill myself onto the tile.

After taking a few ragged breaths, I remove the shower head and rinse off the wall, watching the tangible reminder of my lust for Sammy circle the drain.

A morose smile crests my lips as I hear those words repeat in my mind.

Circling the drain.

Just like my chances of holding on to the closest thing to a family I've ever known.

Chapter Eleven

DEEP THOUGHTS WITH JAYNIE

Sammy

"I kissed him," I spit out as soon as I burst into Jaynie's office.

"Well, hello to you too. I'm fine, thanks for asking," she quips as she closes the door behind me.

"Sorry. We've got a lot to unpack today, and I'm on the clock, so I'm just diving right in." I clap my hands twice to emphasize my point.

She smiles indulgently. "Fair enough. All right. Hit me. Who did you kiss? Tell me what's going on."

My nails have been chewed down to the nubs over the last four days, and I haven't been able to talk about *the kiss that launched a thousand swoons* with anyone. As you can imagine, I'm chomping at the bit. Jaynie is my safe space, and I need her now more than ever.

"Well, I asked Sawyer to take me to the smash house. He did. More about that later, but —"

She cuts me off. "Remind me who Sawyer is again, please."

Sigh. Doesn't she know everyone in my life by now?

Just kidding. I'm not that big of a bitch.

I know she's got tons of patients. Plus, she's getting up there in years, and it's gotta be hard to keep little details straight.

"Leo's best friend."

Her face softens with understanding. "Oh, that's right. He's a Redleg guard who works with Sue and Leo. He's the one who picked you up from that motel you were hiding out at and took down Craig ninja-style from the back seat." She throws up her own version of *knife hands* and whooshes them in an attacking motion, getting a chuckle out of me.

"You've got it. That's the guy."

"Okay, proceed. Sawyer took you to the smash house, and then what happened?"

I force my knees to stop bouncing by pressing my palms on them. I hope I can contain the adrenaline long enough to get my chaotic thoughts in order. Jaynie gets a pencil from her curly hair and poises it over the notepad, ready to take notes on this clusterfuck of emotion I'm about to dump on her.

"The next night, he came in to see me at the Sassy Parrot. He was with two other guards from Redleg, having a few beers. No big deal. But he was acting... off. Cold and dismissive, and that's the furthest thing from how he normally is — especially with me. He's usually flirty and funny. So I figured something was really wrong."

Jaynie leans forward like she's on the metaphorical and literal edge of her seat. "He was acting *off*. Got it. What next?"

"I told him to follow me to the back because I wanted to talk to him. I confronted him about why he was acting so strange and being a dick to me."

She interrupts, raising her hand in a miniature old-lady fist pump. "Good for you. Standing up for yourself."

A smile befalls my face at her encouragement, and yeah, I deserve that praise, so I relish it for a moment. I *am* proud that I stood up for myself. I'm not going to be anyone's doormat ever again.

Fuck you, Craig and Dad.

"So I'm trying to get him to answer me, but he was not saying anything. He was so uncharacteristically stoic. I don't know why, but I put my hand on his really super, mega-firm chest and squeezed. I think his proximity and general hotness must have short-circuited my brain. When he finally spoke, he said I was *driving him crazy*, and then he kissed me. Like... really freaking kissed me."

The look on my therapist's face is as gleeful as a golden retriever going for a ride. She tilts her head to one side knowingly. "And you liked the kiss?"

I cock one brow and look at the ceiling, as if I need to contemplate the answer. "Hmm. Let me think about that for a second." With a roll of my eyes, I melodramatically break character. "Yes, Jaynie. No doy! In fact, I *loved* it. It was the best kiss of my entire existence. I'd wager there will never be another kiss like that for the rest of my life. It was... perfection."

An honest-to-God sigh comes out of my mouth as I fall backward onto the sofa cushions. My chest heaves with frantic breaths, and I get hot and bothered just thinking about how good it felt to finally kiss that stallion of a man.

"Wow," she sighs, leaning back with her palm against her chest. "That's wonderful, Sammy. What happened next?"

I feel my brows wrinkle as I recall how it ended. "A customer walked by and ruined the moment. I pushed Sawyer back a little so I had some space to think."

Jaynie frowns, but I continue, "I can't be sure exactly who said what because it's all a blur of excitement, nerves, and hormones. But I'm pretty sure we decided it was a mistake and it can't happen again."

Her lip actually juts into a full pout as she sets her pencil down with a huff. "Oh poop. Why not?"

It's hilarious how invested she's become in my kiss with Sawyer in just two minutes' time.

With jaw to chest, I protest, "Because he's my brother's best friend. My *extremely overprotective* brother's best friend and his coworker. That's a double no-no."

"But isn't Sawyer your friend too?"

"Well... yeah. I guess so. But he was Leo's friend first. His closest Army buddy. I only know him because of Leo."

"And you aren't allowed to have a relationship with any of his friends? Who decided that?"

My head pops backward, and my jaw drops a little with her question.

Who *did* decide that? Isn't it just an understood absolute?

My mouth opens and closes a few times in quick succession as words fail me. Jaynie leans back in her recliner and extends the footrest with a pleased smile on her lightly wrinkled face.

My hands fly to my sides. "I can't have a relationship with Sawyer. I just can't."

"Why not?"

"It's against the rules." This excuse is starting to feel as flimsy as wax paper.

Jaynie shakes her head at me, pinching her lips up to one side. "Whose rules, Sammy? I'm still waiting for an actual reason."

Is this a generational difference between Jaynie and me? Why isn't she getting this? Did people date their siblings' best friends in the baby boomer era, all willy-nilly without respect for the code?

"I don't know who makes the damn rules, Jaynie. But there's a bro code or something. A sibling code, too. Probably. Maybe. Sawyer and Leo... their friendship would..."

I don't know how to finish that sentence, so I don't.

"Sawyer and Leo would what?" she asks.

Well, dammit. Didn't I just say I don't know how to finish the stupid fucking sentence? Newsflash: I still don't.

"I don't know. It's just wrong. They'd fight or something."

Apparently, I'm entertaining the hell out of her today because she lets loose a deep chuckle that makes her entire belly and chest shake.

"That's the most ridiculous thing I've ever heard in my life," she says between laughs.

Feeling petulant, I cross my arms at my chest and wait for her to finish.

It's not ridiculous... is it?

"Sammy, I don't think that's the real reason. Not buying it, honey. Try again."

"What?" I huff.

"You can't possibly tell me that you're afraid your brother and Sawyer would fight — physically or otherwise — if you and he were to enter into some type of *consensual* romantic relationship. Why on earth would you think that? Talk me through your thoughts. Help me understand because from what I know about your brother, I don't see him reacting like that. If Sawyer is good enough to be his best friend, why isn't he good enough to date his sister? Come on."

I'm going to have to talk more about what happened in Maine half a decade ago. The events that led to me faking suicide and running off with Craig.

And I freaking hate talking about that shit. It was such a dark time.

"Jaynie, you first need to understand something fundamental about my brother's relationship with me. Leo has always been *extremely* protective of me."

With a forward lean, I widen my eyes for emphasis. "Ever since we were kids, when Dad treated us like his little punching bags, Leo made it his mission to take on the lion's share of the abuse. He coddled us like we were fragile, and sometimes we were. Especially Mom." I pause, searching for the shortest path to get to my point.

It's critical that Jaynie understands how protective Leo is so she can help me deal with the fact that my attraction to Sawyer can't be acted upon. My feelings be damned.

"As an example of this protectiveness, Leo would hide us in the closet and go downstairs to provoke Dad, drawing his focus away from Mom, Drew, and me. It was... I don't know, sweet but also fucked up. He wasn't any more deserving of the beatings than the rest of us, yet he felt the need to protect us. Like it was his duty as the oldest sibling or something. And that protective duty didn't end when we were no longer subject to Dad's drunken fits. It followed us into adulthood."

I run my palms over my upper thighs, trying to provide myself with some type of comfort to stop the onslaught of bad memories from pricking away at my skin.

"How so?" she asks.

"Leo was gone for so long while he was a Ranger, and he lived through a lot of horrible shit. While he was away, the rest of us were just flitting through life. After he left the Army and came home, he needed us. We needed him too. Things finally started to get settled, I guess you could say. Drew bought a house with his wife, Tara. I got the job at Banks Software. We helped Mom make the *final* break from our father, and our family spent so much quality time together. In a way, it was a healing period while we reconnected."

"Sounds healthy," Jaynie surmises.

"It was, and it wasn't. That's when Leo's role as the family savior sort of came to a head. Maybe the way we all suddenly got our shit together made him feel like we were powerless without him. Or maybe we truly needed him to lead us. Like it or not, things improved when he got home, somehow making him even more protective of us. And when I started dating Craig, it got really bad — his overprotectiveness. He was over the top. Nothing I did or said was ever taken at face value. He was all over my shit. In a way, I felt like he almost pushed me further into the hole I found myself in with Craig."

My voice cracks. I don't want to blame Leo for my choice of a romantic partner, but that time was so confusing.

"On one side, I had Leo undermining me and hovering so damn much it made me feel like a child. And on the other side, I had Craig filling my head with how controlling my family was and how I needed to set boundaries, push them away. What I know now is... Craig only wanted those boundaries with the family so he could control me."

Wrapping my arms around myself, I put my head down, and let my eyes fall to the floor. I hate what I'm about to admit. Hate that I did this. How could I be so cruel?

"And before I faked my suicide, I said some horrible things to Leo. I knew he was right about Craig, but I didn't want to be the victim anymore in Leo's eyes. I was tired of him always having to save me. So I lied, making excuse after excuse for Craig. Denying all the signs of abuse and control that were clear as can be. I blamed Leo for everything. But it was all my fault."

Tears fall in earnest. She hands me the tissues, and I dab at my eyes and nose while the room fills with a heavy silence.

I need to get to the point, though. I need to make her understand.

Meeting her eyes again, I say, "I'm telling you this because it's why I can't be with Sawyer. I'm getting to the point, I promise."

She nods encouragingly with a sad half smile on her sweet face.

I swear, I could tell this woman all my darkest fears. *Shit*. I think I have. Most of our sessions focused on Craig's treatment of me during our so-called marriage. And there's a lot to unpack there. And now I'm spilling all my dark thoughts about the fake suicide and how I blamed Leo for it.

How does Jaynie do it? Is it the scented oil in here or something? Does she put truth serum in her outlet scent diffusers?

"Go on. When you're ready."

"I already proved Leo's point when I left with Craig — I'm incapable of making my own decisions about a partner. I chose someone just like my father, which is exactly what Leo told me I was doing. And my choice almost cost us everything."

Steadying myself, I add, "Leo wants me to be alone now. To find myself. To heal from... everything. He's found his person, and I'm sure he wants that for me too, deep down. But he's been explicitly clear about how I need to be on my own for a while. And I just know that if I tell him I want to try something with Sawyer, he won't believe I'm ready. And he'll do what he does best — overprotect me. He'll tell Sawyer to steer clear. And Sawyer will because he's loyal to Leo. Leo saved his life in Afghanistan. He'd never go against Leo."

I want to add *I'm not worth their friendship ending,* but that's not something I can bring myself to say. Especially when Leo's right, and I'm probably not ready to date. And let's not forget, my taste in men is shit, and I'd probably turn Sawyer into a miserable asshole who'd also feel the need to control every aspect of my life because that's what *I* do best.

My tears have stopped falling, and I think I'm ready to listen to whatever wisdom she's about to spew.

Sock it to me, woman.

Jaynie nods solemnly and finally speaks. "Remember that our frontal lobes don't finish developing until we're around age twenty-five."

"Okaaay." I draw out the word while I try to guess where she's going with this.

"There are many ways people cope with trauma — we've talked about that quite a bit. Some methods are healthier than others. Even with our fully developed frontal lobes, adults often make poor choices when it comes to coping."

She sits up taller, straightening her shoulders. "Leo was a child, without a fully developed brain, living through an unimaginable trauma — just like you and Drew. The likelihood of any of you choosing a healthy coping mechanism is slim to none in that situation. Slim to none." She claps three times to accentuate each word of her dramatic restatement.

Say what you want, but Jaynie is a riveting speaker when she's on a mission to deliver a life lesson.

"At the end of the day, he did what he did to survive. Likely, he was able to get through each day by putting himself into this *savior* role." She holds up air quotes around the word savior. "That's how he coped. It gave him meaning and purpose in the midst of a horrific adolescence. Was it healthy for him? No. Did it put him into the habit of protecting you from everything? Yes. But did he do the best he could to survive? Also, yes."

She sits back, letting her words float around the room.

After her message has permeated a bit, I feel the need to defend myself. "Jaynie, thank you for that explanation. I hadn't ever thought of Leo's protectiveness in that context before. But I don't blame my brother for how he handled things or the choices he made back then. That's not what I'm trying to say."

"I didn't think you were pointing fingers, dear. I just wanted to make sure we looked at his overprotective behaviors through the lens of science." She points to her forehead, then to her chest, above her heart. "And with some compassionate forgiveness for how you and he got to where you are today."

I nod, understanding more of her point. "I see. And yes, you're right. I'll be sure to give him some grace as we work through this issue."

Part of me loves to watch the genius of my therapist unfold before me. I don't always know where she's going at the start, and sometimes we take a detour or two, but she always seems to get me where I need to be.

"And give grace to yourself too," she adds.

My gaze trails over the coffee table as I nod thoughtfully.

Grace to myself? What a novel concept.

My first reaction is to recoil from that since it's an automatic response to blame myself for my failures, regardless of the cause.

But don't I deserve the same grace I'm willing to give my brother? He was coping by being the savior, and I was coping by being the victim and clinging to the slightest shred of protection anyone could provide.

The roles we've taken in life were forged through the blood and tears of our childhood — literally.

Grace for myself.

I think I'd like to try that.

Perhaps sensing that my moment of epiphany is ending, Jaynie guides us back to the topic at hand. "Now that we've gotten that out of the way and established the how and why of your brother's overprotective behavior, where does that leave us?"

And isn't that the million-dollar question?

Chapter Twelve

GOT ANY LUBE?

Sawyer

My eyes flash to my cell phone as it buzzes and lights up with an incoming call.

Nope. Sending to voicemail.

Just like the little punk bitch I am.

A few weeks ago, when I first got assigned to lead my own security team, I had mixed feelings about it. On one hand, I was stoked that Big Al thought so highly of me and recognized my hard work. But on the other hand, I knew I would miss the assignments with Leo. I've always loved being his right-hand man, and we have fun together on the job.

This week, however, I'm not conflicted about it at all.

I'm 100 percent ecstatic that I don't have to see my friend every day.

He's been back for a few days from his little weekend getaway with Sue, and he's tried unsuccessfully to catch me in the office a few times before or after our shifts. I've also been successful at dodging him by phone, declining calls and sending a text asking if we can message instead since I'm with a client or busy with something else.

Let the record show, those were not lies.

They also wouldn't usually be reasons for me to avoid his calls, but I'm still not sure what to fucking say about this whole shit show.

Call me a coward if you must. I won't disagree with you. Make me a button that says, *Chickenshit*, and I'll wear it on my chest for a week. Change my door placard like I do for Tomer — err, Chuck No-fun-fuck — and I won't even take it down.

But I don't want to lie to Leo. Scratch that. I *won't*.

I'm not looking forward to telling him about what happened with Sammy and me.

You're probably thinking, *Sawyer, why do you need to tell him? If he doesn't ask, there's nothing to lie about. He probably doesn't suspect a thing.*

Unless he does.

What if Sammy told him? She probably did, and that's why he's trying so hard to contact me. He probably already knows and is ready to pound my face.

Sure, I'm a Ranger and can hold my own. In fact, some might say they'd be hard-pressed to find someone I couldn't subdue in hand-to-hand since it's my specialty along with stealth. But Leo is a fucking beast of a man. Plus, my heart wouldn't be in the fight. I'd just take the beating I know I deserve.

My only defense right now is employing my top-secret ninja skills to sneak in and out of the office only when needed and avoid him the rest of the time.

It's called self-preservation. Look it up.

But I can't let it go on much longer. The guilt and shame are doing exactly what I thought they would — eating away at my soul, much like my all-coffee diet erodes my stomach lining.

In case you didn't follow, my soul is my stomach lining in that scenario.

I've been popping antacids like candy — could be the aforementioned coffee consumption or the guilt. Probably the guilt. I'm a damn train wreck without a station to crash into.

And that metaphor doesn't even make sense, but I don't give a shit right now. See above... I'm a fucking mess.

I still haven't talked to Sammy. I can't because... reasons.

My cell lights up again, vibrating itself across the table. It's Leo, the relentless fuck.

Man up, Sawyer. Face the music.

With a tight breath, I answer the damn stupid freaking phone call. "Hey man, something wrong? I'm in the soup."

My eyes are pinched shut as I wait to hear what he's going to say.

"Are you busy, or are you just saying that so you don't have to talk to me?" he asks in an annoyed tone.

I look around the green room where I'm waiting for my charge to get done with her stage makeup. She's a film star about to do a press junket for her upcoming movie release.

"I can give you five minutes," I hedge.

"Why are you avoiding me?"

Insightful bastard.

"Been busy. Sorry about that." Once again, not a lie. Being busy hiding from him is still being busy. Hashtag facts. "You and the future Mrs. Mason enjoying engaged life?" Nice job at deflection, soldier.

"It's fantastic. That's why I'm calling."

Relief floods my veins. He's not calling to chew me out for nearly dry humping his sister in a dark dive bar hallway.

"What's up? Are you having concerns about the wedding night? Need some instruction on how to please a woman?"

If I joke, he won't know I'm hiding something, right?

Right.

"Very funny, shithead. But I've got something important I need to ask you. Are you free this evening around seven for dinner? Just you and me."

The press junket will be done by then, and I'll be able to hand off starlet protection duties to the next shift. She's low-key and will likely want to decompress in her hotel room for the rest of the evening anyhow.

"Sounds romantic, you stud. Since you're the one asking me on a date, I expect you'll be paying. And by the way, I don't put out unless we're having surf and turf."

His returning laugh is warm and genuine, which makes me think he doesn't know a thing about what I did with Sammy.

Or is that *to* Sammy?

Nah. It was *with* Sammy. She gave back as good as she got.

And now my dick's getting hard again. Dammit.

"Let's meet at the Sassy Parrot for a drink first. I want to check in on Sammy. We can either eat there or head someplace else."

"Sounds good," I lie.

It sounds terrible.

He's taking me to the scene of the crime.

And fuck me in the ass with a chainsaw, I'm going to have to see Sammy tonight.

Wonder if I can fake a case of smallpox to get out of going.

Nope. That won't work because the damn military vaccinated us for everything under the sun. Leo would never believe it.

Welp, I'm screwed. Better stop at the drugstore on the way to stock up on lube.

Chapter Thirteen

TONIGHT'S SPECIAL IS HOT AND SPICY DRAMA

Sawyer

"Big Al might join us later if we end up hanging out for more than an hour," Leo says after we've ordered drinks.

We're at the Sassy Parrot but haven't seen Sammy yet. He also hasn't punched me, so things are going better than expected.

"More than an hour, huh? Can you be away from your lady friend that long?" I tease while making my brows dance suggestively.

"Sue's shadowing a detective from Clearwater PD tonight. So she won't be home until late."

"No shit. Your Sue? The same woman who won't even go to a staff meeting because she detests people is doing a ride-along?"

He levels a playful glare at me. "Yes, smart-ass. One and the same. She's tagging along with their detectives for a few weeks, gaining more on-the-job experience to make her an even better profiler."

"That's freaking awesome, man. Did Big Al hook that up?"

"Actually, it was her brother Nick. He helps train police K9s, so he had the contacts."

Pressing my spine against the back of the chair, I study my best friend's posture and facial expressions more closely. Happiness looks freaking good on him.

"You're really proud of her, aren't you?"

"Of course I am," he says with a short nod. His cheeks get a touch ruddy.

"Oh man, you're such a sap. I'm so happy for you and Sue. Truly. In fact, I'm so touched by your love that I forgive you for not telling me about the proposal yourself."

Our beers are dropped off a few seconds later. Perfect timing. I hold my bottle up toward his. "Cheers!" Feeling more like myself, I take on a German accent and add, "To my *Freund* und hiz *Freundin*, *prost*! *Zur Mitte, zur Titte, zum Sack, zack, zack!*" A crude toast used only by the classiest of soldiers.

We served in Germany for a few months, and as Army Rangers, it's essential to know how to give a proper toast in several languages and communicate with the locals off post. So we know all the good toasts, among other key phrases like *Don't shoot* and *Where's the bathroom* and *I'll take a beer*. You know? The important phrases.

"*Zum Wohl!*" he replies in flawless German with a sheepish look on his face. His cheeks grow rosier, probably from the emotions Sue has stirred up in him these last few years.

For such a big tough guy, he's as mushy as a marshmallow. With all his tattoos, he's more like a toasted marshmallow.

Once more, I survey the bar looking for Sammy, who's still MIA. Leo's eyes frequently dart around the room like mine. It's an occupational hazard to always be on the lookout for trouble. We try to disconnect from our jobs at the end of the workday, but it's not easy. And it's not always a bad thing to be vigilant.

After some meaningless blabbering — mostly on my part because I'm trying to avoid telling him I stuck my tongue in his sister's mouth... *repeatedly* — he finally says, "I've got two things I want to talk to you about."

"The floor is yours, my good sir," I say, using my go-to British accent.

When I'm nervous, my default is British. And no, I don't know why that is, but here we are.

"As you know, Sue has agreed to marry me and —"

"A terrible decision on her part," I interject.

"Agreed, but she said yes, and I'm going to hold her to it." He laughs, but it sounds a little high-pitched. Is he nervous? He's normally not fidgety, but he's peeling at the label on his beer, so maybe he is on edge about something. But that doesn't make any sense.

He clears his throat. "Anyway, I was hoping you'd be my best man.

You're like a brother to me. I can't think of anyone I trust more, and there's no one else I'd want standing beside me."

A guilt-laced dagger slides directly into my shameful sister-kissing heart. "Absolutely. Of course. I'd be honored."

Even if I am a pond-scum-level friend and don't deserve this honor.

He beams at me as the tightness of his shoulders relaxes.

Holy shit. He *was* nervous about asking me. Huh. That's so weird. Of course I'd say yes.

"Excellent. Thank you, Sawyer. That means a lot."

"Do we need to hug it out, man?" I spread my arms wide because even if I feel like a piece of shit, I can still make a joke. I'm a soldier, after all. Making jokes at inappropriate times is part of our creed.

He tosses the wadded-up bottle wrapper at me, and we laugh together.

After scanning the room for Sammy again, I turn back to my friend and find he's doing the same thing.

"What was the other thing you wanted to talk about?"

"My sister," he answers flatly.

Squeak.

Shit you not, hand to a bible, I just fucking squeaked in response.

But like the true badass I am, I cover it up with a cough and expediently chug a few swigs of beer down to make it seem like I had a tickle in my throat.

Leo watches me through wide eyes with his mouth cricked open a half an inch or so. Probably wondering what the fuck is wrong with me.

Same here, pal.

"You okay, man?"

"Oh yeah, just a frog in my throat." I cough again to sell my bullshit, but I don't think he believes me. Or that might be my guilty conscience talking. "So what's this about your sister?"

"She's been acting strange lately. I've got a gut feeling something is wrong. I asked Ma about it, and she confirmed Sammy's been unusually quiet and avoiding her at the house these last few days. I've tried reaching out to Sammy to see what's going on, but she hasn't opened up to me. I'm just concerned about her. After everything she's been through, I get worried when I see a shift in her. It might be nothing, but..." Trailing off, he shakes his head and strokes his beard.

I'm half expecting a server to approach our table to tell us tonight's specials are drama, hot and spicy drama, and for dessert, a guilt fudge sundae.

"Maybe she's just busy."

He purses his lips and shakes his head. "I think it's more than that."

"How can I help?"

"Well, Mom said you took her somewhere last weekend. Did she seem all right then?"

Sure, if by all right, he means unleashing a shitload of rage in a smash room, breaking an industrial-strength sledgehammer, and collapsing on the floor.

"Well, did she tell your mom where we went?"

With a crick of his head, he shifts his eyes to the ceiling as if trying to recall. "Actually... no. I just assumed out for a bite to eat or shopping or something. Where did you take her?"

I don't want to betray Sammy's confidence, and I don't know if she wants her family to know she has these anger issues and went to a rage room. She asked me to keep her little rage breakdown between us.

Then again, those places are for entertainment purposes and not really therapy. And she didn't ask me to keep where we went a secret.

"We went to one of those smash places. For fun."

"What the fuck is a smash place?" He looks a tad enraged and a lot scandalized. "You don't mean smash... like... *smash, smash*, do you?" He raises his brows suggestively.

A guffaw busts from my chest. "You think there is a place of business where people go to have sex?" My head bobs from side to side as I hear what I just said out loud. "I mean, I guess there are those pay-by-the-hour motels and sex clubs. But no... that's not what I meant at all."

"Oh, thank God!" he says, sinking back into his chair in apparent relief.

And there you have it, folks.

The very thought of Sammy and me hooking up was abhorrent to him. Just as I knew it would be.

"What is a smash place then?"

"It's a facility where you pay to break stuff. With a baseball bat or sledgehammer and shit. They give you all the protective gear and put you in these rooms where you can just go ham and smash old appliances and glass bottles. We even smashed watermelons. It's fun."

The look of utter disbelief on his face is quite comical. "Are you serious? You and my sweet, innocent sister went to a rage cage?"

"She's not as innocent and sweet as you may think," I toss out without thinking.

I wonder how fast I can get my boot off so I can shove my foot in my mouth. One thing I know about Leo is you don't joke around about the women in his life. And usually, I don't. It's a line I happily don't cross. The fact that I just did proves how I'm *not* myself right now.

"What the hell is that supposed to mean?"

Instantly, the lighthearted, joking vibe we had — like we usually have — is gone.

I put my palms up in front of me, facing him. "I didn't mean it like that. She's very sweet and innocent. Sorry."

I'm trying to play it off like I normally do when I say some shit I shouldn't. But images of how she nipped at my lip and sucked on my tongue fill my mind, making it hard to be chill about this. My tongue suddenly feels swollen, and a lump forms in my throat.

Shit.

This is exactly why I've been avoiding him all week.

He visibly calms, takes a swig of his beer, and searches the bar again. "Where the fuck is she, anyway?"

I shrug but stay silent, too afraid to make things worse.

Leo steers us back on track. "Anyway... for some reason, you guys thought it would be fun to go break stuff. And how did she seem that day? Acting normal?"

I can't answer that without betraying Sammy's confidence or lying to Leo. I'm officially fucked.

"Hold that thought. I'm going to look for her. I'm getting worried," I announce before immediately leaving the table.

Marching over to the bar, I ask a server who's loading her tray with drinks if she's seen Sammy.

"I don't know, but she's been gone for a while, and we're getting busy. She needs to get her ass back here." She leaves in a huff.

I ask the bartender but get a similar sentiment in response.

Likely, I shouldn't be heading into the kitchen since I don't work here, but now I'm worried about her safety. The hiss of the fryers and steam from various cooking surfaces fills the air. Two cooks are frantically working at their stations, but there's a dude who looks like he's in charge grabbing dishes from the window and throwing fries on plates. I head over to him and clear my throat to signal my approach.

When he sees me, his eyes widen. "What the hell are you doing back here? You can't be in here."

"Sorry, sir. But I'm looking for Sammy Mason. She's supposed to be here, but no one can find her. Do you know where she is? I'm concerned about her safety."

"And who are you?"

Well, I'm sure as fuck not a condescending prick like you, I think to myself.

"A friend. Her brother is out there too. He's with me."

"I haven't seen her for a while. She's got orders ready, though."

My pulse jumps, and adrenaline courses through my veins. Hairs stand on my arms. This isn't good.

"When's the last time you saw her?" I ask him.

"About thirty minutes ago. She was taking trash out to the dumpsters."

Without waiting for another word, I race through the bar toward the rear of the building. I muscle past a customer coming out of the restroom without apologizing.

With a violent shove of the door, I pop it open and storm outside into the dark alley. "Sammy! Are you out here?"

I call out two more times, but there's no response. By this point, Leo has caught on to the problem, and he's on my heels.

"Sammy!" he yells, then meets my eyes.

Wordlessly, we begin working as a team. Just like we've done a million times before. We split up, him heading left and me to the right to look down the back alley for any sign of her.

That's when I see it.

A cell phone lying on the ground beside the dumpster. One bag of trash is on the ground near it.

"Is this hers?" I call out to Leo.

He runs over and drops down to one knee beside me. "Fuck. Yes."

Holy shit. Someone has taken my Sammy.

And just like that, my best friend finding out I kissed his sister is the least of my concerns.

Despite my heart shattering into a million pieces with the thought of something bad happening to her, I quickly slide into operator mode. "Call 911. I'll get the manager out here and start looking for possible witnesses." I stand to get a better view of the area around the dumpster, looking for other clues. Time is of the essence, and they've already got a thirty-minute jump on us.

Leo's frozen in place for about three seconds before his training takes over, and he pulls his phone out of his pocket and dials.

"Boss, we have a problem. Someone's taken Sammy," Leo hisses into the phone.

If anyone harms so much as a hair on her head, I'll fucking kill them this time.

No hesitation and no regrets.

Chapter Fourteen

CUE THE GLORIA GAYNOR

Sammy

I wake up disoriented with a throbbing head and the scent of motor oil filling my nose. There's a steady humming sound and a subtle, continuous shaking coming from beneath me like I'm being rocked to sleep.

Blinking, I struggle to focus my vision. A faint red hue falls over the small, dark space, but it's not enough to help me see where I am.

What the hell happened? Why is it so dark? Where am I? And why does my head hurt so badly?

Think, Sammy. Think.

The last thing I remember was taking out the trash at work. Yeah, I was at work. And then what?

Fuzzy memories tickle the back of my subconsciousness, and I try to piece them together like a puzzle. I was bending down to pick up the last bag of trash to throw it into the dumpster when I heard footsteps. Right as I turned toward the source of the sound, a splitting pain took me down.

My head.

Someone must have knocked me out. And then... they must have taken me somewhere.

Oh, fuck. Where am I now?

A familiar squeaking sound pierces my panic-filled thoughts as my body rolls gently like a log.

I know that sound. Bad brakes. I'm in a car.

Oh no, no, no.

My hands shoot up to feel around me, immediately hitting a hard surface over my head, about six inches from my face. To make matters worse, my hands seem to be tied together at the wrists. The more I try to pull my hands apart, the more I feel something cutting into the skin of my wrists, like rope or twine.

Worried about my feet, I force my legs apart and feel no resistance around my ankles. Thank goodness. Since my legs and feet aren't tied, at least I'll be able to run if given the chance.

As my vision comes into focus, having adjusted to the darkness, I see I'm in the trunk of a car. The reddish tint to the darkness appears to be coming from the taillights.

My breath comes fast and shallow as panic blooms. I'm not claustrophobic, but this is still scary as hell.

Amidst the rising fear, thoughts race through my mind at breakneck speed. Who could have done this? Why me? What do they want from me? Am I going to die?

Craig.

It has to be him. He's come for me, just like he always said he would. And I'm restrained... just like before.

He's going to kill me this time. He's probably furious since I helped send him to jail.

Wait.

That doesn't make sense. Craig's in jail. I'd have known if he got out. They'd have had to contact me, right? When he was sentenced, my lawyer said they would notify me if he ever got released, given the circumstances of the case.

Tears fill my eyes, and I'm tempted to scream in terror. Somehow, I manage to keep my mouth shut except for my shaky breaths. I don't want to let whoever took me know I'm awake. Drawing his attention doesn't seem like a good idea.

What am I going to do? I don't want to die. Not when I'm just finding my way back to my old self.

I can't do that to my mother, Leo, and Drew.

And Sawyer.

Making them lose me all over again seems like the cruelest torture.

At this moment, when I'm alone with my screaming thoughts, one thing is perfectly clear. I will do anything to get back to my family.

And to him.

I don't want that to be our only kiss. I want more, so much more.

Gritting my teeth, I suck in a deep breath through my nose, then force a cleansing breath out of my mouth. Then another and another.

Inhale, exhale, inhale, exhale.

A steadying sense of calm comes over me, and I recognize the feeling immediately. It's a survival mechanism, and it's been triggered like muscle memory. A skill I honed over years and years of being around volatile people.

My father at first, and then Craig.

When he would get in his rage mode, I'd have to channel all my calm to defuse the situation. That's what this feeling reminds me of.

It's an artificial sense of calm with the sole purpose of survival.

And I will survive. Like Destiny's Child and Gloria Gaynor said, I'm a survivor, bitch. Or however the songs go. You know what I mean.

Shaking off my stupid thoughts, I shift my focus to getting myself out of this situation and back to my family.

The red light illuminating the tight space triggers a memory. I saw a movie once where a girl was thrown in the trunk. She had her phone with her.

My phone. Do I have it on me?

Thinking back, I remember I had my phone in the back pocket of my jeans when I went outside. I can't move my hands around to my back to feel for it, but I can roll my body. So I shimmy and rub my ass against the trunk floor, but I don't feel a phone poking me.

Whoever took me must have gotten rid of it before we left the alley. Probably so I couldn't be tracked by GPS.

Fuck.

Okay, what else?

In the movie, the 911 operator had the girl smash out a taillight and wave her hand through the opening, hoping someone would see her and call the cops.

I try repeatedly but can't break the taillight out. I can't get my feet or hands into the right position or put enough force behind the movement to break through. I need something sharp or pointy to shove in there.

Rolling over, I search the trunk's interior for a tire iron or a wrench or fucking anything, but there doesn't seem to be a thing in here except me.

Something bright green catches my eye as I spin onto my back. There's writing on it. I lean toward the object, squinting to read the small print.

Jackpot.

It's a glow-in-the-dark emergency hatch lever.

The car is still moving, so it doesn't seem like a good idea to open the trunk now. Perhaps I can pull it as soon as it slows down or stops, then I can jump out — hopefully before he gets around to the back of the car — and I'll have to run.

Run for my life.

Chapter Fifteen

THAT'S WHY HE'S THE BOSS

Sawyer

My fist hits the counter, shaking the silverware tray and making the manager jump. "What do you mean there are no cameras in the alley? What the hell kind of place are you running here, fucko?"

"We have one for the front entrance and a few for the interior of the bar because that's the only place customers go."

"Fuck!" I run my hand through my hair again and take a step away from him because it's getting pretty damn close to throat punch o'clock.

Honestly, for a dive bar, I'm surprised they have cameras at all. But not having one overlooking the back alley won't help us find Sammy.

Time to adjust fire and come up with another idea.

I've already questioned all the customers, and no one saw or heard anything. The cops just arrived, and Big Al's rounding up Redleg resources. For about twenty-minutes now, Leo's been on the phone nonstop with who the hell knows who. Everything has been moving at lightning speed since the second we discovered she was taken.

Taken.

Sammy was fucking taken.

She's in danger. Gone. Again.

A-fucking-gain.

"I'm going to the businesses nearby to ask about security footage that might show a vehicle pulling in or out of the alley," I tell Leo as I shove past the cops. He responds with a nod.

One of the Clearwater cops falls in stride with me. "You should let us handle that."

Fuck that.

"She could be halfway to Georgia before you get around to doing it," I snap without slowing my pace.

"Then I'm going with you," he huffs. "You Redleg guys are something else."

I'm not going to respond to that because now is not the time to get in a pissing match with the cops. Big Al's networking ability allows Redleg to enjoy a friendly relationship with local law enforcement. It needs to stay that way, especially now.

We're out the front and heading toward the Shark Bait bar next door when he puts his hand on my forearm, trying to stop me. "Hold on."

I shrug his arm off and keep advancing. From behind me, I hear him say, "Go for Daniels."

"Copy." Louder, he announces, "Stop. They've found her."

My feet grind to a halt, and I spin to face him. "What?" The pulse beating in my ears might have distorted what he said. Did he say what I think he said?

He's pointing at his ear to indicate the message he got through his police radio. "They've got her. She's alive."

My heart pounds frantically with a mixture of relief and dread about her condition. "Is she unharmed?"

He angles his chin toward the radio hanging from his shoulder. "Can I get a status on her condition for next of kin?"

To me, he adds, "Let's head back inside so we can tell her brother the good news." We start moving back into the Sassy Parrot to rejoin the rest of the team.

"Copy that. Show us en route," he speaks into his radio.

"Well?" I prompt.

"Bump on the head and shaken up, but she's okay."

More relief mixed with concern. How bad was this bump on the head? I've had my bell rung enough times to know you don't fuck around with head injuries.

"Where is she?"

I need to see her.

Now.

"Paramedics are taking her to the hospital."

Bowing my head, I close my eyes and try to shake off some of the fear gripping me for the last half hour.

When we get inside, he waves over Leo and the other officers, who are still questioning some of the customers. Leo meets my eyes, and I immediately tell him the news. "She's alive. They've found her."

"Where is she?" he asks, then looks at the cop on my right.

As the officer answers Leo, I have a morbid thought, and my pulse accelerates again with worry. If she escaped her abductor, then he might still be after her. She might not be safe even in an ambulance or at the hospital.

"Do they have cops with her?" I ask.

He radios my question to whomever is on the other side, then relays the response. "Yeah. They sent one officer with her in the ambulance. He'll stay with her until we get there."

"Let's move," Leo announces.

Big Al and Shep walk into the bar as we're leaving. We quickly get them up to speed. Tomer's behind the wheel of a Redleg SUV waiting to take us to the hospital.

When we arrive, a uniformed officer walks us into the ER along with officer Daniels, who's been somewhat in charge of things thus far.

A plain clothes cop waits outside a curtained area. "Officer Daniels," he says with a nod.

Daniels responds, "Detective Patterson. This is the brother of the victim." He points to Leo, then to me. "And this is... who are you again?"

"I'm her... *friend.* Can we see her?" I'm absolutely 100 percent sure no one noticed how I stumbled over the word *friend.* Trust me. I'm a professional at playing it cool.

"Yeah. Go ahead. Don't leave until you see me, though. We still need to ask her more questions, and we might have some for you guys too." The detective pulls back the curtain a little, indicating our path. "The doctor should be in to check her head shortly."

Leo and I offer curt nods as we move past him. She's on a stretcher, with paramedics on each side. She must have just arrived if the paramedics haven't even had a chance to leave or transfer her to a hospital bed.

Sammy's eyes light up when she sees us. "Leo. Sawyer," she says with a relieved sigh.

She holds her arms open, and Leo goes in for a hug while I hang back at the edge of the stretcher. Our eyes meet over his shoulder, but I can't hold her gaze. I press my palms against my eyes, suddenly overwhelmed with relief. It's nearly too much to handle.

Thankfully, she looks unharmed for the most part. She's wearing her Sassy Parrot T-shirt, and her blond hair is tied back in a messy ponytail with strands hanging loose from all sides. She's got a bandage on her forehead, and it looks like she's bleeding through it.

Relief turns to rage at the sight of her injury, and I feel my fists clench at my sides. I bite my lip to hold myself back from firing questions at her. I want to find this asshole right now and end him.

"Are you okay?" Leo asks her as he pulls out of her embrace and looks closely at the wound on her head.

She bats his hand away. "Yeah. I'm fine. Your future brother-in-law took good care of me," she answers with a half smile as she tips her head toward one of the paramedics.

Leo's eyes widen with realization as he takes in the man at the head of the stretcher. "Callum? Holy shit. It's good to see you." They shake hands. "You remember my buddy Sawyer?" He nods in my direction.

It's the one and only Callum O'Malley. One of Sue's million brothers. I've met him a time or two before, but I didn't notice him at first since I was so focused on Sammy.

"Leo, trouble seems to follow you and the women in your life. I gotta tell you, it's seriously making me reconsider the blessing I gave you to marry my sister," he jokes.

"Cut him some slack, Callum," Sammy says playfully.

I'm comfortable enough with my sexuality to admit Callum is a handsome man. The ladies probably love his big blue eyes and immaculately groomed dark blond hair. I can also say with absolute certainty that I do *not* like how he's looking at my girl. I instantly want to punch him right in his handsome face.

He rolls his eyes, then says, "We'll step outside so you can talk." He catches the gaze of the other paramedic and angles his head away from the tight space we've infiltrated.

As he passes me by, he sticks out his hand. "Sawyer," he says as we shake.

"O'Malley number seven-hundred and twenty-three," I tease, surprising myself that I'm even capable of joking at a time like this. Must be the O'Malley effect. They're all good people, and Callum's a lighthearted and funny dude. Even if he was a touch too close to Sammy a moment ago.

Oh, hello, jealousy. Nice of you to stop by and pay me a visit while I'm in the midst of a crisis. Excellent timing, you piece of shit emotion.

Callum taps me on the chest with the back of his hand before he leaves. Leaning in close, he whispers, "You gonna catch the piece of shit who did this?"

"Absolutely," I answer without hesitation.

"Good." He leaves the room, and my focus shifts back to Leo and Sammy.

"What happened?" he asks her.

"I was taking the trash out, and I heard footsteps approaching. He must have hit me over the head with something because I blacked out, and the next thing I knew, I was in the trunk of a car."

"Son of a bitch," I hiss under my breath. She must have been so scared.

"Hey, I'm okay, Sawyer. I got away." She's soothing me like I'm the one who was just fucking abducted.

I force myself to relax so she doesn't feel the need to expend any energy worrying about me. "How did you escape?" I ask.

"Well, I found the emergency trunk release latch. I waited until I thought he was slowing down and pulled it. My hands were bound together, but nothing else was restrained. I guess he didn't expect me to wake up before he got me to wherever he was taking me. When I popped the trunk, we were at a traffic light. I got out and sprinted as fast as I could. I ran into a restaurant and had them call the cops. The cook cut me free of the wrist bindings."

Her wrists have deep red lines around them, and I want desperately to kiss the pain away. The last thing she needs is more marks on her body.

Leo's concerned eyes meet mine briefly, then turn back to his sister. "You're so lucky that you weren't out in the woods or somewhere remote when he stopped the car."

"I know. I'm very lucky for so many reasons."

Leo takes a deep breath and seems to be shifting from compassion mode into business mode. "Sammy, did you see who took you?"

"No. I'm sorry. I didn't. Hell, I don't even know if it was a male or female. I didn't even get a look at the type of car. I was so laser-focused on running away without looking back." Her voice becomes more distraught as she speaks. "As soon as I saw I was at an intersection, I bolted before the car started moving again. I didn't look back because I was terrified I'd see him about to jump me." By the time she's done, her tears are falling.

Leo pulls her in for a hug. "Shh. You're fine, Sammy. You did the right thing."

My jaw aches due to the prolonged teeth gritting. I want to push Leo aside and take her in my arms. Hold her to my chest, smooth her hair down, and whisper soothing words in her ear.

She buries her face in his chest while her shoulders shake with silent tears.

I can't stand being in here and not comforting her, so I leave the room. She's safe, and she doesn't need me hovering over the bed. Leo's got her.

She's safe. I saw that with my own eyes and heard her sweet voice with my own ears. I'm not the man in her life. It's not my role to do anything else to help her get through this right now. Instead, I'll find another way to help resolve the situation. Like figuring out who hurt her.

I've heard enough to know we've got our work ahead of us to find this fucker and bring him down.

With a tip of his head, Big Al beckons me over as I come out from behind the curtain. I join him, Shep, and Tomer. Shep hands me a cup of coffee.

He knows me so well.

"Thanks," I tell him.

"She okay?" Boss asks.

"Yeah. Looks like it. Bandage on her head."

Shep puts his hand on my shoulder in a comforting gesture. "You okay?"

This fucker has been a little too suspicious of my feelings for Sammy lately.

I deflect. "Yeah, why wouldn't I be? I'm not the one who was thrown in a trunk."

He narrows his eyes at me but doesn't prod further. "Thank fuck she's okay," he says before heaving a deep sigh.

"She say what happened?" Big Al asks.

I relay what little info Sammy was able to share.

Tomer pipes in with his own questions. "What restaurant? Where was she found?"

I can see his wheels turning, and likely, his thoughts are going to the same place as mine. For starters, we need to find witnesses and surveillance from the area to try to get a tag number or description of the vehicle she escaped from. I'm sure law enforcement will be doing their own investigation, but we can work much quicker than they can and have more resources at our disposal.

"She didn't say, and I didn't ask." My head falls in shame. I'm barely a step away from being considered a wreck. It's a miracle I haven't lost my shit yet.

"Go ask her," Tomer suggests.

My brows furrow in annoyance, and I grit my teeth some more. His lack of social skills and tact is exhausting at times. "I'm not going to pelt her with questions right off the bat. She was fucking attacked and kidnapped. Let's give her a few minutes. Let Leo comfort her."

Shep speaks up. "I'll go ask the detective where she was found."

Instantly sliding into command mode, Big Al starts giving orders. "While we wait, let's make a plan. Tomer, you need to get traffic cam footage and track the route he took from the Sassy Parrot to the restaurant where she was found. Then I want to see what kind of surveillance footage we can find from any and all businesses along the way. We need a license plate number or a visual of the unsub. Something we can use to find out his identity because it doesn't sound like Sammy's going to be any help ID'ing him."

Boss turns to me, and I feel my shoulders stiffen like I'm being called to attention. Old military habits die hard, and right now, he's in full command mode. "Sawyer, I'll work with you and Leo to develop a list of potential kidnappers and start checking alibis. We'll divide and conquer once we have a starting suspect pool. We'll need to get with Sammy on that because this could be about her *or* Leo." He pauses, scratching his chin. "Hell, it might even be about Redleg. We'll need to brainstorm motives at headquarters. Look at recent cases we've had or people with axes to grind against Leo. This is his sister, so this could have been payback for something — we'll need to refresh the list we had for when Sue was threatened." His eyes widen. "Fuck. What about Sue? Do we know her twenty?"

"She's doing a ride-along tonight with Clearwater PD," I tell him. "Leo already called her from the bar and told her to wait at the station until he comes to get her later. She knows to watch her back."

His shoulders slump with relief. "That's good."

Shep comes back over, halting Big Al's strategizing. "It was a little grill on the corner of Cleveland Street and Garden Avenue."

"That's excellent. There's a big Scientology Center in the area, so there's bound to be a shitload of security footage," Big Al responds, then keeps right on barking commands without taking a moment to breathe. It's moments like these when he earns the Boss moniker.

"Listen up, Shep. Here's the plan so far. Tomer will pull video footage from traffic cams and businesses near there to try to identify the vehicle. I'd like you to sweet talk the owner of the Sassy Parrot and get copies of all their surveillance archives from inside the bar. Sammy's one of their own, so hopefully, you won't need to twist any arms. Get in there and make copies before the cops take possession of the tapes. I don't want to box CPD out; I just want to ensure we have full access without the red tape. Once you have the tapes, I want you to pore over the last month's footage and look for anything odd. Bring in Kri or Klein to help you sort through the footage — whoever's free."

Shep's deep in thought with arms crossed and one finger tapping at his lips. "What exactly are we looking for? Anything suspicious?"

"Right. Identify everyone you can who came into contact with her. Was someone studying her? Someone looking at her a little too much? Any strange behavior? Who were the regulars? Who were the tourists? Anyone stand out? Any employees acting suspiciously? I also want you to do a deeper interview of all the staff there with similar questions. Find out everything you possibly can about her last few weeks at work. There was likely a reason the perp grabbed her there. They were probably studying her. Looking for opportunities. They likely knew there weren't security cameras in the alley. If we can't get an ID from the traffic cams, then Sassy Parrot is our next best bet."

"You got it, Boss," he replies.

I clear my throat to get Big Al's attention before he moves on to the next assignment. "Sammy will need protection. Around the clock."

"That's a given. I'll leave that to you and Leo to handle — you two are officially assigned to her until further notice. I'll farm out your other assignments." He heaves a deep breath, then keeps going through his mental gymnastics. "I've already sent Henderson to watch Madeline Mason, and I'll relieve him as needed. He's protected her before, and she's comfortable with him." He pauses to look at his watch. "He's already picked her up, and they should be here any minute."

Is this a good time to notice how Big Al's eyes dance when he talks about Leo and Sammy's mother, Madeline? Probably not. But I'm storing that bit of knowledge for a later time. He needs to be teased and then mercilessly grilled about that. And that he already called her and sent protection to her — but not to Sue — is telling.

But I'll save that for later. We've got bigger problems right now.

"Speaking of suspects, what about her ex, Craig?" Tomer asks.

Boss's brows raise. "Far as we know, he's still in prison. No reason to think that's changed. But double-check to make sure he didn't escape or get out without us being made aware. Can't trust a government organization for shit."

"On it," Tomer responds while pulling out his phone and stepping away from our group.

"I'll bring Lionheart and Sammy up to speed now," Big Al says, then turns to leave.

So... yeah. Leo and I will be protecting Sammy around the clock for the foreseeable future.

No problem. Sounds great.

What's the worst thing that could happen?

Stop right there. It was rhetorical. I already know I'm fucked with a dick big enough for an elephant to feel it. I don't need any shitty commentary.

Chapter Sixteen

AM I HALLUCINATING?

Sammy

"Lionheart, Sammy, can I come in?"

"Yeah, Boss," Leo replies.

Big Al sticks his head around the privacy curtain, and I offer him a slight smile as I wave him in.

"How you doing, kiddo?" he asks me.

"Head hurts, but I'm okay."

He stops at the edge of my hospital bed and taps my foot. I've finally been transferred out of that uncomfortable ambulance stretcher.

"It must have been scary. How are you holding up... emotionally?"

My shoulders pull back with a hint of defensiveness, but I force it away. Big Al is a kind man who knows some of my history, so I'm sure he's not implying I'm a fragile flower.

"It was scary, but I handled it. And I'm oddly not all that upset. I'm just glad it's over."

"That's what I wanted to talk to you two about," he starts.

"Got a plan already, Boss?" Leo crosses his big arms over his enormous chest as he shoots a look of interest toward his boss.

Big Al nods with an air of authority that's slightly attractive. Even if he is old enough to be my father, Big Al is kind of hot. How did I not notice this before?

"We've got an initial plan. Are you ready to hear it?"

Leo looks down at me and squeezes my shoulder. "Sammy, you want me to talk shop with Big Al in the hall, or do you want to hear this?"

I think I've woken up in an alternate reality where my brother is treating me like an adult instead of handling everything for me like I'm a toddler fresh out of training pants.

Or maybe my head wound is more severe than I thought. Perhaps hallucinations are a side effect of being clocked in the skull. First, I'm noticing Big Al's hot factor, and now, Leo's refraining from coddling me. What's next? Mom's going to come in with banana bread?

Shaking off my bizarre musings and unfortunate new craving for banana bread, I reply to Leo. "Stay. If it has to do with me, then I want to hear it."

My brother offers me a tight-lipped smile before turning to nod at his boss.

Big Al addresses me. "Right, so until we catch this guy or the cops find him, you'll need protection. We don't know who he is or what he wants, which means you're at risk. I'm assigning Sawyer and Leo to guard you around the clock. Henderson will provide protection for your mother, and I'll give him rest breaks as needed."

"What about Sue?" I interject. "If Mom and I are at risk, then isn't she as well?"

Leo uncrosses his arms and puts his hands on his hips. "I'll handle her protection too. She can work at Redleg during the day — she's safe there — and I'll drive her each day. She'll have to put her dog training and police ride-alongs on hold for now. Unless she's at Redleg, she won't be out of my sight. Sawyer will have to take the night shifts protecting you and Mom. I'll do the days. That way, he can relieve Henderson, and Boss won't have to do much."

I hope no one notices how my throat just bobbed with my tight swallow at Sawyer's name. And now, a memory of his lips pressed against mine floats through my mind. I also recall how gutted he looked when he got here a few minutes ago. I wanted to comfort him so badly.

The next few minutes are a haze of talk about strategies, traffic light cameras, installing tracking software, and more. But my mind is stuck on one thing and one thing alone.

Sawyer will be guarding me each night. Each and every night.

"What about work?"

"You're not going back there," Leo decrees.

Ahh, there he is. There's my overprotective brother making decisions for me like I'm still suckling at the teat.

Before I have a chance to object, Leo's phone rings. "It's Sue," he says with wide eyes.

Knowing how much Sue hates using the phone for actual phone calls, Leo's shocked face makes perfect sense.

"Babe, are you okay?" Leo says, exiting the room.

"You okay with the plan?" Big Al asks me.

Emulating the pose my brother took earlier, I cross my arms. But I do it with a tad more hostility. "I guess I have to be."

"You're Redleg family, and we protect our family. You have my promise, Sammy. We'll keep you safe."

My eyes mist over at his words. *Family. Protection. Safe.*

"Thank you."

For a moment, I wish Big Al had always been in the picture. Perhaps we wouldn't have suffered at Dad's hands all those years, and maybe I wouldn't have fallen prey to Craig's manipulation and abuse.

A familiar sound flutters in from the other side of the emergency room. "Where's my baby girl?"

"She's right this way, Mrs. Mason," Sawyer answers.

I see his hand reach around the curtain to open it for her. Sawyer's standing right outside my room. He's guarding me already.

"Oh, Samantha. Are you all right, my baby?" Mom wipes her eyes as she takes me in from the edge of the room.

"I'm fine, Mom. I'm okay."

She moves quickly into the space and envelops me in her arms. I soak up her loving touch, feeling more relaxed by the moment.

"Did you bring any banana bread?" I tease her.

"I'll make you all the banana bread you want when we get home." She kisses me on my head, and I hiss in pain. "I'm sorry, Sammy." She pulls back and then looks around the room. Her eyes meet Leo's boss.

"Nice to see you again, Madeline," Big Al's deep voice practically purrs at my mother.

"Lovely to see you, Alan."

My eyes bounce from one to the other. My mother's cheeks are turning a nice shade of rosy pink as she stares him down. Big Al rocks back on his heels and eyes her from head to toe, then back up again. I feel like I'm intruding on a personal moment.

What the Kentucky fried fuck is happening?

He just eye fucked my mother.

Leo comes in, breaking the moment. Thankfully.

He looks at his boss and says, "I'm going to pick up Sue. She's been jumpy ever since she heard about the accident. She wants to come and see for herself that Sammy's okay. Tomer will drive me back to my vehicle, then he'll come straight back."

"Sawyer's SUV is at the bar too. And Shep needs to get to the bar to get the surveillance footage. Have them go with you. I'll stand guard until Sawyer gets back."

Leo nods.

"See you in a few, big guy," I tell him.

He grabs my hand and gives it a quick squeeze. "Sawyer will be back in a few minutes. And the cops are still here waiting to question you. We're holding them off until after the doctor sees you."

Leo kisses Mom's cheek before making his exit.

A few minutes later, an older man wearing blue scrubs comes in with a nurse at his side. Big Al takes the opportunity to leave while flashing a quick wink at my mother.

"Hello, Ms. Mason. I'm Dr. Connors. Tell me how you're feeling." Without waiting for a reply, he shines his penlight in my eyes, causing me to blink and pull back. The movement causes my head to throb and pain to shoot down my neck.

"I'm a little dizzy, and my head hurts. A lot."

He pulls back the bandage to examine my wound while continuing his line of questioning. "I'll need to stitch this up. I'll have a nurse come in to clean it out first. Any vomiting?"

"No."

"Ringing in your ears or blurry vision?"

"No."

"Trouble breathing?"

"No."

"Did you lose consciousness?"

"Yes. I was knocked out and put in a trunk. I woke up with my hands tied and a pounding headache."

"That must have been very scary. Follow my finger." He moves his finger from side to side and up and down.

He runs through a list of pointless questions like my name, the current year, the name of the president. I'd roll my eyes, but I know he's just doing his job. Plus, it hurts a little to roll my eyes.

"Where were you before the accident?"

The accident? Is he honestly trying to make it sound like I tripped and fell hog-tied into the back of a trunk?

"Before I was *attacked*... I was at work."

"Do you know how long you were unconscious?"

"Well, I was unconscious, so I didn't check my watch," I reply with a bit of irritation.

Mom's grip on my hand tightens, and she whispers, "Just answer the questions, dear."

"Were you drinking or taking any recreational drugs this evening?"

"What? No. I was at work."

Dr. Connor meets my eyes. "Sorry, sometimes alcohol and drug use can interfere with an accurate diagnosis. I need to ask to ensure the best care."

My irritation recedes, but I just want to go home. I don't like his attitude. He's almost as jerky as the detective who was firing questions at me until Sue's brother Callum told him to back off. He could see how upset I was, and the constant barrage of questions made it worse. I'll need to tell Sue to give Callum my thanks when I see her.

"Is she going to be okay, doctor?" Mom asks him as he pulls away and writes notes on his clipboard.

"I think so. I'm ordering a CT scan to rule out anything serious, but from what I can tell, it's a minor head injury. We'll follow concussion protocol and stitch her up. You'll need someone to stay with her for at least twenty-four hours, and we'll give you a list of things to monitor for."

"Doctor, the detective is impatient about questioning her. Do you want him to wait, or can he do that while we wait for radiology to get her?" the nurse asks.

The doctor earns major brownie points when he turns to me for a decision. He raises his brows in question.

I let out a deep sigh. Might as well get it over with. "I'll talk to him now. But can I get something for the pain? An ice pack, maybe?"

"I'd rather wait until after the CT scan. I'll expedite it so we can get you something soon."

An annoyed huff escapes me. It feels like my forehead is splitting in two.

"We understand," my mother answers. Always the one to try to defuse tension.

"I'll be back to stitch up your head after the scan. We'll go over the results then."

He and the nurse leave while Mom pulls a chair closer to the bed and asks me to tell her what happened.

"Why don't we get the detective in here so I don't have to repeat myself yet again?"

A few seconds later, my mother brings the detective in, along with a uniformed officer.

One last time, from the top...

Chapter Seventeen
PLEASE STOP ASKING ME QUESTIONS

Sawyer

Mrs. Mason puts a folded sheet, pillow, and blanket on the foot of the couch for me. "Are you sure there isn't anything else I can get you?"

"No, ma'am. I won't be sleeping much. So this is great."

Great. Yeah, that's one word for it.

Another word?

Agony.

That's what it's going to be for me to stay here on the couch with Sammy sleeping one room away while tonight's events run through my head along with the memory of the only perfect kiss I'll ever have in my life.

"I put on another pot of coffee, and there's flavored creamer in the fridge," she tells me. "I'm going to bed now."

"Sleep tight, ma'am."

Her lips purse, and her eyes close to slits. "Please stop calling me that. It makes me feel old as hell. Madeline or Maddy is fine."

"Yes, Mrs. Mason," I tease and give her a wink.

She rolls her eyes and brings her pointer finger and thumb together in front of her face. "That's only this much better." Retreating to her room, she offers, "Feel free to wake me if you need anything. I doubt I'll be able to sleep much tonight anyhow." She sounds upset, which is to be expected after the night we've all had.

We got here about two hours ago after an excruciatingly long night at the hospital. Fortunately, Sammy has only a moderate concussion with no bleeding of the brain. She got thirteen stitches to seal the gash at her hairline. She's going to be fine, physically.

Emotionally? That's yet to be determined.

I can tell she's beyond frustrated with everyone hovering over her, so I've kept my distance. She finally forced Leo and Sue to leave about a half hour ago. They wanted to sleep over, but there aren't any guest beds here. The third bedroom has been converted into Madeline's craft room. So, aside from a bedroom for Sammy and another for Mrs. Mason, the modest three-bedroom home is full. As it is, I'll be bunking on the couch.

Then again, I won't bother trying to sleep. I need to keep my focus on ensuring these ladies are safe. Plus, I need to figure out what I'm going to say to Sammy. Once the dust settles from the chaos of her abduction, we'll need to address the mammoth in the room — our kiss.

I've avoided her for the last few days, busying myself with work. She hasn't reached out to me either. But now I can't avoid her. I don't want any residual weirdness between us, so I'll need to bring it up — perhaps tomorrow. We'll clear the air and move on. Pretend it never happened.

Yeah. Sure. I can do that. No problem.

Lies, lies, beautiful lies.

I settle on the couch after taking a quick sweep around the outside perimeter to look for anything suspicious. Leo installed all of the Redleg bells and whistles for security in his mother's home, so it's a secure place, allowing me to rest a little easier.

This place has everything from smart locks and strategically placed panic buttons to floodlights and outdoor and indoor cameras. Hell, the cameras even have motion sensors and alerts. The doors and windows have multiple sensors and chimes that can alert to subtle movements, temperature shifts on the glass, and even breakage.

It's a modern-day Fort Knox.

And it's all controlled through an app I now have connected to my phone and a tablet.

Nothing else to do but sit here and twiddle my thumbs. Stay alert and monitor the perimeter cameras.

I'm on my third cup of coffee when I hear movement from Sammy's room. My head whips around, and I catch her tentatively easing out of her room.

I rise from the couch. "You need something?"

She subtly shakes her head. "I live here, Sawyer. If I need something, I'm pretty sure I can get it myself."

Oh, good. Sassy Sammy is back.

She creeps slowly into the living room, and I take a few steps in her direction. Like I'm being pulled into her orbit.

"How do you feel?" Sliding my hands into my back pockets, I make myself come to a stop a few feet from her. Any closer and I might take her in my arms.

She raises her shoulders in a slight shrug. The movement draws my eyes to her pert nipples, poking out from under the thin tank top. Something stirs in my pants.

Hey, dick, don't get hard. Don't get hard. Don't get hard.

"I'm okay. I was having trouble sleeping, though."

I motion to the couch area. "Want to watch TV?"

She nods, and we move around the couch. I sit on one side, and she moves the folded bed linens to the center cushion and takes a seat on the other end, leaving an empty space between us.

Getting comfortable, she folds her legs under her. I turn the television on, then hand her the clicker.

With raised brows, I tell her, "Ladies' choice."

"Gee, thanks," she teases with a slight smile. "I guess it's the least you can do since I was shoved in a trunk tonight."

My jaw tightens, and my hands squeeze into fists. "Too soon, Sammy. Too soon."

She reaches over and touches my forearm gently. "Hey, sorry. I was just joking. I'm fine. I'm honestly not that upset about it."

My gaze flits from her hand to her beautiful face, so kind with compassion. Even the bandage across her forehead does nothing to detract from her beauty.

"How can you be so chill about it so soon?"

She tucks her arm back across her chest and faces the TV while flipping through Netflix. The rhythmic clicking sound of her scrolling through the options fills the quiet room.

"Well, I thought I should *chill* since we're watching Netflix," she deadpans.

When she inclines her head away from me and flashes a shit-eating grin, I let a chuckle break free.

"Are we Netflix and chilling, Sammy? With your mom in the house? You're such a bad girl," I tease, then add a tsking sound.

Facing the TV, her face falls once more, all traces of the playfulness gone.

Without meeting my eyes, she flatly replies, "Jokes aside, I guess I'm not more upset about what happened tonight because it's not the worst thing that's ever happened to me."

A sour feeling settles in my gut.

The urge to comfort her burns bright once more. Just like it did at the smash house. "Feel like talking about it?"

She shakes her head. "I do enough of that in therapy."

"Fair enough, but the offer is there if you change your mind. Unlike your therapist, I'd be listening because I care and not because I'm on the payroll."

With a tight-lipped smile, she gives me a side-long glance. "Excuse me, sir. I'll have you know my therapist cares about me. She's cool as shit."

I put my palms up in front of me. "No offense. I'm sure she does. But I do too."

Shifting her gaze back to the TV again, she quietly asks, "Is that why you kissed me the other night? Because you *care*?"

Are we doing this now?

Shit ass. I haven't had time to figure out what exactly I need to say about it. Guess I'm going to have to shoot from the hip and just say what I feel.

The truth. But with a few exceptions.

It's not like I can say I fell for her the first time I saw her. And how the stories Leo told me about her kept me alive when I was knocking on death's door in a hut in fucking Afghanistan.

Those secrets I'll take to my grave.

She sets the remote down on the sofa between us and turns to face me, bringing her knees up to her chest and wrapping her arms around them.

My tongue rolls across my teeth as I try one last stall tactic. "You really want to talk about that now, Sammy? After the day you've had?"

I watch her throat bob as she swallows down her fear. I can tell by the set of her shoulders she's feeling more confident and not about to let me off the hook.

"You're going to be watching me every night for the foreseeable future, and I haven't been able to stop thinking about it. Hell, even while I was in the pitch-black trunk tonight, I thought about it. Maybe if we clear the air, I'll be able to get some sleep."

Dragging my fingertips across my forehead a few times, I try to smooth out my wrinkles. "Okay, what do you want to know?"

"Why did you kiss me?"

A dark laugh escapes me. "Just gonna dive right in and lead with that, huh?"

Moving my arm to the side, I throw it over the sofa cushion and angle my body toward her, giving her my full attention.

"Life is short. Might as well get to the point. I could've died tonight, and I'd have never known the answer."

"Fuck, Sammy. That's dark."

"The truth is sometimes dark. Are you going to answer?"

"Such a ball buster, Sammy Mason," I hedge playfully.

"Guilty as charged." She kicks one leg out and digs her toes into my ribs gingerly. "Stop evading the question. Why did you kiss me, Sawyer?"

Dropping my macho bravado and any hint of playfulness, I squarely meet her eyes. "I kissed you because I really fucking wanted to kiss you, and I couldn't stop myself from doing it for another second."

Her voice is raspy as she replies, "That's a damn good reason."

"But it can't happen again. We can't do that."

She ignores my statement in favor of asking more questions. "How long have you wanted to kiss me?"

My gaze falls from her face to her shoulders, taking in the supple skin of her upper arms and how her forearms are wrapped around her legs. My mouth waters, and I force down a tight swallow.

Don't get hard, dick. Come on, stop it. Man up. Err... man down in this case.

"A long time."

"Did you want to kiss me at the smash house after I freaked out when you were on the floor with me?"

"Yes."

"Did you want to kiss me in the car afterward?"

"Yes."

"Did you want to kiss me at Leo's birthday party last year?"

"Yes."

"In the elevator at Redleg after I had lunch with Sue that one time?"

She lists off a half dozen other times I nearly kissed her over the last couple of years. My answers are the same because I've always wanted to kiss Sammy. Let's face the facts. I'm never *not* going to want to kiss her, and I'm not going to lie about that to her. Not anymore.

She must have always known. Apparently, I haven't been as stealthy with my lust for her as I am when I'm evading the enemy.

"Did you want to kiss me when you found me at the motel two years ago?"

"I felt guilty as fuck about it, but yes. I was just so damn glad to see you alive."

The memory of that rapturous moment peppers my mind, and I can almost feel the way my soul sang when I finally confirmed my suspicion that she wasn't dead. That hug she gave me brought something back to life inside me that I thought was dead and buried, just like I thought she was for three long years.

She rests her head across her knees and looks at the back of the couch for a long few minutes.

"Why did you feel guilty?"

"I always feel guilty about it. But that time, in particular, it was because I knew you'd just fled a fucked-up situation, were probably being hunted by that dick bag, and the last thing you needed was me trying to hump your leg."

She laughs at my unexpected joke. It was only a matter of time before my personality returned. I can't silence the loud-ass joker inside me for long. No cage can contain my humor.

"What about any time before that? Did you ever want to kiss me before I... before I left with Craig?"

I tilt my head to the side and nibble at the inside of my cheek. "Sammy, what the hell do you think?"

A sad smile lifts her lips, but it doesn't reach her eyes. "Anything you want to ask me in return?"

A sound comes out of me that's part growl, part groan, and part laugh. Tons of questions I want to ask Sammy race across my mind.

Did you want me to kiss you all those times?

What do you sound like when you come?

Do you like your nipples pinched?

How wet do I make you?

Do you like dirty talk?

How many times can I make you come before you beg for mercy?
Do you feel for me even half of what I feel for you?
Even if I don't deserve you, will you let me love you forever?

"Um... I have questions, but I don't know if I want to know the answers. Nothing you say will help our current situation."

"Our current situation?"

"You're my best friend's little sister. I can't be with you like that. And now I'm in charge of your safety, making you even more off-limits than you already were. You're the forbidden fruit. And it doesn't matter what we want; we can't go there. So anything I ask won't help."

She bites her bottom lip as anger flashes behind her ocean-blue eyes. Her body shifts back toward the screen, and she picks up the remote. After scrolling a bit more, she hits play and sets the clicker down.

Quietly, she mutters, "I wonder how old I'll have to be before men stop trying to make all my decisions for me. Apparently, thirty-two isn't old enough to decide who I can love."

It feels like I've just been punched as a rock lands in the pit of my stomach.

I have no idea what movie she put on. All I can see are vague images flashing across the screen. I can't hear the words or follow the plot. Sounds a lot like Charlie Brown's teacher.

All I can do is think about what she just said. All she's been through in her life. All the men who've controlled her and hurt her. The anger and disgust I feel at myself make it impossible to focus on anything else.

Deciding for her? Is that what I'm doing? Or are we letting Leo decide for us both?

I don't want to control her. I only want her to be free to follow her heart and make herself happy. I want her to find joy anywhere she can. She deserves a full life.

And did she just imply she loves me? Or was it more of a metaphorical love? She probably meant it more in the abstract rather than specifically about me.

About an hour later, she gets up. Without meeting my eyes, she says, "I'm going to bed now. See you tomorrow." She sets the remote down on the coffee table.

"Good night, Sammy," I mumble in the direction of her retreating back.

The door to her room closes a few seconds later, and I let my head fall to the couch. I don't know how long I stay there, frozen in place. I don't sleep. I don't move. I simply exist.

Lost in my mind and feeling like my heart's fractured in two.

One side of my heart longs to offer itself to the woman who's owned it forever.

And the other half fears doing so will hurt the only people who ever made me feel like I mattered.

Chapter Eighteen

JUST LIKE HILARY DUFF SAID, I'M COMING CLEAN

Sammy

My bladder wakes me after a fitful night's sleep. If I even slept at all.

Then again... I know I slept some because I had sweet and naughty dreams about Sawyer. Not that I haven't had them before, but it felt different, given he was outside my room last night.

I wonder if he heard the electric hum of my vibrator or the slight moan I couldn't hold back when I came. It was so damn hard to fall asleep after that tension in the living room, and I had to take the edge off with a little self-care. And given that my house smells like Sawyer, it was pretty damn easy to come. Especially when I thought about what he said to me on the couch.

I envisioned all those near-kisses he wanted to give me over the years. One by one, I fantasized that he'd done what we both wanted him to do. That he gave in to his desires and took what he wanted from me.

That's all it took to send me over the edge.

But then reality sank in, just like it is now, with the subtle, nagging twinge in my lower gut. Trying to ignore it, I roll over, but the pressure won't let me get comfortable. The covers are twisted and hanging off the foot of the bed, thanks to what appears to have been some nocturnal synchronized swimming practice.

After padding over to my bedroom door, I pause with my hand hovering over the doorknob. I don't know what time shift change is supposed to happen for my guard duty, but Sawyer or Leo will be here. Honestly, I don't want to see either one of them right now.

Some of that familiar rage boils to the surface. I'm sick and tired of being controlled by men who think they know better than me and insist on making all my choices. I am *not* an invalid.

And I'm absolutely over it.

My fist squeezes the doorknob to the point of discomfort before I finally cave and exit my room. Without looking down the hallway, I breeze into the open bathroom and close the door behind me.

A few moments later, I'm washing my hands at the sink when I glance at my reflection in the mirror. The shock of my battered face causes me to take a step back. An audible gasp leaves me at the sight of a deep purple bruise peeking from under the bandage on my forehead. Involuntarily, my hand raises to cup my agape mouth, but it's still soapy. The taste makes me flinch again.

Holy shit.

I've been so hung up on the man standing guard outside my bedroom all night I forgot the reason he was there in the first place.

How could I have forgotten?

Who the fuck gets abducted, barely escapes with her life, and then forgets about it by the next morning? That can't be a normal reaction to this type of trauma.

I'll need to see Jaynie as soon as possible.

After leaving the bathroom, I return to my bedroom and get my cell phone off the charger so I can request an appointment.

The smell of fresh-brewed coffee calls to me like a siren's song. Reluctantly, I leave the sanctuary of my room. My steps are tentative as I pass by the couch where Sawyer and I talked last night — where he confessed to *always* wanting me.

Desiring me.

While looking absolutely delicious in his snug fit T-shirt. How does he make a cotton tee look that good? The tanned skin of his arm called to me as it laid over the back of the couch. I wanted to crawl into those arms and forget about everything but the feel of his touch.

Speaking of making basic apparel look impeccable, let's discuss how good he looks in his dark cargo pants. Something about the mystery of all those pockets intrigues me. What's he got in there? Could be a knife or a chocolate bar. A bag of coffee beans or extra toilet paper. A booze-filled flask or a bag of Twizzlers. Who knows? Hell, it could be all of the above. Knowing him, he probably has containers of instant coffee that say: *Break in Case of Emergency.*

Wearing simple utility pants with a zillion pockets shouldn't be that hot, but here we are.

And why am I obsessing over pockets? Damn. I'm *such* a mess.

All I know for sure is that a strikingly handsome, polished, strong man wants me. He has for so long. I always suspected it, but having him confirm it was heady as hell.

But then he immediately decreed that we aren't going to do anything about it and refused to even hear my thoughts on the matter.

He outright refused to consider my wishes or desires.

And now, *angry Sammy* has taken over. Ragey rage monster reporting for duty. Maybe another trip to bang town would help after yesterday's shit show.

Huh. Bang town. Now, *that's* a great name for a smash place. Better than Blow Your Top. I wonder if they have a suggestion box.

My fingers drag along the top of the sofa as I pass. The pillow and sheets my mother laid out are still folded neatly, looking unused. He's former military, like Leo, so if he did use them, it's entirely possible he tidied up after himself.

Speaking of the big brute, my brother is seated at the kitchen table.

He looks up from his phone and offers a warm smile. "Good morning, Sammy. How are you feeling?"

"I'm fine. Good morning."

That's a lie. *I'm filled with a fiery anger and low-grade lust for your best friend who won't touch me — because of you!*

But Leo's actually sweet, so it feels wrong to lash out. Instead, I'll bottle up my rage and shove a cork in it.

Reaching into the cabinet, I pull out my favorite mug and fill it with the piping-hot nectar of the gods.

In case you're curious, the mug says: *Come back later when this cup is empty.*

"Mom at work?" I ask.

"Yep. Henderson is with her," he replies.

"Sawyer's gone, I assume?"

"Yeah. He went home to get some sleep about two hours ago. He'll be back this afternoon, though. Sue and I have an appointment with a wedding coordinator that we couldn't reschedule. I hope you don't mind."

He frowns, then amends, "Well, we could've rescheduled, but this guy is hard to get an appointment with, and it would have delayed our wedding by at least eight weeks. Sue and I don't want to wait that long to get married. But if you need me here all day and evening, considering everything that's going on right now, I'll cancel. Sue will understand."

I join him at the table and wave him off with my hand. "I don't mind. But what's the hurry?"

A dopey smile lifts his cheeks. "I've waited my entire life for Sue. And now that she's finally ready to take the next step, we don't want to waste another minute." He puts his head down, showing a touch of uncharacteristic shyness. "We want to make it official. Life's too short to wait."

My coffee tastes bitter, so I add more creamer. But I don't think it's the acidity of my drink that's the problem. It's my bitter jealousy of my brother's relationship.

Actually, that might not be accurate.

I'm not jealous of him and Sue. In fact, I'm elated for them. I adore them both and wish only the best for them.

What I'm jealous of is that he has the freedom to make his own choices. Meanwhile, I'm at the mercy of whatever the men in my life decide for me.

Leo shakes me from my thoughts, saying, "We need to head to Redleg HQ today if you're feeling up to it. Boss wants to sit down with us and hash out a list of possible kidnappers. He's already doing some investigating, but we need to help where we can. If you don't want to go there, we can ask him to come here to meet with us."

"No, that's fine. I'll shower after breakfast, and then we can go."

He seems pleased with my response.

My phone vibrates on the table with an incoming call. Rising, I leave the kitchen for some privacy.

"Hey, Jaynie. Thanks for calling me back so quickly."

"Hello, Sammy. What's going on?"

"I really need to see you. Yesterday, I was..."

I trail off, unsure of how to say this delicately. This isn't exactly something you can just dump on someone without warning. Talking about this kind of thing requires tact.

"You were what, dear?"

"I was jumped in the alley behind work, knocked out, and tossed in the back of someone's trunk. They took me for a joyride until I regained consciousness, pulled the emergency latch at a stoplight, and escaped."

Judging by her shocked gasp and slight yelp, I don't think I nailed the tactful, delicate delivery I was going for.

"Oh my goodness. Are you all right?"

"Bump on the head and some stitches, but otherwise, I'm physically fine."

"I'll reschedule my afternoon appointments so you can come in and talk through your emotions. I can't imagine what that must have been like. Especially with your traumatic past. You poor dear."

"Yeah, I'm... well, I'm *something* right now, that's for sure."

Angry at life's circumstances. Frustrated with all the men in my life. And perhaps in denial about the attack and what it might mean.

Someone is out to get me.

You'd think that would make me fearful, but that's not even in my top ten emotions.

Weird.

The number one emotion is... sort of stabby.

The sound of rustling papers comes through the line. "Can you come at four? I think I can move my four o'clock to tomorrow. She's usually flexible."

"Sure."

"Great. Until then, just remember your breathing exercises if you get anxious and try to do something that brings you joy. Maybe something creative like drawing or painting."

We say our goodbyes, and I return to the kitchen, where I'm met with my brother's exceedingly concerned eyes.

"Therapist?"

"Yeah. She can get me in today at four."

"That's good. Smart of you to call her. I'll let Sawyer know. He'll need to take you since that's when our appointment with the coordinator is. Unless you'd rather I take you."

"Nah. Go to your appointment. I'll be fine."

"You seem to be handling this well. Are you? Or are you just putting on a brave face?"

I roll my eyes, but the action gives me a twinge of pain. The discomfort only adds to my rising temper.

After grabbing some acetaminophen capsules from the cabinet and throwing them back with a swig of coffee, I face him and level a stern glare at him.

"*I'm. Fine.* For the love of God, please stop treating me like a child.*"*

He has the audacity to look insulted or hurt by my words. Perhaps it was my icy tone.

Whatever.

I don't wait for his response before marching out of the room. "I'm going to shower."

"You can't get your stitches wet."

"Thanks, *Mom.* I wasn't aware of that fact. Whatever would I do without you?" I sass.

After putting some waterproof first aid tape over my bandage, I scan my naked reflection in the mirror. My curves are somewhat curvier than they used to be when I was with Craig, which is a nice change.

But the many scars he left me remain the same.

Most of my injuries weren't from his direct assaults since he rarely struck me. They were from the chaos that would ensue when I'd try to leave, and he'd throw things in my direction. Anything breakable near him was fair game. The pieces often shattered and grazed by my skin, leaving their marks behind.

My gaze rakes over the faint scar on my outer right shoulder. It's about three inches long. Craig stitched it up himself because he didn't want another hospital trip to raise any red flags. He'd thrown a glass vase across the room, and it smashed into the wall two inches from my head. A large chunk of glass ended up lodged in my shoulder.

He didn't only throw things at me, though. Craig was also fond of restraining me to keep me from leaving — that was his primary form of abuse since he was forever terrified I'd leave him.

I look a few inches lower and see the soft pink lines on my forearms. Those are from a coarse rope Craig used to bind my elbows behind my back one night after an argument. The fucker tied them so damn tight the rope cut into my skin.

Maybe I should get tattoos to cover them. I could also get something to cover the smaller scars I got when I tried to fight back.

And now, my wrists are slightly bruised from the rope the kidnapper used yesterday to bind my hands.

My head is going to have a nice jagged scar right at my hairline from that fucker too.

Another injury.

Another scar.

Another horrible memory.

Another person — probably a man — trying to force me to do something I don't want to do.

Great. Just what I need.

My hands are shaking with anger by the time I turn on the hot water in the shower. While the spray washes over me, I try to shake off my hateful thoughts and self-pity.

I'm careful to keep my forehead out of the water as I clean myself because I'm a grown-ass adult and can care for myself, no matter what everyone around me seems to think.

I'm *not* helpless.

I don't need a babysitter and damn well don't need a father figure.

Fuck this.

I'm done being the victim. Starting today, I'm taking what I want, when I want it. My choices are going to be my own.

Mine and only mine.

And if someone doesn't like it, well, that's too fucking bad.

It's time for me to unveil Samantha Mason 2.0. The new and improved model.

As cheesy as it may sound, it feels like the warm water of my shower cleanses my body and washes my soul clean. I scrub and scrub until all my old fears go right down the drain.

When I face the mirror again, a new me stands there. Gone is the victim. A shiny and bright, confident woman has taken her place.

One who gets what she wants.

And I want Sawyer.

Now, I just have to make him see me as worth the effort. Because, dammit, I'm worth it, and he is too.

Chapter Nineteen
EMOTIONAL SUPPORT BEVERAGE

Sawyer

Leo's wearing a shocked expression on his giant face when he sees me already seated in the small conference room. He stops and stares at me with his jaw hanging low like an old lady's braless jugs.

"I didn't expect to see you again so soon. Did you even sleep?" he asks.

I angle my coffee cup in his direction and flash a knowing smirk. "I got about three hours, and I have my emotional support beverage. I feel great. Let's do this."

Sue and Sammy file into the conference room next. They're lost in conversation, chatting amiably. It's nice that Leo's sister gets along with his future wife. He deserves that type of good fortune. No better man than Leo.

Lucky giant fucker.

Shut the hell up, green monster. No one invited you, and you didn't RSVP to this meeting. So get the fuck out of here.

And also, I don't mean he fucks giants. I mean, he's a fucker who is also a giant. But I digress.

I drink in Sammy's appearance as she approaches the conference room table. She's wearing strappy sandals and a multicolored floral skirt that stops just above her knees and flits around with each step, along with a low-cut top in a deep purple shade. Even with the bandage on her head, she looks breathtaking. Damn her for being so freaking irresistible. The audacity.

She sits down across the table from me and meets my gaze. A feline smile plays at the corners of her eyes and lips. My heart rate increases, and I know it's not because of the extra caffeine I've ingested this morning.

"Good morning, Sammy," I tell her, then look at Sue seated on the other side of Leo. "Sue, you good today?"

"Yep." Sue opens her laptop, presumably to take notes. I've seen her do that on several occasions with past cases. She's pretty meticulous.

Big Al comes in, shutting the door behind him and plopping his notepad and tablet at the head of the table. "Thanks for coming in, everyone. Let's get started with our list of suspects. I've invited Sue to help with the profiling. Not sure if we'll get that far, but we need to be ready to move quickly, and I want to keep her up to speed."

Looks like Boss is all business this morning.

"Sammy, how are you feeling today? Head okay?" he asks her.

I detect a hint of her annoyance in her tone as she replies, "I'm *fine*. Thanks for asking." Her smile is tight and obviously forced.

Interesting.

Boss's eyes narrow at her for a split second, but he recovers quickly, glancing back at his notepad. I guess he noticed the snark too.

Getting even more interesting.

Maybe she's in a bad mood because she didn't get enough sleep last night. She must need an emotional support beverage of her own.

"Can I get you some coffee, Sammy?" I ask. "We have the good stuff here — Black Rifle."

"No, thank you, Sawyer. I'm fine." Her smile shoots straight to my gut and reaches down to cup my balls.

That *fine* didn't sound snarky at all like her *fine* to Big Al a moment ago. In fact, it sounded like she put a touch of heat in those words.

Big Al clears his throat, recapturing everyone's attention. "Okay, Shep was able to get a copy of surveillance footage from the last two weeks from the Sassy Parrot before the cops got it."

He pauses, and the slight smile he was wearing falls, replaced by a frown. "Unfortunately, all video files purge from their system after two weeks, so we can't go back any further. Hopefully, it'll be enough. He and Kri will be holed up going through that footage for a few days, at least. Nothing unusual was found as of this morning, but they've only been at it for a few hours."

We all nod in response. When my gaze bounces back over to Sammy, she's staring straight at me while spinning a pen between her fingers a few inches in front of her face. Her fingers are long and delicate, with a light mauve polish on her short, well-groomed nails. I have a momentary vision of her running those hands over my chest while riding my cock.

She catches me watching, and her lips curve as she flashes a wink.

What the hell is she doing right now? This is not the time to be cute and flirty. It's like she knows the dirty things I'm thinking.

Besides, didn't we decide last night that we can't be anything more than friends?

Leo asks, "How did Tomer make out with traffic cam footage and local businesses along the route from Sassy Parrot to where she was found on Cleveland Street?"

"*Escaped* on Cleveland Street," Sammy interjects, cutting a sharp glare at her brother. "I wasn't found. I escaped. On my own."

"Mic drop," Sue mutters under her breath.

I tuck my chin down to hide my grin.

Leo remains silent but tilts his head at Sammy as if he's sending some type of silent warning.

Big Al smirks at the interaction but tries to hide it behind his coffee cup. "If you're asking about obtaining the footage legally, Tomer hit brick wall after brick wall. The Scientologists didn't want to give up any of their footage, unfortunately. And the local government is being... well, the government. I'm waiting for a callback from my CPD contact, and I hope he feels like sharing with us."

"If they're interested in solving the case, they'll want all the help they can get," Leo adds.

"I'm sure you'd like to think that," Sammy jokes.

"And what about less legal methods?" I ask, knowing Tomer is not one to take no for an answer when someone's safety is on the line. He knows his way around the internet better than anyone. If there is a server with relevant footage out there, he has ways of getting it.

"He's working on it. No traffic light camera at the intersection of Cleveland and Garden, so we aren't able to confirm the exact car she *escaped* from." He emphasizes the word *escaped* while grinning at Sammy, then continues, "But Tomer's trying to use the other cameras between the two locations to see who else traveled that route. It takes time, especially considering all the side streets he may have taken. Trying to find someone who was near both locations in the right time frame isn't exactly easy."

"The pub didn't have footage that helped?" Leo asks.

Big Al shakes his head. "Negative. Nothing visible beyond the sidewalk. All we have is her running in from the street."

"Damn," Sammy says softly.

I hate to bring this question up, but we need to know. "Did we get confirmation that Craig Banks is still in prison?"

"Oh, the fuck nugget!" Sue says, then chuckles. "I wonder if his throat is still bruised."

Leo and Big Al snicker.

From the corner of my eye, I see Sammy's face go stark as her hand cups her neck again. And I'm certain it's not because of the reference to how Sue almost took him down by jamming a cell phone into his Adam's apple.

No, that's not why.

Sammy's made that same gesture before when his name came up. Must be some type of subconscious response. Like she's protecting her throat from his mere memory. The possible reasons why make me want to get myself thrown in prison so I can shank him.

"Yeah, Tomer checked last night, and he's still locked up," Leo responds reassuringly.

Sammy drops her hand from her neck and lets out a subtle sigh, but since I'm tuned in to her like an HD radio station, I noticed.

"That's all I have by way of an update, so let's talk potential suspects. Let's start with Craig's family and associates," Big Al says as he clicks his pen, hovering it over the notepad. "Sammy, did he have any close friends? Men he served with who he kept in touch with, perhaps? Someone who might be angry at you for helping put him in jail?"

All heads pivot to Sammy. She nibbles her lower lip and looks toward the ceiling. "He's an only child, and his mother is deceased. Umm... other than his father, I didn't see him interact with many people — certainly no one I would consider a friend. He was a homebody, and visitors at the house were few and far between. I think he was afraid I'd try to get a message sent out with any guests or try to use them to help me escape."

Son of a bitch. She makes it sound like she was a prisoner in her own marriage.

And I guess she was. My blood begins to boil.

She pauses to swallow, and her eyes dart around the table. "He didn't usually take me out to any social events other than an occasional apology dinner, but that was just the two of us. He did have Banks Software employees he managed remotely. The only visitor who came to the house, other than his father, was his personal assistant. She was a petite, older woman, so I doubt she'd have been able to hoist me into the trunk."

Sammy folds her arms across her chest and sticks her chin up, indicating she's finished.

Leo faces Boss. "Since Craig trained to be a Delta, he must have buddies he served with. Perhaps he has some loyalties left over from those days?"

Boss strokes his salt and pepper stubble, deep in thought. "It's possible someone else with questionable morals is doing his bidding —"

Sammy interrupts Big Al. "But why do you think it's him? He's in jail, and we're divorced. What possible reason is there to assume it's him?"

Studying her tense body language, I can't quite tell if she's defending Craig or genuinely not seeing how he could be responsible. In my mind, he's definitely our number one suspect since he's the one most likely to want to capture her or cause her harm.

"Sammy, listen," Leo starts. "We have to consider all possible avenues. Given your past with him, Craig is at the top of the list. Even if he's in jail, there's a strong possibility he's behind this. Probably some type of payback for escaping him and helping put him in jail."

She relaxes into her swivel chair, pushing away from the table and spinning around. Her hands tap on the armrests while she appears deep in thought.

After making a few revolutions, she comes to a stop and abruptly stands. She begins pacing while the others in the room shoot concerned glances at each other.

When she comes to a stop, she leans her arms on the table and meets Leo's gaze head-on. Her voice is determined and icy cold. "Craig has been locked up in a state prison for more than a year and was in county lockup for a year before that. Even though he contested the divorce, the judge granted it. He knows I'll never go back to him, and he's going to be in jail for at least a decade anyway. So why the hell would he come for me now? That doesn't make any sense. It has to be someone else."

Sue jumps in. "I'm with Sammy on this one. Craig has no motive other than revenge, and that's not something he would want someone else to exact on his behalf. He'd want to deal the death blow himself. That's how people like him typically operate."

Heads nod around the table as we all take in her commentary.

Sue purses her lips, then thoughtfully adds, "This was a kidnapping, not an assault. Kidnapping of a woman is typically motivated by money, trafficking, or an underlying sexual deviancy. Since she doesn't come from money, we can rule out ransom. She's a bit old for human trafficking, but she is beautiful, so that's always a possibility. But my money is on someone abducting her for sexual reasons. Maybe a customer who was a little obsessed with her or a coworker who she turned down. Sammy, did you reject any sexual advances lately?"

Apparently, Sue has no qualms about talking about uncomfortable things. I crick my neck from side to side, trying to shake off the building tension in my shoulders.

Three words fly through my mind on repeat.

Sexual deviancy reasons.

The thought of someone taking her for that makes me queasy and gives me full-Gallagher-level rage times three. And don't even get me started on the trafficking comment. Just fucking don't. My head will probably explode if I let myself think of that.

Sammy glances at me, but I put my head down, acting like I'm deep in thought. Damn, I feel guilty for kissing her now. Was that what the phrase *sexual advance* made her think of? Is that why she's looking at me right now? Or is that just my guilty conscience?

Although, she didn't even come close to *rejecting* my advance a few days ago at the bar. She gave me exactly what I wanted. She was soft and pliant in my arms, running her hands through my hair and pressing herself against me. *Perfection.*

No. If anything, I rejected her advances last night when I didn't let her tell me that she wanted me to kiss her. I knew that's what she was going to say. I also knew it would make it even harder to resist kissing her again. So I didn't go there. I shut it down like I'm supposed to.

Like a loyal best friend to Leo — a man who's saved me more times than I can count.

Like someone concerned with the emotional wellbeing of a woman he's in love with. Putting her needs above his own wants and desires.

Yep. That's me. Captain selfless.

Fuck. This sucks big saggy balls.

Sammy recaptures my attention when she clears her throat before answering Sue. "No one stands out more than others. From time to time, a few patrons may have too much to drink and say things they shouldn't. But I don't think anyone is *obsessed* with me. That's ludicrous." She makes duck lips and shakes her head in disbelief.

I think she drastically underestimates how beautiful she is and how she affects people.

I think Sue might be on to something, so I ask, "Sammy, are there any customers or coworkers who give you an uneasy feeling? Anyone creep you out?"

Sammy hits me with a playful glare, her eyes tight with annoyance, but her lips tilted in a grin. "Seriously? Every customer annoys the hell out of me. I get groped on a daily basis by handsy men and the occasional woman."

My hands ball into fists.

Before I have a chance to say anything that would reveal my anger, Big Al speaks. "I hate that you have to deal with that type of behavior, but it means we'll have some potential suspects based on Shep and Kri's review of the bar security footage. Once we get a list, we'll eliminate them one by one."

"I'd like to eliminate them, all right," I grumble to myself.

Leo must hear me because he looks over to me and offers his fist for a bump.

Sue taps her fingers on the table in a rhythmic pattern. "Any arguments or issues with friends lately? Any recent altercations, even if they seem to have been resolved?"

Sammy shifts in her seat, appearing a tad uncomfortable with the question. Not for the first time, I wish I were seated beside her so I could give her shoulder or leg a reassuring squeeze. Although considering the company we're in, that kind of familiarity might not go over well for me.

Sammy shakes her head. "The people in this room and my mother are the extent of my friendship circle."

Big Al picks up on Sue's train of thought, taking it a step further. "I hate to ask this, Sammy, but what about recent..." he pauses as a look of discomfort passes over his features, something resembling indigestion, "boyfriends or romantic acquaintances? We'll need a list of names so we can look into them. Even if things seem fine on the surface, it's worth investigating."

Leo stiffens beside me while my gut does an Olympic-level triple back-flip and sticks the landing in my chest. I try not to let my inner rage show, but I'm not sure if I'm being successful.

The thought of hearing about her recent sexual encounters takes me right up to my breaking point. My left eye twitches, and my jaw clicks audibly in the quiet of the conference room.

I wonder if I can fake a stroke to get out of hearing the answer. If this line of questioning goes on much longer, I won't have to fake it.

Sammy's eyes meet mine before shifting to her brother's and then falling to the table. She looks ashamed — that's the only way to describe it. Her shoulders hunch forward, and her chin drops to her chest. "No. There isn't anyone like that."

Big Al doesn't seem to buy it. "You have to be honest with us, Sammy. No judgment here, kid. We've all —"

I feel the sharp flare of my nostrils as my restraint snaps. "She said no, Boss. Fucking move on. Next question."

All heads snap in my direction. For whatever reason, the only person I can face is Sue. I guess it's because she's the least likely to pass judgment on me. Her eyes bulge as she draws her head back quickly. Her gaze flip flops between all the meeting participants repeatedly before facing the laptop screen in front of her.

Oh fuck. What did I just do?

Leo's eyes are burning matching holes in the side of my face. I ignore him and take a chug of my emotional support beverage, letting it soothe me as only those magic beans can.

"Let's shift gears," Big Al announces after clearing his throat. "Let's look at our own threats. Up first, Redleg adversaries."

The rest of the meeting goes by in a blur. The tension I caused with my outburst is slowly replaced with our focus on actionable items. Thank goodness our history as a team has lent itself to short bursts of testosterone followed by a swift return to business. It's like a micro-detonation of the male ego.

Tick, tick, tick, boom.

It happens in high-stress occupations like ours. You explode your man juices all over the place, clean up the mess, and move on. Hopefully, it doesn't come back to bite me later.

Really, Sawyer? Hope? That's your strategy?

If you put a big pile of hope next to a big pile of shit, they'll both smell foul in the heat of the day.

And no, I don't know what that means, but it sounds good.

Anyway, I'm brought back to the discussion by a few questions Boss asks about recent Redleg clients and things we might have observed on the job. We try to find something that might tie directly to Leo, in particular, before going broader.

We end up with a short list that includes some local gun smugglers and suspects from a meth lab we helped take down when we were protecting an informant. That was a few months ago, but some powerful people probably lost millions when that operation was taken out. Big Al is going to work with Tomer on following the money trail.

It's always the money.

"Terrorist cells with stateside contacts from our Ranger days?" I ask.

Leo and Big Al start ticking off potentials, using code names, of course, considering we're in mixed company.

A pang of discomfort always sets in my shoulder when we talk about our time in the service. And today is no different. I reach up and rub the scar on my upper chest to soothe the ache.

Sammy must notice the movement because she leans across the table and whispers, "You okay?"

"Who, me? I'm fine," I deflect, trying for a playful vibe. But today, I feel anything but playful.

I'm horny on account of sitting across from this beauty and fucking disgusted and enraged at all the people who could possibly mean her harm. It's confusing to have these feelings at the same time.

Big Al and Leo are lost in conversation about our more sensitive Ranger ops when Sammy gets my attention by leaning across the table.

In a hushed voice, she asks, "I have a therapy appointment this afternoon at four. Leo said he and Sue have a wedding-related appointment at that time. Can you take me?"

"Of course. Anything you need. I got you."

She leans back, nods, and offers a shy smile in thanks. My heart squeezes.

Now that we've moved away from Craig's possible involvement, she's much less annoyed. She's even gone back to flashing me those *fuck-me* eyes. Each time she does, my balls get fuller and bluer, and my dick gets harder.

Dammit, woman. Can you stop being so fucking enticing for one hour?

Leo, Sue, and Big Al chatter on about the possibility of Sammy and Leo's father being behind this. Sammy rolls her eyes while shaking her head dismissively before pulling out her phone.

I try to follow the conversation, but my head is still swimming. Being in her orbit is intoxicating. I think I need more coffee to sober me up.

I'm about to get up for a refill when my phone buzzes in my back pocket, distracting me. My eyes widen at the name on the screen.

Looking up from my phone, I'm hit with the intoxicating blue eyes of a smirking Sammy McFlirterson.

Fuck me and my blue balls.

Chapter Twenty

FROM THE TEXTS OF SAMMY AND SAWYER

Sammy: This meeting has gotten boring. I know I should be concerned about my safety and all, but I'd rather be doing other things.

Sawyer: Like what? <thinking emoji>

Sammy: Things with you. And your tongue. And your hands. And your <eggplant emoji>. Should we bounce?

Sawyer: Sammy, your brother is sitting right next to me. And I thought we talked about this last night. What the fuck are you trying to do to me here?

Sammy: Who, me? I'm an innocent little <angel emoji>.

Sawyer: More like a <devil emoji>. Pay attention to the meeting. Your life is on the line here, you know.

Sammy: <gif of spazzed out Nicholas Cage that says: You don't say!>

Sawyer: <gif of Elliot Page that says: I'm here today because I'm gay.>

Sammy: <gif of Steve Carrol saying: I understand nothing.>

Sawyer: Sorry. I tapped the wrong gif. Not gay. I'm pretty sure you, of all people, know that.

Sammy: Well, you could be bi. That would be kind of hot, actually. But okay. Not gay. Good to know.

Sawyer: I'm going to focus on the meeting before I accidentally confess to some other untruth since my attention is spread thin here.

Sammy: I thought of you when I touched myself last night. Did you hear me when I came? Were you listening at the door? I imagined you were right outside with your ear against the door. Did you hear my vibrator humming?

Sawyer: Dammit, Sammy. Don't do this now. Please.

Sammy: What do you think of this swimsuit I'm thinking of buying? <pic of Sammy wearing a bikini in a Target dressing room>

Sawyer: Fuck.

Sammy: So is that... fuck yes, I should get it? Or fuck no... it's terrible?

Sawyer: Yes, I want you to buy it. But not if you plan on wearing it for anyone else.

Sammy: Anyone other than who? <gif of woman confused with numbers and algebraic formulas flying everywhere>

Sawyer: You fucking know who.

Sammy: No, I don't. I want you to say it. Say the words, Sawyer.

Sawyer: Fine. I only want you to wear it for me.

Sammy: So are you staking some sort of claim on me? I thought you didn't want me.

Sawyer: I never said that. Don't put words in my mouth.

Sammy: What can I put in your mouth?

Sawyer: If you don't stop this, I'm going to drag you out of this room, bend you over my office desk, and spank your ass.

Sammy: If you don't man up and take what you want, then I'll be the one doing the spanking. Or I'll find someone else who will. Is Shep single?

Sawyer: Fuck, woman. You're driving me crazy. I only have so much control where you're concerned.

Sammy: Good. Because I want to be the one in control.

Sawyer: What is that supposed to mean?

Sammy: It means I'm done letting men make decisions for me. I'm calling the shots for once in my damn life.

Sawyer: Is that why you're texting me like this out of the blue? Because you're taking control?

Sammy: Yes, because I know what I want.

Sawyer: I know what I want too. But that doesn't change anything. If you insist on having this conversation again, let's not do it via text with your brother straining to look over my shoulder.

Sammy: That's fair. It was just easier for me to get started over text. We can finish later. And trust me when I say I really want us to "finish" together.

Sawyer: I'm going to put my phone back in my pocket now. I can't get hard in the middle of this meeting. To be continued.

Chapter Twenty-One

I'M LIKE A WHOLE MOOD

Sammy

I've never seen a brighter shade of red on a man's face before. Sawyer's obnoxiously handsome face went from a bashful blush to full-on solid maroon with a dash of purple when I asked if Shep was single.

My inner voice is totally like *giggle, giggle, snort, snort.* Which is a nice change from s*tabby, stabby, anger, growl.*

Obviously, I have no interest in Shepherd, but that opportunity was just too tempting to pass up. As the youngest child of three, I've always been a bit of a shit disturber, and it feels good to stir the pot once in a while. It's like riding a bike — the muscle memory is clearly there.

A little good-natured bear poking makes me feel like my old self.

The version of me who found joy in all types of situations and was a world-class joker.

I miss *that* Sammy. Shit-disturbing Sammy is a whole mood.

Anyway, I'd be a liar if I said I didn't find it incredibly hot how jealous Sawyer got at the mere mention of another man's name. His jaw clicked audibly for the umpteenth time today, and he nearly burned a hole in the cell phone in his hand with that death glare he was giving it. I hope the device is under warranty.

My therapist would probably say that Sawyer's jealousy is a red flag or a sign of a potentially controlling partner, but I don't give a frickity fuck at the moment. I mean, it's not like I'm looking for trouble or going to throw caution to the wind. I *know* Sawyer is a good man. Being with him isn't dangerous, no matter what he may think.

And this isn't going to be like last time. I'll *never* get myself in that situation again — under the thumb of some psychotic man.

Never.

Period.

"Sammy, if you think of anything else that might help us identify the person who took you, don't hesitate to speak up," Big Al tells me before turning to my brother and Sawyer. "Lionheart and Sawyer, you'll need to let me know if you need backup or notice anything while you're on watch. Copy?"

"Roger that," Sawyer answers.

"Ten-four, Boss," Leo chirps.

Such good little soldiers. *Giggle, snort.*

"I hope you don't ever expect me to answer you like that," Sue tells Big Al with a sly grin playing at her lips, and her eyes firmly on her laptop screen.

I sort of love how she just says whatever is on her mind. Her lack of filter and awkwardness are refreshing. I can see why my brother loves her so much.

Big Al's answering chuckle is deep and rich. Once again, I'm struck by his attractiveness. I wonder if my mom is hittin' that. If she is, then good for her. I bet he's an attentive lover.

Fuck, I'm horny. All the testosterone in this building must be messing with me. Walking in here is an assault on my senses. So many hot men... and hot women. All of them are badasses. It's distracting. As are all my dirty thoughts about the tall drink of water across the table.

And I'm freaking parched.

My raging hormones have helped cement my decision to entice Sawyer to give in to his desires.

Damn, he's delectable.

I'm still shocked that someone who looks like that is attracted to me. That jaw and those cheekbones must have been carved from stone, then covered with the silkiest tanned skin. The contrast of his skin with his shiny, dark brown hair — almost black — is mesmerizing. He's always so clean-shaven too, and I bet he uses the good skin care products. His skin is radiant, and I dream of rubbing my cheek against his and dragging my lips all over him. It's a marvel how healthy he looks, considering his diet is predominantly coffee.

And he's almost got a metrosexual vibe in how he takes care of himself and dresses, but he's still all man.

Even when he's tired like today, he still looks 100 percent edible. Like a sexy man popsicle just aching to be licked. By me.

And no one else.

Welp, it looks like he's not the only one with a jealous side. Oddly enough, I never felt jealousy with past boyfriends.

Wait. A boyfriend, Sammy? Settle down, girl. He's not your boyfriend.

Not yet, anyhow.

"That's it for now, then. Let's get to it." Big Al's palm hits the table twice to signal the meeting is over. I flinch a little, then bring my thoughts back to the meeting instead of thirsting over Sawyer like I have been.

I think Sawyer's hotness has created a horny monster to live alongside the rage monster inside me.

When Big Al stands, Sawyer and Leo jump to attention at virtually the same time, looking like toy soldiers. Sue's eyes travel to mine across the conference table, and she makes an awkward face. Her nose and lips scrunch to one side, and her gaze bounces from Sawyer to Leo, then to Big Al, before rolling her eyes. She draws the side of her hand up to her forehead in a mock salute, drawing a giggle out of me.

Leaning forward, I silently mouth the words, "We should do that."

She covers her smile, then widens her eyes with a quick nod to signal she's down with the plan.

At the same time, she and I lurch out of our chairs to stand at attention. I add an over-the-top salute and yell, "Sir, yes, sir."

She copies me a second later, but her words are cut off by her laughter.

Sawyer and Leo chuckle and shake their heads at our playful stupidity. When Big Al leaves the room, more of his deep laughter echoes from the hallway, fading as he goes.

Leo puts his hands on my shoulders, giving me a light squeeze. "Let's head home, kid. Unless you have somewhere else you need to go before your appointment."

"Home is fine with me."

"I can take her, Lionheart," Sawyer offers.

Well, well, well. Looks like someone wants to be alone with me sooner than planned. I haven't the foggiest idea why that might be. It couldn't possibly have anything to do with the photo I sent him a few minutes ago. Or all the dirty talk.

Ah, sarcastic Sammy, my dear friend. She always shows up when shit-disturbing Sammy is here. They're best buddies.

And wow. I'm embracing my crazy side and moving straight into multiple personality territory. So much to discuss with Jaynie this afternoon.

I try to hold back my smile so I don't look too eager for one-on-one time with Sawyer.

If I'd known it would be so easy to get alone time with him, I'd have been sending him swimsuit pics since I first met him when I was like twenty. Maybe even a side boob shot now and then.

A morose thought hits me, tanking my mood slightly. Things could have been so different for me if I'd gotten with Sawyer back then. I might not have been available when Craig came around. Imagine not having that mistake staining my past.

Stop that line of thinking, Sammy.

There's no sense going down that road. I don't have a time machine. If I did, there'd be a million things I'd do differently.

"That's okay, we can —" Leo starts, only to be cut off by Sawyer.

"It's no problem. I'm already caught up on emails, and all my personal shit is handled for the day. I can take over from now until tomorrow morning. Why don't you and your fiancée enjoy the rest of the afternoon together?"

Sawyer adds some icing to his manipulation cupcake by asking Sue, "Wouldn't you like an afternoon with your man? Maybe you two can go for a ride up the coast on the Harley."

Sue slams her laptop closed and feverishly shoves it into her messenger bag. "I'd have to be a fool to say no to an offer like that. I may be awkward as hell, but I'm nobody's fool."

Leo looks from Sue to Sawyer, then down to me, where I've taken my seat back at the table, enjoying the show. Wish I had some popcorn.

"That okay with you?" he asks me.

I put on a saccharine sweet smile and flit my lashes at him. "It's perfectly fine with me. I hate to break it to you, but Sawyer's just as good a babysitter as you."

"We're not babysitting you, Sammy," Leo starts, a somber look on his face. "You were abducted and attacked yesterday." His voice is low and chock full of seriousness. "You need *protection*, not a babysitter. That's what we're doing."

Feeling a touch guilty for my sarcasm and petulance, especially considering how worried Leo has been about me, I apologize. "I'm sorry. You're right. And I *am* grateful for everything you and the Redleg team are doing for me. I promise I'll behave and be a good girl."

Except when it comes to trying to get Sawyer's tongue in my mouth again. I'm abso-fucking-lutely going to be a bad girl about that.

We all walk out to the parking lot together before parting ways. Sue looks positively gleeful at the idea of bonus time with my brother. And when I look over at Sawyer, I can relate.

After inspecting the underside of the car with a mirror on a stick and some type of scanning device, he wordlessly opens the passenger door. He positions himself behind the door, keeping that precious inch or two of metal and glass between us. As I weave around him, I intentionally let my hand trail across his forearm. He lowers his sunglasses; I presume to let me see how his amiable expression shifts into something darker — a mix between frustration and arousal with his eyes as slits, a furrowed brow, and a slight nibble of his bottom lip.

I've never been an expert flirt, so I'm just winging it. Fortunately, I know he's attracted to me. That alone makes what I'm planning so much easier. If he rejects me, I know it's because of his loyalty to my brother and not because he finds me lacking. So, in a way, I'm not going out on a limb with this attempted seduction.

Well, at least it's not a rotted and frayed limb. It's a good, sturdy limb on a thick branch on a tree with deep roots.

And that's enough tree metaphors for one day. Not sure where those came from, but whatever.

With my prolonged touch, Sawyer's face has morphed into a mask of seriousness, and his posture stiffens. I remove my hand from his arm, not wanting to anger him. He hasn't made any jokes or used any of his fake accents since I started flirting with him in the conference room, which just feels wrong. A serious Sawyer doesn't sit right with me. It's like we slid into an alternate reality. A darker version of the world.

After he joins me inside the SUV and starts the ignition, he twists to face me, leaving one arm tossed casually on the wheel. Why is that position so sexy?

Dammit. Can he ever *not* be sexy?

He remains silent for a few seconds, as if he's collecting his thoughts.

Instead of cowering or backing down, I just hold my position, facing him head-on, chin up, and eyes wide.

Kiss me, Sawyer. Fucking kiss me. Make like Nike and just do it. Make like rain and fall for me. And other dumb puns.

Thanks to his dark sunglasses, I can't see what his eyes are doing, but I can *feel* them. He's allowing himself to drink me in — no, not drinking but gulping me down like an athlete chugs water at the end of a triathlon. His being stoic since the second half of the meeting makes sense now. It's not sadness or anger.

It's frustration.

Sexual frustration.

Same, Sawyer. Same. There's a cure for that, though.

"Do you understand why we can't be together? I thought I was pretty clear." His voice is barely a whisper.

With a touch of defiance, I respond, "You were clear. Leo is your friend, so you think I'm off-limits. But you didn't listen to my side, so I don't consider the matter settled."

"You're right. I didn't, and I'm sorry for that. Go ahead. I'll listen now."

Crossing my arms over my chest, I press my breasts up, enhancing my cleavage. I get a little thrill when he bites his lower lip. I can't see his eyes, but I know he noticed the movement.

Am I playing dirty? Maybe a little.

And the next time we're home alone, I have an idea of how I can play even dirtier.

"Leo doesn't get to make my decisions for me, Sawyer. I'm thirty-two damn years old, and I can be with whomever I want. Are you going to let him control you, making your decisions?"

He shifts in his seat and curses under his breath.

Nerve. Struck.

"It's not about control. It's about respect, honesty, and loyalty. He saved my life, for fuck's sake. More than once, and I know he wouldn't want me with you. He's the closest thing I have to family, and I don't want to lie to him or hide something this important from him. It's already killing me that I'm hiding that fucking kiss. It's a line I never should have crossed."

His hand rakes through his silky dark locks. My hand itches to do the same. I remember how soft his hair was when I ran my hands through it while his lips were fused to mine.

Recalling some of Jaynie's advice, I ask, "Why don't you just tell him you want to be with me? What's the worst that could happen? He's your friend, so he likes and trusts you. It makes sense he'd want someone like you to be with me. I think we'd be good together, and he'll see that."

The way his head kicks back a little at my words seems to convey something. Does he not believe me? Disagree?

"Now is not the time for that. Someone is trying to hurt you, Sammy. Did you forget you were taken last night? This is serious shit, and I need to focus on your protection. What if Leo pulls me off your detail because he thinks I'd be too distracted?" He grits his teeth and growls, "I want... no, that's not right. I *need* to protect you, and I can't do that if he won't let me near you. It's too big of a risk right now."

Oh, my heart. It's beating so fast. This moment feels so heavy. His honesty and vulnerability make me feel like I can be open with him too. And that's not easy for me.

"And after the threat passes, what then?"

"After that... we'll see."

My head lolls back with a hint of annoyance. "We'll see? That's your plan? What is it that might be different after the threat passes? What might *you see?*"

He shrugs, then forces a deep exhale. "Uh... I guess we'll see if we're both in a position where we're ready to have that conversation with him. And if you're in a place — emotionally — where you're ready for me." Flinching, he shakes his head as if negating his words. "I mean, if you're ready for a relationship."

I see red.

A little voice in my head says, *rage monster reporting for duty. Who do I stab first?*

Trying to replace my anger with sarcasm, I quote the SNL Church Lady, high-pitched voice and all. My mother used to do that impression all the time. "*Well, isn't that special?*" Then my anger returns, so I seethe, "You don't think I'm ready for a relationship, and obviously, you know that better than me. Good to know where *you* stand on *my* readiness for a relationship."

Bringing his arm off the steering wheel, he lowers his sunglasses. I'm met with the most striking dark eyes known to man. And there is pain there, hidden behind the dark embers of his desire. This is hurting him.

He's aching. I can feel it.

It diffuses my anger in seconds, like a candle's flame under a snuffer.

"I know you, Sammy. I always have." He sounds so sincere. "Even before we met, I knew you since Leo talked about you endlessly when we were serving together. And ever since then, I've been watching you. I pay attention. Each conversation we've had has mattered to me, and I remember them in painstaking detail."

He pauses only long enough to catch his breath before continuing, "I know you — the real you. And I don't want to rush you into something you're not ready for. I'm telling you right now that my feelings for you are intense and run deep. I don't know if I can hold back once I have you. I'm going to be all in. That's how much I feel for you." He pauses, shaking his head before adding, "What if you're not ready for all that?"

Oh, that's hot. And also very telling.

If I weren't seated, I'd probably have swooned.

Thanks to all my therapy, I can hear what he's not saying. The hidden meaning in his words. Even if he doesn't see it.

"You're afraid."

He cocks his head to one side and wrinkles his brow. "What? No, I'm not. This isn't about me. It's about you — you're not ready, and there's also your brother to factor in."

"You're scared, Sawyer. You're afraid I'm going to hurt you. That you'll go all in, and I won't be ready. And that I'll end up hurting you."

I'm met with stunned silence.

He pulls away, shifting back like I've hit him in the gut. He slides his sunglasses back on to cover his expressive eyes. He doesn't want me to see how much my words hurt. It's not easy to be so exposed.

Oh, Sawyer. I feel that way too. But I'm willing to go out on that limb for you.

And now we're back to tree metaphors. Excellent.

I reach over and take his strong hands in mine, running my palms over his knuckles before threading my fingers through his.

"Sawyer, listen to me. You can trust me to know when I'm ready. I realize my past is... complicated and a little traumatic. I'm healing, though."

Around the edges of his sunglasses, I can see the beginnings of his manly crow's feet, signaling he's squinting with disbelief. I jut my chin out even more. "*I am.* And I don't need or want you to make decisions for me. Or Leo. Or Big fucking Al or even my mother. Nobody. I can make my own decisions. Me. No one else. Never again."

"A *little* traumatic, Sammy? You were essentially held captive for three years. That's not something you can just get over by snapping your fingers or smashing a fucking watermelon." He shakes his head, pulls his hands out of mine, and then shifts toward the front of the car.

"Okay, so it was *a lot* traumatic. Your past was traumatic too — bouncing around foster homes and never knowing family. I get that. But that doesn't mean we don't deserve to be happy now."

"You do deserve that, Sammy. You deserve the world, but I can't give that to you. Not right now. Maybe not ever."

My stomach sours. He's giving up on me.

On us.

And I don't understand why.

He clearly has feelings for me. *Strong* feelings. He's admitted it multiple times now. And he knows I want him too. But he still won't do anything about it.

Am I not worth it? Or does he think he's not worth it?

The way he glazed right past the *we* when I said *we deserve to be happy* and focused only on me... is quite telling.

I don't think that's a problem I can flirt my way out of with sexy selfies.

But I'm going to show him I'm serious about this. And I'm going to prove that we're worth the risk.

Somehow.

Chapter Twenty-Two

WHO'S THE DUMBASS WHO CREATED THESE RULES?

Sawyer

S ammy is quiet most of the drive to her place. So am I — which is so fucking weird I don't even know where to begin with that shit.

When I was a kid, silence was the enemy. A wasteland where my dark thoughts would take over and the loneliness swallowed me whole. I learned from a young age that if I was outgoing and funny enough, I had a better chance of sticking around longer in the good foster homes. I was only a quiet, brooding asshole when it was a shitty placement, hoping they'd get rid of me sooner rather than later.

Silence is uncomfortable now for a multitude of reasons.

It's painful how I can't think of a single joke or a funny voice to lighten the mood.

Nothing.

It's like my funny bank has been robbed by a masked bandit named life. *Fuck you, life. Give me back my funny funds.*

Aside from her insightful words, all I can think of is that fucking picture of Sammy in a bikini. I've still got a semi, and my balls ache like hell.

When we turn onto her street, she heaves a deep breath so loud it overpowers the old-school punk rock coming from the radio. Her body language has grown increasingly jumpy these last few miles, like she's itching to say something. I suspect she's not done pleading her case.

But I need her to be done. I really freaking do.

My ability to resist her is hanging by a very thin thread. I've never wanted anyone like I want her. I want to make her happy. Comfort her. Please her. Love her.

But I *need* to keep her safe. That's what matters most. Not my wants. I've got to give her what she needs. I must focus on that.

Our feelings and desires will still be here after we bust the bad guy.

Well, I'm not sure about hers... but I know mine will be. I've been pining for her for over a decade. A few more weeks isn't going to do anything to stop that.

"I can't believe you've gone this entire ride in silence," she finally says. "This must be a record or something."

Her lighter tone and teasing words bring something back to my soul, jump-starting my playful side. Without thinking, I adopt a Yiddish accent and reply, "Oy vay! Thank God you finally broke the silence. I was dyin' over here. Enough already, right? Silence schmilence. It's foy the boirds."

Her quiet giggle dances around the car until it lands in my heart. Making Sammy laugh is akin to that first cup of coffee in the morning.

"That's more like it," she cheers. "There's the Sawyer I know... and love." She says the last two words so quietly, I almost don't hear them.

Almost.

But that's just an expression. It's not a declaration of love.

From the corner of my eye, I see her head cock to the side. "Sawyerrr..." she draws my name out. "That's your *last* name, isn't it?"

"Yes."

Don't ask. Don't ask.

"What's your first name? Why do you go by your last name?"

Fuck.

"Is it bad?" she asks. "Judging by your face, I bet it's bad."

When we pull into the driveway, I turn to her with my face masked in seriousness. "Not only did my parents not want me, they cursed me with a hideous name. It's a secret I'll take to the grave. You'll never get it out of me. So just accept that and move on."

Her eyes flash with a hint of sadness, or maybe it's pity. With a down-turned mouth, she says, "I can't imagine how hard it was for you, growing up as an orphan."

"It wasn't great, but I got by." I offer a simple grin to hide my pain. "Give me a second to check the alarm and sensors, and then we can get you inside."

I pull out my phone and open the app to make sure nothing is amiss with the home security system before we enter. I would have gotten a notification if something were triggered, but it eases my mind to verify by giving the cameras a quick look.

The delay gives me a moment to clear my mind of depressing thoughts. My childhood isn't something I like talking about. Bouncing from foster home to foster home, hoping to find a place where I belong. A family.

Nah, screw talking about that. No sense dredging up all that baggage. Certainly not today, when we've already had our fair share of uncomfortable and deep conversations.

I escort her inside with my hand on the small of her back. The feel of her body heat blends with the Florida sun rays, raising my body temperature in response.

She sets her purse down on the entryway table. "Looks like Mom's still at work."

I enter the code on the control panel on the wall to silence the alarm and put it in *home-occupied mode*. "Stay here while I check the house." Better safe than sorry.

I start in the kitchen, and she follows behind me, not listening to my instructions to stay in place. That's one strike. I shake my head at her, and the grin she shoots tells me she did it on purpose. Because I'm confident the house is clear since I checked the cameras already, I let it slide.

Once the kitchen is cleared, she says, "I'm going to get a drink of water while you check the other rooms."

I do a quick sweep from room to room. When I return to the living room, she meets me at the end of the hallway. "Everything okay?"

"Yep. All good."

Keeping her gaze on mine, she glides backward, deeper into the living room. Seductively.

No, no, no. That look she's giving me is trouble.

"I guess we have the place all to ourselves for a few hours. Plenty of time to... do whatever we want." She purses her lips and raises her brows, batting her lashes.

I'm so damn screwed right now.

I press my lips into a hard line and watch her back up, powerless to look away. She props herself up onto the back of the couch and spreads her legs almost imperceptibly. That flowing skirt inches up just enough to tempt me. She must have removed her sandals when I was checking the house.

Why are bare feet paired with a skirt so fucking hot?

Have mercy.

And if you read that in the voice of Uncle Jesse, then you get three bonus points.

What I wouldn't give to drop to my knees in front of her and bury my head under that skirt. I'd camp out and make a meal out of her sweet pussy, have her screaming my name, grabbing a fist full of my hair, and shoving my face deeper into her center.

But I'm a good friend and a responsible fucking bodyguard.

Instead of doing what I want, I tell her, "Sammy, I think we should set some ground rules."

"For what?"

I force a lump down my throat with a tight swallow. "Rules for how we behave around each other. Especially when we're alone."

Her gaze drops to the floor, then slowly works its way back up to meet mine. An air of sadness suddenly surrounds her, but it's quickly replaced with a mischievous smirk.

This woman. Testing me every chance she gets.

"Are rules really necessary? We've spent a crap ton of time alone together over the last few years without issue. It seems silly to have rules now."

As if I can't stop myself, I take a step forward.

You know that saying, *feet don't fail me now*? Well, my feet have fucking failed me right now.

"Things have changed, though. We both know we like each other and have chemistry together. But we can't act on it. Not right now. So having some ground rules will make it easier for me to protect you without getting... distracted."

That's right. Focus on her safety. Good job, asshole. Listen to your head, not your balls. Can't trust those fuckers when she's looking at you like this.

She rolls her eyes. "What type of rules did you have in mind?" Her tone is a mix of skeptical and accepting, an interesting blend.

"Well, for one, no more dirty texts or flirty innuendo. That nearly fucking killed me today."

She folds her hands in her lap, settling them between her thighs, right where I want to be. "Okay, fine. What else?"

"Limit our touching to only what's absolutely necessary for your safety. No kissing. And absolutely no sex."

With an arched eyebrow, she presses, "Anything else?"

"I think that should cover it. Do you have anything you want to add to the list? Anything you want me to stop doing?"

"Aside from resisting this thing between us?" She leans forward ever so slightly, giving me a view right down her fucking shirt.

Hell.

Well, don't look, asshole.

Easier said than done.

"Yes. Aside from that," I force out through gritted teeth as I shift my eyes back up to hers.

"Then I have nothing to add."

"Okay, so to recap, no more flirty texts or innuendo, we limit touching, there's no kissing, and no sex. We good?"

An almost coy smile lifts her cheeks, and something wild dances across her heart-shaped face. "I think I can make that work."

"Good. So with that in mind, perhaps don't sit like that."

"What's wrong with how I'm sitting?" she asks as she inches her thighs open the tiniest bit wider. Why is she doing that? My dick is getting harder by the second, making resisting her nearly laughable.

I'm not a religious man. After all, it's hard to believe in God when you've seen some of the shit I've seen in my life. But right now, I'm three seconds away from praying to some type of god. I need strength. Buddha? Allah? Yahweh? God? Zeus? Poseidon? I don't fucking care which one. Someone, please lead me away from this forbidden temptation.

Slowly, she unclasps her hands, placing one on each thigh and dragging her palms upward. The movement lifts her skirt a little farther, revealing more of that silky peach skin.

My breath quickens, and my lips suddenly feel dry.

She's beckoning me, and I'm powerless to resist. Against my wishes once more, my feet drag me forward, bringing me even closer to her.

"I'm just sitting comfortably. In my own home. Is there a rule against sitting?"

With a subtle shake of my head, I take a step, then another. And one more.

What am I doing? *Hey, feet, knock that shit off.*

I halt about six inches from her. Even though I'm looking into her eyes like a proper gentleman, I can still see her raise her skirt up farther.

This woman will be the death of me.

"Is it warm in here, or is it just me?" she asks innocently as she looks around the room.

Grabbing a handful of her blouse from her chest, she wafts it out in front of her. Her scent stirs around us, a gentle flowery aroma that makes my mouth water. It's a baggy shirt, so when she stops waving it around, it hangs off her shoulder, exposing some of her supple skin and a black bra strap. She did that on purpose. The vixen. I want to run my tongue along every curve of her body, starting right there.

Did I say she was acting innocently? I was dead wrong.

"I thought we agreed to no innuendo."

"Oh, we did. This isn't innuendo. I'm genuinely hot right now. Aren't you?"

Any of those gods feeling generous? I could desperately use that strength right about now.

My voice is thick with lust when I finally choke out my reply. "Yeah, I am."

While looking me dead in the eye, she runs her tongue over her lower lip and lifts her skirt up the rest of the way, waving and shaking it out before settling it at the very tops of her thighs, giving me a glimpse of black lacy panties.

Making borderline obscene eye contact, she draws out each word slowly when she rasps, "So damn hot in here."

It takes all my fortitude — and I mean every ounce of it — not to reach forward and cup my hand over her core to feel her warmth for myself.

Mustering what's left of my resolve, I try again, "Sammy, we agreed to no flirting. What are you doing?"

With the sweet smile of a siren, she replies, "Just trying to get comfortable despite the stifling heat. I think I'll feel better if I remove a layer of clothing."

Oh, hell no. No, no, no, no, no.

Gracefully, she lowers her feet to the ground and bends down, dragging those fucking black panties to her ankles in the process. I step backward and force my hands to remain at my sides.

Holy freaking hell.

The gods have forsaken me.

"Sammy," I warn, my voice like gravel. My eyes are stuck on the panties on the floor, and something tells me to grab them and shove them into my pocket.

So I fucking do.

It's like I'm taking the only part of her I can have right now. I make eye contact with her as I shove them in my back pocket. She raises her brows in shock but doesn't say anything other than a subtle gasp and a half chuckle.

She returns to her perch on the couch, spreading herself before me again. "That's better." She immediately resumes inching her skirt up until she's fully exposed to me.

This time, I don't even pretend not to look. I can't. Nothing short of someone gouging my eyes out could stop me from looking at what she's offering.

May Leo forgive me for what I'm about to do to his little sister. The thread I was hanging on was officially shredded when I slid those panties into my pocket.

My legs lurch me that final step forward until I'm smack dab between her welcoming thighs. Without reservation or even a fraction of a second's hesitation, I fall to my knees before her to get a better look.

She's perfect, and I'm at her mercy.

Waxed to perfection, with glistening pink folds peeking out from the soft white skin on either side. My hands reach up to spread her wider, but she stops me, jerking her legs closed.

"Ah, ah, ah, Sawyer. No touching," she scolds.

"Are you fucking kidding me right now?"

"Nope. I'm totally serious. You do *not* have my consent to touch."

Confusion fills my mind. Why is she bare in front of me if she doesn't want me to touch her? What is this madness?

I *need* to touch her.

"Sammy, I want —"

She cuts me off. "No touching. However, you can watch since that wasn't against the rules."

Ah, so this is the game we're going to play.

Dirty, naughty, beautiful woman.

I lean back on my heels, running my palms over my denim-clad thighs, and exhale a jagged breath.

With a slight nod, she makes an encouraging humming sound, like she's acknowledging my obedience.

Seemingly pleased with my restraint, she moves her thighs out of the way again. My eyes are locked on her perfect pussy as she inches a hand down and slides two fingers through her folds, drawing them up and down a few times before zeroing in on her clit. She swirls her fingers around and around a few times, but her hand obscures my view.

I'm in physical pain right now. It's nearly killing me not to spread her thighs and lips apart and lick right up her slit to her clit. I'm salivating to the point that drool is going to start dribbling out of my mouth any moment now.

My voice is a barely restrained groan when I say, "Spread your lips open. Give me a better view, babe."

"Ask nicely," she says coyly but with authority.

I meet her eyes, expecting to see confidence and dominance. But I see something else.

Vulnerability.

She's unsure about doing this. I sense a hint of fear reflected too.

I'm not sure if she gets off on this power dynamic or if she's testing me. Then again, maybe she's not testing me, but herself.

Either way, I'll happily do anything she wants as long as she keeps giving me a show like she's doing.

"Please," I beg.

"Please what, Sawyer?"

"Please give me a better view of your gorgeous pussy. I want to watch you touch yourself. Please, Sammy. For me."

A beautiful smile spreads across her face like a warm caress, and she nods. She bends her leg and lifts one foot onto the couch, exposing herself to me like a priceless work of art.

Or more like a canvas I want to coat with my own personal paint.

One hand leisurely moves toward her center, drawing out the anticipation for us both. She runs the flat of her palm across her entire center a few times, slowly stroking her outer skin up and down, until she lands at the top, where she digs her fingers into the wet pink flesh. Spearing her fingers into an upside-down *V*, she opens herself up to me.

Heaven.

I'm looking directly at heaven.

My spank bank runneth over.

My straining cock is pressing against my jeans so fiercely, I'm afraid the zipper is going to cut into the overly sensitive tip, maiming my lower head forever. I shift my position, trying to free up some space in my pants.

She must notice my change in position or discomfort. "Are you hard, Sawyer?" Her voice is breathy and hot as fuck.

"Yes, babe," I rasp. "I've never been this hard in my life."

"Show me."

Her wish is my command.

I rise to my knees without reservation. Literally, I would do anything she asked right now. With shaky hands, I fumble around, unbuckling my belt and lowering my zipper. I shove my jeans down to my knees, followed by my boxers. My aching cock bobs around due to my expeditious movements as I rest back on my heels with my hands back at my sides. Her widening eyes take it in greedily while she licks her lips.

A swell of pride fills me when she swallows audibly, obviously impressed with what she sees.

"Holy shit. You're so thick, Sawyer."

I flash a devilish grin. "Do you see how hard you make me?"

A soft moan escapes her lips as she nods quickly, then increases the tempo she's been keeping with her ministrations. My hand wraps around my cock, and I give it a squeeze.

"You can't touch yourself yet," she decrees.

Like a dutiful sex slave, I remove my hand and just freaking sit here with my cock out and my hands at my sides.

What the fuck is happening right now? I've never taken orders from anyone in the bedroom.

Never.

Well, *technically,* this is the living room. Therefore, I guess I can still say I've never taken orders in the bedroom. Apparently, that's the highest level of logic I can operate on right now.

The fact that she's denying me is making me want it so much more. It's like telling a kid they can't eat sweets until after dinner, and now all they can do is think about candy.

Well, if I can't touch myself, maybe she wants to do it. "Are you going to touch me?"

Her eyes are locked squarely on my erection for a solid three seconds before she looks up at me. "That... that's... that's against the rules," she stammers between breathy pants.

Fuck the rules. Absolutely fuck them. I don't know what I was thinking when I came up with them. That was the dumbest thing I've ever done in my life.

Stupid, stupid past-Sawyer.

It's clear now, her intention is to torture me with those rules.

And hell if I'm not loving every second of this game.

Her breath is coming quicker now, matching the tempo she's keeping with her fingers dancing across her swollen clit. I've never wished I could shape-shift into fingers so badly in my life.

This is easily the hottest thing I've ever seen. She's so damn wet I can see the slickness all over her fingertips.

I didn't know I had a voyeurism kink. Then again, I didn't know how raging hard I could be from being denied touching my own dick, and yet here I am. Rock hard and drooling.

My hips are subtly rocking of their own volition, seeking any relief for my angry cock. Even the air rubbing against my erection is enticing at this point.

A frustrated growl erupts from deep inside my chest when she dips her middle finger inside herself, then withdraws it slowly. She does it again, faster and harder, about five more times until her hips start to pulse in time with her fingers. A soft keening sound comes from her beautiful mouth, but my eyes are locked in on her sweet spot where she's speeding up her pace.

My cock is literally *aching* for the slightest friction. I wonder if a dick has ever broken off from being this hard with no relief. I'm being edged without even being touched.

"Do you want me to beg, Samantha? Is that what this is about?"

"Begging won't help. I'm following your rules like a good girl."

She releases a deep moan and throws her head back as she continues pleasuring herself. She's pressing the base of her palm against her clit while thrusting her finger in and out of her tight heat. It should be my hand there. Fuck. I want to do that. With my fingers. My face. My mouth. My dick.

I have to mash my hands into fists to stop from squeezing my cock, but I manage to hold back.

I'm willingly letting this little vixen control me from a foot away, and I've never been more turned on in my life.

Knowing what I do about her sexual past, I think she needs this — the control. So I'm just resting here on my heels with my dick out. Waiting for permission to stroke it.

I meet her gaze. With both my eyes and my words, I beg her to let me jack myself off. "May I stroke my cock, babe? Don't you want to see how I fuck my hand when I'm alone and thinking about you?" Softer, I add, "*Please.*"

Her eyes flash wide with approval *and* arousal. "Yeah, I really do. I want to see it so badly. You can do it now."

Based on her expression and the eagerness of her tone, I can tell she fucking loves it when I ask for permission. *Filing that away for later use.*

Without delay, I wrap my fist around my throbbing cock and squeeze from root to tip.

Fucking relief.

Finally.

Sweet, sweet relief. I can't hold back a deep moan as I start stroking myself with vigor. As long as I live, I'll never take touching myself for granted again.

After gathering some moisture from the tip, I rub it across the head. Dammit, my cock is freaking weeping for her. The lubrication helps me go faster and squeeze harder, and my hips keep rocking me into my hand.

The room is silent with the exception of the slapping of skin, gasping breaths, and desperate moans as we stare into each other's eyes and inch closer to nirvana.

"You're beautiful when you touch yourself, Sammy. So fucking beautiful."

She points her chin at my fisted cock. "Is that how you do it when you're alone?"

"Just like this, baby." I hiss, trying to hold back the impending eruption. I don't want her to think I'm a one-pump chump.

"Mmm," she moans. "I like watching you do that. It's so hot." Her leg falls from the top of the couch as she rocks a bit more wildly into her hand.

Meeting her eyes now, I ask, "Did you really touch yourself last night while thinking of me?"

"Yes."

"Just like that?"

With a high-pitched voice, awash with pleasure, she replies, "Yes. And then I used my vibrator."

"Good God, woman. You're so fucking hot, talking like that. Are you close? I'm close."

"Wait for me," she demands. "Do *not* come yet."

My head falls back, my eyes meet the ceiling, and I curse under my breath. Her fucking telling me I can't come only brings me even closer to climax.

I pull my hand off my dick and stand, buying myself a few seconds in hopes I can hold off and do as she asked... more like demanded. Two more strokes, and I would have been gone.

My clothes are burning up my skin. I run hot anyway, and being clothed in proximity to this ethereal goddess as she finger fucks herself is liable to make me self-combust.

After throwing off my shirt, I kick off my shoes and jeans from around my ankles so I don't fall flat on my face. Buck naked now, I inch as close to her as possible without touching — stupid fucking no-touching rule — and lean down, inhaling her skin. I hover my nose inches away from her shoulder and neck so I can get another hit of her delicious scent.

"Ah, ah, ah. No touching," she warns.

Deeper this time, I inhale again, then move my head over to the other side. "Yes, ma'am. Just getting a whiff of your skin. You smell so damn good."

As my gaze falls to the exposed skin of her shoulder and that sexy as fuck black bra strap. My vision catches on an exposed scar on her shoulder. My mind tries to process what might have caused an injury like that. I've seen scars on her lower arms before, but seeing that one on her shoulder does something visceral to me.

Unbidden, my teeth press together in anger instead of arousal. Whoever hurt her and left that scar will pay — whether it's Craig or her father or someone else. I'll find them and make them sorry they ever hurt my girl.

My girl. *Mine.*

Whether or not I ever get the courage to do anything about it, she'll always be mine. Then again... hasn't she always been? Even if she doesn't know it.

She distracts me from my momentary lapse in focus by removing her shirt, revealing her luscious breasts spilling from the top of that sexy black bra. Her hard nipples poke through the soft, lacy fabric, and I can see the top halves of her rosy areolas. They look positively mouthwatering. I would sell my left nut to be allowed to take one in my mouth while squeezing the other.

Her eyes drink in my naked form, sweeping across my skin from head to toe. Suddenly, she reaches out toward my chest like she's going to touch me. I lean forward into her touch, desperate to feel her skin on mine, but she pulls back and levels a glare at me. Her hand stays about an inch away from my skin as she moves it over my shoulder, my chest, and then my stomach, before pulling it away altogether and closing her hand in a tight fist.

She didn't even touch me, but I felt her skin on mine all the same.

"Dammit," she hisses.

"It's okay. You can touch me, baby."

"No. I can't. We have rules against that." Her voice is harsher now, taunting and dominant.

Hot, hot, hot.

"Maybe we should amend the rules," I offer, utterly desperate for her touch.

She's sitting spread eagle on the back of the couch again, gloriously naked, except for the lacy bra and the loose skirt pooled around her waist, and hitting me with the most shit-disturbing grin I've ever seen. Even more devilish than my own.

Fuck me running, she's absolutely perfect for me.

Her sarcastic and sassy attitude.

Her fiery spirit.

Her curvy body.

All of her. Absolutely made for me.

"Are you telling me you've had some profound change of heart? Perhaps you've done some soul searching in the short time since you laid out the ground rules?"

Her hand moves back down to start toying with her clit again, so I grab my shaft and resume stroking as we stare each other down in a bit of a mutual masturbation standoff of sorts.

"I've reconsidered our situation, and I think we should be allowed to touch each other. I now believe we can handle it."

"So this was what, like a moment of personal growth on your part?" she says, playing along while knowing full well she's already won the game.

"Yes, absolutely." My head nods wildly, like a bobblehead on the dash of an old truck with worn shocks on a dirt road.

Clearly, my dick is doing the talking for me.

Her lips quirk when she says, "An erection is not considered personal growth, Sawyer."

We laugh together, and I lean in for a kiss. But she denies me, turning her head to the side.

"No kissing, remember the rules?"

Fuck. The. Rules.

With a groan of frustration, I let my hands fall to each side of her body, caging her in but still not touching her — respecting the dumb-ass rules concocted by a dumb-ass man.

Her breath catches, and I pull back, expecting to see her awash with arousal, but I'm met with a fearful expression instead.

"What's wrong?"

"Take a step back, please," she says, her voice tight.

Instantly, I follow her instructions, concern for her spiking.

"Better?" I ask.

"Yeah, thank you," she says, looking a little unsteady. She's stopped touching herself and won't meet my eyes.

Did I scare her?

Oh, my sweet Sammy. What did he do to you? I'll fucking kill him.

"Sammy, you know I'd never hurt you, right?"

"I know," she whispers.

"We can stop, if you want. I won't be mad."

Her gaze flits from the floor to my eyes, and she studies me carefully. It's like she's looking for the deceit hidden in my words.

She must believe me because one corner of her mouth raises slightly and her chin lifts with determination. "I don't want to stop until we've both *finished*."

"It's fine, Sammy. We can stop," I repeat.

A determined look settles across her features. "Take my panties out of your jeans."

My brows lift in disbelief at her sharp return to commanding dominance. I'm not sure if she's going to put them back on or do something else, but I do as she says. She holds her palm out for the panties. Before I release them, I bring them to my nose so I can smell her arousal.

My rock-hard dick becomes Mount Everest once her tangy scent hits my nostrils. I smile deviously at her before I place them in her outstretched hand. She twirls them around her finger while eyeing me closely.

"If I touch you with these, it's not breaking the rules, is it?" A wicked smile plays on her lips.

"I guess it wouldn't be *you* touching me. It would be the fabric of the panties. Seems like a fine loophole to me."

"I'm sure it does," she quips before wrapping her hand inside the panties.

Encased in silk and lace, her hand runs across my chest and down my stomach. Her eyes meet mine when she encircles my cock. My breath hitches.

This is better than any fantasy I've ever had. *Ten stars. Would most definitely recommend.*

She gives me a firm stroke, and the silk of her panties mixed with the roughness of the lace feels like heaven and hell have joined forces. A dash of pain to mix with the warm softness of her touch. My hiss quickly turns to a moan.

I'm not going to last long like this. I need to get her off so she'll let me come.

After murmuring nonsensical words softly, I nod at her chest. "If I touch you over your bra, I'm not really touching you, am I?"

She resumes playing with herself with one hand and stroking me with the other. "I guess you wouldn't be breaking a rule if you were only touching my bra."

"May I touch you there?" I ask.

"You're being so good, Sawyer. Asking nicely." With her breath increasing, her head lolls around her shoulders again as her fingers blur across her clit, then disappear inside her body.

I'm torn between watching her fingers work her into a frenzy or watching her panty-covered hand fist my cock. Either way, I can't lose.

My balls draw up tight as she moves faster around my shaft. Trying to hold back my own pleasure, I focus on her and grasp both breasts in my palms, giving them a gentle squeeze over her bra.

The pace she's using on me increases as she arches her back and shoves her tits deeper into my hands. Through the thin fabric of her bra, I find her pebbled nipples. They feel exquisite. I pinch one with light pressure to test her response.

"Squeeze harder, Sawyer."

"Anything you want, baby," I tell her, then squeeze both nipples simultaneously.

Literally, anything she wants. I'll give it to her.

With jerking hips, I steadily increase the pressure on her tight buds until she throws her head back and keens. "Coming. I'm coming."

And then *I'm* coming. Directly into her fucking silky black panties.

Chapter Twenty-Three

NO ONE NEEDS TO KNOW

Sammy

We haven't talked about it.

The thing we did.

The naughty, deliciously hot thing that instantly became a core memory.

Wordlessly, we took turns using the bathroom to clean up. I went into my room for new panties. And when I came out, he was completely dressed and acting like nothing happened.

Only it *did* happen.

It was hot and forbidden, and oh my freaking God, I'll never be the same.

No one could remain unchanged after seeing that man gloriously naked, stroking himself, and coming into a handful of black silk. If it wasn't disgusting, I'd keep those panties in a little zipper bag. However, I realize it *is* disgusting, so I'm not gonna do it.

But I could.

He's doing a perimeter sweep outside, but I know it's merely an excuse to get some space from me. Sawyer's probably freaking out right about now.

In truth, I am too.

I feel a little guilty for manipulating him. He didn't want to cross that line; that's why he made those stupid rules.

And what did I do?

I immediately shat all over his rules — metaphorically speaking, of course. I'm not into doing the *Dirty Sanchez*.

Disclaimer: if you don't want to be grossed out, you might want to avoid googling that term. And if you already know what it means, and you're into that sort of thing, then more power to you. Not trying to yuck your yum. It's just not for me.

But I digress.

Technically, I didn't break any rules.

Nonetheless, the guilt is hitting me, souring my stomach and ruining my post-orgasmic high.

I'm not usually a manipulative person. I've spent my life being controlled by others, and I don't want to force that on others because I know how much it freaking sucks.

It's just that I am so damn tired of everyone else making decisions for me. So I took control for once.

I want Sawyer.

That being said, I certainly didn't force him to do anything. He could have left the room. But he didn't. He dropped to his knees right in front of me. *Damn, that was hot.*

And he absolutely respected every boundary I put in place in the hottest way possible.

I tested out exerting some power over him — something I've most certainly never done before — and he responded beautifully. It's like he knew I needed that.

The way he instantly followed my directions was liberating in a way I never thought possible. I was free to take charge, without fear of repercussions or judgment.

Sawyer always makes me feel safe enough to let down my guard.

Sure, I felt vulnerable and exposed.

But at the same time so very safe.

He's without question as good a man as I thought. Suspicions confirmed.

The timing isn't great for us; I'll admit that much.

But fuck it. Life is short, and we might as well be happy before time runs out.

In this house that Leo has secured like Fort fucking Knox, we're safe for the time being. So why not explore our attraction and have a little fun?

Don't I deserve that much after all I've been through in my shitty excuse for a life?

The front door closes, distracting me from the mental yoga I'm doing to justify my reckless behavior. I flip through the channels mindlessly.

"What time do we need to leave for your appointment?" he asks.

Oh yeah.

"Uh, about quarter 'til four should be fine."

"Let's go a little early so I can check out the facility to make sure you're safe there."

I nod, understanding his concern and check my watch. We've only got a half hour to kill.

A kitchen chair scrapes across the floor. I guess he's going to completely avoid me until we leave.

Not if I have anything to say about it — and I sure as hell do. Sammy 2.0 isn't the type of gal to let life happen to her.

"Ready to talk about it?" I holler over my shoulder in the direction of the kitchen.

He sighs loud enough for me to hear it thirty feet away, bringing a reluctant smile to my face.

Setting down the remote, I rise and head to the kitchen. When he sees me enter, he squints and purses his lips like he's in pain.

I approach cautiously and take a seat beside him. I *need* to comfort him. "Hey, it's okay. We didn't do anything wrong. We're consenting adults."

His gaze fixes on the table. "Feels wrong."

"Why?"

Frustrated now, he groans and throws his head back, lifting his shoulders almost up to his ears. "Nothing has changed from what I said earlier." He ticks off the reasons on his fingers. "Your brother and family. Your readiness for a relationship. Your safety. All those things make what we did wrong."

I scoff and roll my eyes. "Bullshit. Leo doesn't control my life choices. I'm ready for a relationship when I say I am — and I'm saying I am. And we were perfectly safe here. You didn't compromise my safety in the least."

He finally meets my eyes. "Even if Leo doesn't make your decisions, he still outranks me at Redleg. He could pull me off your detail if he finds out." His voice has softened, compassion and sadness laced together. "Big Al would agree with him because it's a conflict of interest for me to guard someone I'm romantically involved with. We can't do this, Sammy. Even if we both want to."

He's right.

I hate it, but he's right.

Unless...

"Sawyer, I don't think I'm strong enough to fight my attraction to you anymore. And I don't want to. Not since you kissed me in the back of the bar. The switch has been flipped, and I can't turn it off now."

I pause, giving myself one last chance to back out. But I don't retreat from this path we're on. He doesn't say anything. Just stares at me with longing, giving me the last bit of courage I need.

With deliberate slowness, I angle my head to the side and softly add, "What if we didn't tell anyone?"

He cocks his head, mirroring my pose. "You want me to keep a secret this big from my best friend in the entire world? The closest thing I have to family? And my boss? My whole team?"

I gulp down my fears and steel myself to whisper what my heart wants me to belt out fortissimo.

"You don't have to decide right now. But yes... that's what I'm suggesting. I'd be keeping it a secret from my family too, which isn't easy for me. Especially after how badly I hurt them before."

I put my head down, feeling shame for asking him to make this sacrifice. For me. Old habits and years of feeling insecure return, making me feel like I'm not worth this sacrifice.

Shit. Maybe he's right, and I'm not ready for a relationship with him. This could be a colossal mistake.

"Let's not decide now. Just think it over," I hedge, trying to buy myself some time to think.

His warm eyes meet mine. He isn't that good at hiding his feelings from me, and I can tell he's strongly considering throwing caution to the wind and claiming me.

I want him to.

But I also don't want to hurt him.

"Speaking of secrets, I erased the cam footage from the server so no one sees what happened earlier."

"Cam footage?" I ask.

"From the living room when we... you know."

"Oh my God." My hand smacks my forehead. "How could I forget about the nanny cams? Is someone at Redleg monitoring that in real-time? Did they see us?"

When I moved in two years ago, Leo told me he had cameras recording the front door area, driveway, front and back yards, living room, and hallways. Just in case someone meaning us harm was to get inside.

"No one is *actively* monitoring it, to my knowledge. But anyone with access to the app can tap in whenever they want to see what's happening live or review the recorded footage. But I deleted that time frame."

"Thank you."

"Of course, I want to protect your modesty. But I'll admit, it wasn't *only* for you. The caveman in me sure as hell doesn't want anyone else to see you come, and I also did it so your brother didn't see it. I don't have a death wish," he jokes humorlessly.

"Well, regardless of the reasons, thank you."

He nods, staring at his hands on the table. His nails are perfectly manicured and always so clean. I can't help but want those fingers inside me.

Rising brusquely, I brush my hands down the front of my skirt as if I'm symbolically ending the conversation. "Can we stop by Starbucks on the way? I need some coffee before therapy."

He levels a playful glare at me. "Sammy, quit trying to sweet talk your way into my pants."

Chapter Twenty-Four

ALL MY LITTLE MONSTERS ARE HERE

Sammy

My head feels like it's splitting in two. The ache is coming from my stitches and reverberating around my entire skull.

Idly, I wonder if such a thing has ever happened to anyone. Has there been a traumatic brain injury so painful it caused a skull to crack open? Not like a crushing injury that physically splits a skull, but merely from a sheer desire to do anything to end the pain. Like a self-destruct button. Is that about to happen to me? Freaking feels like it.

Oh man. Now I have guilt for thinking so flippantly about someone who might have suffered something that horrible.

And now I've got *guilt* on top of the headache from hell. *Super-duper party pooper.*

The events and heavy conversations of the last twenty-four hours run through my mind at Mach speed. There's so damn much to process, and when you add in the stupid head injury, it just makes me want to crawl into a bottle of ibuprofen and sleep for a few weeks.

My inner rage demon taps the microphone and says, *looks like someone took her overdramatic pills today.*

I think I'm losing it. Good thing we're on the way to see Jaynie now.

I felt better earlier, probably thanks to the endorphin blast from the orgasm. But that nagging ache has come back with a vengeance as the day warred on. I wonder if that's normal after a concussion. I should have asked the ER doctor more questions last night. But I wasn't in the right frame of mind for productive Q&A time.

Sawyer's been quiet on the drive thus far. He only spoke to ask for my drink preference and then to order his *two* trenta black coffees — one for now and one for later — along with my iced vanilla latte.

Who would have thought that a little mutual masturbation would make him so reserved? I thought guys got happier after they came.

Then again, what the hell do I know about men? I've only had five lovers in my life. Hardly enough for a proper case study on post-orgasmic male behavior.

"Open the glove compartment," Sawyer whispers after turning off the radio.

Why is he being so quiet?

I pop it open and survey the contents. "What do you need?"

"Nothing. Grab that bottle of ibuprofen and take a few."

Curious, I ask, "What makes you think I need them?"

"Sammy, I've told you before. I watch you. I know you. And you're hurting right now. How long has it been since you've had something for the pain?"

After checking my watch, I reply, "About six hours."

He nods in the direction of the bottle that's hanging out with a handgun. I don't know guns, so don't ask me what kind it is.

"Thank you," I say quietly, still feeling a bit shocked at how easily he can interpret my body language.

When I was with Craig, I worked hard at schooling my features to keep from letting emotions show. I didn't want to reveal any weaknesses for him to exploit. Perhaps being away from him these last few years has helped me feel safe enough to let my guard down.

Or maybe it's just Sawyer who makes me feel safe enough to be myself.

After I toss the capsules in my mouth and wash them down with a few sips of my latte, the only sounds are the low hum of tires on the road.

I can't stand this awkward silence, so I tap into my mischievous side. "Is it Edward?"

He whips his handsome face over to me. "Is what Edward?"

"Your first name. Is it Edward?"

"Ha ha. No. That would've been okay. I could've made Eddie work. And Twilight was all the rage for a while, so that would have been dope."

"You're not team Jacob, huh?" I tease, not expecting him to fully get the reference.

"Team Edward all the way." He drops his voice. "You're like my own personal brand of heroin."

I can't hold back my smile. He's so damn cheeky with all his impressions. And he either read or watched *Twilight*. That's hilariously unexpected and a tad sexy, if I'm being honest.

"Humperdink?" I tease, raising my brows high.

A boisterous laugh jostles his shoulders, and then he shakes his head.

"Jeremiah?"

"That's not a bad name. It's biblical and shit. Plus, *Jeremiah was a bullfrog*." He sings the line, sounding just like the song. He actually has a good singing voice. My clit must agree since she's pulsing away down there.

"And he was a good friend of mine," I add in my own less-impressive singing voice. We share a chuckle.

A sensation of warmth coats my skin as we return to our typical playful interactions. My headache even dials back from a twelve to a nine. And I don't think it's because the pills kicked in yet. So it must be him.

In the style of Mark Wahlberg in that classic meme-worthy scene from the movie *Ted*, I rapidly rattle off a laundry list of names without taking a breath. "Henry, Samuel, Otto, Ralph, Stanley, Wilfred, Bruce Wayne, Abraham, Barnaby, Bartholomew, Cecil, Cornelius Oggleberry the third, Winston, Wilfred?"

Through deep guffaws, he holds up his hand and stops me. "You said Wilfred twice."

Playfully, I toss my hands, fall deeper into the seat, and let my body go slack. "I give up."

"Good," he teases. "Now, we can have a moment of silence for all the names that were offended by your rant."

Well, now I'm not going to stop.

"Hmm..." I drawl slowly, tapping my finger across my lips. "How about Gordon?"

"Gordon, huh? Do I look like a Gordon to you?"

No. You look like whatever you'd call someone who should have his face buried between my legs.

Easy, horny monster. Settle.

"Not really. I always think of that as an old man's name. Not a young, studly name for a handsome buck as yourself." I wiggle my brows at him.

Pretty sure we've already established that I find him incredibly hot, so I guess he's not going to comment on that part like he used to.

"I bet there are thousands of Gordon Ramsay mega fans out there who would disagree *hard* with that sentiment."

"Oh, that's true. I forgot about him. He *is* pretty hot for an older dude. But I'm not a huge fan because of his yelling and throwing dishes across the kitchen." My shoulders lift in a visible cringe.

When a man raises his voice in anger, it reminds me of Craig or my father. On TV or in person — it doesn't matter. I'm anti-yelling. And throwing shit in anger? Hard pass.

Sawyer's face sobers, and I realize I just tanked the mood by referencing my traumatic past. Well, I *indirectly* mentioned it.

Shit.

Getting us back on track, I ask, "I think it's Percy. Or Percival."

Sawyer lets loose a slight chuckle, just a little one, but it's reserved and tight.

"Hmm. I think I'm getting close. That reaction was telling."

He leans a little closer to my side of the car and talks out of the side of his mouth like he's telling me a secret. "You know that even if you guess it, I'm going to deny it, right?"

I scoff. "Oh, I think I'll be able to tell when I get it right. I know you."

"Oh really? You think so, huh?"

Nodding, I reply, "Yep. I do. You're not the only one who's been watching. Learning. Paying attention. I know your tells."

"I don't have any tells. And even if you figured them out..." He shifts into a southern drawl and says, "Frankly, my dear, I don't give a damn." Punctuating his *Gone with the Wind* line, he winks at me, the handsome fucker. Instantly, my nipples pucker.

He's so damn sexy.

"Persephone, Perkins, Perty!" I shout excitedly. "Oh! I got it! Pertalicious. It's Pertalicious, isn't it? I knew it. Nailed it."

His answering laugh does the waltz between my legs and directly to my cervix.

I could ask Big Al or my brother what Sawyer's first name is, and they'd probably tell me. But where's the fun in that?

When we pull into the parking lot a few moments later, I heave a deep breath and wait for him to tell me when it's safe to get out. I've learned enough from my brother and Sawyer to know better than to jump out of a car without checking the area first. Heaven forbid.

I can hear an amalgam of their voices in my head as clear as day. *Sammy, if someone were following us, they could immediately pull in behind you and grab you before we could react.*

So I sit dutifully and await instructions. Mentally, though, I'm doing it under protest. My inner rage monster is holding a picket sign.

"Sit tight," he mutters.

No shit, Sherlock.

Responding with a nod, I offer a salute, then fold my hands in my lap like a good little girl. My rage monster pokes me with the edge of her picket sign and yells: *Fuck that. We don't listen to men anymore. Do what you want, Sammy!*

Ignoring the little angry voice because it's highly possible she has zero regard for my safety, I literally twiddle my thumbs while I wait. Sawyer exits the vehicle, locks it with his remote, and swiftly walks to the building entrance. He meanders around for a few moments before heading back, checking over his shoulder the entire time like he's got eyes on all sides of his head.

He's back in a matter of seconds, coming right to my door. I hand him his *later coffee* since he chugged the first one on the short drive. The handsome stud sure loves his java. I feel the same way about wine — like my mother before me.

With his free hand, he ushers me out of the vehicle, giving my hand a gentle squeeze before letting it go. My heart and pussy clench in unison. *Just* from that minuscule contact. Oh my freaking hell. I'm wrecked for this man.

I *need* to get a grip. But how can I now that I've seen him naked and know what he sounds like when he comes?

Hot as fuck. That's how he sounds. It was a gentle grunt, heavy panting, and a hushed curse of *fuuuck* that will forever live in my mind rent-free.

Don't get horny before therapy. Don't get horny before therapy.

With a hand on my low back, he guides me to the entrance. He has a slight spicy smell about him, and when the wind blows just so, I get a good whiff, nearly tripping on my own feet from the onslaught of deliciousness. It's some type of masculine body cleanser or cologne. It's probably called: *I'm about to take your girl.* Or maybe it's just him and his potent pheromones. I wouldn't be surprised if it's just his natural aroma that makes me salivate.

He should come with a warning label. *Caution: Don't sniff too closely. Will make you horny.*

His head swivels from side to side and over his shoulder with each step we take.

"Relax, man. It's just therapy. You're making me nervous," I tell him.

"Your safety is my number one focus, baby. I'm not going to compromise on that. I might cave on some of the other *rules*..." He trails off and catches my eye over the rim of his sunglasses, raising his manicured brows suggestively. "But I won't slack on my duty to protect you. When we aren't at your house or Redleg, you're in danger. And I'm what stands between you and fuck knows who or what means you harm."

He just called me baby. And I wasn't half-naked in front of him when it happened like the last time. But I'm not going to comment on that little slip.

Yet.

I'm storing that bit of information for later just like a Tilikum squirrel with a nut (if you know, you know).

"Is it possible you're more paranoid than my brother? Survey says..." I raise my voice, dragging it out dramatically, and finish with, "Yes. Ding, ding, ding."

A slight grin plucks at his cheek, and his damn sexy dimple pops. Fuck me.

Don't get horny walking into therapy. I try one last time to command the little horny monster to stay at bay, but she's banging at the bars of her cage with her metal cup like a disgruntled inmate.

"Can you put that away, sir?" I ask him once we're safely inside the building.

Puzzled, he looks at me with narrowed brows while hanging his sunglasses on his shirt collar. "Put what away?"

"Your sexy dimple. I just want to stick my tongue in it and swirl it around a little to see if it feels like what I think it does."

"Jesus," he curses under his breath. "You are out of control."

"Guess I've decided the no flirting rule can go straight to hell."

"In a handbasket," he finishes for me with a sexy shrug.

Snickering, I head to the elevator and mash the call button twice. Because reasons. Does anyone just push it once?

"Eh... I'd rather we take the stairs. Third floor, right?"

"Oh my gosh. An elevator is dangerous now?"

"You never know. Where are the stairs?"

I scoff but lead him toward the end of the hall to the dank stairwell. "I thought staircases were dangerous. They always tell women not to go into them alone."

"You're not alone. Besides, I can control what happens on a staircase better than in an elevator."

Shaking off his overprotectiveness and trying to remember that I actually like him — even though I'm feeling a little stabby at him right now for treating me like a child — we head up the stairs together.

My mind sorts out my thoughts as we trudge upstairs slowly.

What the hell is so risky about an elevator? I've seen him use the elevator at Redleg before. Does he have control issues? Is this a bodyguard thing or a Sawyer thing? Or is it something else?

He lets me lead, following right on my heels. I can tell he's looking in front of and behind me simultaneously. Probably also checking out my ass, but the skirt is too flowy for him to see much. When we hit the second landing and turn the corner, heading to the third, I pause and eye him from over my shoulder. My abrupt stop brings him up to the same step as me, and he brushes against my back.

His head whirls around as he inspects the tight space around me for danger. "What's wrong?"

I don't try to hide my eye roll.

"Nothing is wrong. I think I figured it out."

"You're not going to guess my name, so you might as well give up. *Surrender, Dorothy!*" he teases with a witch's cackle.

Through a giggle, I say, "No. Not that. I just figured out why you didn't want to take the elevator."

This time, he's the unabashed eye roller. "Enlighten me, gorgeous."

First baby and now gorgeous? Swoon.

Turning to align my body with his, I softly reply, "You don't want to be alone in an elevator with me." Nibbling on my lower lip, I draw my fingertip over the collar of his shirt and run it up his neck toward his bobbing Adam's apple.

"Touching rule," he cautions. His eye glints as his gaze moves from my hand to my lips. When he smiles at me, his ovary-killing dimple pops. "After that stunt you pulled in your living room, can you blame me?"

I lean closer, rising to my tiptoes, desperate for a kiss. "Well, we ended up all alone in the stairwell. So it looks like your plan backfired."

His warm breath, minty with the gum he always chews, feathers over my cheeks while his free hand wraps around my waist, pulling me close to him. I can feel the beginnings of an erection against my belly. It grows and twitches against me the longer he holds me and gazes into my eyes.

"Yeah, I guess my plan backfired," he says, running his nose across my cheek with only the slightest touch — just barely grazing my skin. Fever burns along the path he takes across my cheekbone toward my ear, then back down my jaw toward my mouth. His lips are inches away from mine when I feel his grip on my waist loosen, and he pulls away a few inches.

Without warning, he swats my ass, drawing a yelp from me that echoes around the stairwell.

"I told you I'd give you a spanking if you didn't stop messing with me. Now, up we go, little miss rule breaker."

Scoffing, I try to recover from the hormones he doused me with. "I'm rubber, and you're glue. Because you just broke the no touching rule."

"Excuse me, but you obliterated the no flirting rule. Whereas I *gently* stretched the no touching rule. It's not the same. Come on. Let's go. You're going to be late." He points toward the top of the stairs, and I start moving upward, hiding my smug smile from him.

"There are only two rules left to break. Kissing and... the other thing," I mutter mostly to myself. But it's so quiet in here, except for my heavy footsteps — his freaky ninja steps are oddly silent — he must hear me because he sighs loudly, letting loose a mildly annoyed groan.

When we get to the third floor, I grab the doorknob, ready to pull the door open, when he stops me with his hand on the crease between the door and the wall.

"Turn around. Eyes on me," he murmurs darkly in my ear.

Instinctively, I obey, getting a secret thrill from the commanding tone of his voice. It's not the tone he'd use if there were danger; it's huskier and breathier.

That's a bedroom voice right there. *My kitty starts to purr.*

When I meet his eyes, they're practically burning into me.

So much for not getting horny right before therapy. That ship has sailed. *Bon voyage!*

He's got me partially sandwiched between his firm body and the cool metal of the door. But this time, I don't feel trapped by his presence. He's given me one side of freedom to my left since he's keeping his right arm at his side. How does he know my needs so well?

Instead of telling me how many ways he's going to make me scream his name when we get back home, he drops a different kind of bomb on me. "You need to knock it off. *Please.*" His voice is less bedroom and more anguished now. "We can't do this, Sammy. Especially when we're not in an environment I can control."

"Do what?" *Innocent as a cherub — yep, that's me.*

My hands slide behind me, resting over the curve of my bum. Oddly, I notice I don't feel the need to have my hands up in front of me for protection like I normally would. Even when he looks upset, I feel safe.

His head tilts to the side. "We can't flirt like this and be..." he can't seem to find the words. I merely wait for him because I don't want to jump to any conclusions or put words in his mouth.

Although, there are other things I want to put there.

At times like these, I miss my inner rage monster. The horny monster that has taken her place is certifiably insane. Sawyer was right. I'm out of control.

After stammering a bit, he finally decides what to say. "We can't behave like we've been behaving today. Acting like this thing between us is going somewhere right now. It can't happen. It's dangerous for so many reasons. It's not just you. We both need to stop."

My heart hits the stark concrete floor of the stairwell and rolls down the steps, feeling as though he's practically kicked it down a flight or two.

Preparing myself for any response — even one I don't want — I confirm what he's saying by asking, "So you've made your decision, then? You don't want to try to keep *us* a secret. You're not willing to do that. I'm not..."

My eyes and chin drop. I can't say the last two words.

Worth it.

I can sure as hell think it, but I can't say it.

I'm not worth it. I'm not enough for him.

Once again, someone else is in charge of my life, and I have to go along with whatever they feel like dishing out to me. Whatever scraps they deem worthy to feed me.

He lifts my chin with his smooth hands, tilting my head, but I can't meet his eyes right now. I'm too ashamed, and I feel sickened. With myself. With him. With this situation. With everything.

So I mash my eyelids into tight lines. He runs his hand across the bottom of my cheek before dropping it.

Side note: How does he have soft hands considering his background? Is it sorcery? If he's a wizard, that might explain the pheromones. Does he exfoliate with sea salt taken from the Sea of Galilee or something? What type of moisturizer does he use? Twenty-four-carat gold melted down, kissed by an angel, and blended with holy water by a fairy princess from a land of enchanted creatures?

If Jaynie were listening to my inner thoughts right now, I know she'd say, *you're using humor to hide your pain again. Why don't you try feeling your feelings for a change?*

Bingo, imaginary therapist. Bingo.

His husky voice shakes me from my bizarre musings, but I keep my eyes closed. "This doesn't mean no *forever*. It just means no *for right now*. Okay, baby?"

His ridiculously soft hand strokes my cheek again, tugging it down and opening my eyes a little in the process.

"Look at me."

I do as he says. Not because he's in control of me — fuck you, rage monster — but because I can't keep my eyes off him for another second. My body craves it like an addict.

With an almost palpable tenability, he whispers, "Believe me when I say this because I've never meant anything more. I will make you mine one day. When the time is right."

"When will that be?" My voice cracks, and I want to punch my own face for being so pathetic — like I'm begging him for scraps.

"Sammy, I don't know. But I've waited more than twelve years for you, so a little while longer isn't going to kill us."

I almost died last night.

His job is dangerous.

Tomorrow isn't guaranteed for anyone.

I want to yell these thoughts at him, but he's already made up his mind. So I save my breath and nod.

Rage monster, are you still here? Take your seat with the sad monster, pathetic monster, and horny monster. We're all going to therapy.

I hope Jaynie's ready for me. We've got a lot to address today. Like how I think I'm officially going nuts by naming my personality traits little monsters.

And also how I'm using self-deprecating *inner* humor now to deal with my issues, rather than just outwardly doing that.

Yep. Lots to unpack here.

Chapter Twenty-Five

BUSTED

Sawyer

While I'm pacing outside her therapist's door, Sammy's words won't stop running through my mind. On a freaking loop. Over and fucking over again.

So you've made your decision, then? You don't want to try to keep us a secret. You're not willing to do that. I'm not...

I can't help but wonder what the last words were that she didn't say.

I'm not... what?

She's *everything*, so for the life of me, I can't figure out how that sentence was supposed to end. I should've made her finish that sentence, and then I could tell her how wrong she was for thinking she's less than perfect.

I think I'll ask her when she gets out of her therapy appointment. And I hate that I can't be in there with her.

Is that weird? It feels strange to want to sit with her while she talks to her therapist, but I do. Partially because I want to make sure she's safe, but I also want to comfort her if she's upset. And surely talking about what happened last night will be hard for her. I just want to support her in any way I can. Even if I can't claim her the way I want, I still intend to be there for her.

My phone buzzes with an incoming call. "What's up, Shep?" I answer on the first ring.

"We need to talk, man."

His tone isn't good. He sounds... worried. And that's not his typical vibe unless shit's about to go ass up. Ah hell, what now?

Bend over, here it comes again.

I clench my jaw, then ask, "What's wrong?"

"Let me start by saying that if you get pulled off Sammy's detail, I'm going to volunteer to take your place. And not because I'm trying to get with her — because you know I'm not — but because I know you'll trust me to keep her safe."

My gut twists into a knot.

"What the actual fuck are you talking about right now, Shep?"

His deep breath comes through the receiver loud and clear. "We saw you with Sammy."

No, no, no.

All I can think about is what happened today in her living room. Were they watching? Did they see it before I erased it?

"Clarify."

"At the Sassy Parrot. The night we met for drinks. In the back hallway."

Oh fuck. The kiss.

Heaving a partially relieved sigh that he didn't see us today, I ask, "Who all saw it?"

"Just Kri and me. *For now.* We're scanning the footage from the bar, looking for potential suspects, remember? I'm supposed to tell Boss everything of note we find regarding Sammy, and that's a pretty big fucking note. Even though I know you have nothing to do with her abduction. But I still think I need to tell him."

Okay. I can work with this. I don't think I'm *totally* screwed. It's salvageable.

"Listen, man. It was a one-time thing." *Technically, not a lie. After all, I haven't kissed her again. Letting her jack me off into her panties is totally different, right? Thanks for your agreement.* "Can you just keep it quiet? If Leo or Big Al finds out —"

He cuts me off. "You need to tell Lionheart. I know you've had feelings for her for a while now. He'll understand. You're like a brother to him."

"Ever heard of the bro code?" I scoff. "Now is not the time for that conversation with him. Too risky. If he doesn't like it, he'll have me yanked from her detail."

"That's why I said I'll try to take your place. You can trust me with her."

"Shep, listen. Let this go, please," I plead. "I promise there's nothing to worry about with this. Sammy and I are good. We talked about it, and it's not happening again." *Now.* "No reason to tell Boss or Lionheart. Once this mess is over and she's safe, I'll talk to him. Just not right now. Can you just pretend you didn't see it? And I'll ask Kri to do the same."

He makes a groaning sound like it's hurting him to give me this. I'm not asking much, am I?

"You know we have rules against being involved with our clients for a reason. You're compromised."

"And I just told you we're not involved. It was just one kiss." *And a hot as fuck mutual masturbation.* "Plus, that rule is bullshit. Big Al's allowing Leo to protect his own sister *and* his fiancée right now. That's a bigger risk than trusting me with Sammy."

"Yeah, I guess you have a point. But good luck getting Leo pulled off Sammy or Sue's detail. I think you'd need a thousand tranq darts and a backhoe to accomplish it with that giant fucker."

One corner of my lip quirks at the image his words paint, but I need to stay on point and get him to commit to keeping this secret for me. The thought of someone ripping me away from Sammy's side makes my blood boil. Especially after the last few days. Something changed at the smash house, and we haven't been the same since.

She's mine to protect as much as she is Leo's.

My temper is rising, and so is my voice. "Shep, it's the same for me with Sammy. Good fucking luck getting me reassigned."

"Wow. And can I just say... I'd like brownie points for not giving you a big fat *I told you so* right now."

My labored sigh makes the phone line crackle. Rubbing the bridge of my nose, I squint and try to find the right words to convince him to keep this on the down-low.

"Told me what?"

Am I playing dumb? A little. So what?

"That you're in love with her. I knew it." He laughs, and I want to punch him. Like a friendly punch, of course. "Fuck it. You know what? I can't hold it in. Screw the brownie points. *I told you so.* I called that shit the day she got back, and I saw how you looked at her at the cabin in Ocala. I might have been about to bleed out, but I knew that look. You sorry sap, catching feelings. Poor bastard. You love her."

No sense denying it. I'll let him have his gloating moment.

Still pacing around the empty waiting room, I head to the glass overlooking the parking lot and brace a hand on the windowsill.

"Okay, Gloatasaurus Rex, what will it cost to keep this hush-hush? Name your price."

"You know, I think I want my own door sign, and you need one too."

"Done."

"*And* I get to choose what they say."

This fucker.

However, he knows me so well I can't help but laugh. The way to my heart is a great joke. Even if I'm the butt of said joke.

Still chuckling, I say, "Fine. What do you want them to say?"

"I'm not sure yet. I need to think about it. But after this shit is done, I'll tell you, and you have to do it without bitching. Is that a deal?"

"Yeah, it's a deal. We both get signs of your choice, and you keep this quiet."

"And you have to promise me you're not too involved to keep her safe."

A lump appears in my throat, and I choke it down. "I promise. I won't let anything happen to her."

"Good. And don't worry about Kri. I'll handle her."

Interesting way to put that. Filing that away. Now's not the time to turn the tables on him.

With the issue seemingly settled, I need an update on the progress from HQ. "Did you guys find anything else in the bar footage yet?"

"We've only gotten through a handful of days' worth of footage, but *man*. There are a lot of fucking perverts out there."

"Explain," I order. Once again, my blood pressure spikes.

"She gets groped or smacked on her ass at least four times per shift."

My vision wobbles in and out. "What the fuck? Tell me you're kidding."

"I wish I were. We've given still shots of the sickos to Tomer to run through facial recognition, and he's preparing a suspect list for Boss. Between that, all the traffic cams he's hacking, and the Langley S&D gig, poor Tomer is losing his shit."

"No-fun-fuck sign still hanging on his door?"

"Yep. I suspect he's too busy to even notice it."

"Well, at least I have that to make me feel better. What's going on with Langley S&D? I haven't heard that name in a while."

Sue's brother Nick married into the Langley family in some fashion. I think he has a brother-in-law who's the CEO, if my memory serves. Redleg protected them a few years ago from a stalker. Cool family. Good to know they hired Redleg again.

"New security system installation for some of their distribution centers or some shit. Tomer's in charge of designing *and* implementing. And that's on top of all the shit Big Al's dumping on him for Sammy's case."

"We need another guy in the chair. Poor Tomer."

"Klein's chomping at the bit to get called up to the big leagues. You know how much he loves intel work and all that hacking shit. But Big Al has a former spook he's considering for the role."

"Huh. Interesting." We don't have any former CIA operatives at Redleg. Someone like that could come in handy.

The topic fizzles out as my mind keeps returning to the image he painted of men touching my Sammy while she's at work.

"So we've got a lot of grope-happy customers who need broken wrists. I assume you'll get me that list so I can pay them visits later. Anything else? What about other avenues?"

He snickers. "Weren't you just in a briefing this morning about this?"

"A lot can happen in half a day."

"Nothing new. Stay sharp out there. I gotta go. I'll talk to Kri for you."

"Thanks, man. I owe you."

We say our goodbyes, and I slide my phone back into my pants. Still staring out the window, I notice someone lurking around my Redleg SUV. He's tall, broad, and wearing a hoodie with the hood pulled up. That's certainly suspicious, given the warm weather.

I watch him closely to see if he attempts to put anything on the vehicle, like a GPS tag or explosive. So far, he's not doing anything wrong, per se. But I don't like how he's hanging around. What is he waiting for at an office building? It's not a shady area or a place to loiter.

I pull the phone back out and snap a picture, zoomed in as far as it can go. Not a great shot of his face, given the forty-five-degree angle he's standing at. But all the same, I'll send that to Tomer in a minute to see if it matches any of the pervert customers.

I glance at my watch to mark the time. *1643.*

What the fuck is he doing there?

By 1646, I'm contemplating going down there to confront him. But what if it's a trap? He could be trying to draw me away from Sammy.

My heart rate spikes. It's quiet behind the door to the therapist's office, and I hate not having cameras in there. There was an external window that didn't appear to open and no other doors or means of egress. I checked the closet before she went in. She should be safe in there, but I can't shake the uneasy feeling.

I take another look at the lurker before turning around and knocking on the door.

"One minute," the older woman answers.

She opens the door a crack, sticking her head out. "Yes?"

"Everything okay in there?"

Studying me, she wrinkles her forehead, then pats her wild hair down oddly. "Everything is fine in here." Her eyes bounce from side to side. "Everything okay out there?" Her voice has a humorous lilt to it that makes me smile.

"Fine, ma'am. Sammy, you good?" I holler, wanting confirmation.

A muffled voice answers back. "Good, Sawyer."

She does *not* sound good.

I press past the sweet older woman gently to poke my head inside. Sammy's eyes are red rimmed, and she's dabbing her nose with a tissue. Like they have a mind of their own, my feet bring me the four steps to the couch where she's seated. I take the seat beside her.

"You okay?" I set my hand on her thigh, near her knee, and squeeze softly. I hate seeing her cry.

Fucking despise it.

"I'm fine. You can chill. Get out, though. We're not done yet." Her voice has that same muffled quality, thanks to the tissue that's still covering her mouth and nose.

Oh. That makes sense. She's not being held against her will. Just crying.

Feeling only marginally better, I tell her, "I'm going to go downstairs to check on a suspicious character. Can you wait inside here until I get back?"

Her shoulders roll back, and she sits up straighter. "What's going on? What suspicious character?"

"I don't know. Don't worry about it. Finish your session and wait inside with the door locked until I get back. Okay?"

She nods, and I can't resist comforting her. Leaning forward, I place a kiss on her forehead, gently so as not to hurt the area around her stitches.

"Be right back."

As I rise and turn to the door, I'm met with the sly smile and knowing eyes of her therapist. It makes me wonder if Sammy told her what we did earlier today.

The beautiful, kinky, unspeakable thing.

I close the door behind me and wait to hear it lock. Once it does, I check the window and verify that the guy is still there. Yep. There he is.

Double-timing it, I take the stairs two at a time and jog through the lobby, then through the exit doors.

When he sees me approaching, he takes off briskly, walking toward the road. I pursue him slowly at first, trying not to startle him any further.

"Hey, wait up, man. I just want to ask you a question!" I yell.

He increases speed until he's at a slow jog. As his hands pump, I notice he's got on gloves.

Yeah, this guy is definitely up to no good. This is freaking Florida. We don't do gloves here.

"Stop!" I try again.

That definitely didn't help. He's in a full-on sprint now. I might be able to catch him, but this big fucker is surprisingly fast.

We're racing down the sidewalk that runs parallel to the road. I hear tires squeal behind me, coming from the direction of the office building where I left Sammy.

Left Sammy. I just left Sammy.

Bodyguarding 101: Don't leave your charge.

Fuck. What if it *was* a trap to draw me away?

I reach for my sidearm while sprinting back at full speed and turn off the safety. When I get back to the parking lot, there's no sign of any new vehicles, which I'd kept track of while looking out the window earlier. It's not a large building. Only three floors tall and a handful of offices inside. Three short rows of cars, half of them empty.

Since there's no parking lot around the back of the building for a car to hide in, I guess the car was a false alarm. After ensuring no one is about to jump me, I race upstairs to make sure Sammy is okay.

My lungs burn as I suck in a few ragged breaths.

I try to calm myself by rationalizing that it's possible the tires squealing came from the busy road. It might be completely unrelated. And maybe the guy outside was guilty of something else, and that's why he ran. It's probably just a coincidence.

Keep telling yourself that, asshole.

Rushing into the office, I knock roughly, pointing my gun to the ground so I don't give Sammy's therapist a heart attack.

"Again, Sawyer?" I hear Sammy yell playfully.

Thank fuck. She sounds okay. The death grip on my gun loosens, and I shift it behind me. I'm not putting it away until I see her with my own eyes.

Through the door, I reply. "I'm back. Just making sure you're still okay."

This time, it's her who opens the door. Her face is considerably less tearful than it was before.

"Sawyer, do I or do I not have a GPS tracker on my person?" she asks.

"You do."

All Redleg clients get them. Earrings, bracelets, shoe tags. We've got all kinds of them. Sammy has two, actually.

"And didn't you tell me to stay inside this room with the door locked until you returned?"

"I did."

"And do you think I'm incapable of following your simple instructions?"

"No. It's just the guy outside ran and the tires..." I stammer, then trail off.

Her eyes widen.

Shaking my head, I tell her, "Forget it. Sorry. I'll be out here when you're done."

I put the safety on and slip the gun into my holster. She watches me carefully with one brow arched.

"You're serious, aren't you? This isn't an overreaction. You were actually scared. Something's wrong."

My lips press in a firm line. "Nah. It's fine. Finish up. Talk later." I nod back into the office behind her, signaling her to go.

"Five minutes, okay?"

"Take your time. It's fine." I give her forehead another kiss and push her back into the office, closing the door behind her.

As I turn, I heave a calming breath and head to the window once more. No one out there now.

I prepare a text with the photo to send to Tomer, along with a height and weight estimate, basic description, and summary of the incident.

He replies with a ten-four a few seconds later.

And now I have nothing else to do but wait. Empty-handed.

Should've gotten three coffees.

Chapter Twenty-Six

THESE ARE A FEW OF MY FAVORITE THINGS

Sammy

"Okay, so you have your plan, then?" Jaynie asks, bringing our session to a close.

"Yes." Grinning, I hold up my fingers and tick off my action items one by one. "I'm going to make a list of five good things in my life and read it three times each day until my next session. I'm going to list my irrationally angry thoughts so we can try to figure out what's truly causing them. I'm going to try *again* to find something creative that sparks joy." I can't hold back my eye roll at that one, but at least she chuckles with me. "And four, I'm going to follow Leo and Sawyer's instructions for my own safety without being a petulant child." Another eye roll for good measure.

"Perfect. And call me on my cell if you need me urgently. You've got a lot of stressors right now, but you're not alone anymore. You not only have your family, but I'm here for you too, and I care about you."

My returning smile is genuine because she's just so damn sweet. How could I not smile? "I know you do. I care about you too, and I appreciate everything you do for me."

And it's entirely possible I might need some extra help this week. We unearthed some deep feelings of fear today relating to how I felt when I was trapped in that trunk and how it reminded me of all the times Craig restrained me. That feeling of being powerless and at someone else's mercy is something I thought was a distant memory.

But I was wrong.

"Something tells me you might not need me much this week, though. Looks like you've got someone out there who cares deeply for you and who'd be willing to listen to anything you want to vent about. Not sure I've ever seen a forehead kiss like that in real life, but my old ass swooned a little." She puts the back of her hand to her forehead in jest and mocks falling backward.

I cover my giggle with my hand like a freaking middle schooler. "No comment," I joke with a closed-lip grin.

And we only scratched the surface of what's happening with Sawyer. We didn't have time to delve into all my feelings and what transpired. By the time we got through the abduction, fears that resurfaced because of it, and how moody I've been since, time was up. She offered to cancel her next appointment so we could continue, but I can't in good conscience do that to someone. I feel good enough to get through the next few days on my own.

Plus, she's right. I have Sawyer to talk to. Not to mention Leo, Sue, and Mom, if needed. I could also call my other brother, Drew.

Speaking of which, he texted me earlier, and I should return his message. He's worried about me, having heard about last night from my mom.

She walks me out to the waiting area where the aforementioned swoony forehead kisser is waiting patiently. Or is that impatience? Hard to tell with that tight expression he's wearing.

When Sawyer and I exit the building, he puts his hand on my low back again. The gesture leaves me feeling a little conflicted. Part of me is miffed because I don't need to be led around like a toddler. But the other part of me really wants him to let that hand drift lower to give my ass a squeeze and relishes the way he's guiding me. It might be just a bodyguard thing to do, but it's also sweet. And let's face it. Anytime he puts his hands on me is a good time.

He does the typical sweep around the car, keeping me locked onto his side the whole time. His scent is going straight to my nipples once again. Damn nipple stiffening pheromones of his.

He checks underneath the SUV with that stick thing. It beeps when we get near the trunk, and he bends down to grab something from under the rear of the vehicle.

"I fucking knew it," he snaps. "Dammit."

"What is it?"

"Tracker," he responds, more calmly this time. He squeezes the small black circular piece of plastic, snapping it with his bare hands.

Boy, that's hot.

Not now, horny monster. Someone put a tracker on our vehicle. This is time for a panic monster. Quit thinking with your clit.

My mind swirls with questions and worries as we finish a second loop around the SUV.

As I shuffle along with him, I ask, "Why did you break it? Don't we need it for evidence or something?"

"My first priority is always to protect you. Evidence is secondary. We can't let anyone track you. *Period.*"

"Well, you touched it. What about getting fingerprints off it?"

He brings us to a stop at my door. "He had gloves on. We aren't getting prints off it."

After ushering me into the car. "Any other questions?"

I shake my head, feeling sorry for aggravating him. I should've known he'd already have thought of everything.

Leaning over me, he wordlessly grabs the seatbelt and fastens it.

Again, I'm torn on how to feel about the gesture. Inner rage monster is annoyed because I'm not a freaking child. Meanwhile, my horny monster has all but rolled over and spread her legs.

I'm erring on the side of the horny monster since I got another good whiff of his nipple erecting aroma when he leaned over me.

Getting in and starting the ignition, he turns the air conditioning on full blast before turning to face me, offering an explanation.

"When we're out in public — which I'm going to suggest we drastically limit to necessities only from here on out — you need to follow my every instruction immediately. The abduction clearly wasn't a one-time attempt. Someone wants to hurt you, and this is proof." He holds up the pieces of the black disk, then slams them into the console.

Gulping down a lump in my throat, I force out, "I will. I promise."

"Thank you for understanding, baby," he says, raising his hand to cup my cheek.

Baby again? My panties can only take so much.

But more importantly... Why would someone be tracking me? What did I do to deserve this? Why is this happening to me? What is it going to take to make this guy stop? What does he want from me?

I want to pelt Sawyer with these questions, but his furrowed brow and tight-set jaw tell me this isn't the time for lamenting my woes. He's deep in thought, and I'm not sure I'm ready for the answers to those questions anyhow.

The tears I let out during therapy have left me nearly dry, but my sinuses sting with the need to spill more liquid emotions, and one or two spill free.

Can I just say this quickly? Sometimes, I detest being a woman. If you're considering becoming a woman, I'd strongly advise against it. Why? Menstruation aside, it's because I cry at the worst freaking times. Not just when I'm sad. It could be anxiety, happiness, or a million other emotions. And cue the waterworks. Even when I'm freaking mad and shaking with anger, the urge to cry can be overpowering. Men probably think it's a weakness, and I hate appearing like a delicate flower.

I'm *not* weak, dammit.

I feel emotions so deeply they overwhelm me and then leak out of my eyes. It's not fair. But that doesn't mean I can't handle a situation or kick some ass — despite my past.

And honestly, that should make me more fierce than fragile. There. I said it. Someone had to.

Damn hormones.

Ugh. I'm so stuck in my head today. It makes it hard to focus on what's actually happening around me. Shit.

Once we're on the road, I muster the courage to ask, "What happened when you ran out? Who did you see? What got you so upset you pulled out your gun?"

"I need to call Big Al with an update. I'll do it right now on speaker so I only have to explain once, if that's okay with you." He gives me a questioning side-long glance.

His seeking of my consent is so fucking hot, and it's taking all my strength not to jump him. I much prefer this to the babysitting treatment I get from Leo.

I agree with his plan with a sharp nod. "I'm going to text Leo too. He'll want to know what's going on."

"Good idea. Ask him to call me when they get out of their appointment with the wedding planner."

With a slight tremor in my hands, I tap out a simple text to Leo, asking him to call us without ringing any alarm bells. Sawyer places the call to Big Al.

"Status," he commands, answering without any pleasantries.

"We've got new developments, Boss. You ready?"

"Fire away."

"I transported Sammy to therapy for an appointment at 1600 hours, and at approximately 1643, I noticed an unidentified male in a hoodie, head covered, hanging around my SUV and acting suspiciously. After several minutes of observing him, I secured Sammy in a locked office and went downstairs to confront him. When I approached, he fled. I pursued on foot but didn't want to go too far away from Sammy, so I let him go. Sorry I didn't catch him."

"That was the right call. Could have been a trap. Description?"

"Yeah, I snapped a picture from the upstairs window and sent it to Tomer a few minutes ago along with basic details. Not sure how much help it will be, though. He was good at staying incognito."

Snapping a picture was smart thinking on Sawyer's part. Not sure I would've had the foresight to do that.

"Good. You heading to Sammy's place now?"

"Yeah."

"Show the picture to Sammy when you get there to see if she recognizes him. Anything else?"

"Yeah." He pauses, shaking his head. "When we got back to the vehicle, I found a GPS tracker under it."

"Son of a bitch. Well, that proves last night wasn't a random grab."

"Yeah, I know," Sawyer responds despondently.

Something sounds odd to me, so I speak up. "Why would he linger around after placing the tracker? That seems really stupid. Shouldn't he have just tagged it and left?"

"Hey, Sammy. Didn't know you were listening," Big Al says, then adds, "Sawyer, thanks for telling me I was on speaker, asshole. I would have watched my fucking language in the presence of a lady."

We all share a tension-relieving chuckle. Having been around military men for most of my adult life and enjoying a good F-bomb myself, I'm no stranger to *colorful* language.

"And yeah... you make a good point, Sammy," Big Al continues. "It seems like he wanted you to pursue him, Sawyer. The hoodie in this freaking heat was like waving a red flag. Hanging around out in the open, then running off. He wasn't trying to be slick, that's for sure. I suspect he was trying to draw you away from Sammy or lead you into a trap with the foot chase. The tracker could've been a backup plan in case the trap failed."

Sawyer replies, "Yeah, maybe they would've followed us and tried again to get me away from her."

My stomach sours, the earlier vanilla latte no longer agreeing with me. Sawyer getting hurt because of me or being lured into some trap is beyond unsettling. It's downright nauseating.

"I'm almost scared to ask, but anything else I need to know?" Big Al asks.

"That's all for now. You got any news for us?"

"We're pulling together a decent list of suspects. Tomer already has about a dozen potential license plates he's running from cars that appeared to be near the appropriate intersections by the Parrot and the other pub at the right times — or at least thereabouts. He's going as fast as he can but says he needs more time. There's a lot of footage to cross-reference." He pauses for a breath.

Sawyer jumps in. "Tell Chuck to hurry his no-fun-fuck ass up."

A deep chuckle echoes from the car speakers before Big Al continues, "Shep and Kri are making good progress on the bar footage today — it's taken them far less time than I expected. They'll probably finish by tomorrow. Quite a list of ass-grabbers developing. Sammy, while he's got you, why don't you have Sawyer teach you how to grab a wrist and put someone in a submission hold? That shit is unacceptable."

"Yeah, you can say that again. But I do work on tips, you know, and I do need some form of income. Can't go around breaking wrists all night and expect to make rent," I snark.

My mind takes a trip through all the drunks who have thought my ass was there for their entertainment and makes a sharp detour to how much I want to have Sawyer's hands on me instead.

Having him teach me some moves sounds like fun. Leo's taught me a few, but I don't think I know any fun wrist grabs. Playing with Sawyer in that way could be like foreplay.

Dammit. Still horny.

"Sawyer, I know you didn't get much sleep last night and came on duty early today. You good for tonight's shift or do you need someone to cover? I could send Klein."

"I'll be fine, Boss. Thanks for worrying about my beauty sleep."

"Screw that. I just need you alert."

"Don't worry about that. I've got my coffee to keep me company during the wee hours of the night shift. Plus, Leo has more security in his mom's house than you have in yours."

"I also added those front yard sensors last month and upgraded her window locks."

My eyes nearly bug out of my head. I didn't realize Big Al was putting time or effort into securing my mom's house.

"Sawyer, I assume you disabled the tracker in case this guy doesn't know where she lives?"

"Yes, Boss," Sawyer drawls, adding an eye roll for my benefit.

Now he knows how it feels to be treated like a child. *Welcome to the kids' table, chief.*

"Tomorrow morning, on your way home, bring what's left of it to the office so we can see if we learn anything from it, and then we'll turn it over to CPD."

"Roger that."

"Got to run. Keep me posted on any new developments and continue with heightened protocol."

"Will do, Boss."

"Take care, Sammy," he adds.

"Thank you," I respond. "Oh, and Big Al?"

"Yeah, kiddo?"

"What's Sawyer's first name?"

"Tell her, and I'll resign," Sawyer snaps.

Big Al doesn't even respond, other than his rich laugh, before hanging up.

As funny as the end of the call was, I'm still a bit of a wreck thinking about everything that's gone down. The guy Sawyer chased. The GPS tracker. My hopes of last night being a one-time thing have been dashed, and it freaking sucks sweaty balls.

Silence lingers after the call, so Sawyer turns the radio on, then whips us through the streets of Clearwater. I feel some good old fear resurfacing, cutting off some of my airflow.

Rather than launch into a full-blown panic attack, I focus on the advice Jaynie gave me today, pull out my phone, and open up the notes app. I create one list titled *Good Things* and another titled *Rage Thoughts*.

I'll start with all the good things and add rage thoughts as they come.

Good Things:

1. My family's love and support.
2. I have a safe place to live.

3. I'm in good health.
4. Craig's in jail.
5.

My fingers fall away from the screen as I run through my options for a fifth item. My mind whirls around all the things that make me happy. Sharing a bottle of wine with my mother during dinner on my days off. Smashing the watermelon was fun. My therapist is awesome. I could also put that I'm *not* broke — although, if I'm not able to go back to work soon, my savings will run out in a matter of weeks, if not days.

My fingertips tap on the armrest as I deliberate.

"What game are you playing?" Sawyer asks, nodding at my phone.

"No, I'm not playing a game. I'm making a list."

"Shopping?"

"No. It was an assignment from therapy. I'm supposed to make a list of positive things in my life to draw focus away from the bad stuff happening."

"That seems like a good idea. Need help coming up with more? I'm sure I can help you find lots of nice things to focus on." His smile is warm and slightly intoxicating.

I don't think he meant to lace his words with innuendo, but I can't help letting my mind go there.

"No. I think I've got it, thanks."

5. Sawyer.

Chapter Twenty-Seven
GUESS WHO'S COMING TO DINNER

Sawyer

"Hey, Lionheart," I answer on the second ring and head out to the front porch to take the call. No sense in upsetting Sammy's mom with what I need to tell him.

We've just gotten settled at Sammy's place. Henderson is here, along with Mrs. Mason. She's in the kitchen starting dinner, and it already smells fantastic. That woman can cook. Considering she's been feeding him all his life, it's no wonder Leo is such a huge mofo.

"What's up, man? I got Sammy's message. Everything okay?"

"Yeah, don't worry, but we did have some developments this afternoon at therapy."

I give Leo the rundown, and he's understandably concerned. He grumbles through some self-flagellation about not being the one who took her to therapy. For some dumb reason, he feels like he failed her.

"Would you have done anything differently?" I ask.

He sighs, then says, "No. Not really."

"And she doesn't seem upset, so don't worry. Ease that guilty conscience, buddy."

"Thanks, man. Does she want us to come over this evening?"

"Have you even met your sister?" I tease. "She's one of the most independent people I've met. She's handling things fine and doesn't want you fussing over her any more than you normally do. I'll let you know if she starts to struggle. I'm watching her closely."

Probably too closely, if I'm being honest.

"Thanks, man. I'm lucky to have you. I know I can trust you with her."

Ouchity, ouch, ouch, ouch.

Silence stretches for a few seconds as I remove the cinder block from my gut.

He adds, "I still think Craig is behind all this. Who else could be this fixated on her?"

"To what end, Leo? The fucker's got a few years left before he's even eligible for parole. Why are you guys so hung up on him?"

He and Big Al need to quit fixating on that douche nugget. If I have to see Sammy's reaction to hearing his name one more time, I will lose my ever-loving shit.

"Just call it a gut feeling. I can practically see him orchestrating something like this from behind bars merely to screw with us. He's got enough money to throw around and way too much time on his hands. He's a sick fuck."

Wait. *See* him?

"You just gave me an idea. Hear me out."

"What are you thinking, bud?"

"Well, maybe you and I should take a ride up to Raiford and pay him a little visit tomorrow. Let's confront him about it and see how he responds," I suggest, my grip on the porch railing tightening. "Between the two of us, we could tell if he's involved or not based on his reaction."

"Not a bad idea. We might be able to eliminate him as a suspect if he's genuinely surprised. Hmm." He makes a low grumbling noise like he's chewing on the idea. "One problem with this plan. I doubt he'll want to see either of us."

"True. He does have the right to refuse visitors. And the last time he saw us was in court, and we looked pretty fucking smug as he was escorted off in that orange jumpsuit."

Dammit.

"He won't see either of you, but he'll see me." Sammy's voice startles me. Whipping around, I see that she must have followed me to the porch to eavesdrop. I guess I said enough on my end of the call for her to put it together.

"Sammy, you don't have to. I would never ask that of you," I start.

"Well, I guess it's a good thing you're not asking," she replies, crossing her arms.

Leo chirps in my ear, "Tell Mom to set two more places for dinner. Sue and I will be over in a half hour to talk about this."

The line clicks, and I spin around to face Sammy. "Guess who's coming to dinner."

True to his word, Leo and Sue arrive twenty-eight minutes later.

"There's my gentle giant and his sweet angel," Mrs. Mason gushes, bringing them both in for a hug like she didn't see them yesterday. And probably the day before that.

I wonder what it was like for him to grow up with her. A mother who was always happy to see him. Effortlessly loving and kind.

"Sorry for the last-minute notice, Madeline, but someone insisted we come over without asking," Sue says, throwing a side-eye at Leo and backing away from Mrs. Mason's hug with a touch of discomfort written on her face.

I'm going to get her a shirt with the picture of a cactus on it that says: *I'm not a hugger.*

"No need to apologize, love. I'm thrilled to have a full house. I've got two of my three sons here with both my girls and my temporary fourth son." She winks at Henderson as she says that last bit. "What could I possibly need an apology for?"

A lump forms in my throat at how she casually referred to me as one of her three sons.

"Why are you here, you big lug? We could've talked over the phone about this. You should be spending time with your woman." Sammy pouts at her brother but hugs him anyway. The way she sets her cheek against his massive chest and closes her eyes warms my blood.

Not with anger, nor with jealousy. But with a sticky emotion I can't quite place. I'm glad she has that relationship with her brother. I want her to soak in all the love she can. She deserves it.

Henderson and I rest with our backs to the counter, out of the way. Casting everything else aside, I find myself silently watching the interaction between the family members with a slack jaw and blank expression.

The Masons have always gone out of their way to include me, but for some reason, I'm still waiting for the moment when they'll brush me aside. When you've been passed from family to family all your life, I suppose it's only natural to expect the other shoe to drop.

"Well, we can give everyone a wedding update at the same time we talk about if it makes sense to go see..." Leo trails off.

Sue finishes the sentence for him. "The fuck nugget," she whispers, probably hoping Leo's mother doesn't hear her swear.

"I heard that," Madeline sing-songs, her back to everyone as she pulls a roast out of the oven.

"Sorry, ma'am," Sue says, tucking her chin down.

Turning around from the stove and tossing the pot holders onto the counter, Madeline beams at her future daughter-in-law. "Not sure why you think I'd give a damn if you cuss or not, doll. We're all adults here. And Lord knows I've called that piece of shit garbage excuse for a human way worse things than a fuck nugget." She clasps her hands together and looks around the room. "Now. Who's hungry?"

Everyone grabs a serving bowl or platter of food from the counter and brings it to the dining room table.

"Thanks to whoever set the table. But this is backward," Sue says, scrunching up her nose, then rearranging the order of the cutlery beside her plate. Leo looks on with utter adoration. The poor smitten sap.

"My bad. I didn't know there was an order as long as it was all on the table," Henderson says with his brows drawn to a sharp point.

Sue's answering chortle is hilarious, and I can't help but join her in laughter.

"Oh, there is most definitely an order," she says between high-pitched and fast-paced guffaws. "From left to right, it goes salad fork, regular fork, plate, knife, spoon." She makes a gruff sound of disgust, then moves her cup from the left to the right of her plate. "And cups on the right, for heaven's sake. Were you raised by wolves?"

Mrs. Mason, seated at the head of the table, watches with an amused grin. Leo looks at Henderson, awaiting his reaction. Knowing my best friend and how much he loves Sue, I'd bet he'd be the first to grab Henderson by the collar and drag him outside if he so much as raised a mocking eyebrow at Sue's quirkiness.

Fortunately, Henderson is a smart guy, and no one is forcibly removed from our meal.

Sammy's quiet throughout dinner, picking at her plate. Outwardly, she appears to listen intently as Leo and Sue talk about their appointment with the wedding coordinator. She nods encouragingly as they describe the small beachside venue. A soft smile caresses her face when they explain how they were able to pick a date just five short weeks away, thanks to a cancellation.

But I know Sammy, and she's not paying a bit of attention. She's full of anxiety — probably about seeing Craig.

And I can't blame her.

"Everything was delicious, Mrs. Mason," Henderson says once he's cleared his plate.

"It really was, Mom," Leo adds.

"Thank you, boys. I'm glad you enjoyed it. Finish the rest for me." She cuts up the remaining roast into three portions before rising and refilling my plate, along with Leo and Henderson's. "And I have a confession," she adds sheepishly.

Folding up her napkin and placing it over her nearly untouched roast — what a waste — Sammy asks, "What's up, Mom?"

"This was a guilty-conscience meal. I'll be leaving tomorrow for a week. I've got to fly to California first thing in the morning."

"What?" Leo asks, his voice full of concern. "It's not a safe time for travel —"

She raises her hand, cutting him off. "One of our directors is participating in a conference, and his assistant — who was supposed to travel with him — was in a car accident on her way to the office this morning. She's in the hospital with two broken legs. She'll be fine but obviously isn't up to making the trip. Unfortunately, I'll be filling in."

A sour look befalls Mrs. Mason's normally pleasant face, and her eyes fall to the empty serving platter in front of her.

"Dammit. There's no one else who can go, Ma?" Leo pleads.

Sammy piles on. "Yeah, Mom, listen to Leo. Today, someone followed Sawyer and me to therapy and put a tracker on his SUV. It's definitely not a good time for a trip."

Madeline silences them both with her outward-facing palms. "It's nonnegotiable. I was told to make it happen or find another job. With the market the way it is, I honestly don't have a choice." She steeples her hands in front of her face and pins me with a look. "Sawyer, I trust you and Leo to keep my only daughter safe while I'm gone. And Henderson, I realize you won't be able to travel with me, given your family situation. I don't want you to feel a bit of guilt about that. It's my problem to deal with, and I'm not pulling you away from your wife and newborn on such short notice. I'll be fine."

Henderson starts to speak, but Mrs. Mason cuts him off with a tight smile and brusquely asks, "Who's ready for dessert?"

Indigestion. That's what we're all having for dessert.

"Leo, you're going to chip a tooth," Sue mutters from the side of her mouth at him, her hand rubbing his leg under the table.

Either that or she's rubbing his dick, and I don't really want to picture that. So thigh it is.

He looks over at her, a soft smile tugging at his lips. Sammy rises swiftly, fills her arms with plates and empty bowls, and stomps to the kitchen. I do the same, trailing behind her. But with slightly less stomping.

Once we're at the sink, I lean close and ask, "You okay?"

She turns on the faucet and starts rinsing off the plates. "Yep. Fine. My mother is going to be flying across the country without protection, someone is trying to kill me, and I'm going to willingly see my abusive ex-husband in the next day or so. Everything is peachy fucking keen."

She picks up a sponge and starts violently scrubbing the roast pan clean. Reaching over, I shut off the water and still her hand. She finally meets my gaze.

"First off, your mom is going to be fine. Big Al will come up with a plan for that. Second, no one is going to hurt you. I won't let them. And third, we don't have to see your ex. We'll figure it out without putting you through that."

Her eyes widen, and she presses up on her toes, bringing her face closer to mine. "Yes, I am going to see him. I need to find out if he's behind this." With a humorless laugh, she quotes her mother's earlier words. "It's nonnegotiable."

She flips on the water and proceeds to physically assault the dishes, signaling she's done with this discussion.

Such a ballbuster.

It's part of what I admire about her. Tough-as-nails Sammy Mason. No matter how life knocks her down, she gets back up and dusts herself off.

Once the dishes are done, Henderson heads home with the rest of his week unclear. Leo texts Big Al to tell him about his mother's bombshell. Mrs. Mason begins packing for her trip.

While we wait to hear back from Big Al, Sammy and I join Leo and Sue in the living room to strategize for the prison visit.

Once all the plans are decided, Sammy kicks Sue and Leo out for the night and excuses herself to get ready for bed. Her silence and curtness are so damn loud that I can barely hear the coffee machine percolating as I prepare for a lonely night on the couch.

A little after midnight, the silence of the house and my lack of sleep make me nod off. Rather than fall asleep on the job, I get up to stretch my legs, padding my bare feet down the hall. After using the restroom and tossing some cold water on my face, I pause to listen at Sammy's door.

Unless my ears are deceiving me, I hear whimpering coming from her room.

Shit. She's crying. What should I do here? Leave her to cry in peace? Go talk to her?

I want to comfort her. But if I go in there, I'll probably end up doing something stupid. *Something most definitely against the rules.*

Her muffled cries get louder, all but making my decision for me. It physically causes me pain to think of her crying alone in the dark.

Opening her door without knocking — because she'd only send me away — I sneak in and close it behind me. No sense waking up Mrs. Mason.

She's on her side, facing away from the door, buried in the covers. With the moonlight sneaking in around the edges of her curtains, I can see the outline of her head pop off her pillow as I come in.

"Sawyer?" she asks, her breath raspy from her tears.

"Yeah, it's me, baby. I heard you crying. Scoot over. I'm coming in, and don't try to stop me."

"Uh... umm," she stammers, obviously embarrassed. But she should know better than to be ashamed of having emotions in front of me. She's been through a lot these last few days.

Lifting the covers on one side of her queen-size bed, I crawl in behind her. In one swift motion, I pull her back to my front and wrap her in my arms.

"It's going to be okay, Sammy. Cry if you need to," I whisper into her ear.

"I wasn't crying —" she starts, but I cut her off.

"You don't always have to be tough with me. I already know you're strong. So just let it out. You're safe in my arms."

Her shaky breath hitches, so I run my palm up and down the smooth skin of her arm a few times to soothe her, then bring it to rest on her waist.

Her extremely bare waist.

The warmth of her supple skin nearly stings my palm.

I assumed she was wearing a tank top or short sleeve top since I could feel her silky arms. But now I'm not so sure.

My hand — like it has a freaking mind of its own — travels a bit higher, searching for a scrap of fabric. I can feel the rise and fall of her breath under the weight of my arm. My fingertips get all the way up to the bottom of her breast and then shoot back to her waist like I touched a hot stovetop.

She's not wearing a shirt. Fuck me running.

Now *my* breath hitches and my dick swells in my jeans.

Please have on bottoms. Please have on bottoms.

Sleeping only topless is a thing girls do, right?

Right? *Right?!*

My foolish hand is determined to get an answer to the question I'm afraid to ask. I hold my breath, afraid to suck in another tempting whiff of her freshly washed hair while my hand moves ever so slowly from her waist to her hip.

Any second now, I'm going to feel the waistband of her low-slung sleep shorts.

Aaany second now.

Nope.

Just satiny smooth skin, curvy hips, and a thick, juicy ass.

"Sammy?"

Through staccato breaths, she answers, "Yes?"

"Tell me you're not naked."

"Okay. I'm not naked," she responds dutifully, but I can hear the heavy sarcasm in her words.

"Who lies naked in the dark while crying? Isn't that an activity for clothes?"

Is it a dumb question? Yes.

Do I have any other words coming to mind that can get me out of this shit show I've found myself starring in? No.

I start to pull my arm away — now that I know she's naked, I can't stay here — but she grabs my hand, not letting me leave. With a determined grip, she yanks me back to the big spoon position.

"I told you I wasn't crying."

"But I heard you."

Her sigh isn't laced with arousal or tears this time. It's packed with annoyance.

"And what exactly did you hear?"

"Soft moans and whimpers," I answer, then hear the words I've just uttered.

Oh, shit. Things are about to go from bad to worse.

Chapter Twenty-Eight

SWEET DREAMS ARE MADE OF THESE

Sammy

I think all Sawyer's brains are in his biceps. In his defense, he has substantial biceps.

Did he actually think I was in here crying rather than warming myself up to my second orgasm in five minutes?

Apparently so.

I don't normally sleep naked, but after the first climax, I had a hot flash and stripped down for number two. One wasn't enough to take the edge off.

After all, said edge has gotten remarkably sharper lately. Sharp. Just like Sawyer's chiseled jaw. *Dammit.* Merely visualizing his jaw makes me hornier, which I didn't think was possible since I'm already naked and wrapped up in a deliciously scented Sawyer cocoon.

"Maybe I should go," he whispers, but even in the darkness, I can easily tell he doesn't mean those words.

"Or you could stay and help."

I snake my arm up, trailing it over his, then settle my hand on the back of his neck. Tilting my head deeper into the pillow, I leave my neck exposed, hoping he'll take the hint. I give him a tug, bringing his mouth to the curve of my throat.

Now that he realizes I'm not letting him slink out, his grip on my waist tightens. I can feel his growing erection poking my behind, so I arch my back and press my bare ass into the scratchy fabric of his jeans. He pulls back slightly, hisses into my neck, then runs his nose along my fevered skin.

"What kind of help do you need, baby? It's my job to take care of you, after all." His husky voice causes a tidal wave to start brewing deep inside me.

"I can't seem to fall asleep. Do you have any idea how to fix that?" I arch back again, pressing my ass into him once more. This time, instead of shying away, he grabs my hip and pulls me harder into his erection. A sly grin breaks across my lips. If he could see me, I'd be ashamed of how happy that little break in his resistance made me.

Since he's no longer trying to leave, I release my hold on his neck and bring my arm to rest on top of his, where it sits on my hip.

"Maybe you could start with getting out of those jeans and that shirt," I suggest, like the helpful bitch I am.

"How is that going to help you fall asleep?" He presses a kiss on my pulse point, and I can feel him smiling against my skin.

"Your pants are coarse against me. I want to feel your skin on mine. It'll help relax me. Skin on skin contact is a known muscle relaxant," I fib.

He runs his slightly open lips along my neck outward, then over the round edge of my shoulder, leaving goosebumps in his wake with the feel of his warm breath on my skin. It feels so damn good I have to hold back a groan. My breath is coming shaky and fast now, and I'm burning with need.

"Baby, if I press my naked front to your sweet naked ass, I seriously doubt you're going to be *relaxed* enough to fall asleep."

"Oh? How will I feel?"

"Excited." He places a kiss on my shoulder. "Aroused." Another kiss on my upper arm. "Hot, like your skin is on fire." Running his lips all the way back up the same path, he takes the skin at the juncture of my neck into his mouth, sending a delicious thrill coursing through me. "Soon, you'll feel very full." A kiss on the same spot. "Because I'm going to bury my cock so deep inside you, you'll still be able to feel me there with every step you take tomorrow." He gives me a small nibble before adding, "If we're both naked in this bed together, you'll feel more pleasure than you've ever felt in your life, but *relaxing* isn't how I'd describe it. At least not at first."

I have no clever response to that. No snarky comebacks. No sassy taunts. I'm far too horny to form coherent thoughts.

Instead, I mutter, "Yes. That's what I want. Please do that."

Simple. To the point. And only slightly begging. I can live with that.

"But all those things are against the rules," he teases with a playful quality to his deep timbre.

"Shut up and touch me, Sawyer."

I can hear the smile in his voice as he says, "I am touching you, Sammy. It's against the rules, but I'm holding you and touching you."

"Damn you," I huff.

Desperate for relief, I lace my fingers through his and inch our joined hands lower down my body. I'm going to put his hand exactly where I want it.

"Touch me like this," I order him. That domineering tone I used the last time we were intimate returns, bringing with it an arousing boldness that I could swear makes his dick twitch behind me.

"Teach me how you like to be touched," he answers, and I almost flood the room with arousal.

Fuck, fuck, fuck. That's so hot.

I lead his hand to the sensitive spot between my legs and hear him groan when he comes into contact with my wet, tender skin. Moving his fingertips through my folds, I zero in on my clit and press his digits into my flesh. I gasp and whimper softly when he makes contact.

"You like that?" he asks. The cheeky bastard knows I like it.

"Rub it harder." I press his fingers firmly into my clit and begin swirling them. "And faster," I command, increasing our pace.

"Yes, baby." He buries his mouth in my neck and nibbles at the skin there.

I'm awash with pleasure, and my hips start bucking into our joined hands.

His voice is like velvet, caressing my ears like he's caressing my clit. "I think you like that. Tell me how it feels."

Halting the swirling motion, I begin moving our fingers up and down while my hips rotate in a circular movement. My thighs press together, trapping our hands. The whimpering sounds falling from my mouth turn into a garbled cry when I bring my free hand up to mute myself.

"It feels good," I answer him.

"You can do better than that, baby. Describe what it feels like." He licks beneath my ear before tugging my earlobe into his mouth and sucking gently.

"Waves of tingly sparks. It's so good, but it makes me feel empty, though. I'm clenching. Aching to be filled."

"That's better. Good girl. What do you want to be filled with, baby?"

"Your cock. I want your thick cock inside me while you do this with your hand, grinding it against me."

"And what will happen when we do that? Tell me."

"I'll come for you, Sawyer. I'll come."

My moans turn into a keening sound. My back arches and my thighs squeeze even tighter together as the first tingle of my climax rocks through me.

"Move your hand, baby. I'll take it from here," he rasps, his breath jagged while he thrusts his erection against my ass over and over.

As I buck back against him, his hand brushes mine aside and rubs frantically across my clit.

"Come for me, baby," he orders.

On command, I absolutely detonate in his arms, convulsing and shaking with my release.

As I struggle to catch my racing breath, I hear him say, "You sing so fucking beautifully when you come."

I feel heavenly. Sawyer makes orgasming a celestial experience — and I don't mean the tea brand.

It's perfection. Being in his arms, riding the euphoric high, and listening to him praise me.

He places butterfly kisses along my jawline from behind me, and I let my head fall into him, reveling in his touch, his kisses, and his affection.

Like a starved child at a feast, I take it all in.

And I have been starved. Deprived of loving touch for so many years. Now all I want to do is become a glutton for this man's skin, soaking it all in and letting my famine become a distant memory.

"We have to stop meeting like this," he whispers, drawing a chuckle from me.

I twist in his arms, spinning until I'm facing him. A stream of moonlight falls across his handsome face, and I can just make out his probing gaze. He's studying me, looking at me with so much raw emotion.

"Sawyer," I start, but he silences me with a kiss on the tip of my nose.

"Shh. Quiet baby. Close your eyes; you need rest."

My eyes must bulge out of my face. "What about you?"

No guy has ever been that selfless with me.

"Don't worry about me. I'm used to blue balls around you," he deadpans.

My returning chuckle is way too loud for this time of night, and I bring my hand up to cup my mouth.

"Shh," he hushes me again. "Are you trying to get caught naked with a man in your bed? Your mom is right down the hall."

"Oh, to be sixteen again," I joke.

"Did you sneak boys into your room when you were in high school, Sammy? I know you were a wild child, and I can see you doing that."

Pretending not to feel his thick cock pressing into my waist, I snuggle in closer to his chest. He feels so good pressed close against me. I could die like this, *happily*.

"Not often, but sometimes on the weekends. Whenever my dad wasn't around, that is." My orgasm-high dissipates with the sour thought of my father. "Mostly, I would sneak out. Easier to have fun at someone else's house than my own."

"When you'd sneak out, where would you go? A boyfriend's house?"

"Sometimes. Why do you want to know?"

"Leo wasn't at home with you during that time of your life. So I didn't hear many stories about your upper high school years."

Oh, this man. Did he truly pay that much attention to a bunch of Leo's dumb stories?

"Did he really talk about me?"

"All the time. All the good stories starred you."

We spend the next few minutes pillow talking about my high school days. I tell him about the prom dress I made for myself. The time I got suspended for organizing a student walk-out. Related: We weren't protesting anything in particular; we just wanted to leave school.

I also tell him about the summer between my junior and senior year. My brother Drew and I went to my aunt's farm because Mom was in the hospital after a "slip and fall." We knew Dad did it to her but never made her admit it. She suffered enough at his hands, so there was no reason for us to make it harder on her.

"What about you?" I ask him after I run out of interesting stories and get tired of talking about myself. "What were you like in high school? I bet you had all the girls chasing you. Probably captain of the baseball team or something."

"Not even close. I was tall, scrawny, and had weird patches of facial hair that I thought made me look cool, but looking back, it just made me douchey. And I wore ragged, hand-me-down clothes from whatever foster home I was in. So... no, I wasn't exactly popular."

I give him a little squeeze to ease the tightness I hear in his voice. "Your personality is so effervescent, though. I'm sure you still had friends. It's impossible not to like you."

He scoffs. "The funny-guy personality developed over time as a necessity of survival. Moving from one group home to another was rough, and I changed schools quite a bit as a result. I made myself laugh enough to cope with the bad times, and eventually, other people started to find me funny too."

"Especially the impressions?"

His white teeth catch the light as he smiles. "Yes. Especially those."

"I'm quite fond of them," I tell him honestly. A flicker of something crosses his expression, making me want to amend my statement. "To clarify, I like you with or without the silly voices."

"Thank you, Sammy. And I like you with or without your ragerific tendencies."

I giggle softly, hiding my face in his thick neck. So warm and strong. Inviting.

"Now, go to sleep," he says. "I'll hold you until you fall asleep." He presses a kiss against my forehead.

Oh, the forehead kisses this man gives. Chef's kiss.

"And you're sure you don't need some," I raise my brows, then add, "relief?"

"Good night, beautiful."

"When will you sleep?" My voice grows groggy with drowsiness.

"I'll nap when your brother relieves me in the morning and then catch a few hours on the way to Raiford."

"Okay. Good night, Sawyer. I'll see you in the morning."

His voice is the softest sigh as he breathes, "Good night, my love."

Chapter Twenty-Nine

PRISON BLUES

Sawyer

My head shoots off the back seat the moment I feel the SUV come to a stop.

"Coffee!" I yell before I've even opened my eyes or know where I am.

Leo and Sammy cackle at me from the front seat.

"Good morning, sleeping beauty," Leo teases.

"Fuck off, you giant motherfucker," I toss back without mirth and scrub the sleep from my eyes. "Where are we?"

Taking in the parking lot around me, I see the answer to the question before they can respond.

"We've arrived at our destination," Sammy says in the monotone voice of the GPS lady.

She's doing voices now, which makes me happier than I have any right to be. Like I'm rubbing off on her.

Hmm. Rubbing off. Like I did last night.

Come on, dick. Don't get hard with her brother around. That won't end well for either of us.

I check my watch. Looks like I got three solid hours of sleep on the ride up here from Clearwater. Sweet. I should be good to go for another twenty hours. Let's do this thing.

While I yawn and shake off the last of my grogginess, Leo turns to his sister and puts his hand on her arm. "You sure you're up to this, kid? No shame in changing your mind."

"I'm fine, Leo. Trust me. I've got this." Her voice is steady and calm. She shows no trace of fear, and since I can't see her face from this vantage point, I can only assume she's not just putting on a show for Leo. If she is scared, then she's hiding it well.

After pulling my sunglasses out of my hair, I slide them on and get out of the car, feeling the crack of my bones when I arch my back to get out the kinks.

Sleeping in the back of the SUV — I recommend you avoid it at all costs.

"Your weapon," Leo reminds me, pointing to the glove box where he's secured his firearm.

Oh right. No weapons inside the prison.

"Sorry. Still groggy. Think we can get some coffee in there?" I ask while adding my gun to the box. Once it's inside, Leo locks the door closed.

"Here." Sammy hands me a small black coffee. "Chug it on the way in. I doubt you can bring in outside drinks."

"Oh, you got me coffee? I'm touched. Will you marry me?" I kid, playfully.

I've always teased and flirted with beautiful women around him, and Leo expects a certain level of flirtatious sarcasm from me — even with his sister to a certain extent. If I stop now, he'll figure out something is up. And I can't let that happen. Not until she's safe.

I finish the small cup of mediocre nectar in three large gulps and toss the empty cup into a trash bin near the entrance. We file into the prison visitor's center with Leo on point and Sammy safely between us. My heart rate increases with each step. Something about exposing her to the presence of that dirtbag is clawing at my chest from the inside out. Even if she's going in willingly and it's a safe environment, I don't want her to risk one more emotional scar from him. My fists clench at my sides, but I need to trust her to be strong enough to handle him.

Plus, Leo and I will be watching on closed-circuit TV from an adjoining room. Big Al pulled some strings with the warden to not only get our visitation request fast-tracked but also made some arrangements to ensure her safety and that we could watch the visit without him being aware.

And Hades help me, if he so much as brings a single tear to her eye, I'm taking out whatever guard stands between Craig and me.

After going through the scanners, getting a pat down, showing our IDs, and handling the other formalities, we're finally shown to our observation room.

"Sammy, we'll be right here, watching the entire time," Leo reassures her.

The corrections officer gives us some basic instructions, then turns to Sammy. "Ma'am, I understand there is some history between you and the prisoner. He'll stay cuffed and chained to the table. We'll bring him in first, then you. You'll be safe the entire time."

She rounds her mouth and exhales sharply, then gives him a curt nod.

I add, "You remember the questions we talked about?"

She gives a stiff nod, gritting her teeth.

"And give the signal if you want out or need a break. We can come and get you if you get scared," Leo piles on. He steps in front of her, bends down to meet her eyes, and rubs her shoulders.

I can see the frustration boiling inside her.

She shrugs him off and takes a step backward. "Oh my god. Fucking chill, you guys. You're making it worse. I got this." She meets Leo's concerned gaze. "I'm not scared of him." To the guard, she says, "Let's go. I'm ready."

"Yes, ma'am. I'll be back to get you in a few minutes. I'm going to bring him in now."

Silence fills the room after he departs. I want to comfort her, grab her shoulders or hold her hand. Do something to show her I care, but she's not in the right frame of mind. Instead of cowering, she looks like a soldier ready for battle.

I'm so proud of her.

"Your sister is a bit of a badass, Leo," I murmur, trying to get him to notice her bravery instead of the vulnerability I think he sees.

One cheek lifts with a forced grin on his gruff face.

Sammy stares at the screen, waiting for them to bring him in. When he finally appears on screen, shuffling in his prison slippers and shackles, she arches one eyebrow and smiles. Fucking smiles.

"Look at that pathetic shithead," she jokes. "So strong once. But now, he's chained like a dog. Exactly what he deserves." With a shake of her head, she adds, "I think I'm going to enjoy this."

"See? Total badass," I repeat with a shake of my head. Leo offers a half chuckle in response.

After securing him to the table, the guard exits the screen and enters the viewing room a moment later. "Ready?"

"I'll be back in a minute, guys. Enjoy the show."

She doesn't meet our eyes again as she leaves, following the guard to the next room. As she goes, her shoulders lift and roll back as she infuses strength into her body.

So damn proud.

Once she's gone and the door has closed behind her, I slap my hands together and rub them a few times. "Ladies and gentlemen, please silence your cell phones. It's time for our feature presentation," I joke, impersonating an announcer of sorts. Not my best work, but I'm tense. So you get what you get.

A haughty grin crawls across Craig's face as Sammy enters the visitation room. He taps his fingers on the table as he studies her every move, like he's sizing her up.

"There's my beautiful wife. The months have been kind," Craig says when she sits down. "Except it looks like the food on the outside is a bit better than it is in here. What is that, twenty pounds? Thirty?"

"I despise that fucker," I mumble under my breath, hating the condescending way he's judging her.

With a shake of his head, Leo adds, "He's already trying to manipulate her."

"Thirty-five, actually," Sammy replies with a saccharine smile. "Never felt better in my own skin."

"Well, enjoy it now. When I get out, I'll want you thinner."

She tilts her head back and laughs. "Oh, delusional Craig."

He leans forward and lets his slimy gaze crawl over my girl. So glad for that table separating them and the cuffs that bind him, even if I wish there were plexiglass between them. I cross my arms over my chest and root my feet in place. Leo bristles beside me, heaving a sigh that's part growl.

Yeah, neither of us wants him that close to her.

"To what do I owe the pleasure of this visit? Miss me, darling?" the snake asks.

"Zoom in. I think she's going to start her questions."

Leo uses the joystick in front of the screen, which controls the camera. He pulls in for a tighter shot of the shitbag.

"I think you know why I'm here," she starts.

Craig's brow furrows, but he doesn't respond.

Sammy continues, "Your plan isn't working. I escaped the first time. And we found the tracking device on the second attempt. Why don't you just give up and save us all the trouble?"

Leo zooms in a touch farther, eliminating Sammy from the frame entirely.

Craig tilts his head to the side and narrows his eyes. His body language isn't quite revealing anything yet. If he knows, he's hiding it well thus far.

"Sammy, did something happen to you?" His voice sounds thick with concern, and I don't fucking like it.

"Don't play dumb."

"Darling, I never want to see you hurt. Despite our divorce, I still love you. Now, tell me what happened. Maybe I can help."

"I'm not telling you shit," Sammy seethes. "And you never loved me. You only loved controlling me."

In a low voice tinged with rage, he tries again to get her to talk. "Tell me what happened to you. Tell me now."

"Zoom out a little. I want to make sure she's okay," I tell Leo. He's already reaching for the controls.

Sammy looks a little shaken, and even with the dim lighting and grainy image, I can tell she's gone ashen.

Fuck, fuck, fuck.

"Come on, Sammy. Stay strong," Leo mutters under his breath. I put my hand on his shoulder to steady him. He's vibrating with something — anger, probably.

Stammering this time, Sammy answers him, going off-script. "I... I was abducted. Thrown into the trunk of a car." She lifts her hair, revealing the bandage hidden under her bangs. She intentionally styled it to hide the injury, in hopes he wouldn't see she was hurt. I suspect it's because she doesn't want to appear weak in front of him.

Craig gasps when he sees it, his breath catching in his throat a little. "What the fuck? That doesn't look good, darling. Does it hurt?" He moves to reach for her, but his chains halt his movements.

Balling his fists, he bangs them against the table, shaking the metal. It startles Sammy, and she jumps in her seat before quickly settling. She rolls her shoulders back and shakes her head slightly, appearing to shake off the fear.

"Dammit," Leo whispers, his voice a steely calm.

"I saw it too," I reply, referring to the way she startled. "But she got it back together. She's fine. Trust her to handle this. She's good."

Leo nods and takes a deep breath.

Sammy clears her throat, recapturing our attention. "It's okay," she tells Craig. "Doesn't hurt anymore."

Craig looks like he's getting agitated. His demeanor has shifted from playful manipulation to simmering rage. His jaw is ticking, his fists clenched, and there's unmistakable tension in his shoulders. "Whoever did this will pay, Sammy. No one hurts what's mine."

Fury turns my vision black. "What the fuck?"

"Interesting. I'm starting to think it's not him," Leo says. Oddly, he's the calm one.

I was supposed to be the steady one. But Leo must be channeling his Lionheart *gentle giant* moniker right now. He tilts his head, examining the screen closely, and zooms tight on Craig's face.

"Look at him," Leo says. "He's absolutely furious someone hurt her."

"Doesn't mean it's not him," I start. "He might just be pissed they hurt her in the process. Maybe that wasn't part of the deal."

"Possibly. She needs to keep asking questions to get him talking."

Sammy must realize this because she takes control of the conversation. "Someone also put a tracker on my vehicle. You wouldn't happen to know anything about that, would you?"

"That's odd. I didn't realize you were driving again. When did this happen?" Craig asks.

"How does he..." Leo trails off.

"How did you know that?" Sammy asks, echoing Leo's musings.

Craig shifts back in his seat, the chains rattling slightly. "I might be locked up here for the time being, but that doesn't mean you're out of my life. You know I don't like repeating myself, but maybe you've forgotten. So let me say it once more." He levels a glare at Sammy, his eyes like a predator. "You belong to me and always will. I always know where my assets are and what they're doing. I'm always watching."

Yelling now, Sammy demands, "Who did you hire? Give me a name!"

"Good girl," Leo says.

"I don't answer to you. It's the other way around. Now be a good girl and look after that head wound. I don't want it to scar and tarnish your beautiful skin."

"Oh, so you only like the scars you personally give me?" She lowers her collar, revealing a patch of skin on her shoulder. "Like this one?" Quickly righting the shirt, she jabs her arms out in front of herself, pointing to the scars above her elbows. "Or these?"

Craig cringes, but it's not with regret. It looks like disgust. His mouth purses, and he turns his eyes away from her injuries.

Without meeting her eyes, he says, "I already apologized for those. But you and I both know you wouldn't have those marks if you'd behaved."

My teeth mash to the point of pain. "I'm going to kill him."

Leo bangs his fist on the table. "Get in line."

I can't stand for her to be in there another second. "I think that's enough. He's obviously still our main suspect — he's clearly not done tormenting her. I want her out of there."

Leo meets my eyes, his brows raised. "Easy, man."

"Now, Leo. Get the guard." I move to the door and rap on it three times.

In the five seconds it takes for the guard to come in, Sammy has already stood and called for the guard. *Thank fuck.*

"Done?" the guard asks me as he sticks his head in.

"Get her out. Now." Shoving him right back out into the hallway, I point to the door to the visitation room where Sammy is with that sick fuck.

With the guard gone, Leo turns to me. "What the fuck is happening right now? I thought I'd be the one losing his shit. You need to calm down."

"I'm trying but come on, she's..."

I can't finish the sentence. Leo just eyes me cautiously for a few seconds before letting out a haggard sigh and facing the door to await Sammy's return.

I pace in the small room, heaving shaky breaths. I'm so filled with rage, disgust, and hatred for that man.

Why didn't I kill him when I had the chance?

He's a monster. He'll never stop. Even if he does move on from Sammy, he'll find someone else to prey on.

I have to end him.

And I will.

Chapter Thirty

IT AIN'T JUST A RIVER IN EGYPT

Sammy

"I'll accept an apology in advance," Leo jokes, nudging me with his mammoth shoulder. Like a trooper — or someone who was expecting it — I don't fall to the ground of the prison's parking lot. I'm on some type of odd high after managing to have a visit with Craig without crumbling into a ball.

I am woman. Hear me roar!

"I'm not apologizing. I'm still not entirely convinced," I respond, jutting my chin with an air of petulance.

"It's more than likely him," Sawyer adds. "He's obsessed with you."

"And in jail," I hedge.

Leo jumps back in. "Where he can get visitors and messages out. He's wealthy and a deranged psycho. It's him, Sammy."

"Agree to disagree."

Leo inspects the car with the stick thing. Sawyer keeps his hand on my back, his head rotating like the Exorcist kid.

"Seriously, guys? It's a secured parking lot."

"For all we know, he knew we'd come here and had a plan in place for that eventuality," my brother replies.

My eye roll is so emphatic that my head follows suit and circles in time with it.

"Clear," Leo announces.

Sawyer opens the door to the front seat and ushers me in.

"Are you going to sleep again? If not, you can have the front," I offer.

"I'm nothing if not a gentleman." He winks at me and grins with that stupid dimple making a reappearance.

My panties explode, and a little voice inside yells, *let's jump his bones and ride his face all the way home! Tell your brother we'll meet him there.*

Oh, good. My horny monster is back now that I'm no longer in a heightened state of panic.

On the way home, Leo calls Big Al on speakerphone, relaying the highlights of the visit. Big Al and Sawyer completely agree that Craig is the number one suspect, despite my objections. However, they'll still consider all other possibilities and look for other leads, leaving nothing off the table. After the call, Sawyer and Leo take turns trying to convince me of his guilt.

But I'm still not sure.

"Here's my theory," Sawyer starts. Because of the fantastic orgasm he gave me last night — and for no other reason — I decide to hear him out. "He's bored in prison and wants to get you to come to see him. So he stages a few things using his money and influence, and *bam*. You came running, just like he wanted. We walked right into his little trap. He wants to prove he's still controlling you."

My fist punches the dashboard, the rage monster fully back in control. "The fuck he is!"

"Easy, kid. Sawyer's got a good point. We all know he's not in control of you anymore. You're free of him and living your life. This was just a little setback."

"Congratulations, we played ourselves," Sawyer murmurs, mostly to himself, then lets loose an annoyed groan.

He's seated behind me in the SUV, so I can't see him, but I can envision him wiping his face from forehead to chin in that sexy way he does. Damn his hotness. I'm trying to be angry, and he keeps distracting me via my imagination.

He's a horniness-invoking wizard. Which Harry Potter house is that? Slytherin maybe? Let's face it. We all know Slytherin had the sexy ones. They can probably make you orgasm with a spell. Something like: Expectrum Orgonum Climaxus.

Focus, Sammy.

Shaking off my insane thoughts, I ask, "You guys honestly think this was all for fun for him?"

Leo looks over at me, giving me a knowing side-eye. "Absolutely."

"Yep," Sawyer adds, popping the *P* sound.

"Then why on earth was he so mad about my head injury?"

That's the part I don't get. I know Craig, and that was a genuine reaction. He didn't like that someone hurt me.

No. That's his job.

A chill creeps up my spine, and I have to physically shake off the uncomfortable sensation and the memory of his hands on me.

"I agree with you that it was a genuine reaction at seeing your head," Leo responds. "I think he paid someone to abduct you to mess with you, give you a scare. He didn't expect them to hurt you in the process. That anger was directed at whomever hurt you."

Even I can admit that seems valid. "Okay, I guess that makes sense. Maybe you guys are right. This just doesn't seem like his style. It's like Sue said the other day. He's much more hands-on."

Sawyer's voice is regret-laced when he says, "Damn, I wish we'd have brought her with us. Maybe she could have seen something in his body language that we missed."

Leo shakes his head ardently. "I don't want her anywhere near the shitbag ever again. She had nightmares for a long time after everything went down at the cabin." He rolls his broad shoulders, then adds to me, "It took all my strength to let you go."

"It's not like I gave you a choice. And for the record, I'm glad I did it. I feel good about it."

I grin to myself at the memory of me flipping him off and telling him to rot in hell as the guard led me out of the room.

That felt good.

"New subject. Can we talk about your boss and our mother?" I ask Leo.

He cricks his head at me so sharply, I'm worried he's going to swerve the car off the road. "What about them?"

"You haven't noticed?" I ask.

"Noticed what?" Leo looks absolutely dumbfounded.

Wow. Just wow.

"Where to begin? The way they look at each other. The way they call each other by their first names," I start.

Sawyer chimes in. "How Big Al always seems to know what your mom is up to and where she's at."

After a soft giggle at Leo's perpetually shocked expression, I add, "Oh, and let's not forget how he growled when you informed him of her business trip. You weren't even on speaker phone, and I still heard the growl loud and clear from beside you."

Shaking his head fervently, Leo says, "You guys are nucking futs. He's just her friend, and he knows how much she means to me, so he takes her safety seriously. He does the same for Sue and you, Sammy. And for Henderson's wife and kids. That's just Big Al. You guys are dead wrong on this."

"And what if we're not wrong?" I test him. "How would you feel about your boss dating your mother?"

His cheeks turn ruddy. "Well, it doesn't matter because that ain't happening."

I want to test his reaction a bit more for purely scientific reasons. It has nothing to do with how I feel about *General Jawline* in the back seat.

"And what if it did happen? Hypothetically. Would you be okay with someone you work with being with one of the most important women in your life?"

I'm holding my breath, and I bet Sawyer is too.

Leo's deep in thought for five or six long seconds. He scratches his beard, then finally answers, "I guess if it made her happy, then I'd be okay with it. As long as his intentions were good. Mom's had a hard life, and I think someone like him might be good for her."

Glee pours into my soul. *Not the show, but the feeling, weirdo.*

"Wow, that's very mature of you, Leo. I'm surprised."

"I'm an exceedingly mature and reasonable person, Sammy. You know that," he jests.

"Yeah, but that protective streak is a mile long and twice as wide."

"Well, maybe life has mellowed me out."

"A certain lady, you mean," Sawyer teases.

Leo flips off the back seat. "But listen... it doesn't matter because it's definitely not happening. Big Al's interest in Mom is merely platonic."

"Okay, sure." I nod a few times, then tap his arm with as much condescension as I can muster.

"Shut up. You can trust me on this."

"Mm-hmm. Totally. Uh-huh."

"Get the hell out of here, sis." He gives me a slight shove toward the side of the car.

A deep chuckle comes from the back seat. "And up next, we have Leo Mason. Auditioning for the role of Cleopatra, the Queen of Denial."

My shoulders jiggle with my laughter. "Okay, thanks for that, Pam Tillis."

He taps my seat from behind. "You knew that? I never took you for an old-school country music fan."

"My aunt loved the stuff. Sang the classics all the time. Everything from the eighties and nineties."

Leo adds, "And she loved Johnny Cash too."

I nod in agreement, but my mood sours almost immediately.

I miss her. Aunt Tilly.

She and Mom had a falling out a while back. I figure she had come to Mom's aid one too many times after Dad hurt her. Eventually, Aunt Tilly had to take a stand. She was trying to get Mom to leave him. At some point, you have to put your foot down and protect yourself from toxic situations — even if that means you lose your sister in the process. I don't blame her; I just miss the shit out of her.

Does she even know I'm alive? I wonder if she'd take my call. Probably. I was innocent in the matter with my father, as Jaynie often tells me. After all this time, I finally believe it.

But I'm not able to believe Jaynie when she tells me that how my family reacted when I faked my death wasn't entirely my fault.

Nah.

No matter what she says, I know I'm solely to blame for the devastation my mother faced and the wedge that surfaced between my brothers.

"Did you talk to Drew yet?" Leo asks a few minutes later, right before the silence starts to get uncomfortable.

Damn, I was just thinking of my other brother. Maybe I'm finally back in sync with Leo after all this time. We're sharing a brain again like we used to.

"Yes. Last night before bed. Sawyer reminded me to call him back." I try to suppress my grin at how doting Sawyer has managed to be these last few days. Yet it's not smothering.

In fact, it isn't only these last few days. He's been a supportive presence since I got to Clearwater. The calm in my storm.

"Good. He was really worried," Leo replies.

"I'm so glad you guys are on good terms now," I tell him.

"Yeah. Me too. I've missed a lot these last few years. His kids have gotten so big."

"They're coming for your wedding, right?"

"Yeah. I checked with him before confirming the date."

I smile, genuinely happy with how much my brothers have overcome to forgive each other. I didn't know it at the time, but Drew blamed Leo for my "suicide" since he was smothering the hell out of me leading up to it. Leo blamed himself too, and they came to blows over it. Once I was back, they were forced to deal with their issues.

And then I dealt with mine.

Well, in a large way, I'm still dealing with my issues over the disappearing act I pulled with the fake suicide and how everyone I loved was hurt in the process. Probably always will be.

Guilt racks me when I think about all the anguish I caused my family. Back then, I was so wrapped up in what Craig wanted that I barely considered what my family would go through when I left. What Craig said was gospel to me. And he wanted us to move away together, to start our life free from my family's *interference*, as he called it. Once Leo saw the signs of the emotional and then physical abuse, he tried to get me away from Craig. I was so stubborn and messed up at the time, I reacted poorly. A large part of me wanted to hurt my brother. Not everything in the letter was Craig's idea.

My stomach swirls with disgust, so I roll down the window to let in some fresh air.

Jaynie seems to think I blamed Leo in my letter because I knew he could handle my burden. His shoulders were broad enough — no pun intended — to carry the weight of what I couldn't bear myself. I'm not sure if I buy it, but it does make sense on some level.

Whatever.

Fortunately, Leo and I have made our peace for the most part. I know I'll never stop feeling guilty, but I can't change the past. So it's best to move forward. That's all I can do.

"Drew and the family are still coming down for Christmas again this year, right?"

"Yeah. That's the plan," Leo answers me, then whips his head over his shoulder toward Sawyer. "And you're spending the holidays with us this year. Not just Christmas, but Thanksgiving too. And I don't want to hear shit about it. I still can't believe you bailed on us last year."

"The overtime was hard to pass up," Sawyer says. "Plus, it was good for you to spend time with your family after everything went down."

"You're part of our family, Sawyer. I don't know how many times I need to tell you that before you finally believe it."

"Maybe a few more times. Seventeen or eighteen, tops," Sawyer jokes, but there's pain in his voice.

Or is that guilt?

If it is, it's because of me. Or, more accurately, because of his feelings for me.

Damn. You'd think we were raised Catholic with all this guilt. It's so thick in here, it's practically choking us all.

Chapter Thirty-One

ISN'T IT ALWAYS HAPPY HOUR?

Sammy

Sawyer pats my brother on the shoulder and gives him a squeeze. "We'll be fine, Leo. I'm sure Sue is sick of being at Redleg HQ. Go get her and head home. It's been a long day. I've got everything covered here."

While we went to see the douche today, Leo hid Sue away at Redleg so he could rest assured his angel was safe.

How sweet.

Gag.

I'm not in the mood for sweet. I want to get a little tipsy, take a shower, have an orgasm, and then pass out. In that order.

I plop down on the couch with an empty wine glass and a bottle of chilled Riesling with a corkscrew sticking out of the top while Sawyer tries again to get Leo to leave. He's acting like cheap plastic wrap right now. Fairly clingy, but ultimately useless.

"You good, Sammy? I can come back after I get Sue if you need me."

I'm not responding to that. I've already told him to go home three times in the last half hour. He isn't even listening at this point.

And don't roll your eyes at me. I get it. I'm his baby sister. He loves me and is worried I'm emotionally damaged from our visit to the prison today. But I'll tell you the same thing I told him all damn afternoon. *I'm fine.*

To be clear, I truly am fine. This isn't the *I'm fine* that we reserve for our spouses or partners when we're really not fine, but don't feel like telling them what the problem is because *they should already freaking know!*

No. It's not that kind. I'm legitimately fine.

After I pull the cork out with my teeth and spit it out onto the coffee table, I pour myself a very large glass — a mega pint, if you will. I can feel Leo and Sawyer's eyes on me as I chug for the count of two, three, and four.

"Ah," I say, enjoying the chill and nip of the delicious beverage as it burns a little down my throat on its way to my empty belly.

"Sammy?" Leo prods.

Channeling my bodyguard's British accent, I say, "Sawyer, be a sport and escort the giant from the premises. Chop, chop." I wave my hand in the direction of the front door as if I'm shooing him out the door.

Leo takes three quick steps, eating up the distance between us, and presses a kiss just above my hairline. "I love you. I'll see you tomorrow. Call me if you need me."

"I love you too. Give Sue a fist bump for me."

He and Sawyer grumble to each other as he takes his leave — freaking finally. I polish off the first glass of wine and pour another, not bothering to put the bottle back in the fridge.

So crisp and delicious. The liquid dinner of champions.

I earned this shit today.

"Are you sharing that, or am I on my own?" Sawyer asks over the beeps of the alarm resetting.

I make a *pfft* sound, then reply, "As if you'd drink alcohol on duty."

"Yeah, fair point. I guess it doesn't feel like work to look after you. Besides, it just looks damn good."

"You look damn good," I retort before I have a chance to filter my words.

Guess the wine is already doing that thing that alcohol does. You know... where it turns you into a moron?

"Damn, woman. Your brother isn't out of the house for sixty seconds yet, and you're already starting shit. He's probably still in the damn driveway." He pulls out his phone and taps a few times. "Yep. Still sitting there." He flips the screen around to show me the security camera feed from the front porch.

I take another sip to disguise my chuckle.

"Want something to eat?" he hollers from the kitchen. "Your mom said she'd leave food for us, or I can cook something. Oh, look. She left a note."

He throws his voice to impersonate my mother. "Kids, I prepped a meatloaf this morning before my flight so you'd have something to eat after a long day in the car. Just cook at three-fifty for about forty-five minutes. There are mashed potatoes and vegetables in the fridge you can warm up in the micro. A loaf of banana bread is in the bread box too. I'll see you Saturday. I love you."

He returns to his normal voice and says, "And then in parentheses she put, 'I love you too, Sawyer.' Aww, your mom is so sweet. You're so damn lucky to have her."

"Very lucky indeed." I finish my second glass and debate filling up a third.

Let's go with a half glass. That's a good compromise. Enough to finish taking the edge off this day without making me a sloppy embarrassment. Perfect plan.

After putting the cork back in the bottle, I stroll to the kitchen to put it in the fridge.

Sawyer holds the raw meatloaf covered in tin foil out in front of him, brows raised in silent question.

"Sure. Go nuts," I say indulgently with a shrug.

He fires up the oven and throws in the meatloaf, then sets the timer. When he spins around, I'm watching him closely over the rim of my glass.

"Milady." He does a half curtsy, and I bust out laughing, too buzzed to resist his silliness.

Not that I'd want to. The resist-Sawyer-ship sailed right off a cliff before he even touched my clit.

My laugh fades into a quiet giggle, and I take another sip.

"Happiness looks good on you," he tells me after returning to his normal height, towering over me in the best way.

Setting the glass down on the counter beside me, I pad two steps across the kitchen to meet him in the middle.

"No cameras in here, right?" I ask, lifting my brows suggestively.

His gaze shifts to the ceiling as he draws his teeth across his lower lip. "You are *not* going to make this easy on me, are you?"

I pantomime putting a phone to my ear, and in a higher-than-normal-pitched voice, I say, "Hi, Sawyer. It's me. You should come over tonight so we can make out. My mom's out of town."

I bat my lashes at him as I hang up the fake phone, flipping my hand closed.

Apparently, when I'm buzzed, my hand phone is a Motorola Razr.

With a soft hiss, he grabs my upper arms, running his palms up and down over my skin. "You're not drunk already, are you?" he asks, looking me over carefully.

"Nope. Barely a wine buzz. Just relaxed and feeling good."

"That's good to hear." His hands sink down and wrap around my low back, hauling me closer. "Because I want to ask you something."

"Whatever the question, the answer is yes," I tease.

He laughs silently and shakes his head. "It's not a yes or no question."

"What is it?" I run my hands up his chest and bring them to rest over his strong shoulders, feeling absolutely safe in his arms. There is no place else on earth I'd rather be.

His pheromones must be working overtime right now, and my panties are going to have to burn the midnight oil to keep up with output if this continues.

"Let's sit," he says, taking a step away from me. He suddenly seems very serious, and I can't help but worry why that might be.

"The other day on the way to therapy," he starts once we're both seated.

"You mean yesterday?" I ask.

"Was that only yesterday?"

With a chuckle, I nod.

"Wow. These last few days feel like weeks."

I feign offense. "Ugh, I'll try not to take that personally."

He grins, popping that stupid nipple-hardening dimple again. Treacherous thing.

"So... yesterday on the way into therapy. In the stairwell."

"Yes?"

"You started to say something but then stopped yourself. I want to know what you were going to say."

Like a dog hearing a whistle, I cock my head to the side. "Do you remember what we were talking about?"

He nods, fiddles with his hands, and looks down at the table separating us. "I remember it exactly." He pauses and meets my eyes. "I'd just gotten done telling you that we needed to stop flirting. And you said, 'So you've made your decision, then? You don't want to try to keep us a secret. You're not willing to do that. I'm not.' And then you stopped. I want to know the rest of that sentence. You're not what?"

I pinch the bridge of my nose. Of all the things he might have asked, I didn't expect that.

But I should have.

Sawyer knew I was holding back something significant. After all, *he knows me* so well.

"You can tell me anything, Sammy. I hope you know that." His dark, beautiful eyes implore me. "You're not what?"

"As I recall, the conversation we had earlier in the day was about us keeping things between us a secret. And you were clear that you didn't want to keep it from Leo or your team. I told you that I'd do it for you. Because I think *you're* worth it." I take a deep breath, preparing myself to say the rest. The part he wants to know so badly. "But obviously, I'm not worth it for you."

Silence falls heavy in the room for two short seconds before he has any reaction.

His throat bobs, and fire ignites in his gaze as it seeps through my skin, right into my bones. My every sense of being prickles with electricity under the intensity of his stare. I can tell he's made a decision, and I suspect it's the one I've wanted him to make so desperately.

He cricks his finger at me while backing his chair away from the table, making room for me.

With my heart pounding furiously, I rise and glide around the table. He grabs my hand as soon as it's within reach and pulls me close. I climb onto his lap, straddling his hips.

Face to face and chest to chest, I slide my arms around his shoulders. His scent engulfs me, wrapping me up in an intoxicating blanket. He's like catnip, and I want to rub myself all over him.

As he stares into my eyes, he tells me in earnest, "You're worth everything."

I think my heart is about to explode.

And then he brings his lips to mine, brushing them gently before sweeping his tongue across my mouth. I open for him, letting him claim me.

Because I'm his.

That's what's happening, right? We're starting something special. We know the risks, but we're choosing each other over everything and everyone else.

The kiss starts tentatively but grows and blossoms, just like our feelings for one another have been doing all along.

He commands my mouth, both domineering and submissive at the same time. It's deep and shallow. Soft and hard. Too much yet not enough.

This kiss is profoundly beautiful — unlike any kiss I've ever had. Not born out of lust or anger. It's honest and true. I feel him taking root in my soul with each swipe of his tongue and nip of my lip.

I also feel his erection growing beneath me, and I can't help but rub myself against him. Slowly and rhythmically. Back and forth.

So much for these panties.

Dun, dun, dun. Another pair bites the dust.

I'm beginning to suspect none of my panties will ever be safe around Sawyer.

His large hands rub up and down my back while he owns my mouth. They settle around my waist, and he pulls me forward, dragging my core over the thick ridge beneath his jeans at his own leisurely pace. I bear down, pressing harder as I undulate my hips, giving my clit the friction it begs for.

He breaks the kiss with a groan, then steadies my hips, locking me in place. "Slow down, baby." His voice is deliciously raspy and sends a bolt of electricity directly to my nipples.

"I guess I can't help myself. I want you so badly, and this feels so right. After so long."

Sweet, poignant honesty.

Sharing my feelings so openly is entirely liberating.

"I know it does. But if you keep doing that, I'm going to need to get inside you. And we can't do that right now."

"Why not?" My eyes narrow. "Don't you dare bring up those rules because I'm fairly certain those are now moot."

Sawyer grins brightly. He's happy again. Back to his usual self.

And he proves that he's back when he uses his go-to British accent. "Well, for one, milady, I don't have a johnnie."

I can't hold back my chuckle. "A johnnie?"

With his regular voice, he says, "Yeah, I think that's a slang term in England for a condom."

"Oh, I see. So you don't have one, huh?"

"Negative."

That's disappointing. After everything we've shared, I'd like to see if it feels as good to take it to the next level as it did to feel him spooned against me last night. I'm not entirely sure if I'm ready for sex with him, but I'm certainly ready to try.

He gives me a quick peck, and I dive in for one more. Then another. I love the feel of my lips on his. They're just as smooth and supple as they look.

"I guess you weren't a boy scout since you're clearly not always prepared," I tease.

He smiles, and his eyes dance with mirth. "No, I most certainly was *not* prepared for this. For you. Seducing me."

"But what about having one on hand for other... dalliances?" I tease, using my own British impression.

He smiles at first in response to my silly accent, but then his face sobers. "There hasn't been a chance of that happening for quite some time, Sammy."

Drawing my nose across his, I close my eyes and breathe him in for another moment. His words register slowly but surely.

"What are you saying? How long has it been?"

Instead of answering, he throws my question back at me, raising his well-trimmed eyebrows. Damn. He's so sexy from this angle — underneath me. With a voice as smooth as whipped cream, he asks, "Well, how long has it been for you?"

A pinch in my chest makes me wince at the memory of my last sexual encounter. "I haven't been with anyone since... you know who."

"So more than two years?" he clarifies.

Wordlessly, I nod, unable to speak due to the discomfort Craig's memory brings me. Especially regarding sex with him.

It wasn't necessarily violent or overtly forceful. He was far too controlling emotionally for me to fight back when it came to sex. Although I'd say no, I went along with it, more or less. It was easier that way. Yet, at the same time, it also wasn't explicitly consensual for the last few years of our relationship.

Relationship? Ha. That's a laugh.

More like an emotional hostage situation. But... whatever. It's over now. And it's time to move on.

"It's been that long for me too," he says.

I gasp, my head kicks back, and my jaw falls to my chest. "Seriously?" My voice comes out in a near screech, so I dial down my shock a tad. "You're a young, hot, sexy, virile man with a smokin' body and a good job. Why on earth haven't you been breaking hearts all over the coast?"

His head tilts to the side, and the skin at the side of each eye pinches. "Because that's when you came back into my life."

Whoa, whoa, whoa.

"You haven't been with anyone since I came back? Why?"

Something flashes behind his eyes that I can't decipher. "You know why."

I feel like I'm having an out-of-body experience. Is he saying he hasn't been able to take another woman to bed because of his feelings for me? That doesn't seem possible.

"All this time you've..." My words trail off.

I'm not sure how to process what he's telling me, let alone speak words or have some type of logical reaction.

This can't be real.

"All this time," he confirms, then swallows. When he exhales, his breath is shaky, like he's scared of how I'll react to his confession.

I search his expression for any trace of dishonesty, manipulation, or any other tactics Craig used to pick at the scabs around my heart.

There's no deceit.

I only see honesty and vulnerability written across Sawyer's arrestingly handsome face.

I sway forward, pressing my forehead to his. Bringing my hands up, I palm his smooth cheeks and join my lips to his. I can't say anything in response to his profession of... love? Is that love? For me?

No. That can't be *love*.

But it's at least some profound feelings for me if he abstained for more than two years.

Even though I don't have words for him, I do have my body.

My mouth.

My kisses.

My tender touch.

And I use them all.

I kiss him like I've always wanted to kiss him. The way I've dreamed of for years and years — even if those dreams were dormant at times, they were never far away.

Pressing my chest against his, I wrap him tighter in my arms and hold on for dear life. Twirling and twisting our tongues together in a sweet and slow dance.

Damn the consequences.

I'm going to kiss this man like he deserves to be kissed. He's been waiting for me. Watching out for me. Caring for me. Supporting me as a friend, while wanting so much more — but never forcing himself.

My head is spinning. I have to have more of him. I *need* it.

And I don't think I can wait.

Chapter Thirty-Two

JUST THE TIP

Sawyer

Kissing Sammy is like all the good things in my life have joined forces and shoved their tongues down my throat.

Wait. That's not very romantic, and this moment is the height of romance for me. Or at least it should be.

Hell, I'm consumed by her body and those soft moans, gentle sighs, and gyrating hips. I'm holding perfection in my arms. Literal perfection. What could be more romantic than that?

I'm in ecstasy from simply kissing her.

From kissing. *Only* kissing.

Despite living like a monk for a few years while pining for Sammy — I still can't believe I admitted that — I've kissed my fair share of women and taken many lovers in my day. Some long-term and some brief flings.

But in all that time, I've never been swept away with a kiss like this. I don't even think I can speculate how earth-shattering it will feel once I'm finally buried inside her.

Speaking of which, she's inched her hand between us to unbutton my jeans. As she lowers the zipper and snakes her hand inside, she gets a handful of my rock-hard dick and starts stroking. This time, no silk covering her hand.

My thoughts turn carnal — all I want to do is bury myself in her and have her screaming my name. Dammit. I blame the way she's gripping my cock and sucking on my tongue for my less-than-romantic thoughts. The way we're making out has gone from loving and gentle to animalistic and frantic pretty damn fast.

Grabbing her hand, I make a tsking sound to stop her. While smiling across her lips, I tell her, "Sammy, I'm noticing a pattern here. I draw a line, and you walk right up to it and tiptoe right across it. You're a habitual line crosser."

She pulls back and tries to look innocent, but because her hand is down my pants, that's a little hard for her to pull off.

Hard.

Pull off.

Dirty-mind mode activated.

"Sawyer, I have to be honest with you. I haven't wanted sex with anyone for a very long time. Years and years even." She's still slowly stroking me as she speaks, her voice a delicate whisper. "But I want it with you so damn bad right now that I think I'm going to explode if I can't feel you inside me just for a second." She bites her lower lip and bats her lashes at me. "Can you get inside me for just a quick second?"

"Sammy —"

"I've been tested for...well, you know; all clear."

"Me too, but it's still not a good idea." I try again to tell her why this isn't the best course of action. "Sammy —"

"Please, Sawyer. Just for a second. I want to see if I can handle it. It feels so right with you."

My brain is frazzled with testosterone. I'm also overcome with an intense desire to not only make love to her, but to make her happy and fulfill her every wish.

I can't think straight. She's broken my brain.

It's the only possible explanation for what happens next.

"Take your pants off."

"Here?" she asks.

I nod. "Right now. Before I change my mind."

Her eyes widen, but she obeys, rising to her feet between my spread legs.

While she removes her jeans and panties, I finish freeing my cock and shove my bottoms down around my knees. I get rid of my shirt too. If we get that far, I'll have to pull out, so it might get messy. I don't have a change of clothes with me because, as she so astutely pointed out, I'm no boy scout.

And this shirt cost eighty dollars.

I've already seen her gorgeous pink pussy once before when she spread herself open on the couch. And last night, I even touched it, but only a little bit. Now that she's bared before me again, I'm tempted to reach out and cup her delicate core, then slip my fingers inside to see how tight she is.

I'm about to do just that when her earlier words stop my movements, giving me pause.

She said she's not sure if she's ready for sex, and given how she clammed up when I caged her in on the couch yesterday, she probably needs to stay in control for now — until she's sure she can trust me.

I'm not sure if I can handle it, she'd said.

I don't pretend to know everything about sexual assault survivors, but I imagine she's nervous about trying this. So I need to take it slow.

This needs to be entirely about her.

Tamping down my alpha tendencies, I ask, "Can I touch you, gorgeous? There." I tilt my head toward her pussy as she settles herself back onto my lap.

Her lips quirk into a devilish grin. "You want to feel how wet I am for you first?"

"Yes, baby. I *really* fucking do. And I need to slip my fingers inside your pretty pussy and stretch you out so I don't hurt you." I wrap my hand around the back of her neck and pull her close for a quick kiss, one with just a little tongue. She doesn't resist my grip around her neck, leaning in and opening for me like she wants it as bad as I do.

Pulling her mouth from mine, she drags her wet folds across my cock, which is pressed between us. "That's probably a good idea. You're a lot bigger than my vibrator. I'm not sure if you'll fit unless you get me ready."

Good Lord. The thought of her using a vibrator, coupled with her rubbing against me, is almost enough to get me off right now.

"It'll fit, baby." I wink but add, "And I'll be gentle."

Her brow furrows as she grinds against me, her slickness rubbing onto my hard flesh. "Promise?"

"I never want to hurt you, Sammy. I promise. We'll go slow. You set the pace. Okay?"

"Oh, Sawyer. You're just..." My name dances out of her sweet mouth with a breathy sigh, but she can't seem to finish her thought.

"I'm going to touch you now, okay?"

"Yes."

The tension starts radiating from her.

"Just relax and enjoy it."

She nods and rocks her clit against my dick again, taking a deep breath. As her lashes flutter closed, her breath fans across my skin, giving me goosebumps. There's a sweetness to her breath, just like the taste of her kisses.

Kisses I can't seem to get enough of tasting.

Maybe she sprinkled crack in her wine because I'm quickly becoming an addict.

I move my hand between us and dance my fingertips along her wet flesh, dipping them between her folds until I find her clit. I flick the pearl a few times before rubbing the sensitive skin around it. She moans, her breath increasing to a pant.

The angle isn't great for slipping more than one of my fingers inside her unless I can move her back, but I don't want to do that because I like her close to me. I can't seem to pry my lips away from her soft skin for more than a few seconds.

So after placing a few kisses along her collarbone and working my way up to her ear, I whisper, "I want to lay you down across the table. Can I do that? Or do you need to be on top?"

Her subtle movements slow to a halt. "You said *need* and not *want*. It's like you know exactly what to say. How do you know how hard this is for me?"

All my movements cease so I can tell her this as honestly and earnestly as possible. "I told you before. I pay attention to you. I know you, baby. Your cheeks are flush when you're aroused, but they go pale when you get scared. Your breathing changes too."

I wipe her bangs to the side of her face so I can see the shimmer of her eyes as I continue, "I saw you dig your fingernails into your palms with a hard fist a few times too. You also told me you weren't sure you were ready, and knowing what I do about your past, I can imagine why that is. And how you took control on the sofa yesterday gave me a good indication of what you need from me. I'm just trying to give you what you need."

Her eyes get shiny. "I don't deserve you."

Before I can object — because it's me who isn't deserving, not her — she leans forward and nuzzles our noses, then angles her head as she gently swipes her lips against mine. I deepen the kiss, tangling our tongues together and getting lost in her.

I resume circling her clit, then move my other hand to her hip, encouraging her to rock against my hand and dick.

She breaks the kiss. "Okay."

I struggle to remember what I asked her, which is a challenge considering where all the blood in my body is headed.

Ah yes. A position change.

"Okay? As in, I can lay you down. Right?"

She nods and grins shyly. "Yes. Let's try. You'll stop if I tell you to?"

"You shouldn't even need to ask that, Sammy. I'll do anything you say. And we can stop at any time."

She pulls away from me and lifts her luscious ass onto the table. I stand and spread her legs, squeezing her inner thighs a few times. She's gained some weight since she got back home — thank fuck. Now she's truly perfect, inside and out.

With one hand around her upper back, I lean forward slowly in time with her, helping her recline onto the cool, hard surface.

"You okay?" I ask her once she's laid out before me.

I'm keeping about a half foot of space between us while hovering over her. I intentionally only have one hand bracing on the table beside her head so she doesn't feel restrained or locked in by me.

"Yes, keep going." I watch her throat bob. "I need you to keep going. Please."

She sounds so scared. It breaks my heart.

With my other hand, I reach down and resume massaging that tight bundle of nerves. Even though she's nervous, she's still soaking wet for me. I'll take that as a good sign.

She reaches up and pulls my face down to hers for a suddenly rough kiss. It's like she got renewed with a shot of her formidable strength and is determined to chase her fears away. Somehow we've moved from sweet right back to scorching without so much as a warning. She nips at my lip and sucks my tongue into her mouth.

Sweet Jesus. She's trying to kill me.

As our kiss continues to build, my erection throbs, and I'm sure if I looked down, I'd see a bead of precum leaking from my tip.

But this isn't about me. This is *all* for her.

I break away from her decadent mouth, rise to a standing position between her thighs, and slip one finger inside her slick heat. Her walls pulse around my finger.

Fuck. I groan my approval.

Pumping in and out, I study her face for signs of panic. With her head tossed back and neck exposed, she bites her lip.

There's no sign of panic, so I continue readying her for my dick. Using one hand to work her clit and the other to stretch her out, I slip in another finger. She arches her back off the table and meets my eyes. They flash with a hunger for more.

Even though I'd prefer being pressed flush against her and worshipping her mouth as we do this — especially for our first time — I think this position will be better for her. She can have space between us so she doesn't feel trapped, and I can see her every expression. Plus, I'll have easy access to her clit the entire time to keep her in the moment if her head should get away from her.

"Feels good. Keep going. Faster." That smoldering, sexy voice of a siren she used when she wouldn't let me touch my own cock is back.

"Fuck yes, Sammy. Tell me what you want."

She rolls her hips a little, bucking them gingerly. "Add another finger."

"Your wish is my command." I wink at her, unable to hold back my cheeky nature.

It's a snug fit, but I get a third finger inside her, and she squeezes them so tight that my eyes roll back in my head in pleasure.

"I'm ready. I want your cock now. Just a little bit."

I can't resist a joke. Raising my brows in jest, I ask, "Just the tip?"

She laughs, and her walls pulse around my fingers in time with her soft chuckles.

I can't wait 'til she's squeezing my dick like that.

Replacing my fingers with the head of my cock, I drag it up and down across her pink flesh, soaking it with her wetness. My cock pulses and twitches in my hand at the mere thought of the pleasure it's about to experience once I slip inside her.

What we're about to do might cost me everything — my friendship and maybe even my job.

But she's worth it. My Sammy is worth it.

She scoots her body down the table, getting closer to me until her ass hangs off the edge. I lift one of her legs, wrap it around my left hip, and run my hand along the underside of her thigh. Feels so damn good to have her supple flesh pressed against mine. I'd like to dip my mouth down and lick up her folds, but she's been clear with what she wants, and something tells me not to push her right now. She's given me permission to do what she's ready for and nothing more.

With an aching slowness, I sink my cock inside her delicious body, giving her exactly what she asked for — just the tip. We both sound like we're running a race with our ragged breaths.

She moans softly and squeezes her hands into fists at her sides, pressing them firmly against the table. It might be from pain or pleasure — given my size and how long it's been for her, it's probably a bit of both. By the time my head is all the way in, her eyes roll to the back of her head.

"Eyes on me, baby. Right here. Stay with me," I rasp, barely able to hold in a growl.

Her eyelids spring open, and I'm hit with those same gorgeous turquoise pools I've dreamed about for years and years. She's trying to be strong, but I can see this is emotional for her.

"Good girl," I shower her with praise. "You're so fucking beautiful."

Steadfast, she holds my gaze. We're frozen in time for a few seconds. Barely joined but completely in the moment and ultimately in sync.

I wait for her to give me a signal — to tell me to either stop or go. Red light or green light. Something. *Anything.*

It's killing me not to thrust farther, but this isn't about me. It's all for her. So I'll resist as long as it takes and still consider myself the luckiest man on the planet.

This might be all she wants for now. And if that's the case, then so be it. I'll only give her what she can take.

My head falls back when she squeezes around my cock ever so slightly, making it nearly impossible for me to hold back. I look to the ceiling, count to three, and heave a tight exhale. Channeling my inner soldier, I remember my SERE training.

Not that we trained to resist *this* particular form of torture in the Rangers, but remembering to breathe and focus on something else might help me get through this. I need to channel my inner resolve. The last thing I want to do is give her more than she asked for and destroy this tenuous trust we're building. I want her to know she can count on me to never push her past her boundaries.

She constricts her walls again, choking my thick head. As much as I want to, I don't advance, having tapped into my mental toughness.

I look down upon her prone form, letting my gaze trail over each inch of her exposed flesh until I catch her eyes. "You okay, baby?"

She doesn't answer right away, her eyes pinched closed. I need to bring her back to me.

After running my hand up and down her thigh a few times, I trail it down to her hip and give it a squeeze, shaking her from her thoughts.

"Yeah-yea-yes," she stutters. "I'm okay."

My ego is a little miffed by that answer. I want her to feel light-years better than *okay* when my cock is inside her. Even if it is just the fucking tip.

Bringing my other hand around, I start swirling my fingers around her clit again. After a few seconds, her hips start rocking, and involuntarily, I sink in a little deeper.

I try to pull back out, but she works herself up and down my shaft — going only about an inch past the head each time, never farther. Holding my hips steady, I let her set the pace and get used to the feel of our connection. But she's getting wetter by the minute, and it's getting harder to stay in place.

Pun intended.

"This is all at your pace, baby. Okay?"

"I think I'm ready for more. Deeper."

The feel of her slippery flesh squeezing mine is heaven. My breath grows increasingly ragged, and my balls draw up with the need for release.

"Tell me what you want, and it's yours," I tell her, my voice raspy and coated in desire. "And not only right now. I mean *ever*. Period. I'll give you anything you want. I'm going to treat you like you're my princess."

She raises up on one elbow and reaches around my neck with her other arm. "Kiss me, Sawyer."

"Yes, ma'am," I reply with a grin and bring my lips to hers.

When the tips of our tongues meet, my hips inch forward of their own volition, from either the angle change or my desire for sexual release — not sure which. She doesn't seem to mind, though. In fact, she thrusts her hips forward, bringing me a few inches deeper.

I muffle her moans as I deepen the kiss, sucking her tongue and lower lip into my mouth, ravishing her as our passion ignites more fervently.

Her hand travels from the back of my neck down to my hip, then sneaks around to my ass. She squeezes and pulls me deeper inside her body. "I love your ass," she hisses.

I try to resist, but she's gripping me with both her hand *and* her tight, wet channel. I'm stronger than her physically, of course, but my emotional and sexual resistance are barely hanging on.

After more than a decade of wanting her and two years of actively dreaming of this moment, I'm running short on restraint.

"Sammy, are you sure?" I ask, pulling back to look into her ocean eyes.

"Yes. I'm sure. I want you to fuck me and make me forget everything else but you and me."

Looks like I fell for the oldest trick in the book — just the tip. Didn't know that one also works on guys, but I guess it does.

With a low growl emanating from deep inside me, I reach both hands around her plump ass, lift her slightly off the table, and impale her fully onto my cock.

Hello, heaven. I'm home.

Chapter Thirty-Three
GUESS WHO'S GOT DIABETES

Sammy

Are we doing this? I think we're doing this.

And hello! That's a big, magnificent, thick cock moving slowly inside me as his gentle hands roam over the exposed flesh of my thighs and ass. It feels *amazing* being with him like this.

Nothing between us. Nothing separating him from me. He's giving me all the skin contact I can handle, as if he knows exactly what I need.

As he finally pushes all the way inside my body, I feel like I'm exploding with pain and pleasure, a delicious mixture of both in just the right amounts.

For a moment, we just pause — soaking it all in. Every decadent sensation courses from where we're joined throughout every fiber of my body. And then he kisses me so deeply that for a moment, I think I might cry.

When he starts to move, he's so attentive, staying tuned into my every wish. I honestly couldn't ask for a better person for my first time.

Well, not my *first*, first time. But you know what I mean.

It *should* be beautiful — the joining and succumbing to our mutual desires. And for moments, it is. Truly, it's heavenly.

Yet something isn't quite right.

As cliché as it sounds, it's not him. It's me.

My heart is racing and not in an *oh-my-gosh-I'm-about-to-come* way.

And I totally should be about to come. He's playing my body like an instrument, rubbing my clit with his fat thumb as he drives deep inside me and pulls back, dragging his cock along my G-spot with each powerful stroke.

Although Craig couldn't locate that part of my anatomy — not that I wanted him to — I have found it on my own plenty of times, thanks to some of the best toys money can buy. And I know that Sawyer is giving it his all right now, rubbing against it with each drive.

But it's not happening for me. The big bang. The magical release. The pinnacle. The big *O*.

Nope. Nothing.

Sawyer's standing up as he rocks into me, having given me space so I don't feel trapped. I know that's why he's doing it because, like I said, he's paying attention to my every flinch, every breath, every sound.

Everything.

And when he got too close a moment ago, hunched over the table with me, I clammed up. He instantly pulled back, slowed down, and waited for me to be ready again.

He's so sweet. Complete and utter perfection in every way.

I glance down to where we're joined to watch him drive in and out of me at a languid pace, hoping the erotic sight will get me closer to the goal line. He's not being too rough with me, not going as fast as he probably wishes he could. Hell, I can see how hard he's holding back by the strain of the tendons in his neck and the bulgy veins in his forearms. Each time his fingers dig a little too firmly into my thighs, he remembers to be gentle — like he promised he would be — and he pulls them back, making fists.

He's doing everything right. Positively everything.

I should be exploding in pleasure with my body lit up like a Christmas tree. I should be chanting his name and screaming through double orgasm after double orgasm.

But I'm not.

And sadly, I don't think I'm going to be doing that anytime soon. I'm just not in the right headspace.

I probably shouldn't beat myself up for not being able to climax despite Sawyer's exemplary performance. After all, this is my first consensual encounter in years. And it was supposed to be an experiment of sorts. I only wanted to know if I could tolerate it.

And I can. I'm tolerating it.

How romantic? Gag.

Fuck tolerating it.

I want to be able to *revel* in it. To feel nothing but euphoric pleasure shooting through my body instead of dark memories and fear. To be so in the moment that I bring Sawyer right over the edge with me.

Yet here I am. Merely tolerating it.

I sicken myself.

He was right. I'm not ready for him. For this. For a relationship.

Will I ever be ready? Am I defective? Broken beyond repair?

My heart is pounding so violently now that I need to stop.

I can't do this. I just can't.

He must see the anguish and disappointment written on my face because he slows to a stop. Reaching down, I tap his hand where it's resting on my hip.

"I can see I've lost you. You want to stop, baby?" he asks.

I nod. It's the only response I have for him.

There's no judgment in his eyes as he pulls out, leaving me feeling like a husk of a woman.

And that's what I am.

With his nonjudgmental gaze locked on me, he leans down close to me, moving with clear intentions. Tenderly and with deliberate slowness — like he's afraid to spook a cat — he wraps his arm around my shoulders and pulls me up off the table. I'm gently wrapped in his arms as he returns to the chair and pulls me into his lap.

Fuck. He's so perfect.

Tears prick at the backs of my eyes as my sinuses start to sting. I want to be better for him. He deserves better than me.

I want to make love to him without fear or worry. Without being in my head like this. Without being scared.

What man wants a woman he can't fuck without mercy? What man wants a woman who bursts into tears after she stops him in the middle of the first time?

This is too much baggage to deal with, even for someone as spectacular as Sawyer.

Burying my head in his neck, I whimper, "I'm so sorry. I thought I was ready." Tears pool and overflow, running down my cheeks and spilling onto his neck, then down his chest.

"Shh. Shh. It's okay, princess." One arm holds me close while the other hand runs up and down my spine. "You don't have anything to apologize for. I'm the one who fucked up."

I sniffle and pull back to meet his warm eyes filled with concern. "What? You don't have anything to be sorry for. You are amazing. It's me. I'm the..."

The downturn of his lips looks so foreign on his normally happy face that my words trail off. "Yes, I do. I shouldn't have done this. I shouldn't have let it get this far. I knew you weren't ready, but my lust for you clouded my judgment. I'm so sorry, Sammy. Please forgive me." His voice cracks, giving me a glimpse of his pain.

I muffle my sob and choke out an apology. "No. I begged you. I manipulated you. I'm so sorry. It was me. Not you."

He brushes my bangs aside and kisses the injury-free side of my forehead. "How about we say we both fucked up? We moved a little too fast. But it's fine. We're fine. I still want you. And I'll still wait for you. Just like I have been waiting for you for years."

He's trying to ease my guilt. I can see it so clearly. Once again, I'm hit with how much I care for him but don't deserve him.

Shifting my body to straddle him, I take his cheeks in my hands and fuse my lips to his, tasting the saltiness of my own tears.

Gripping me around my waist, he pulls me flush against him so there isn't even a millimeter of space between us and kisses me back. He hugs me tight, but I don't feel trapped. I only feel Sawyer.

Safe.

Protected.

"I'm sorry," he mumbles against my lips. "I'm so damn sorry, Sammy."

"Shh," I hush him, hating the sound of his unnecessary apology. "Shut up and kiss me, Sawyer."

Slanting my lips over his, I stroke my tongue against his lips, beckoning him to open for me. As we savor each other, twirling and swirling our tongues together, his cock starts to press up into me as it hardens once more.

Overcome with passion again and emboldened by this new position, I shift back to give myself space to reach between us, grab his cock, and notch it at my entrance. Looking down to where we're joined, I shudder as I sink onto him.

I meet his hypnotic dark eyes. He studies me carefully, searching for any signal. I know he'll stop if I need him to.

Without breaking the hold his eyes have over me, I let out a shaky breath as I start rocking against him. Not up and down, but back and forth. I rub my clit over the thick base of his shaft over and over. I feel my inner walls pulse and grip him as he flexes his hips upward, driving himself deeper with short thrusts, matching my tempo. Our breaths grow ragged as we grind and writhe against each other.

Oh, this is much better.

Pleasure, pleasure, pleasure.

I feel it everywhere. My entire body is lighting up.

"You okay?" he asks me softly.

I nod and smile between nipping kisses as relief mingles in my blood along with unyielding pleasure. Our bodies move in concert with each other as I feel myself fluttering closer to ecstasy.

Before I have time to register the thought, I grab his hands, removing them from around my hips. He lets me control his movements as I grip his wrists and bend his arms behind his back. The compassionate fucker even leans forward so his arms can fit between his body and the back of the chair. He could easily overpower me without batting an eye. But he's letting me dominate him.

"This better for you, baby? You want me restrained?" His voice is breathy and filled with heat. I think he likes it when I'm in control.

I do too. Dammit. I *really* like this.

It was hot before on the couch yesterday when I was calling the shots, but this is a whole new level of excitement.

As I nod my response, my core floods with renewed arousal, and I start moving on him again.

Faster.

Harder.

Rougher.

He keeps his hands locked behind his back as my pace increases. Moving my hands to brace myself on his shoulders, I ride him harder still, grinding and taking my pleasure from him.

Slamming our lips together, I claim his mouth, and he gives himself to me willingly. I feel the telling flutters of my orgasm start deep inside my stomach, blossoming and growing as my hips move frantically to chase my orgasm.

He gasps out, "I'm gonna come, baby. You need to get off. I can't hold back much longer."

I don't want to get off of him, although I do want *us* to *get off*.

Together. I need this.

Making a split-second decision, I tell him, "I want you to come inside me, Sawyer. I want to feel you."

"Are you sure? Is it safe?"

I slow down my movements so I can think. Considering the probability of pregnancy based on my cycle timing, I give him an honest answer. "Let's say 75 percent chance it's safe based on timing."

"I'll take those odds," he growls into my neck. "Tell me to come right before you do. I want you to order me to finish."

Oh my fucking hell. He's getting off on me dominating him as much as I am.

Heat unfurls all over my skin, and jolts of pleasure start shooting from deep in my core. My pace picks up until I'm right back at the precipice. "Come for me, Sawyer. Come. Now."

He growls and pumps up furiously, jostling me a tad in the process. But the bumpy movement causes me to fall harder onto his cock, rubbing my clit in the most electrifying way.

Tingles skate across my skin.

Lights dance behind my eyelids.

Screaming out his name in ecstasy, I dig my nails into his shoulders as my back arches and legs stiffen. I feel myself convulse around his cock, locking him in place deep inside me. He pulses and swells tight against my walls as he erupts, filling me with his release.

Our movements slow to a stop, leaving our heaving breaths as the only sound.

When my eyes open, his are still closed. Beads of perspiration roll down in rivulets across the smooth planes of his cheek. His hair is matted across his forehead with sweat. He looks positively breathtaking with the muss of sex glow.

"Shower with me?" I ask him while running my fingertips through his damp hair. I want to explore every inch of his body and watch sudsy bubbles flow across his supple skin and chiseled features. I feel like a dam has been breached now that we've finally given in to our desires.

His eyes pop open, and he starts rambling adorably, his voice getting higher pitched the longer he goes on. "We should talk about what just happened. Shouldn't we?"

Assuming he means the big finish, I try to ease his fears. "I'm sure it'll be fine based on my cycle timing. We're probably in the clear."

"Still risky. We shouldn't do that again," he says, pulling his hands free and placing them around my hips.

My heart falls to the ground, shattering into bits. He doesn't want me again. Was this just a one-time thing for him? Did I misread things *that* badly?

He must see the expression change on my face. He cups my cheeks, looks deep into my eyes, and whispers, "I mean without protection. We shouldn't do *that* again. We're definitely doing the rest again."

My slow smile gives way to shaky laughter. "Oh, I thought you meant —"

He cuts me off, taking my lower lip between his teeth and tugging gently before letting go. "Princess, now that I've had a taste of you, I'm never letting you go. You're mine."

Without pausing for my reaction, he seals his lips around my mouth, swiping my tongue with his. My toes curl, and my clit purrs at the way he's gripping the back of my neck.

As he breaks away, he pulls back and studies my face carefully. "Sammy, does it bother you when I say things like that?"

Honestly, that kiss was so fucking epic I can't remember my name right now, let alone what he said.

"Like what?"

"That I won't let you go. Or that you're mine. I never want to make you feel the way he did. I don't know exactly what your relationship was like, but I promise you that ours will be nothing like it. I'll never hurt you or take away your free will. I meant it when I said I want to treat you like my princess."

Once again, my eyes fill with tears.

"No."

It's all I can say because he's such a damn cinnamon roll. I'm going to happily get diabetes if he keeps this shit up.

"No what?"

"No, it doesn't bother me. I know you're nothing like him."

The skin between his brows is pinched. "Why are you crying then?"

"Because I'm happy," I choke out.

Sometimes the simple truth is all you can say.

He presses another kiss to the good side of my forehead and leans my head across his chest, patting my hair down and comforting me.

My heart pounds with excitement for what the future holds.

If we could only figure out what to do about my brother and whoever the hell is out to get me.

Chapter Thirty-Four

CONSIDER THE WARRANTY VOIDED

Sawyer

I work Sammy's coconut-scented shampoo into a lather and scrub my fingers across her scalp, drawing a satisfying moan from her. She stares up at me with a dopey look on her sweet face. I can't resist pressing a quick kiss onto the tip of her nose.

She's already washed my hair, so she grabs a sponge, pours shower gel on it, and starts working it all over my body. My dick takes notice of her movements, twitching and growing hard a-fucking-gain.

Settle down, soldier.

Reaching above her, I grab the handheld shower head and begin rinsing her hair. Her gaze moves down my soapy arms and pauses on the underside of my upper arm.

She runs her fingertips across the mark. "How did you get this scar?"

"That's from a chute mishap during airborne training. My arm got twisted up in the ropes of my primary chute, and I had to pull my emergency chute."

"At least you walked away," she says with a sly grin.

"Wrong. I ran away."

She cocks her head in confusion, so I explain, "My landing was way off target, so I had to roll up my chutes then double-time it to rejoin my team."

"What about this one?" With the sudsy sponge, she points at another scar. This one's a thin white line under my chin.

"To be honest, I have no recollection of that one. I've had it as far back as I can remember."

"And this one?"

I track her eye line and see she's looking at a spot about two inches above my navel. My dick, growing stiffer by the moment, bobs like it's waving at her, trying to get her attention.

Damn, dick. Fucking settle already.

"That one is boring — gallbladder surgery. Along with this one." I point at another small line in my midsection. "And these two. Laparoscopic, so just small holes."

She trails her fingertips over my sudsy abs, resting them on a small scar around my waist. "And here?"

"Grenade shrapnel."

Her lips pull tight. "Yikes. That's scary."

"Nah. I was lucky. Lots of soldiers were hurt way worse."

She draws her fingers over my shoulders. I have to stifle a moan — her touch is enough to send me reeling. "This is a gunshot, right? Leo was with you for this one."

I feel my throat bob as the memory begins its assault on my senses. That day is burned into my memory, and the slightest trigger takes me right back there.

"Yes."

"He told me a little about it. That must have been scary."

Should I tell her how bad it actually was?

Nah. No sense in upsetting her.

"We were hunkered in a dilapidated building for hours, sweating our balls off, but I was in and out of consciousness for most of it. They kept pumping me full of morphine, so it wasn't that bad for me." It's just a tiny fib.

Her nose wrinkles, and she makes a clicking sound.

"What's that look for?" I ask.

"I feel like there's something you aren't telling me."

Buying some time, I return the showerhead to the wall attachment so I can start with her conditioner. I love caring for her this way — it's doing something profound to me — opening me up and making me feel safe enough to be vulnerable. And not just because she's perusing every inch of my skin. It's because this moment is so raw and real.

As I work the smooth pink cream through her tresses, the need to tell her one of my deepest secrets becomes overwhelming, like it's clawing to escape. "You're right. There was more to it than that." I don't want to hide this from her any longer. She deserves to know how much she means to me.

After placing the sponge on the ledge, she brings her palms to my chest as I add more conditioner to my hand. It's like she knows this is going to be significant, so she wants to give me her full attention. "Tell me," she prods, her voice replete with tenderness.

My pulse spikes. "My team thought I was going to die that day." I shake my head and start again. "*I* thought I was going to die. And I'd made peace with it and was preparing to insist they leave me behind. No sense in all of us dying. There wasn't anyone who was really going to miss me. I had no family outside my battalion brothers."

A tightness in my throat makes it hard to swallow, so my eyes shift from her hair to her eyes, hoping to find the strength to continue. I need to get this out. Purge it from my system. I've been dying to share this with someone for years, but I haven't had someone I could tell until now. "Sammy, I think that's the day I started falling for you."

"Me? How? Why? I wasn't even on the same continent as you."

"When my vitals dipped into dangerous territory, your brother came and sat beside me. He wouldn't let me fade away. Kept smacking my face and wouldn't shut the hell up." My breath hitches in my chest. I glance at the shower wall, afraid to look into her eyes. "He told me stories about you to make me laugh, like he'd done so many times before. But while I was bleeding out on a dirty floor in the middle of hell and preparing to leave this earth... his stories made me realize that I wanted to live. I wanted to get back to you. You gave me something to fight for. Something worth living for. For the first time in my life, I felt like I had a purpose. And it was you."

Reaching up to my chin, she turns my face back toward hers. Her eyes have red rims around them and glisten with more than the wetness of the shower.

"Sawyer, I had no idea. Does Leo know?"

I shake my head. "I've never told anyone what I just told you."

With a quivering chin, she says, "I don't know what to say. I'm touched. But why me? We'd only met a few times. Back then, I was just a dumb twentysomething with daddy issues and far too much sarcasm."

Bringing my shoulders up in a shrug, I shake my head subtly. "Maybe we were kindred spirits. Every story he told about you was better than the last. I felt like I *got you* — your pranks, your spirit, your spunk. You made a great impression on me the few times we'd met. *Hell*, I remember when I saw you with my own two eyes for the first time..." A sigh leaves my lips, and I give my head a shake at the powerful memory. "It was like I was shot in the chest with cupid's arrow. I knew I had some type of feelings developing for you. But it wasn't until that day, when I was knocking on death's door, that it all clicked." I feel my cheeks warm when I hear the cheesiness I'm spewing. "I know it's stupid. I'm sorry for being such a sap. Forget it."

Her eyes shine like sapphires as she looks at me with the warmest affection. "No, it's not stupid. I'm so glad I could be that for you and that you were able to hang on. The world would be a much darker place without you in it."

My eyes roll hard and fast. "I don't know about all that."

"Okay, maybe not the *entire* world, but I know for a fact *my* world would be darker without you in it. It would be... empty."

She squeezes my pecs like she did the night I kissed her in the back of the bar. I don't have anything else to add, so I lean forward and give her a quick kiss.

"It's time to rinse your hair," I tell her as I grab the showerhead again.

I'm not sure why, but the intimacy of washing each other like this far surpasses that of our sexual moments. I think it has to do with the way we're cherishing each other.

It's beautiful.

Once her hair is free of conditioner, she asks, "Why didn't you ever tell me? Back then... I saw you so many times before I met Craig. Things could've been..." She trails off, and her eyes fall.

I hate thinking about all the *what-ifs*. When I thought she'd killed herself, the guilt of those damn *what-ifs* almost buried me. If I hadn't needed to be there for Leo, I'm not sure I would've made it. I couldn't leave him when he was barely hanging on. Especially after his only brother had it out with him.

Since I've already splayed open my heart, I might as well keep it going with another confession. "I never thought I was deserving of you."

Her lips pucker into a pout, making her expression sadden. "And what about now? Has your misguided belief system determined I'm finally damaged enough that you're worthy of me?"

I run my hands up and down her arms, pulling her close. "No, I don't think you're damaged at all. You proved it this morning when you walked into a prison and pumped that fucker for information. And let's not forget all the other times you've been strong as hell. Like when you escaped from him in the first place. And how you've been working hard to put your life back together these last few years. You, Sammy Mason, are a badass."

"What else do you think about me?"

I'm tempted to answer with a resounding *I love you*, but I'm worried she's not ready. I've essentially told her how I feel without saying those three words. But once it's out there, it can't be taken back. And what if it spooks her?

"What do I think about Sammy Mason? Hmm," I tease. "Let's see. I think you've got a body made for sin." My hips tilt forward, slipping my erection across her abdomen so she can feel the proof of how hot I think she is. Curves and all. "You're tough, confident, and funny as hell. You're beautiful and smart. Most impressive of all, you're a fighter."

My hand travels up her back, resting on the side of her neck. I can feel her pulse beating wildly under my fingertips.

"To answer your earlier question... no, I don't think I'm deserving of you yet. But I'll work hard every day to become the man you need because I don't want to spend another day without being yours."

"You already are," she whispers.

I hope so.

It's still hard to believe I'm standing here with her, naked and vulnerable. The way the water slides across her flesh, shiny under the shower's spray, is intoxicating. I let my gaze trail over her skin as my hands follow their path.

Now that I can see her entire body in full light, she's marred up more than I expected. I want to ask about her scars like she did about mine. But I think we've shared enough deep shit for one shower.

She lets her hands slide around my slick body until they come to a stop on my low back. She pulls herself close to me and lays her head on my chest, facing the wall.

"I have to warn you," she starts. "I'm probably going to be a little clingy since we've broken the rules and touch is on the table. Jaynie says I'm touch starved."

"What the hell does that mean?"

She lifts her head off my chest and smiles before elaborating. "Think of it like an old well, but instead of filling with water — it's love. Some people fill theirs by spending quality time with people they love or with material possessions. But for me, my reservoir needs to be filled with physical touch. My well is empty, and that's where you come in." She waggles her brows and gives me a toothy grin.

"So it's like a loneliness thing? I can relate to that."

She pulls her lips to one side of her face, looking as adorable as possible. "Yes and no. You see, the entire time I was with Craig, the only human touch I received was via cruelty. Since I associate love so strongly with touch, it was an incredibly dark time for me — beyond the obvious reasons of being isolated from my family and living with an abusive, narcissistic sociopath. And since I've gotten home, I've been trying to refill my love well, but I can only hug my mother and brother so much before they start thinking I'm strange. I haven't wanted a relationship with anyone," she widens her eyes and adds, "until now. So I'm going to be stockpiling your touches. I hope you can handle that."

With an overdramatic huff, I drop my hands and let them fall to the sides, pretending to be annoyed. "You mean I'm going to have to deal with you putting your hands on me all the time? Like touching me and stuff? Gross." I add an eye roll for good measure to sell the joke. "I suppose you'll probably want to have more sex too. Ugh."

Her laugh is rich and full of joy, filling my own *love well*.

Reaching up, she wraps her hand around the back of my neck and pulls me down to meet her. Her supple lips press against my mouth, and I open for her, letting her take all the love she can get from my kiss.

If she needs affectionate touch to feel love, then that's what she'll get from me. As much as she can handle and then even more for good measure.

"Sammy, I've wanted to touch and caress you since I've known you. So it'll be my pleasure to make sure you're never starved for touch again."

You can bet your sweet ass when I say — and I mean this with as much punny innuendo as possible — I'm going to fill her love well up more than it's ever been filled before.

Her answering coy grin dazzles me. "Be careful, or I'm going to fall in love with you."

Those are the magic words. "Good. I've been waiting for you to catch up."

The groan reverberating from her chest as she yanks my lips down to hers makes me feel dizzy. She tastes so damn good. I'll never get enough of this. Of kissing my Sammy.

She's finally my girl.

And I'm never letting go.

My hands roam over her silky back, shooting electricity through my fingertips, up my arms, and through my chest. Having her in my arms like this, naked and vulnerable, is the most precious gift, and I'll never take one second with her for granted.

Sammy runs her hands down my spine, trailing them lower until she reaches my ass. I break away from her lips and hiss when she gives it a firm squeeze, pulling my lower body flush toward hers and driving my erection against her slippery flesh.

"I'm going to need to have you again if you keep this up, and like I said, I don't think we should do that again until we can get supplies."

She appears a touch repentant, looking at me from under her thick, dark lashes and worrying her lower lip. "Are you mad at me for what I did earlier? For how we... finished?" Her gaze drops to the floor, and her chin falls to her chest.

"Well, it was hot as hell, so it's hard to be mad about it. You're not on birth control, huh?"

Slowly, she brings her eyes back up to mine, then shakes her head.

I grin, trying to get that beautiful smile back on her face. "Thanks for telling me the odds first. To be honest, I probably wouldn't have changed the ending even if it was only 10 percent safe."

She squints like she doesn't believe me, drawing her brows in tight. "What if it was a mistake? Wouldn't you feel trapped?"

How can I say what I'm thinking without freaking her out? We've already said so much to each other in such a short time. Although my feelings have been developing steadily over a decade, that doesn't mean we can go from the first kiss to forever in less than a week.

"Before I answer that question, I'm going to ask you something. I need you to be honest with me. Tell me the truth and not what you think I want to hear."

I take her cheeks between my palms and run my thumbs over her lips, tugging them slowly. Unable to resist, I lean down for another taste.

Fucking hell. I just want to kiss her all the time. Now that we've started, it's like an avalanche has been triggered.

Reluctantly, I pull away from her addicting mouth. "Do you want to be a mother one day?"

She expels a deep breath, making the water sputter around her lips. My grin spreads while I await her answer.

"Yes. I've always wanted kids... with the right man by my side."

The warmth in her expression gives me the courage I need to drop another truth bomb on her.

"Do you remember when we were talking the other day, and I told you how strongly I felt for you? And how once I had you, I was going to be all in?"

She nods as her lips spread in a wide, beaming smile like she knows what I'm going to say.

"Part of what I meant by *being all in* was a hope that you'd want to have my baby one day. I've dreamed about it. Pictured you round with my child growing inside." I drag my hand down and run it across her soft stomach. "Assuming you wanted the same, that is."

"Really?" she asks, her voice barely a whisper and her eyes wide with an emotion I can't quite decipher.

"Yes, really. So if you end up pregnant, I'll be the happiest man on the fucking planet. But only if you're on board. I never want you to feel trapped by something like that. So if you want to get some Plan B, I'll support your decision. You have all the power here. Always."

"Sawyer..." She cuts herself off when she brings me close for a kiss. One quick peck turns into another, then another. The kiss builds until we're writhing together and moaning into each other's mouths.

I've got her pressed against the tile wall, and she doesn't seem the least bit afraid or fearful like before, so I build our intensity with deliberate slowness in case she gets spooked.

"Can we have sex again right now? You can pull out or don't. I honestly don't fucking care. I just need to feel you."

"We can run to the store after our shower and have sex when we get back."

"I can't wait. I want you now."

"Need me to take the edge off, baby?"

I run my lips down her neck, then bend down to take one of her nipples into my mouth. While swirling my tongue around the tight bud, I hollow my cheeks and increase suction until she arches her back, letting out a breathy moan. My other hand snakes down between us, and I drag my fingertips across her pussy lips before delving inside.

"Please," she whimpers.

My lips find hers once more as a plan takes form. Grabbing the showerhead, I adjust it to the strongest setting and bring it between us.

"What are you doing?" she asks once she sees my intention.

I wink and pull back, dropping to my knees in front of her. "Taking the edge off."

With a cheeky grin, she replies, "I think using it that way may void the manufacturer's warranty."

"That's a risk I'm willing to take, princess."

She leans back against the cool tile, placing her hands on my shoulders, but she looks on with rapt fascination.

"Put one leg up here," I say, then help hook her knee over my shoulder.

With her spread open before me, I use one hand to massage her pink flesh and aim the stream of warm water at her clit with the other.

Sammy's mouth falls open wide when I make contact, and her hips jerk back. "Oh my God!"

"My friends call me Sawyer," I joke, looking up to catch her eyes.

"Funny guy," she says on a shaky breath before moaning and tilting her hips forward and back a few times to chase the water stream and her pleasure. I move the jet spray back and forth, then around in small circles, testing a few angles.

Once she's panting heavily and cursing under her breath, I pull it away. She looks down, wearing a bereft expression.

While holding eye contact, I lean forward and gently kiss that sensitive bundle of nerves, carefully judging her reaction with every breath. I pull back and raise my brows at her, silently asking for her consent.

She adjusts her weight and squeezes my shoulder tighter to hold her balance. Her slight nod gives me permission to lick her sweet pussy. *Thank fuck.*

I alternate using my mouth and the showerhead, giving her a few seconds to acclimate to each sensation before switching it out again. I throw in my fingertips occasionally, stroking inside her silky walls while sucking on her clit.

On the last time I revert back to the showerhead, she bats it away. "Your mouth. I want you to make me come with that perfect fucking mouth of yours."

Lord have mercy. She's using her dominant voice.

There is nothing sexier on the planet than a woman who tells you exactly what she wants and when she wants it.

The shower attachment clatters to the tile floor, and I dive in with both hands, spreading her open and nuzzling my face into her sensitive flesh. The way her hips undulate as she rubs herself against my mouth while chasing her climax is all the encouragement I need to keep going — not that I'd need any.

Just like Captain America said, *I could do this all day.*

From the corner of my eye, I see her making a fist and shaking it out a few times with her free hand.

Releasing her clit briefly, I tell her, "Baby, use your hand to grab my hair and move me however you want me."

In between pants, she asks, "What?"

A devilish grin on my face and her taste on my lips, I rumble, "I'm asking you to grab my head and fuck my face, princess."

Getting immediately back to work, I stroke and suck and nibble at her clit until she's cussing like a sailor, screaming my name. At the last moment, she *finally* takes a fist full of hair in her grasp and pulls my face even deeper, running my nose, chin, and mouth through her folds as she bucks and jerks with her release.

"Fuck, fuck, fuck," she rambles, her voice keening with ecstasy.

"That's it, princess. Good girl," I shower her with praise.

Sorry about that unintentional pun.

Her grip loosens a few seconds later, then she awkwardly pats my hair down, stroking it as if she's trying to brush it with her fingers. The gesture is so damn funny but also sweet.

Before standing, I put two fingers back inside her while looking directly into her beautiful blue eyes. I pump a few times to get them good and coated with her arousal. Without letting the water wash them clean, I shove them into my mouth, licking and sucking each one clean.

"You're fucking delicious, baby."

After rising to my feet, I bring her into my arms and hold her close. The water has long run cold, but neither of us seems to care much.

"Holy shit, Sawyer. I think you could get me pregnant just by doing that."

Chapter Thirty-Five

HOT AND SPICY NEWS

Sammy

Wrapping my hair in a twisty towel, I toss it back over my head and rise to a stand. My eyes immediately focus on a six-pack of abs with sharp hip lines sticking out just above the towel he's got wrapped low on his waist.

I stifle a giggle when I think of a recent meme that had funny names for that *V*. Since it's not fair that only I get the laugh, here are a few of my favorites. Devil's arrow. Peen root. Cock cleavage. Cum gutters. Dick branches.

You're welcome.

Whatever they're called is irrelevant because they render my brain a pile of mashed potatoes with lumpy gravy.

"We've got news, more news, and spicy news." Sawyer sets his phone down on my bedroom dresser.

Was he holding his phone? Odd. All I remember seeing was his chiseled body on display for me like a *Playgirl* spread.

Where are we? *Abs.* What's my name? *Pecs.* How did I get here? *Shoulders.* What day is it? *Biceps.*

He snaps his fingers in my direction. "Sammy."

I blink three times before finally meeting his eyes — which, for the record, are about three feet higher than where I was staring. "What? Sure. Yes."

His eyes dance, and he puckers his lips like he's sucking on a lemon. "I didn't ask you a yes or no question." His expression turns feral. "Are you distracted, baby? See something you like?" Gesturing toward his physique, he strolls a few steps in my direction, like he has all the time in the world.

Gulping, I nod repeatedly and plaster a maniacal smile on my face — partly to be funny, but also because I'm feeling pretty damn insane right now. I blame the orgasms. Probably orgasm hysteria. That sounds like a real thing and totally *not* made up.

"*Oh yes.* I like what I see *very* much. You should only wear a towel from here on out. All the time." I nod even faster. "I like this plan. It'll make you a better bodyguard."

He holds up one finger and opens his mouth, preparing to argue.

With hands perched on my hips, I keep going, rattling off my nonsense before he speaks. "In fact, you had your rules. Well, these are mine."

Looking playfully affronted, he starts, "That's not how —"

Not letting him finish, I add, "And they're not up for negotiation. Glad that's settled."

His deep chuckle pebbles my bra-covered nipples. Stupid bra. All I can think about is taking it off and dragging my breasts all over his taut skin.

Because I'm finally free to touch him, I stride up to him and trail my hands all over his body, feeling every ridge, divot, and corded muscle. The smooth, the rough, the patches of hair. I feel all of it, and yet it's still not enough.

I groped him for at least a half hour in the shower. Or probably longer. And then in the kitchen before that. But like a greedy hussy, I still want more. I *need* more.

Touching him is refilling my tank, but that sucker was running on fumes for so long. I'm starting to think I'll never get enough of his skin on mine.

Flashing a cheeky grin at him, I tug gingerly on his towel. "I think I need to do some laundry. You better give me this."

He grabs me around my waist and hauls me flush against him, bringing my roaming hands to rest around his shoulders.

"You weren't listening to me, were you?"

"Honestly, I can't focus when you look like this. I didn't even realize you were talking."

His teeth sink down onto his lower lip as he shakes his head. "Hurry up and get dressed so we can go get some condoms. I need to run by my place to get some clean clothes too. And I want to be inside you for as long as possible. Leo's coming at 0700 to relieve me. That only gives us about eleven more hours."

"Okay."

Not the most articulate or thorough response, but it's all I can manage with him looking at me like that. All that heat and intensity in those stormy dark eyes.

He gives me a light swat on my panty-clad ass, then rubs the smarting flesh. He follows that up with a hard squeeze. My brain reverts to some type of cavewoman state. *Must get condoms. Must leave. Get dressed. Put on shoes. Grab purse. Go. Come back. Bang all night.*

Once we're both dressed, Sawyer leaves me locked inside the house while he runs outside to check the vehicle. I take the opportunity to wrap up the dinner we didn't eat — no regrets — and put it in the fridge. Left-over meatloaf can be our breakfast tomorrow. Or maybe a midnight sex snack.

He comes back a few minutes later to escort me out, quickly putting me in the SUV. When he joins me in the confined space, my mouth waters. He smells so damn yummy. He didn't have clean clothes, so he had to put his dirty stuff back on after our shower. So instead of smelling like my boring coconut body wash, he's back to smelling like a delicious mix of laundry detergent, spicy aftershave, and common sense-obliterating pheromones.

On the way, he tries again to tell me whatever news he had. Since he's clothed, I'm able to focus this time. *High five to me.*

"First bit of news: the team has a list of three strong candidates based on the footage from the bar. Shep and Kri are already digging into backgrounds, alibis, phone records, criminal history, and so on. He told me to expect an email later tonight with a summary, and we can review it together."

"That sounds promising."

"Speaking of Shep and Kri." He pauses, crinkling his nose and the skin around his eyes, looking like he ate expired sushi. "They saw us kissing. In the back of the bar that one night when my brain broke."

I want to laugh at the broken brain comment, but I'm too shaken. Eyes widening, my jaw goes slack, falling to my chest. "Oh no."

Status of secret relationship: Compromised before it even began.

"Don't worry. He didn't tell Big Al or your brother. He said he'll trust me to tell them when the time is right. And Kri won't say anything. We can trust them to keep it a secret."

An uncomfortable sensation pricks at my chest, but I push it down. "That's good." The words taste funny on my tongue. Not funny *ha-ha*. More like funny *uh-oh*.

Like a lie.

Sawyer's left leg starts bouncing. "The next thing is regarding your shitbag ex." A low rumble escapes him, and for some reason, it makes me smile.

My fingers dig into the fabric of my shorts resting on my thighs. "What about him?"

"Tomer is digging into his finances, work associates, extended family, and shit like that. He's found two items of note. The first thing is that ten grand was transferred to an offshore account about two weeks ago."

That's not a great sign.

My throat tightens, and my clothes suddenly feel scratchy against my skin. I cross my legs as my gaze goes hazy. Attempting to calm myself, I focus on the hypnotic passing of streetlights running across the windshield.

"And the second thing?"

"Your ex-father-in-law is in town."

My hand covers my shocked gasp as a memory assaults me. "I think I saw him. The day we went to Blow Your Top."

Sawyer tilts his head to the side in thought, his eyes bouncing from side to side before settling back on the road. "When we got back in the car?"

"Yeah."

"I knew you were lying." His words hold no anger, only acceptance.

"Sorry. I thought it was my imagination or an attack of paranoia. I'd shown you enough emotional damage that day to pile on more."

He looks at me with a softness to his chiseled features that warms my heart. "Babe... come on."

I shake off the guilt and ask, "When did he get to town?"

"He got here the same day as the funds transfer."

"That's a pretty big coincidence."

"With you and Redleg putting his son behind bars, he certainly has a revenge motive."

"Mr. Banks doesn't need money, though. He's loaded. Why would he need to move around his son's money?"

"True. The money doesn't entirely make sense." He screws his lips to one side, deep in thought. "Unless Craig transferred the funds to hire someone to grab you, and his father is facilitating it down here. In that case, it might make sense for Craig to be paying."

"Fuck," I hiss, punching my thigh. "Does that mean they took a hit out on me? If I hadn't escaped the trunk, would I even be alive right now?"

For the first time, the gravity of my situation truly hits me. Right square in the throat. It's suddenly hard to breathe. My hand lifts to cup my throat, and a throbbing sensation thumps wildly under my palm, so I try to rub the skin to soothe it.

Sawyer must notice because he reaches over, pulls my hand away from my throat, and then threads his fingers through mine. "Hey, it's okay. I've got you. You're safe." He presses a kiss to the back of my hand, letting his lips linger against my flesh.

My spine stiffens with defensiveness, my customary armor shifting into place. "I know. I'm not scared."

If I say it enough, maybe I'll believe it. Seems legit.

"You don't always have to be brave with me, baby. You know that. I won't see you any differently."

Heaving a sigh, I force my muscles to go limp and sink my body into the plush seat. "Thank you." My voice is so low and weak that it's almost inaudible.

I feel so grateful for his calming and understanding presence right now. The air returns to my lungs, and my throat loosens as he squeezes my hand like he's transferring his strength to me through his touch.

Maybe I don't have to put on an act in front of Sawyer the way I do with everyone else. I can be strong when I'm feeling able. Weak when I need him. And sad when the memories of all I've missed or lost are too much.

I can just *be*.

No matter the emotion... I'm allowed to show it. Without artifice.

Just Sammy.

No rage monsters. No horny monsters or pathetically sad monsters. No monsters at all. Only me.

Pulsing my hand around his, I bring it up to my mouth and run his knuckles across the smooth pout of my lips, loving how it steadies me.

And for real! What type of moisturizer does he use?

He grins. "Are you ready for the spicy news?"

Releasing his hand, I sit more upright, readying myself for another dose of bullshit. "That wasn't enough spice for us?"

Sawyer snickers. "Oh, not even close."

Judging by his happiness level — ten thousand — this won't be another bite of a shit sandwich. I raise my brows, waiting for him to continue.

"Guess who caught a flight to California?"

"My mom." I wrinkle my forehead because this isn't news.

"That was this morning. I meant this evening."

"Who?"

I know the answer before he says it.

He gives me an incredulous look. "Big Al."

"He's going to guard my mother? Personally?"

Nodding furiously with a downright gleeful grin, he replies, "Yep."

Shifting in my seat to face him, I swat his shoulder with my hand, unable to contain the excitement. "This isn't just spicy news; this is *juicy*. Oh my God. They're *definitely* hooking up."

His brows gather, and he scoffs. "Big Al doesn't hook up."

"Well, what would you call it?"

"I don't know, but that doesn't sound right for him. And I don't think it's what your mother does either. They aren't exactly the Tinder generation."

I lean one elbow on the console between us, resting my chin on my hand. "Nice ageism, Sawyer. But are you suggesting it's *more*?"

"I'm not suggesting anything." He tries for innocence, failing spectacularly.

"Psh. The hell you aren't, Mr. Spicy Newscaster." In classic news reporter style, I put my fingertip to my ear and hold my water bottle up like a microphone. "This just in, a new bombshell report reveals people in their fifties can, in fact, have sex. The study goes on to conclude that strings need not necessarily be attached for this theoretical sex to occur. More on this shocking development as the story unfolds. Back to you in the studio, Tom."

When he's done laughing, he says, "Listen, all I'll tell you is this. One, I've never seen Big Al look at any woman the way he looks at your mother. And two, he almost *never* goes out in the field. And to fly across the country, leaving the entire operation behind to guard someone who doesn't even have a credible, known threat? Unheard of. You do the math."

"Fuck that. I hate math. You do it."

His chest and shoulders shake with his laughter.

A few more minutes into the drive, his demeanor shifts from animated to reserved. An air of seriousness falls over us. The tiny hairs on my arms stand on end. Not because I have a sixth sense, but because of Sawyer's drastic change in behavior.

"Princess, if I tell you to get down, you do it. Okay?"

"What's the matter?"

"Pretty sure we're being followed."

My head whips around, but there are several cars behind us. "How can you tell?"

Seriously, how? We've been joking and laughing the last few minutes. I'm not even sure what street we're on.

"I'm a professional, baby. He's been behind us since we left your neighborhood. Now hold tight. I'm going to make a sharp turn up here onto the bridge to see if they follow."

A second later, he dives into the turn lane, slams on the brakes, then makes an abrupt turn, nearly tilting us to two wheels. I have to brace myself on the dash with one hand and grab the *oh-shit handle* with the other.

Once we've completed the turn, he hits the accelerator. I feel the horsepower kick in as my back hits the seat with gusto. Turning around, I see a large utility vehicle make a similar move.

"Grab my cell, babe. Dial Tomer. He's in the recent call list." His voice is calm. Steady.

There's a slight tremor in my fingers, but I do as I'm told. When the call connects, Tomer's voice comes through the car's audio system. "I just got home. What the fuck do you want?"

"You got your laptop, right?"

"What the hell do you think?" Tomer snarks. There's a rustling sound in the background.

"I've got Sammy with me, and we're heading east on the Courtney Campbell Causeway. We've got company. Can you activate the cameras on the rear of my vehicle and see what info you can get us about the driver of the tan Chevy Tahoe behind us?"

Sawyer lets off the gas, slowing us to a more reasonable speed.

"Sixty-seconds." Tomer's voice is crisp but devoid of the earlier hostility.

Sawyer looks over at me briefly before training his eyes back on the road. "You okay?"

Wordlessly, I nod and grip the seatbelt. My eyes travel to the side mirror. The Tahoe has caught up and is riding our ass.

Sawyer's jaw clicks, and his knuckles turn white under the force of his death grip on the wheel. Other than that, he looks perfectly calm and collected. "Hurry up, Tomer. I don't like letting him get this close for too long when I've got her with me."

"Going as fast as I can. It's not like I sit around all night waiting for you assholes to call me."

"Yeah, but it's not like you have a life," Sawyer teases.

"Fuck you."

"Aw, same, Chuck." Even with someone chasing us down the highway, Sawyer still manages to be a shithead.

Damn, he's absolutely perfect for me.

"Okay, I'm in. I've got a visual on the tango. No front-facing plate, but I'm zooming in and switching to night vision to get a better view of the driver. Let him get a little closer for me."

Sawyer presses his lips into a tight line and shakes his head but slows down. The Tahoe gets right up behind us, then swerves slightly to my side, like he's preparing to pass. Sawyer dives into the right lane to block his path.

My heart is practically in my throat. Or my stomach. One or the other. Perhaps both.

"Okay, I have a good screenshot I can run through facial rec. He looks familiar. I think he's one of the guys Shep sent me from the bar footage. Not sure yet, though. While that's running, any chance you can get me a plate number?"

"You don't ask much, do you?"

"I seriously wish more people in Florida had plates on the front of their vehicles," I muse.

"Shit! Sammy, get down." Sawyer reaches over and shoves my head down toward my lap, folding me in half. He guns the accelerator again.

"What's happening?" Tomer asks, echoing my own thoughts.

"Aren't you watching?"

"My attention was on my other screen. I see it now."

"Someone tell me what's happening," I beg, sounding a touch hysterical.

"He's trying to come up beside us. If he does that, he could get a clean shot at us or try to run us off the bridge."

"Shit. Shit. Shit."

"I've got 911 on the other line. Sending law enforcement to your position," Tomer breaks in.

"Tomer, is the front camera on?" Sawyer asks.

"Affirmative."

"Make sure you're recording. He's coming up beside me. As soon as we get off this bridge, I'll slam on the brakes and let him sail by. You should be able to get a plate and another look at him."

"Slamming on your brakes in the middle of a high-speed chase? Are you trying to get a safety brief? Because that's how you get a safety brief! Besides, that's a move from *Top Gun*. Get original, at least."

Through his grim concentration, Sawyer's unable to hold back a grin. I need to ask him what a safety brief is after this mess is over.

"Very funny. You ready?"

"Ready. Go ahead and *Top Gun* him."

"Brace yourself, Sammy," Sawyer orders.

I do as he says. A second later, he slams the brakes, burning up the tires and fishtailing slightly.

"Did you get it?" he asks Tomer while simultaneously punching the gas and making the tires screech again. I'm tossed toward the door as he makes a sharp left, turning us around in the middle of the freaking highway. As soon as we're facing back toward the bridge, he hammers the accelerator down.

"You can get up now, Sammy."

When I rise, I see we're going in the other direction, and we've left the Tahoe somewhere behind us.

"We're going in the other direction now, T. We got out right in front of a line of traffic. He's not getting through right away."

"I see that. And yes, I got the plate. Running it now. Where did this drive originate?"

"Sammy's house."

"Safe to assume he followed you from there, so I don't think you can go back there. Where are you heading?"

Sawyer doesn't answer; he just drives faster. His eyes dart from the road to the rearview and side mirrors on a loop.

"Sawyer!" Tomer yells. "Destination?"

"I'm thinking. I'm thinking." He rolls his head, loosening up his shoulders.

We take a series of turns as soon as we get to the other side of the bridge, making it nearly impossible for anyone to follow us without it being obvious.

The clack of the keyboard in the background drowns out my pounding heart and the loud sound of the tires thumping across the potholes.

Sawyer finally answers Tomer's earlier question. "My place. We can hide out at my place. Let's hope he doesn't know where I live."

"Ten-four. I'll get the perp's info to the cops so they can try to find him. In the meantime, I'm sending Shep and Kri to your place for backup. I'll track you on GPS until you get there. Call me back if you need me. I've got work to do."

"Thanks, Tomer."

The call disconnects, and Sawyer sighs. "Well, baby. It looks like our plans for tonight have changed."

That sucks.

Chapter Thirty-Six

I KNOW

Sawyer

"This is not at all what I expected." With bulging eyes, Sammy looks around my living room with her mouth agape.

Even shocked to the point of being dumbfounded, she's still cute as hell.

"You're sure you've never been here?"

I'm fucking with her. Your dream girl in your personal sanctuary is not something easily forgotten.

She arches one eyebrow and looks at me with heaps of incredulousness. "Oh, I would have remembered this."

"What's the big deal? It's just a house."

After ensuring all my security sensors and cameras were operating properly and no one was following us, I finally felt secure enough to bring her inside my house. I'm still on high alert but feel safe and sound here for now. So I'm content to let her explore my humble abode.

"Sawyer, oh my freaking hell. This is *not* just a house. It's... breathtaking." She puts her hand to her chest. "It even smells heavenly in here. Did you decorate it yourself?"

Now that I know she's impressed and not horrified, my chest puffs with pride. "Maybe," I hedge while fighting back a smile.

She moseys from the living room to the kitchen, and I trail behind.

Having her in my home is doing something funny to my insides. I want to say it's butterflies. But I'm a bodyguard, a former Army Ranger, and an all-around badass, so I shouldn't be getting butterflies. I'm going to consider it hunger pangs since we skipped dinner.

However, that snack I had in the shower was pretty damn filling. I lick my lips at the memory of her taste, and my dick pulses.

Fuck.

Hey, dick, don't get hard. You can't do that right now. Shep and Kri will be here any minute to cockblock us.

She runs her hands over the granite countertop of the enormous center island, and I have a vision of spreading her out on it and feasting between her thighs, then fucking her into oblivion.

"This kitchen. *This kitchen.* I have no words."

I lean against my fridge and cross my arms, watching her enjoy her self-guided tour. I take in the room, trying to imagine it through her eyes. Sleek and modern design with slate gray cabinets, stainless steel appliances, and an exposed range hood over a six-burner stovetop.

The more she explores my space, the more I see her here... permanently. Visions of her sitting on a stool at the center island, wearing nothing but my old Army T-shirt as we make omelets together after a night of passionate lovemaking. Another vision of her reaching for a glass from the cabinet while I walk up behind her, kiss her neck, and wrap my arms around her body, round with our child.

A few seconds later, she finds some words. "These are high-end as fuck." She inspects the Le Creuset pots and pans hanging from a rack over the island. "Are you secretly a billionaire?"

I scoff. "No. I just had a run of exceptionally good luck investing a few bonuses I got for re-upping my military contracts. And I'm a first-rate saver."

Truth? Partly. But mostly because I've never had anyone to spend it on or with.

"I had no idea someone could be a saver and have fancy-ass appliances like this. This kitchen screams spender, not saver."

"I didn't have any nice things when I was young, so I have them now. No big deal."

She pauses her inspection, pulls her head out of one of my cabinets, and shoots me a triumphant glare. "I knew you were secretly bougie. I fucking knew it." With a finger pointed at me, she decrees, "No one has skin and hair as nice as yours without being at least a little bougie."

At least the Kiehl's face cream is doing its job.

Her gaze falls back to the cabinets. "A hidden dishwasher? This is so freaking cool."

Unable to resist touching her any longer, I move in close, wrapping my arms around her waist from behind, and press my semi-hard dick against that delicious ass. She lets her head slump backward, falling against my chest. I breathe her in, sticking my nose into that freshly shampooed hair and pulling it deep into my lungs.

Sammy spins around and threads her hands around my neck. Her big blue eyes beckon me closer.

I run my tongue over my lips as I prepare to claim her mouth. Our alone time is about to expire, but I'm not ready to share her with anyone else yet.

"Shep and Kri should be here in about five minutes. I need a little something to hold me over until the next time we're alone."

"You can have anything you want," she whimpers as I run my lips over her pulse point, then bring them up over her jaw.

A second later, our lips converge, needy and desperate. My hand journeys up to the back of her neck, thumb under her ear. I tilt her head to the side with the gentlest of pressure, and she opens for me. When our tongues touch, my gentlemanly restraint snaps. A growl comes from deep in my chest as I suck her tongue into my mouth.

I try to quench my thirst for her through the kiss, but deep down, I know I'll never be entirely satiated. I'll always want more of her.

Her smell.

Her taste.

Her touch.

As our intensity and passion ignite, she lifts her leg, running her calf over the back of my thigh. I run my hands under her ass and scoop her up, desperate to get closer to her. Her legs wrap around my hips, bringing her hot center right up against my waist.

I set her down on the edge of the counter to let my hands explore her sumptuous body. Soon, we're nothing but a wash of bodies grinding against each other, tongues and hands roaming. Gasps and moans fill the air.

In the back of my mind, something tells me to go slower. Be more cautious. The last thing I want to do is overwhelm her.

But she puts that worry to rest when she yanks my hair at the roots and takes my lower lip between her teeth, dragging me forward. Her breath is low and seductive when she says, "I want to ride your big, thick cock right down on the floor of this fancy-ass kitchen."

My erection strains at the back of my zipper. I *need* to be inside her again. It's not a want anymore. It's a fucking need. I need Sammy's sweet pussy squeezing my cock just like I need air and coffee to survive.

Do we have time?

I break the kiss. "Hang on, baby. Let me see if I can buy us a few minutes."

Her shuddering breaths echo in my eardrums as I pull my phone out of my pocket and call Shep.

He answers without a greeting. "You okay? We're only about six minutes out."

I school my voice to mask my arousal, trying to sound nonchalant. "Yeah, we're fine. Take your time. My house was clear, and we weren't followed. Listen..." I catch my breath and think of something plausible. "Can you swing by the store for a bottle of wine? Something white and sweet. Sammy's nervous, and I don't have anything she likes on hand. She needs something to take the edge off." I wink at Sammy, hoping she catches the innuendo.

Of course she does.

"Wine? Are you for real right now? Tomer calls me all flipped out, we rush over, and you're asking for wine?" His voice gets quieter as he mumbles under his breath, "Unbelievable, this guy." Louder and sarcasm-filled, he adds, "Do you want anything to eat with that? Five-course meal? Fresh flowers? Tylenol? What else can I get you, my liege?"

"Food sounds good. We skipped dinner. I'm pretty hungry."

"Fine, asshole. Be safe in the meantime. If something happens to you guys while I'm rummaging around Publix, Boss will have my ass." He makes a grumbling sound. "You know what? I could go for a sub. You want subs? Kri, you want a sub? I fucking love Publix subs."

Genius. The Publix sandwich line moves slower than a herd of sloths stuck in I-4 construction rush-hour traffic.

"Sure. Buffalo chicken tender sub for me." I turn to my girl. "Sammy, what kind of sub do you want?"

"Turkey and cheese, mustard and mayo with lettuce and pickles."

I relay the order to Shep.

"Done," he replies. "See you in a half hour or so. We'll hurry."

"We're fine. Take your time."

Kri's voice comes over the speaker. "In that case, I'll get my nails done before we come over."

As soon as I disconnect the call, my mouth is back on Sammy's. Gasps, moans, and breathy sighs reverberate around the kitchen, the tile doing nothing to mask the arousing sounds.

"Condom, baby," I gasp into her mouth when she sneaks her hand into my jeans, grabbing my cock.

"I thought you didn't have any."

"I might have some in my room. Not sure if they're expired, though. Do you care?"

"I was planning to ride you bare, so an old condom is fine with me."

"I'll be right back." I give her a quick peck and pull away.

Sprinting to my bedroom, I open the bedside drawer, finding it empty of what I need. "Dammit!"

My feet carry me into the bathroom, where I'm opening cabinets and flinging out drawers, looking for even just one.

Nope. Nada. None. Zip. Zero.

Fuck me.

Or, in this case... no fuck for me.

"No luck, huh?" Sammy's voice startles me.

With my hands braced on the bathroom counter in frustration, I look up and see her gorgeous face in the reflection of the bathroom mirror, her lips still swollen from my unforgiving kisses.

"Sorry, baby. I can't find one."

Holding my gaze, she shrugs as if it's no big deal and removes her shirt, tossing it on the floor behind her, then she removes her shorts. "What are you waiting for? Take your clothes off, Sawyer. You're wasting time."

Her voice has that smoky purr of a dominatrix again. Standing behind me in only her bra and panties, she looks like something from my darkest fantasies. My hand goes to my waistband to start fumbling with my fly.

"You sure, baby?" I ask. "Are you willing to accept the risk?"

She nods. "I am. Are you?"

She strolls up behind me, her head poking around my bicep, holding my eyes in the mirror. I can feel her breasts press up against my back. My mouth waters.

My pants are gone in the blink of an eye. My shirt is next. *Poof.* Gone.

"If you think I could ever turn down a chance to be inside you now that I know how good you feel wrapped around my cock, then you've sorely overestimated my willpower." Spinning in her arms, I find her cheeks and hold them between my palms.

Our lips reconnect, and our tongues touch, reigniting that passion as if no time has passed and we're right back where we left off in the kitchen.

"We need to hurry." Her hands roam lower, removing my boxers and giving my length a good, firm stroke. I release her cheeks and trail my hands down to return the favor.

With her propped up on the bathroom counter and her thighs spread to welcome me home, I bury myself inside her warmth again and again. Each stroke brings me closer to heaven and gives us the tension release we need so desperately.

Once we're spent and satisfied, our ragged breaths eventually calm. I kiss her forehead gently, then give her another on the neck. She grabs my cheeks, presses her lips to mine, and spears me with those blue orbs I love so much.

It's not just her eyes, though. I'm in love with the entire person. This complicated, drama-filled, sarcastic, beautiful, loyal woman.

I love her.

We simply stare at each other for a few moments, content to soak up the afterglow.

Reluctant to break the moment, I eventually whisper, "We should probably get dressed. They'll be here soon."

I'm still not ready to let her go when she slides off the sink, so I hold her in my arms, resting my hands above her plump bottom. Rising to her tiptoes, she brings me in for a sweet, gentle kiss. She tastes a little salty, her face slick with small beads of sweat. Mine is too.

"I have something I need to tell you," she starts before sucking in a breath like she's gathering courage.

"Anything, baby. You can tell me absolutely anything." I kiss her forehead, her nose, and those full lips once more.

"That was incredible. I *love* having you inside me." She breathes the words across my mouth while running her fingertips through the hair at the nape of my neck. "More importantly, I think I'm falling in love with you."

"Well, you let me know when you're sure." I can't help but tease her.

She laughs deeply, making her breasts heave across my chest. "Okay. I will."

I squeeze her tighter into my chest, wrap her in my arms, and surround her with my love. Our noses rub together.

My voice is soft but steady when I finally confess, "Samantha Mason, even if you're not ready to say it back, I want you to know I'm head over heels in love with you."

"I know," she says, a hint of playfulness in her tone.

"Did you just Han Solo me?"

"Maaaybe."

"And did you just Peter Griffin me?"

We're laughing and kissing when my phone starts going off like crazy from somewhere on the floor behind us.

Shit. What now? Can't I enjoy this perfect moment before it goes tits up?

Apparently not.

Chapter Thirty-Seven
NOW I WANT CAKE

Sammy

Twenty-five minutes after Sawyer officially told me he loved me, four of us are seated around the kitchen table, half-eaten sub sandwiches spread out in front of us.

"And you're sure?" Sawyer's velvety voice has a calming effect on me, despite the upsetting topic. It's like a warm hug traveling from his vocal cords straight to my nipples.

Tomer's response crackles loud and clear from the phone sitting in the center of the table. "One hundred percent. That's your guy."

"Sammy, do you recognize him?" Sawyer turns the laptop screen around to show me the picture of the guy who tried to run us off the road. Tomer sent a photo he took during the chase and put it side-by-side with a driver's license photo.

Thomas Ian Jones.

"Yes. I've seen him at the Sassy Parrot before. Hard to forget that neck tattoo." It depicts a dagger slicing his throat. I remember thinking it was seriously fucked up.

Shep agrees. "Yeah, he was asshole numero uno on the list we compiled from reviewing the Parrot footage. He spent a lot of time studying Sammy during the week leading up to her abduction. One night, he was even messing around near the employee door leading to the alley where she was grabbed."

A chill shoots down my spine, and goosebumps raise on my skin. "Was that the night I got locked out back?"

Three pairs of wide eyes meet mine.

"You got locked out in the alley?" Sawyer asks.

"Yes. One night, there was supposedly a delivery out back because the doorbell rang. I went to get it, but no one was there. The door closed behind me, and the latch didn't work. I was locked outside for a few minutes until my manager came to let me in. In fact, it was the same night that..." My voice trails off at the memory of Sawyer's hand heating my skin when he grabbed my wrist and slammed his lips against mine for the first time. But I quickly recover. "The night y'all came in for a drink."

Shep's eyes sparkle with mischievousness. I can tell he's itching to tease us. I know he knows about the kiss. He knows I know that he knows. Sawyer knows he and Kri know. We *all* know. But no one is talking about it. It's not just an elephant in the room, it's more like a T-rex with its tiny arms trying to put on a fitted sheet. We all see it and can't look away, but no one is discussing it.

Tomer takes control over the conversation. *Hallelujah. There is a God, after all.* "Kri and Shep got a real creepy vibe from him, so they had me dig into him, and he's got a hell of a criminal record for someone so young. He's only twenty-four, and he's been arrested twelve times."

"Twelve fucking times. And yet, he's still on the streets," Kri grumbles, a look of disgust on her face.

Same, girl. Same.

"That's arrests; not convictions," Tomer clarifies. "I was able to find out lots more. Let's see here." He clears his throat before continuing, "Suspected ties to the STK gang. In and out of juvie starting at age thirteen. Started simple with petit theft, criminal mischief, and vandalism. Then he got violent. Escalated to grand theft auto, assault, assault with a deadly weapon, and attempted sexual assault charges. Always getting off on technicalities, like witnesses not showing up and evidence going missing. He also got a really good plea deal for one of the charges and entered a diversion program for another. His adult record is even worse."

"It gets worse?" One of my hands falls to the table, clattering the ice inside my water glass. "And hold on a damn minute. The STK gang? Like steak?" My eye roll is so fierce that I think I can nearly feel my eye socket stretching and straining.

"Stands for *Shoot to Kill*, baby," Sawyer says, his lips quirking.

Shep whips his head over and glowers at Sawyer, raising a brow. Slowly, his shocked expression morphs into a Cheshire cat grin.

Shit. Sawyer just slipped and called me *baby* in front of our guests. Oh, well, we're fucked. At least they bought me dinner first.

Sawyer catches Shep's reaction but makes a show of ignoring him, pulling the laptop back over, and plastering a tight grimace on his face.

Before they arrived, Sawyer dropped the bomb on me that although Shep and Kri know about the kiss, they're not aware it's gone any further. So we're supposed to keep it friendly, but not *too* friendly, lest it get back to Leo or Big Al. Heaven forbid.

And I'm not sure how I feel about that.

Fuck that, my inner rage monster roars, making a sudden reappearance front and center in my psyche. *Unacceptable. He needs to publicly claim you.*

Oh, I almost missed her. But not really.

Kri elbows Shep in the side, scolding him with a sharp glare. He tries to play dumb, his mouth forming a perfect *O* shape and giving a full-body shrug. Meanwhile, I bite the inside of my cheek and try not to throw my turkey and cheese at someone.

Would you settle for throwing a pickle or two?

Shut up, rage monster. Those pickles are for me. They're fucking delicious. We will not be committing crimes against deli items in the name of rage. Not tonight, anyway.

Unaware of the odd looks being tossed around the room at Sawyer's slip-up, Tomer returns to reviewing the esteemed history of the *lovely chap* who's out to get me. "It gets much worse, guys. When he was eighteen, he was arrested for kidnapping and sexual assault of a minor — she was a fifteen-year-old. According to the initial police report, he left her for dead in a ditch, but she survived, thanks to a jogger who found her early the next morning. The fucker never served hard time for it, though, because she later recanted her testimony, refusing to press charges. The case was dismissed, and he was released from county lockup three days later. And we all know why that happens."

"Victim intimidation. Probably from his STK brothers," Sawyer answers.

Kri pops her knuckles. "This guy sounds like a peach. Respectfully, I'd like the first crack at him once we find him. When do we leave?" Her eyes dance around the table to see if it's time to kick ass or not.

Not gonna lie, I'm a little attracted to Kri right now. She's tough as nails. Even if she might be younger than me, I want to be her when I grow up.

I study the laptop over Sawyer's shoulder as he taps through the information Tomer sent. When I see a photo of the Tahoe, something clicks into place. "Wait. It's clear this is the guy from tonight, but how do we know he's the guy who grabbed me? I didn't escape from an SUV. It was a car. I don't know the make or model, but it sure as hell wasn't a big-ass SUV. It had a trunk, for shit's sake."

Sawyer leans back in his chair and drags his hand through his hair. The sight of his bicep muscles rolling with that movement could cause a nearly blind woman to climax.

Shep leans toward the cell phone. "Tomer, did you get a plate number on the Tahoe?"

"Oh yeah, thanks for reminding me. The Tahoe was reported stolen two days ago. So that's not his vehicle."

"Shocking. Another failure of the justice system." Kri's eyes lift to the ceiling, and her hands clench into fists. "He's still stealing cars, so he's probably still kidnapping women." She shoots a sympathetic gaze at me and mouths the word *sorry*.

Shep pats a fingertip across his lips. "T, does he have any cars in his name?"

"Nothing registered in Florida, but with his record, he probably stole a car specifically to grab Sammy, then dumped it to upgrade to the Tahoe."

Sawyer adds, "That tracks with our timeline. Plus, it makes sense he'd want to get a new car after she got away. Tomer, can you check to see if CPD has any recently recovered cars that might fit with our timing?"

"Already checked with them and Pinellas Sheriff's Department. Nothing yet. And I've got Klein checking with surrounding jurisdictions for stolen sedans that have since been found. Sammy was bleeding from her head, so there's a trunk somewhere with her blood in it. It's bound to show up, and when it does, I hope they can get some DNA from him so they can send him to jail for a long time. Can't let this fucker keep running around grabbing innocent women, knocking them out, and throwing their bodies in trunks. Given his record, I think it's pretty clear what he intended to do with Sammy. Sick bastard."

All three of my table mates gape open-mouthed at the phone.

"What the hell?" Kri yells at the phone, her voice full of outrage on my behalf.

The blood drains from my cheeks, and a wave of dizziness rocks my gut.

Instinctively, my hand raises to run along the healing gash and bruise on my forehead. I'd almost forgotten about it. This is all starting to feel like too much. I press away from the table and stand. I need some space. Everything feels like it's closing in on me.

"Easy, Tomer. Shit!" Sawyer scolds, his voice tinged with anger he normally doesn't show. "Sammy's sitting right here, man. Dammit."

"Oh, sorry, Sammy." His apology sounds sincere, but I can't respond. The image he painted was too vivid for me to speak yet. Especially after the car chase tonight.

Shep intercedes, trying to smooth things over. "Tomer's not used to dealing with our clients directly. Or humans. He usually only talks to us."

With no small amount of snark in my voice, I finally manage to answer. "I can see why." Pacing now, I shake my hands out in front of me to dispel my rising anxiety.

When I spin back to the table, Sawyer watches me intently. On my next pass near him, he reaches out and grabs my hand, halting me in my tracks.

He dips his chin and looks up at me from under his lashes. "You okay, Sammy?"

My gaze falls to our joined hands, and I force down a tight swallow. Wordlessly, I nod.

I want to crawl onto his lap and let him surround me with his arms, pushing all the thoughts of this nightmare away as I soak in his touch to refill my love well. But I can't do that because he refuses to tell anyone about us.

I'm the first one to let go.

I rejoin them at the table. "So what happens now? We go after him? Let the police handle it? What?"

Tomer answers for the group. "I'm waiting on Big Al to call me back so we can discuss. He'll probably want us to report this new information to CPD, and if they don't act right away, then we'll handle it. His flight is touching down in... twenty-three minutes. In the meantime, who's briefing Leo?"

"We'll do it," Sawyer announces. "Tomer, while you're waiting, can you try to find any connections between this disgusting piece of human filth and Craig Banks or his father, Edwin?"

"Nothing jumped out at me so far to link them, but I'm just getting started. Oh, we discovered that Edwin Banks met with a Florida State Senator the other day."

"His visit is probably business-related if he's meeting with politicians.

Maybe they're expanding Banks Software to Florida," I muse, picking at my sandwich and no longer feeling hungry.

Since the sandwich isn't going to be eaten, now can we throw it at someone?

Oblivious to how close he is to wearing turkey, Sawyer brings the call to a close. "Keep looking and let me know if you find anything else, Chuck."

Sawyer and Shep grin at each other like fucking toddlers.

"Copy. Talk soon. And also, fuck you very much."

Sawyer reaches to disconnect the call, but before he hangs up, I add, "Thank you, Tomer." Am I the only one with manners?

My knee bounces rapidly under the table as Sawyer swipes to find Leo's contact information and places the next call.

After four long rings, my brother answers. "This better be good. I was just about to have some angel food cake."

Sawyer cricks his head and cringes. "Wait. You call Sue your angel. Is that a euphemism?"

"A gentleman never eats his angel's cake and tells." Leo is *exceedingly* smug.

Laughing, Shep says, "That was definitely a euphemism."

"Oh my God! Gross, Leo. My poor ears!" I cover my ears and stick out my tongue like I'm gagging.

"Sue's a lucky gal," Kri mutters. "I wish someone would eat my cake."

Shep smirks at her. "Is that an open invitation?"

"I swear to God, Shepherd, if you don't stop that shit, I'll rearrange your spinal column one vertebra at a time." Kri jumps up, making a show of getting away from Shep. "I'm going to check the perimeter while you talk to Leo so I don't get fired for workplace brutality and/or charged with homicide." She marches off, leaving Sawyer and me in stunned silence.

Shep calls out to her retreating back. "What did I say? Was it the cake thing? To clarify, I thought you meant you were into baking. And I happen to love dessert." When the front door slams, he looks over at us and shrugs, a smug grin on his stupid face.

Sawyer chuckles right along with him, but I hold mine back in preparation for my own joke.

Leaning forward, I move closer to Shep to get his attention. "What's her problem? I thought you guys were already banging."

Shep's eyes bounce from mine to Sawyer's, and he whispers, "I could say the same about you two."

Without warning, Sawyer reaches over and grabs Shep by the collar, forcibly removing him from his seat. The chair scuttles to the tile floor behind him. Before my eyes can even focus on the ensuing chaos, Sawyer has him in a headlock and is cutting off his airflow.

Welp, that's one way to shut him up.

"What the hell is going on over there?" Leo asks.

"Oh, nothing. Just boys being boys." I try to cover, feeling optimistic that he didn't hear Shep's accusation.

A *true* accusation. But Shep doesn't know that for sure.

"Listen," I continue. "We've had all kinds of drama tonight. We were calling to update you."

Leo's voice sobers. "You okay, kid?"

My eyes roll. At this point, it's an automatic response to almost anything he asks. "Yes, I'm fine. We're all fine. I'm at Sawyer's, and Shep and Kri are here too."

Having finally let Shep go, Sawyer returns to the table. Shep hangs back in the space between the kitchen and living room, coughing and struggling to get his airflow back. Poor guy's face looks like a maraschino cherry.

"Listen, buddy. Here's where we are with things." Sawyer takes over and proceeds to run through our news.

While he does, my blood simmers until it's at a rolling boil. By the time he gets to how we're waiting for Big Al's flight to land in California to determine our action plan, metaphorical steam is coming out of my ears.

He put his friend in a headlock and nearly choked him unconscious to stop him from saying something about us to my brother. For fuck's sake. I knew Sawyer didn't want Leo to know about our relationship, but knowing and seeing it played out in real-time are two very different things.

It makes what we shared earlier feel cheap.

He said he wanted to treat me like a princess. Well, he's failing. Princesses are not treated like dirty secrets.

Rage Monster, reporting for duty. Knives are freshly sharpened. Point me toward someone, and I'll happily cut a bitch.

Damn. My rage monster just said that with her whole damn chest.

Grabbing my cell phone, I open the notes app and scroll to my *Rage Thoughts* list. Frantically, my fingers mash the screen. Hopefully, this little exercise helps me get these feelings out so they don't consume my every fiber and burn me from the inside out.

1. Being Sawyer's dirty secret. Fuck that!

Chapter Thirty-Eight
NEEDLE AND THREAD

Sawyer

"Wineglasses are in the next cabinet, Sammy."

She's already popped the cork and is pouring heavy-handedly into a tumbler.

A *giant* tumbler with an attached lid.

And a straw.

The way she arches a brow at me over the edge of the cup as she presses the straw to her lips tells me she is not the least bit interested in my wineglasses.

Or in me.

Or anything coming out of my mouth.

Fuck.

Here I am, in a "relationship" for less than a week, and I'm already singing the song of my forefathers: *What the hell did I do wrong now?* In the key of E flat.

She was quiet for the second half of the call with her brother. And barely spoke when Tomer called us back a half hour later. He had Big Al and Leo conferenced in so we could discuss our action plan.

Shep smacks my shoulder with the back of his hand. He nods toward where Sammy is standing, trying to flay me with her death glare. "Looks like it's back to your right hand, champ."

"Get the fuck out of here with that shit. I already told you it's not like that. We're just friends."

Like the obnoxious asshole he is, Shep gives me a slow wink and whispers, "Sure. Whatever you say."

I blow him off, refusing to let him get me riled up again. I inject a Boston accent into my voice. "Get fucked, ya jagoff."

"Oh, but he can't do that, Sawyer," Kri interjects, wearing a mocking frown. "He suffers from a very severe medical condition that makes fucking impossible. It's called *noballsatall*. Sadly, it's permanent, and there is no cure." She clicks her tongue and shakes her head despondently.

My shoulders shake with silent laughter, finally glad to have someone else busting his balls for a change. I've carried this heavy load on my own for so long.

Shep raises one brow at her, then flips her off. "I guess I'm the designated asshole tonight. That's fine. But I'll remember this, ya friggin yahoos."

I feign a cringe. "Leave the accents to the professionals, Shep."

After the teasing has dried up and Sammy has polished off the bottle of wine, Shep and Kri share a look before rising from the table.

"So are you guys staying here tonight?" Shep looks from me to Sammy while sliding his phone into his back pocket.

I nod. "I think it's safest. We have to assume he knows where she lives. No sense risking it."

Kri jiggles her keys, slinging them around her pointer finger. "Okay, we're going to see if we can find him. Do some recon. We'll do a perimeter check on our way out. And like Boss asked, we'll use the group chat for updates." She rolls her eyes at that last bit.

Boss was pissed that we weren't on the same page and chewed us up one side and down the other about all the phone tag we've been playing. From now on, Big Al wants us to use our Redleg secure communications app for all nonemergency updates to the group.

Personally, I think he's stressing about being on the other side of the country, away from Redleg for the first time in probably... forever. And his control-freak tendencies are going berserk. But whatever. I'll use the app if it keeps his panties from twisting.

I walk them out, chatting as we go. Once they're outside, I lock the door and reset the alarm. When I spin around, Sammy isn't where I left her.

"Babe?" I walk past the kitchen and living room, then head down the hall, looking for her. "Sammy?"

My heart rate spikes, fear pooling in my gut. How could she have disappeared from a secured house in less than five minutes?

She couldn't, asshole. Just relax.

"Princess, where are you?" I yell again.

A door slams back toward my bedroom. "Don't you dare call me that!"

Even if she sounds pissed, it still instantly lowers my blood pressure to hear her voice. I'll take *angry Sammy* over *no Sammy*, any day and twice on Friday. I never want to feel that sense of loss I did the other night when she was taken.

When I enter my bedroom, it looks like she's just come out of the adjoining bathroom. Her hair is tied up in a messy bun, and her face is pink and shiny, looking like she's scrubbed it clean. Seeing her make herself at home in my space is beyond intoxicating.

She's thrown on one of my T-shirts, and the sight of her shapely bare legs below the hem causes a surge of blood to flow south. Muscular, yet soft. I know how they feel wrapped around me, and I'm aching for more.

I try for playful. "I can't call you princess now?"

She folds her arms across her chest, tension radiating from her every pore. Instead of answering me, she redirects. "Where am I sleeping? Which guest room?"

"Guest room?" I level her with a confused glare. "With me. My bed." My head tips toward the bed beside us, pointing her to where she belongs.

"*I already told you it's not like that. We're just friends.*" She throws my earlier words to Shep back at me. "Oh, and don't mind me while I put you in a headlock to avoid admitting my feelings."

Fuck.

My hands lift in front of me, palms to ceiling. "What was I supposed to say? *Yes, we're involved, but I need you to keep that secret for us. You don't mind lying to the rest of the team, do you?*" A groan leaves me. "Besides, you're the one who suggested we keep it between us for now. I don't like it either, but I also don't want to burden anyone else with this. I can't make them lie for me."

"For you?" She takes in a deep breath, a slight hitch in her exhale.

"Well, for us..." I trail off as my mind races.

How is she not seeing this? If Leo or Boss finds out, they'll pull me from her detail. Leo will be furious, and Boss will definitely reprimand me, or maybe worse. I won't be able to protect her, which would kill me. If anything happened to her, I'd never be able to move on from that.

Hands to her hips now, she looks up at me with a quivering chin. Her jaw wobbles a few times as she searches for a response. When she finally starts to speak, her voice cracks, splintering my heart in the process.

Damn, damn, damn.

"I realize your primary goal is to keep what we have hidden in a locked closet, but —"

I interject, "No, my primary goal is keeping you safe."

She shakes her head solemnly. "I know I said we could keep it a secret, and this feels like a departure from that. But I when you denied me *semi*-publicly like that, I felt cheap, used, and dirty. I'm only telling you how I feel. I don't want to hide my feelings from you."

I'm speechless, utterly unsure of how to respond to her words.

She stiffens her spine and juts her chin. "Now, where am I sleeping? I'm tired. It's been a long few days."

Raking my hands through my hair, I give a few strands a tug, pulling at the root. I force my hands to unclench as I take the two steps to approach her, aligning our bodies from chest to toes.

Softly and earnestly, I tell her, "Sammy, I never meant to make you feel that way. I'm sorry." I bend my knees slightly so I can meet her eyes, and I bring my palms up to caress her arms. "That's part of the reason I didn't think this was the best time for us to get involved. It complicates things. But I truly am sorry for making you feel that way."

She forces a swallow, nodding slowly. "Fine. As long as you know how it made me feel. Even if it is irrational, that's how I felt."

"I hear you, baby. But you understand what I'm saying, right? About us not being able to *out* ourselves yet?"

Her eyes sparkle with unshed tears. "Yes, I understand. Your friendship with Leo and loyalty to Big Al are more important than me. Message received."

"What? No. Not even close."

"I'm tired. Which bed —" she starts again, but I cut her off.

"Sammy, you're not less important. If anything, you're *more* important. We have to keep this a secret so I can continue to be here for you. To protect you. Don't you see?"

A tear finally breaks loose, spilling down her cheek. "I guess so," she says, still sounding unconvinced. "Regardless of your reasons, my feelings are still what they are. And they are valid. I felt... cheap. Unworthy. Angry. Turns out I don't like hiding us... even if it was my stupid idea."

Bringing my hands up to cup her face, I rub her free-falling tears away with the pads of my thumbs, then tuck a loose strand of hair behind her ear. Reaching up, she circles my wrists while looking deep into my eyes.

"I'm sorry, baby. I'll figure something out, okay? Just give me a little time. It won't be long. We're getting close to catching this guy. Then we'll tell Leo. Okay?"

"You promise?"

"I promise."

"Okay."

She rises at the same time that I lower myself to her, both of us feeling an unmistakable urge to connect. Our lips press together, fusing pieces of our broken spirits in the process. Her arms wrap around my waist, pulling me close. I slant my lips over hers, turning her head to the side, and deepen the kiss.

The kiss starts out sweet and healing, but our mutual passion quickly takes over until our hands are roaming eagerly. Our movements become frantic as our bodies grow desperate for each other.

I trail my hands down the back of her body and reach down under her shirt.

My shirt.

With a handful of her silk-covered ass, I pull her up the length of my body. She wraps her arms and legs around me, locking herself in place. A visceral feeling fills my chest and elicits a throaty groan from somewhere deep inside me. She captures it in my mouth, whimpering back into mine.

Taking a few steps, I lay her down on the bed, then crawl on top of her. She scoots back toward the headboard, and I follow, pursuing her like a lion about to claim his lioness.

Something wild is breaking inside me as we kiss and caress each other. My touch gets more intense, more punishing. My grip grows tighter as I pull her to me.

I *need* her closer.

I don't know if it's her wearing my shirt, being in my house, in my bed, or how she bared her emotions to me, showing so much vulnerability and having the courage to call me out and stand up for herself. I'm so damn proud of her. No clue what's causing this beast to rage, but here it is, none-theless. The urge to connect with her is frantic and runs through my blood like wildfire.

My tongue strokes against hers, twirling and spinning, sending bolts of arousal straight to my balls. Positioned between her hips, I find myself thrusting against her core. We grow wilder and more frenzied as we grind together, our breaths mingling.

Suddenly pushing and shoving at my chest, she yells, "Stop! Stop!"

It takes a full second, maybe two, before her words pierce through the lust clouding my mind. But they finally get in there, and I react immediately.

I rise to my knees and pull away from her, leaving myself feeling bereft. Her skin should be on mine right now. I should be sinking into her tight heat. My body wants to claim hers.

But as my vision clears, I see she's wearing that terrified look again. The one I saw on her face the last time I caged her in. My heart crashes down to my gut.

Fuck.

I was out of control, and it scared her.

Our deep, shaky breaths fill the air.

I'm the first one to break the tense silence. "I'm sorry, Sammy. Fuck. I got carried away. I'm so damn sorry for scaring you. It was my fault. Are you okay?"

Her eyes are pressed in hard lines. She shakes her head a few times and squeezes her eyes tighter. A shaky hand runs down her face, hiding it from me.

Daring to touch her, I let one palm rub along her exposed leg. Comforting her.

Her subtle head shakes eventually change into nods, and the skin pinched on the sides of her face slowly relaxes. She drops her hand, exposing her full pained expression to me.

"Talk to me, baby. Can you tell me what you're feeling? How can I help?"

When she opens her eyes, I'm gutted. Absolutely wrecked. Like I've taken a punch to the stomach from her giant of a brother. It shreds my heart in two pieces.

The anguish written on her face is heart-wrenching and rage-inducing at the same time.

Briefly, I contemplate making a trip to the prison tomorrow morning at first light and bribing a guard to let me in so I can have five minutes alone with her ex.

Craig Banks will be sorry he ever laid eyes on her, let alone laid hands on her.

"Can we stop?" she asks, her voice sounding high-pitched, like she's not sure how I'll answer.

"Of course we can stop. I'd *never* force you."

Her head falls back, hitting the pillow. She throws her forearm over her face and screws her lips as the tears come hard and fast.

"You're safe with me. Always." I'm desperate to comfort her. To soothe those fears away. "I'm so sorry for scaring you. Can I hold you?"

Her voice is so quiet I can barely hear the simple reply. "Yes."

That answer — a single word — begins stitching my fractured heart together. Trusting me to console her, even when she's so clearly shaken by past trauma, means the world to me. When I spoon up behind her and pull her safely into my arms, the healing sewing of my heart resumes.

Stitch by stitch.

But until she's whole and healed, my heart will remain injured along with hers. If she hurts, so do I.

As I hold her, I shower soft kisses on her neck, cheek, around the shell of her ear, and on the top of her head. All while whispering softly and giving her as much love and support as my words and gentle touch can convey.

Let it out. I'm not going anywhere.

I'll never hurt you.

I love you, baby.

I'll never let anyone hurt you ever again.

You're so precious to me.

Eventually, her shoulders stop shaking, and her breath grows steadier as she cries herself to sleep.

In the stillness of the night, as the hours pass, I don't sleep. I simply hold her, gently running my hand over her hair and skin. I keep her tucked close and hope she feels safe beside me as she sleeps. I've never been someone who prays, but I'm so tempted to ask some higher power to make sure her dreams aren't nightmares. She deserves peace.

All night long, I surround her with my body. My protection. My touch. My warmth. My love.

All the things she's needed for years but hasn't had.

I know one night full of kind and tender touching, stroking, and caressing can't erase all the painful memories she has. But that doesn't mean I won't try.

Even when my hands get tired, I keep trailing my fingertips over her skin and hair. Infusing all my love into my touch.

At one point, she spins around and snuggles into my chest. She throws her leg over mine and burrows into me. As I look down at her peaceful face, I brush the hair away from her eyes, check the wound on her head, and press a kiss to each puffy eyelid.

The softest, shaky sigh escapes her lips as she mutters, "Love you, Sawyer."

I know she's asleep, so her proclamation doesn't count, but I still heard it. And those words bring my heart one more stitch closer to being whole.

Chapter Thirty-Nine

DON'T BE A TOOL

Sammy

It shouldn't be this hard to pick. It's not a contest or a game. No winners or losers. The outcome probably doesn't matter.

Yet, no matter what I choose, I feel like a part of me loses.

Ugh. I'm overreacting. No one will care if I ride home with Leo or Sawyer. It's only an issue in my head. Leo probably wouldn't care if I went with Sawyer, and he likely wouldn't read too much into it. He knows we're friends and has never been bothered by me spending time with Sawyer, nor has he accused me of sleeping with him.

But if I choose Leo over Sawyer, will Sawyer feel jaded? Or will he be relieved since he's so nervous about Leo figuring out that we're together? For some reason, I don't want to find out the answer.

Just choose, for fuck's sake, my rage monster says with a yawn.

Fortunately, Leo decides for me when he opens the passenger door on *his* Redleg SUV and ushers me in. Sawyer will follow behind us in his vehicle.

They decided we'd head back to my house this morning to grab clothes and supplies for the next few days. Both of them want to be there when we enter the house in case something goes wrong, which is stupid because Shep and Kri are doing surveillance on the shithead and say he's at his place with no sign of him being awake at this ungodly hour.

But whatever. I'm going along with their plan without acting petulant, just like Jaynie and I agreed.

Will you look at me? Bozo button for good behavior.

During the day, I'll be hanging out at Redleg Security headquarters. At night, I'll be staying at Sawyer's bougie house and sleeping in his silky as fuck sheets.

I suspect he opted for the six million thread count. I've never had such a good night's sleep in my thirty-two years.

Then again, it might have had something to do with the human furnace spooned against me all night long. Like a heated, weighted blanket.

Safe.

I felt so damn safe.

And loved.

The bags under his eyes this morning make me think he didn't sleep last night. I guess he wasn't as comfortable with me in his bed as I was. The thought makes my stomach swirl.

Once we're on the road, Leo says, "I want us finished in no more than five minutes. Think through your plan of attack now so you can double-time it when we get there. Grab *only* what you need."

"Roger that." I give him a mock salute.

He shakes his head, a grin poking at his cheek. "Sorry. I know I'm being even more overprotective than usual. And believe me, I'm *trying* to loosen up. It's just the thought of something happening to you." He mutters curses under his breath, but it's too quiet for me to understand.

My hand falls to my chest, and my lips shift into a pout at his words. "Oh, my sweet Leo." A lump forms in my throat. "I'm going to be fine. You've taught me a lot over the years. And I'm not the same person I once was. I'm stronger than I was, and I'm no longer a victim."

He clears his throat, attempting to brush away the emotional moment. "I know we've talked about how bad it was when you left, Sammy. But I just... I can't go through that again."

Guilt sandwiches are worse than shit sandwiches.

"I'll never be able to apologize enough for doing that to you. I'm beyond sorry. But this isn't like that. Nothing is going to happen to me. I'm never leaving you again. I promise." I add a jab to lighten the mood. "You're stuck with me forever. So might as well get used to it."

Glancing over, he smiles wide at me. "At least I know you're safe when I'm not with you. If it weren't for Sawyer, I doubt I'd have gotten much sleep these last few days. There's no one I trust more than him."

For a moment, I consider telling him that I'm falling in love with his best friend. The words form on my lips, but I can't seem to push them out. It feels like a betrayal to Sawyer. Telling Leo now doesn't seem worth the risk of him removing Sawyer from my protection.

I can wait.

He said he'll tell him after we get through this mess. I can be patient. He's worth the wait.

"You two seem to be getting along well." It's a statement, not a question, but the way he looks over at me with a brow raised suggests he wants me to answer him.

"Yeah. I like him. He's funny, and we have a lot in common."

And he fucks like a champion and licks pussy with the best of them. Even better yet, he likes it when I boss him around.

My legs squeeze together, and heat pools in my lower abdomen.

How many hours until I'm alone with Sawyer? I glance at the clock. At least eleven.

Shit. That's eleven too many.

"You know about his childhood, right?" Leo asks, bringing my thoughts back to the moment.

"He's told me quite a bit about his younger days. All the foster homes. Never feeling like he belonged anywhere. Pretty tragic." I pull a large wave of air through my nose as I stare at the trees whipping past us out the window. "We all have our dark stories of traumatic childhoods, don't we?"

"I think that's one of the reasons we connected. He's known hard times like we have but overcome them. We sort of became found family in the Rangers." He chuckles, then adds, "I don't know why I was so nervous to ask him to be my best man. He's the most loyal person I know. There was no way he would've said no. But I was shaking like a leaf." He looks at me from the side of his eyeline. "Stupid, isn't it?"

"Did you shake when you asked Sue?"

His cheeks grow flaming red. "Uh... no. Not at all. No shakes. Aftershocks, maybe." An uncharacteristic snicker escapes him.

An audible gasp leaves my mouth. "Leo Mason! Tell me you didn't ask that sweet woman to marry you while you were having sex."

His shoulders roll inward, and he scrunches his nose up, baring his teeth a touch.

"Oh my God! You did, didn't you?"

With a shrug, he confirms my assertion. "It just sort of happened."

After my initial shock recedes, I finally tsk and chastise him properly.

"I'm so disappointed in you. Our sweet mother would be mortified if she knew. She raised you better."

We chuckle together and enjoy the last few minutes of the ride. When we pull into the driveway, he goes through the customary security measures, checking the cameras on his phone.

Over the hood of the SUV, he yells to Sawyer. "I'll check the inside. You stay with her."

Sawyer arrives at my side of the car. "You got it, Lionheart."

My nipples harden to stiff points at the thought of getting an extra minute alone with him before we have to separate for the day.

"Don't forget there's a camera out here," Sawyer whispers as he bends into the car and reaches across me to unbuckle my seatbelt.

When he pulls back, he braces himself on the hood of the SUV, one bulky arm with delicious throbbing veins staring at me and causing naughty images to flash through my mind.

And right out of my mouth.

"Tonight, I'm going to shove your head between my legs and not let you up for air until you tap out."

His eyes flash wild at my dirty words. "Fuck, baby. You trying to kill me or what?"

"Oh, stop. You'll be able to breathe. Don't be so overdramatic," I tease with an eye roll.

He smiles, that stupid ovary bursting dimple popping out and begging for my tongue. "That's not what I was implying, princess. I meant that you're going to kill me before that because all day long, I'll be fantasizing about it. I'll die from blue balls. Promise to mourn me."

His haunting brown eyes glance from me to the front door and back again. He leans in, hopefully out of the view of the camera. After pressing a brief kiss to my lips, he tugs my lower lip with him as he breaks away.

He winks at me. "Mmm. I miss you already."

I need to start wearing pantyliners to deal with all the floods he incites.

"Me too. I can't wait to see you tonight. I need to make up for losing my shit last night and not giving you sex." My eyes flit to the floorboard.

"Hey, listen to me." He tilts my chin up. "You don't ever have to apologize for that. Sex is not an expectation. *Ever.*"

I feel my brows scrunch together.

"Sex is not an entitlement. It's a privilege to be inside you, and I cherish every moment we're connected in that way. But you *never* have to give me anything you don't want me to have. I will never be angry or upset or even mildly disappointed in you for having emotions or not wanting to make love. Understand?"

I nod, unable to form any words in response.

He's right. I hear what he said, and I believe the words. Logically, I know it's true.

But I've been conditioned to view sex as something I'm expected to give up on demand — whether I want to or not has never mattered. It was a tool.

A tool Craig used to exert power over me, making me feel weak.

A tool to make me feel like an object.

A tool used to "make up" for his outbursts.

Hell, I even used it as a tool on occasion. Sometimes, I'd instigate sex to stop him from having a violent outburst.

But with Sawyer, it's different.

It's about love. Nothing more. Nothing less.

I can't hold back from touching him, so my hand rises to cup his cheek.

He cups his big hand over mine and looks deeply into my eyes. "I love you, Sammy." He pulls back, dropping my hand. "I'll see you tonight. Be safe and listen to your brother." He winks again.

Mentally, I calculate the time needed for me to change my underwear. This pair is officially decimated.

"All clear," Leo yells from the front porch.

Sawyer walks me inside, hand to my back. I soak in that tiny bit of contact. Hoping the affection goes straight to my love well. The one he's filling with each passing second.

He waits outside, watching the cars passing through my sleepy neighborhood. I run through the house, grabbing my toiletries and clothes at a record pace, along with a dog-eared paperback and my kindle to keep me occupied while I sit around Redleg all day. Tossing everything in a small duffel bag, I make quick work of my tasks. We're back outside and safely in Leo's SUV before my brother has a coronary.

"Mission success," Leo says as he starts the ignition.

When we inch out of the driveway, my eyes catch Sawyer in the side mirror. With a slight wave, he takes a deep breath before getting into his vehicle. An air of sadness surrounds him.

My heart pinches in my chest at the sight of him standing there. Alone.

It shouldn't hurt this bad to leave him.

"You okay?" Leo asks.

"Me? Yeah. I'm fine. Why?"

"Longing looks out the window. You seem sad."

"I'm ready to put this behind me. I hate being a burden to you and Sawyer."

"You're not a burden, Sammy. Has Sawyer said something to make you feel that way?"

The sudden harshness in his voice is comical because he couldn't be further from the truth.

I chuckle. "Not even close. He's been great. I just want this to be over."

So I won't have to hide my feelings from everyone. So I can love him openly and proudly, the way he deserves.

And the way I deserve.

Chapter Forty

DAMN CAMERAS, RUINING ALL THE FUN

Sawyer

I'll kill him.

I'm going to do a reverse prison break and kill him. With my bare hands.

Having to listen to Sammy apologize for not "giving me sex" like she's some fucking sex machine — existing only to please a man — was almost as painful as some of the shit they did to us in SERE training.

Fucking hell.

I'll strangle every last breath out of him. Watch his eyes glaze over while his lips turn blue.

And I'm going to enjoy the hell out of it. Then I'll fucking dance and piss on his grave.

When I get home, I strip out of my jeans and the shirt that still smells like my Sammy. I know I should sleep, but I can't. I'm running on fumes. Even coffee — the miracle juice of the gods — isn't going to be able to keep me up another twenty-four hours unless I get a few hours of shut-eye today.

But I'm too angry to rest.

Throwing on some basketball shorts and a tank, I head to the gym at HQ to release some of this pent-up rage. I think I'll hit the range today too.

When I pull into the Redleg parking lot, I see Leo's SUV in his reserved space, reminding me that Sammy's here for the day. I wonder what she's doing and how she'll pass the time.

Coming here has nothing to do with making sure she's safe, since there isn't a more secure place for her to be.

And it has nothing to do with wanting to catch a peek of her before I go to sleep. I just saw her less than an hour ago.

Nope.

It's merely to get the rage out.

And yet...

I still can't stop looking for her as I breeze through the facility, scanning my badge and fingertip at each entry point along the way. Hoping for a mere glance of her, like she's a balm to my chapped heart.

When I enter the gym, the familiar smells of sweat, rusty metal, and disinfectant reach my nose and settle me. Knowing that I'll be beating the shit out of a punching bag soon helps soothe my nerves. Even if it's not what I wish I were beating — the face of Craig Banks and whoever else is involved in threatening Sammy.

"Hey, man." Klein nods in my direction through our reflection in the wall-to-wall mirrors. He's doing bicep curls.

I return his nod. "Feel like sparring this morning?"

He flinches. "With you?"

My arms open to each side. "I don't see anybody else asking."

Setting down his weights on the rack, he turns and approaches me slowly, a skeptical look on his face. "Let me see. Do I want my face rearranged? I'm going to go with no."

"You can wear gear."

"With the way your jaw is ticking and the vein bulging on your fore-head, I'm going to decline. I know my limitations, and I like my body the way it is. Relatively pain-free."

"Wuss," I taunt, trying one last time to get him to bite.

"If by *wuss* you mean someone who has respect for the handsome lines of their face and wants to avoid a broken rib, then yes, I am a wuss. Loud and proud." He laughs at himself.

Normally, I'd laugh with him. Klein and I get along pretty well. We've been through some shit together. But I can't even force a smile right now.

"My ears are open if you want to talk, though." He raises his brows, angling his head at me.

"Fuck that. I'm fine. Just need to blow off some steam."

I head to the treadmill and hitch up the incline while he returns to the free weights. Once the machine is set the way I want it, I plug in my earbuds and crank the music.

As my sneakers pound the treadmill, speed increasing every minute or so, my mind starts to clear. Soon enough, I feel the music deep in my bones, and I'm dripping with sweat as I sprint uphill at a fifteen percent incline. My lungs burn, and my muscles ache. I don't usually go this hard, but this morning, it's a necessity.

After a half hour of running, I do some light stretching and take out the rest of my frustrations on the punching bag in the corner.

My fists pummel the cracked leather sandbag. Over and over again. Even with the wraps, they'll be bruised, but I don't care. The pain makes it all the more therapeutic.

An hour later, I'm spent. I think I can skip the gun range. After a quick shower, I'll go home and pass out.

As I leave the gym, heading to the locker room down the hall, I nearly plow right into Sammy, who's trying to come in through the doorway.

She looks up at me with her sparkling blue eyes, and a tiny grin lifts at the corner of her mouth. "Hi. Didn't think I'd see you again so soon. Not that I'm complaining." The way she flits her brows at me causes a stirring sensation in my stomach.

"Hey, beautiful." My voice is extra husky since I'm still short of breath from my workout.

Her lip is tucked between her teeth as she gazes at my sweat-covered shirt.

I want to kiss her so fucking bad.

This woman should be kissed every fucking minute of every fucking day.

"Aren't you supposed to be sleeping?" She toys with the lid of her water bottle but isn't trying to hide the way she's drinking me in rather than that water.

"Couldn't sleep. Needed a workout first."

"I was going to kill some time on the treadmill."

Now that I'm no longer dumbstruck at the sight of her, I see she's changed into exercise clothes. A baggy t-shirt hanging over spandex shorts, making her look almost edible. A new pair of Nikes on her feet.

Glancing from side to side to see if anyone is watching, I reach out and run my hand up her outer thigh and over her hip, then around to her ass, giving her tush a light squeeze before letting go.

Her brows shoot up to her hairline. "Are you in the mood to live dangerously or something? I'm betting there are cameras in every inch of this place."

Fuck. Good point.

Except…

"None in the locker rooms." I angle my head to the side, pointing down the hall.

"That's good. I'd hate to think someone would be watching you when you strip out of these sweaty clothes." A coy smile appears as she adds, "Or while you shower. It'd be a shame if the cameras caught someone joining you in there."

"The locker rooms aren't co-ed."

She runs a single fingernail from my pec down across my abs before pulling it away right before she gets down to my stiffening cock. "Pretty sure I'm the only gal around right now. So the women's locker room is likely to remain a ghost town. Just came from there, and I was all alone."

"Is that right?"

"Yep. Nothing to stop you from coming in there with me. So I can make sure you get clean after your workout."

I'm loving this sexually charged banter. We've flirted in the past, having always had that vibe with each other. But this is different. These are no longer empty words.

These are intentions we plan to make good on.

Sadly, it can't happen here, though.

"As tempting as that sounds, there actually is something stopping me."

Her immediate pout is so damn adorable. "What?"

"There are cameras in this hallway, so they'd see us go in together."

"Well, fuck." She exhales forcibly, placing her hands on her hips.

I can't hold back my chuckle. My accompanying grin is so damn wide I feel my dimple pop, and I notice her eyes are drawn to it. "It's okay, baby. We have tonight. And tomorrow night. And every night after that."

Her cheeks redden as she nods and bats those stunningly long eyelashes at me. "Okay. I'm gonna hold you to that."

"Please do."

For a few sweet moments, we stand there in the hallway, looking like a pair of grinning goons. Burning with desire and dying to touch each other.

After a moment, a thought that's been playing at the back of my mind springs forth. She might need time to process this proposition, so rather than wait until we're in the heat of the moment, I'll suggest it now so she has the day to reflect on it.

"Speaking of our nights together…"

"Yes?" She draws out the word, cocking her head to the side and spearing me with a heated gaze.

"I've noticed that you seem less anxious when you're on top and in control."

Pursing her lips together, she swallows a lump down her throat. She offers a tentative nod, indicating that I should continue.

"Well, I've been thinking it might help if you were to…" I pause, seeking the right words. "Restrain me."

One corner of her mouth twitches as she tries to hold back a grin.

"You'd let me tie you up?"

"If you think it would help… yes. Or even if you just want to have a little fun. Test it out. Whatever." I shake my head and cast my eyes to the floor, feeling a sudden shyness I'm unaccustomed to. I gather my courage and meet her gaze again. "I'm only saying I'm open to anything you need to do that might help you gain some confidence in the bedroom."

Her eyes twinkle as her twitching smirk blooms into an ear-to-ear smile, beaming and bright. "I knew it."

"Knew what?"

She takes a step forward, bringing her body within inches of mine. Our combined heat mingles between us. I fist my hands at my side to stop myself from grabbing her and bringing her the rest of the way into me, sweat-soaked clothes or not. The need to touch her is becoming borderline painful.

I'm starting to question whether I'm strong enough to hide my love for her for a single second longer.

Leo's upstairs, my conscience chides me.

He's probably checking live camera feeds to make sure she's safe within the building — even if it's completely unnecessary.

Sammy's slight throat-clearing brings me back to the moment.

"I suspected you liked it when I was in charge, but now… it's not just a suspicion."

Busted.

"Princess, I've never fully submitted to anyone before — commanding officers being the only exception. But never sexually submitted. However, when you've taken control, it was the hottest fucking thing I've ever experienced. If you need *or want* to dominate me, then I'm more than on board with anything you have in mind."

"Damn, Sawyer. That is so fucking hot. You have no idea."

"Oh, I have a pretty good idea. Glance down between us."

She moves half a step back and lets her gaze run down my body. Her eyes flash wild when they catch sight of the growing situation in my shorts. This flimsy athletic fabric does absolutely nothing to conceal how intensely I want her.

A dainty curse falls from those kissable lips, begging for my attention. "Shit. I want to kiss you so fucking bad right now. Are you sure we can't run into the locker room for a minute?"

"Patience. Besides, you know we need more than a minute."

She groans. "Good things come to those who wait, right?"

"So I'm going to head home. I'll purchase some *supplies* on the way."

"Like rope or something?" Her brows shoot northward while she bites down on her lower lip.

"And also protection. As much as I love having you bare, we can't keep playing baby roulette."

She feigns a pout, sticking her lips out like she's impersonating a duck. Breaking character after a moment, she finally acquiesces with a grin. "Fine. You're right. It's probably a good idea if our friends and family actually know about our relationship before I get knocked up."

Fuck. The thought of her pregnant with my child is heady as fuck.

I need to leave before I drag her down the hall and fuck her in the shower.

"I'm gonna get cleaned up, then head home for a nap. I'll see you tonight, baby."

"Are you going to shower?" she asks, flashing a knowing grin.

"Yeah."

Her voice takes on that silky smooth tone of dominance that makes my balls tighten. "Think of me when you stroke your cock in there." She winks as she slowly brushes past me to enter the gym.

"Always, baby. Always."

Chapter Forty-One

EYES ON ME

Sawyer

Sammy looks at me over her glass of white wine, a playful glint in her eye. "I'm beginning to think my brother is choosing to be oblivious."

Raising my napkin, I dab at the corner of my mouth before crumbling it and tossing it onto the table. "About?"

"Us. Big Al and Mom. Take your pick."

I chuckle as I push from the table and gather the takeout containers to discard them. "He's certainly got his head in the sand about Boss and Madeline, but I'm not sure about us. I think we've been doing a good job of keeping it platonic in front of him."

Her head kicks back, and she draws in a deep breath. "Did you or did you not eye fuck me right in front of him for no less than five minutes when you picked me up tonight?"

I scoff. "He wasn't paying attention. He was on the phone with your mother, rattling on about his *whodunit* theories the entire time. He had no idea." I come up behind her and bend down to trail my lips along the curve of her exposed neck. "Besides, you looked so fucking good, and I hadn't seen you in like eight hours. I couldn't help it." I suck in a deep breath, getting a sugar high off her sweet scent.

She reaches up to caress the side of my head, locking it in place. "It was maybe five hours. Six tops. I'm starting to think you're getting addicted."

"Only *starting* to?"

I nibble on her neck, then swirl my tongue over the bite to soothe it.

Fuck. I need to be inside her again. I wonder if she's given any thought to the idea of tying me up. The mere thought of it makes my balls ache.

Setting her wineglass down, she spins her legs to the side of the chair and tugs me to stand in front of her. "I'm ready for dessert."

"I didn't order any with dinner, but I might have something sweet around here."

She gazes up at me from under her lashes, batting them seductively. Drawing her hand over my zippered fly, she says, "You have exactly what I want right here."

Without another word, she unbuckles my belt and works my pants open. I'm rock hard by the time she frees my cock and gives it a firm stroke.

She looks at it in awe, licking her plump lips. "I fucking love your dick."

"As you can see, he's pretty fond of you too."

She gives it another hard tug, making my eyes roll back.

"Damn, baby. That feels good," I hiss through gritted teeth.

Bringing my cock up to her mouth, she gives it a tentative stroke with her tongue while pumping me from the base to the tip.

Before she consumes me any further with ecstasy, I need to know how to approach our intimacy tonight so I don't overwhelm her again. "Have you given any thought to what I asked? About you restraining me?"

Her cheek twitches as a look of uncertainty crosses her features. "I need more time to decide. I've never done that before." She looks back at my dick, slowly pumping as she continues, "Not sure how I feel about being on the other side of that dynamic. Although, I do like it when you respond to my... commands." Her eyes flit back to mine and flash with a playful heat.

"Okay, baby. Take all the time you need. No rush."

"Thank you, Sawyer." Leaning forward, she licks me from the base to my thick head, then takes me fully into her mouth. She pulls back and adds, "You're so good to me."

A garbled sound escapes me when she dives back in, taking me all the way back to her throat. "My pleasure, princess. Pun intended."

With a slurp, she pulls back and adds, "I want you to *fuck* me tonight. Be a little rougher. Can you do that for me?"

Without waiting for my answer, she dives back in, hollowing her cheeks and making my balls draw up tighter with each erotic tug of delicious suction.

She stops and grabs tight at my base with one hand, applying an almost strangling force. Her other hand firmly cups my balls while applying gentle pressure across my taint with her knuckles. An intoxicating wave of pain assaults me.

Her voice is velvety and confident when she demands, "Answer me. Can you fuck me rougher tonight? Not all out, but a little harder. Can you do that?"

She tightens her hold on my balls and cock, drawing a pleasure-filled groan from me. I withhold my answer for a few seconds to prolong the delicious torture. The twinkle in her eye tells me she's enjoying it too.

When the pressure gets to be too much, I stammer, "Yes, damn, baby. Yes. Fuck yes."

"Good." She returns to her task of driving me wild with her warm, wet mouth.

After another few minutes of her working me into a frenzy with a mix of rough and gentle strokes, I pull back, stumbling away from her. "I'd rather come inside your pussy, gorgeous, and if you keep that up, I'm done for."

She rises and invades my space. I take her in my arms and fuse our lips.

"Let's go to your bedroom," she says, her voice raspy and desperate.

Nodding, I offer a wink. She spins around, and I follow her to my room. On the way, a thought hits me of how I might be able to be a little rougher with her while not upsetting her.

Once we're in my room, we quickly shed our clothes. She's down to only her bra when I halt her progress with a passionate kiss. I'm simply unable to keep my lips from hers for another minute.

When I pull back, my gaze rakes across her breasts, nuzzled snug inside a lacy bra. Rather than removing it, I sneak my hand inside the cups and pull them out, leaving her breasts trussed up by the dainty fabric.

Perfection.

I bend down and bring one of her pebbled nipples into my mouth, swirling and sucking on the tender skin. My other hand inches between her thighs, and my fingertips quickly find her clit. I pinch it softly, drawing a feral mewl from her.

I pop off her breast and look deep into her eyes. "I want to take you in front of the mirror. It might help."

Her nose wrinkles adorably. "How?"

"From behind. Facing the mirror so you can always see who's inside you. Is that okay, or do you need to be on top?"

A wicked grin lifts her cheeks. Before I can blink, she spins around and bends over the top of my dresser, putting her backside on display.

"Yes. Fuck me like this. Do it now."

Woman. Of. My. Dreams.

I can't resist grabbing a handful of her generous ass and giving it a quick squeeze. She giggles, and it's the sexiest sound I've ever heard.

I'd love to drop down and taste her again, but she's ordered me to fuck her. And she used that rich voice I'm powerless to disobey.

Fisting my swollen cock, I drag it through her wet pink flesh a few times to moisten the tip. Once it's nice and slick, I tease her entrance for a few agonizingly decadent seconds until my head finally slips inside.

I pause there, luxuriating in the feel of her body's natural resistance to my invasion. That blessed few seconds before her walls soften to welcome me home.

My breath comes heavy as I restrain myself from slamming deep. My plan is to be gentle at first.

One hand goes to her hip, the other bracing me on the smooth wood surface of my dresser. I'm careful not to cage her in. I meet her eyes in the mirror. *Damn, that's so hot.* Impatient now, she arches back, impaling herself onto my shaft.

This position. This location. This woman.

It's all erotic perfection.

Not only can I look down and watch my cock sink in and out, but I can also glance forward to see her eyes roll back into her head as she succumbs to the pleasure of her body taking me inside hers.

Entranced by the vision before and beneath me, my hips flex, driving my cock in and out. Faster, I pump, careful not to push her too much or be too rough yet. Not until she's ready.

"Tell me what you need, baby," I grunt. "I need you to let me know how much you can take. You're in control, remember?"

Her soft moans soon grow into sharp gasps and loud curses. "Harder. Fuck me harder," she orders.

"That's my girl." Like the gentleman I am, I fuck her harder. Slamming my hips into her ass, I watch her flesh jiggle and bounce with each powerful thrust.

"Fuck, Sawyer. Yes! Yes! Just like that."

"You feel so damn good, princess. I *love* fucking you." The sound of our bodies slapping against each other is almost enough to make me come.

Sammy's eyes are shut, lids pressed into tight lines. I'm searching for any signs of discomfort or fear as I remove my hand from her hip and sneak it up under her torso. I grab a handful of one breast, giving her nipple a squeeze. Her pussy walls contract around me.

"Damn, baby. Fuck, that feels good." I continue inching my hand forward until it's under her chin. I'm not choking her — not even close. I only want her to look at us. She's got the most erotic image in front of her, but she's not enjoying the show. It's such a shame.

And the caveman in me wants to be sure she sees who's fucking her like this. Bringing her this pleasure.

Applying the softest, gentle upward pressure under her chin, I coax, "Open your eyes, baby. Look at us. See who's doing this to you."

Her eyes pop open, and she shifts her gaze to the mirror. Her lips part as she drinks in the view. My hand falls away and lands on her shoulder so I can pull her body back into mine with each thrust.

A few moments later, I take one full breast in each palm. "You're so beautiful, Sammy. Look how perfectly your tits fit inside my hands."

She does as she's told.

"So damn perfect. Now, look at my face. I want you to watch how much I'm enjoying fucking you. How much I love worshipping your body. How sexy you are to me. How good you're making me feel." I trail my gaze all over the smooth skin of her back while thrusting at a punishing pace.

When my eyes meet hers again, she's biting her lip and struggling to keep her eyes from rolling back into her skull.

"This is exactly what I wanted, Sawyer. Don't stop. And keep talking dirty like that. I fucking love it."

I move both hands to her waist, resting them right above the swell of her hips. "Watch how I move you up and down my cock, baby. You feel so fucking good. Like you were made to take this dick." I start pumping into her with more fervor, using my grip to help me hammer into her harder, just like she wants.

Even though she's acting brave and not showing any distress with my *rougher* treatment of her, I'm still holding back some. If I laid into her with full force, she might panic.

"Are you ready to come, princess?"

She nods, panting and beautiful.

"Watch how gorgeous you are when you're shaking with pleasure for me."

One of my hands reaches around to rub her clit, while the other tweaks a nipple. Her hips roll as she presses her clit deeper into my fingertips, not afraid to take what she wants. A hiss falls from her lips, but it quickly turns into a high-pitched moan that grows louder and more feral.

I raise to my tiptoes so I can use a downward thrusting motion with my cock, attempting to attack her clit from both the inside and outside.

Through frenzied breaths, she screams, "Holy fucking hell, Sawyer! Right there. Don't stop, Sawyer. Holy shit." Her eyes roll back in her head, and her legs quake.

"Look at me when you come, baby. Eyes on me."

She complies, but only for a flash before losing the fight to keep her eyes open as she comes, gasping and screaming in ecstasy. Her silky walls flutter and clench around my cock, nearly bringing me to my knees.

I'm about to join her when I remember I'm not wearing a condom.

Dammit. How did I forget? I bought them, so why didn't I use one?

Fuck.

I slow my pace enough to hold off my impending release and ask, "I forgot to get a condom. Where do you want me to finish, baby?"

Her voice is a breathy grunt as she replies, "Come inside me. Give me every last drop."

My tempo increases with her dirty words. "Your wish is my command, princess."

I'm pretty sure Sammy Mason is giving me a breeding kink because the thought of impregnating her is *everything*. If a single drop of my release drips out, I might shove it back up inside her.

That last thought does it. A few more deep thrusts as my spine stiffens and balls contract, sending warm waves of pleasure deep inside my woman.

Mine.

Swear to fuck, I never want to come anywhere else ever again.

Chapter Forty-Two

I THINK I'D RATHER BE BORED

Sammy

I plop down in the guest chair in Sue's office, then fold my hands across my chest. "I'm bored. How do you cope?"

Her nose wrinkles in confusion. "What do you mean?"

"Cooped up here all day, like we're being jailed." Raising my hands to each side, I shake my head and huff. "How do you stand it? It's only been three days, and I'm already losing my shit."

Sue shifts back into her chair, the leather squeaking with her movements. A horrified look befalls her face. "That was the seat," she mutters. "I didn't fart."

A snorted laugh escapes me, and I cover my nose and mouth with my cupped hand. "I know, Sue. It's fine."

She shields her face with her hand, but I can still see her cheeks turn ruddy with her blush. "I'm sensitive about that after the... broccoli incident."

"Oh my gosh! Sue, you have to get over that. It was two years ago."

"And yet, the mortification is as sharp as it was the day it happened. Curse my elephant memory."

I indulge her for another moment before I draw her back to my question. "Seriously, though. How do you stand being under lockdown all day?"

"Well, it's a nice facility to be stuck inside. My chair is comfortable — except when it sounds like uncontrolled flatulence — and I have my laptop so I can work on wedding planning, Redleg stuff, and do work for Naughty Dogs."

Sue helps her brother run his dog training business. She's even trained some dogs on her own. She's engaged, has her painting and art, holds down two interesting jobs, *and* just finished a second degree. What a rich and exciting life she leads.

Unlike me.

Hiding a relationship with my brother's best friend, being hunted by a gang-banging asshole for some unknown reason, living with my mother, and holding down a crap job I hate. Pathetic.

Probably need to look over my list of five good things a few more times before this darkness tugs me under.

Oblivious to my internal malaise, she continues, "And Big Al said I could paint in the break room if I want to. But I mostly just sketch when I get bored because I don't want to make a big mess here. I also have my music to listen to." She points at the earbuds on her desk, then grabs her phone and waves it at me. "All I need to entertain me is available in the app store."

She leans forward, making brief but intense eye contact like she's about to tell me a secret. "The best part of being stuck here is the lack of random people trying to talk to me." A whole-body cringe runs through her, and she shakes it out. "The Redleg team knows to leave me alone unless they truly need something. And so I've got all kinds of time to myself. It's kind of perfect for me. Plus, I get to have lunch with my man."

"Lucky you." It's hard to hide the snark in my tone, but I immediately feel guilty when Sue's expression grows dismal.

She sputters a rushed apology. "I'm sorry. I didn't mean that you were bothering me. You're fine. Just because I don't like people in general doesn't mean I don't like you coming in here. You're an exception to my no-people rule."

I raise my hand to cut her off graciously. "My bad. I didn't mean to snap at you. I'm just a little... miffed right now."

She nods. "I see. Well, you've got a lot going on. How are you holding up? Have you seen Jaynie lately?"

"About a week ago. The day after the trunk incident. I'm still processing everything. I think what's bothering me the most is that I'm being watched like a child. Leo and Sawyer mean well, but I feel a loss of freedom. That's hard for me, considering my..." I pause as thoughts of living with Craig as his near-captive rock my gut. "My past with my ex. I had no freedom. So this situation of being under protection is triggering me."

She smacks her palm on the desk, shock on her face. "Oh, girl. I can't believe this... but I can relate to that feeling so hard."

"Why is that shocking?"

"Because I'm relating. I don't do that often. Feeling actual empathy — not logical empathy — or being able to put myself in other people's shoes. It seldom happens. The touch of the 'tism... you know?"

"Oh, I see. And you can relate to what I'm feeling?"

"I wasn't diagnosed with autism until my late twenties. My family always knew something was different about me, but they didn't know exactly what or how to help. So they hovered. Hounded me. Coddled me. It was like I wasn't allowed to be an adult. I felt like a prisoner in my own skin. Is that what you're talking about? Was it that way for you?"

The excitement in her voice brings a smile to my face. I love to see her joy in being able to connect with me like this. It's helping me to remove the focus from myself and all my problems.

Plus, she's right. That's precisely what it's been like.

"Yes. Exactly. I wasn't allowed to make my own decisions when I was with him, and now I'm right back in that scenario. It's so frustrating. I want to scream and lash out, but I have to hold it all inside."

"What does Jaynie say about that? She probably had some good advice for you. Does she have you journaling?"

"Not exactly. Just tracking my rage thoughts and focusing on good things I've got going."

"And you're doing it, right? Sometimes that's the hard part for me. Knowing I need to do something and actually doing it are two separate things."

"I am."

"Good. I also thi —" A ping on the laptop captures her attention. "Uh-oh. Something in the group chat about your case."

"What?"

She holds up one finger while she reads the message. Another ping comes through a second later.

"Looks like your guy is on the move."

My guy? Ugh. "Don't call him that."

"Sorry. Looks like *Tom* is on the move," she amends.

"What's that mean?"

A strong thrumming force runs through my veins as my nervous system prepares for bad news. Sue keeps reading, finger still pointed upward.

The sounds of car keys rattling and heavy footsteps stalking down the hallway snap my spine to attention. Sue and I rise to our feet as if preparing for a battle.

It's my brother, with Tomer hot on his heels.

A wave of relief sweeps from head to toe, my shoulders roll inward, and I release the tension from my jaw with a forceful exhale.

"Good. You're both here." Leo pauses at the doorway, eyes sweeping over both of us warmly.

"What's going on?" I ask.

"Updates from the surveillance team. Thomas Jones has just paid a visit to a shady character known to Redleg."

Sue voices my next question for me. "What kind of shady character?"

Tomer pipes in. "The kind who can make people disappear. At least on paper. A Russian national who specializes in fake IDs, passports, and new identities. That sort of thing. As far as we know, he's currently going by Yuri Zaytsev."

I begin pacing in the small space, unable to hold back the adrenaline. "Does that mean Thomas is planning on fleeing?"

Leo shakes his head. "Hard to tell, but that's one theory. Another could be that he needs new identification for someone else." Leo gives me a stern look, like he's trying to tell me something important. But I'm not sure I understand.

When I don't question him, he continues, "Kri's following him now, and Shep's going to talk to Yuri to see what we can find out."

"Shep's going in by himself?" Sue asks, wide-eyed.

"Is that safe?" I echo her sentiment.

Leo replies, "Shep's dealt with Yuri before. They have an oddly civil dynamic. I doubt he'll get much out of him, though. Guys like Yuri don't squeal on their customers unless they've got a compelling incentive to do so."

My lips press into a hard line as I wrap my head around this new development. "Is that it? Anything else?"

Leo puts his hands on his hips. "That's it for now."

"Leo, what did you mean when you said he might be getting identification for someone else?" Sue asks.

Leo's eyes dart from Sue to me, then he glances at Tomer before answering. When he does, his somber tone sends a chill down my spine.

"It's possible he's getting a new identity for someone he'd be taking with him out of the country. Someone he'd need to hide."

Gulp.

Me.

Chapter Forty-Three

TIME IS RUNNING OUT

Sawyer

Not the way I wanted to wake up.

On the bright side, at least I got six solid hours of rack time before waking to the news that Shep and Kri are preparing to bring in Thomas Jones for interrogation *tonight*.

In other good news, this coffee is fucking delicious.

As I walk into Redleg HQ, freshly showered, shaved, and ready for action, Sammy greets me in the lobby. She's wearing another one of those flowing fucking skirts, putting her sumptuous legs on display for me.

An image of when she spread herself open for me on the couch the last time she had on a skirt like this flashes through my mind, but I summon the strength to push the image away before I end up with an erection at work, aching to be inside her again.

I feel like it'll still happen, given our horny history. But I can still give it the ol' college try.

My eyes scan the room, seeing only our entry point guard nearby. He's an FNG — civilian translation: fucking new guy — and doesn't know his ass from his elbow in terms of the people here.

Well, that's not a fair statement. I should clarify. He knows who everyone is — after all, we walk past him day in and day out, and he makes sure we scan in and all that shit. He knows our names and positions. He just doesn't know everyone's background stories. So the way I'm wrapping Sammy up in a quick embrace a few feet from his desk isn't likely to draw much attention.

"Damn, you smell good," she mutters into my chest.

I press a quick kiss on her head. "Did you have a good day?" I break the hug and pull back. After all, someone is always watching. Not only the FNG.

"Great. Yeah, yeah, sure. Whatever."

I laugh as we stroll to the elevator. "Why were you waiting in the lobby? Is everything okay?"

"I missed you and wanted to see you before everything else stole you away from me. So I asked Tomer to track your car for me."

Fuck. I don't need him to get wise to what's going on between Sammy and me. He's too much of a rule follower to let his suspicions slide.

Damn.

Sammy must pick up on my apprehension because she adds, "Relax. I told him I needed to get something out of your car."

"Oh, cool. Smart. Should we go out to my car to sell it?"

"No, fuck that. This shit is about to be over soon, and then we can come out to everyone."

I pull a sharp inhale through my nose and tap the elevator call button.

As we stride into the elevator, she looks up at me, and a dainty blush caresses her cheeks. "I'm sure Leo will give you the scoop on all the tactical shit when you get upstairs, so I'm not wasting our time talking about that. Aside from stealing a moment alone with you, I wanted to let you know my decision about your offer from the other day."

"My offer?"

The doors close slowly, and the car shakes as it begins lifting us to the top floor.

"About restraining you so you're at my mercy. Over the last few days, I've had lots of downtime to research it and give it some thought."

A surge of arousal shoots through my dick, making it pulse in my jeans. "Ah yes. And what did you decide?"

"Not that I'm not enjoying our time sexually — because I am. But I'm ready to try it. *Officially.* It might not be a silver bullet, but I think it might help me get over some of my residual hang-ups. I even called Jaynie and had a mini-phone session today to discuss it. We talked about how women can use it to overcome trauma like mine. And I watched a few videos on how to tie knots properly. Reviewed safety shit — stuff beyond safe words. And I have some spicy ideas on how we can truly have some fun with this." She nibbles her lip and bats her lashes at me.

"Damn, baby."

I can't hold back from touching her again, but I keep it platonic and simply tuck a lock of hair behind her ear, then I let my knuckles trail down her cheek before dropping my hand.

"I hope you got some rest and hydration. You're gonna need it."

Her eye contact is borderline obscene at this point. If she keeps this shit up, I'll press the emergency brake on this elevator and fuck her right here and now.

When I don't object, she tosses out, "So I need you to hurry the fuck up and get a confession out of this guy tonight so we can get down to business. I can't wait to see you spread eagle on the bed in front of me, hands and legs bound."

"Fuck, Sammy. I was asleep less than an hour ago. Let a guy wake up before you throw all this at him," I tease. "My dick can only take so much blood flow at once."

Her naughty eyes glance down, and she stifles a groan when she sees how much she's affecting me. "Where's the camera in here?" Her voice is breathy and hot as fuck.

"Behind me. Back corner." I tip my head to indicate the direction.

She takes two steps to the right, and I turn with her. "So if I'm right here and your back is to the camera, then no one could see if I touched you?"

"Sammy," I warn.

"Answer me," she demands, sultry and commanding.

"Correct."

"Good." She reaches forward without hesitation and runs her hand over the bulge in my pants, stroking the outline over the thick denim a few times before sinking her hand lower and cupping my balls through my jeans.

"Fuck," I hiss. "Baby, please. This is my job."

"And whose cock is this?" she asks, one eyebrow arched and her hand firmly back on my erection.

And the power games have begun.

"It's yours, Sammy."

"That's right. And I'll touch it when I want to. I want you needy as hell for me like I am for you. I've been drenched all day thinking about what you're willing to let me do to you. I'm soaked again just thinking about it. You should feel how wet I am."

"I wish I could."

Her eyes flit to the lights above the elevator door that indicate what floor we're on. Mine do the same. One more floor to go.

Thank goodness this is a slow elevator.

"Last chance to touch me before we get there. Do it now. Feel me."

Hoping to hell no one is monitoring this camera feed, I reach forward and drag my hand up Sammy's inner thigh, under her skirt.

She lifts the cottony fabric out of the way. "Hurry, baby. Almost out of time."

The elevator grinds to a halt. A second before the doors begin opening, I dip inside her panties and draw my fingertips quickly through her pussy lips.

She wasn't lying.

Drenched.

"Turn around," she orders as she slams her legs closed and unruffles her skirt to cover herself.

Right in the nick of time.

The doors finish opening, and we walk out. I bring the small duffel containing my fresh gym clothes across my front to hide the tent I'm pitching.

This little woman will be the death of me. But what a fucking way to go.

Sammy waits in the hallway outside my office as I enter, flip on the lights, power up my computer, and throw my bag in the empty chair in the corner. I take a few seconds without her invading my space to get my cock under control, running my hands through my hair and focusing on my breathing and un-sexy things like stained Tupperware and dirty sheets.

Things that are definitely *not* bougie.

When I turn around, she's studying my movements carefully, leaning against the far wall. "Ready to do this?" she asks, a pleasant smile on her face, like she didn't turn into an experienced dominatrix less than thirty seconds ago.

"Let's get this over with. I need to get you home as soon as possible."

"Damn right you do."

As we pass by Leo's office — just a few doors down from mine — he rises and meets us in the doorway, folder and tablet tucked under his arm. "We're meeting in the conference room."

He's all business right now, firmly in command mode in Boss's absence.

We take our seats, joining the others around the table. Sammy sits to my right. Unlike the last time we were in this room discussing her case, I'll be able to comfort her. *Subtly.*

"Is he on the line?" Leo asks Tomer.

"You still there, Boss?" Tomer asks, leaning toward the speakerphone in the middle of the table.

"Affirmative. Roll call."

"Lionheart here. In the room, we've got Tomer, Sawyer, Klein, Sue, and Sammy."

"Others on the line?" Boss asks in a clipped tone.

"Shep here."

"Kri here, sir."

"This is Henderson. Jonesy is here with me too."

Big Al takes back over after a brief pause. "That's everyone. Let's get started. First up, Shep, report out on your contact with the Russian."

"As suspected, Yuri wouldn't give up much about his visit with Thomas Ian Jones. He did say Thomas goes by TI, though. Stupid name. Like he's a rapper or something. Idiot."

"Focus, Shep," Boss snaps.

"Sorry. Only thing I got from him was that it was a *typical business transaction* — which is code for an entirely new identity — and, more importantly, Tommy might not have been the only subject for said transaction."

"Did he give you a gender on the other subject or subjects he was shopping for?"

"He scratched his beard when I asked if one of the subjects was a thirty-something female with sandy blond hair. That's his tell. I think we should proceed under the assumption he was shopping for a new identity for Sammy."

Dammit. He's obsessed with my girl.

I pound my fist into the table, unable to check my simmering rage. "We need to bring this asshole in tonight, Boss."

It's possible I'm still a little butt-hurt about not bringing him in sooner. He tried to run us off the road a few nights ago. We should've gone after him by now.

"Stand down, Sawyer," Boss orders. "Let's get all the updates before we make any rash decisions."

Leo shoots me a glare, but there's warmth in his expression too. He's equally enraged.

Sammy reaches under the table and brushes her hand over the top of my thigh, giving me a calming squeeze.

Fuck. I was supposed to be comforting her, not the other way around.

Boss continues, "Kri, you're up. Current status on the tango?"

"After he left Yuri's, I trailed him back home and tracked his internet activity using the bug Tomer planted in his home Wi-Fi. He was searching for flights to Cambodia, Morocco, and Indonesia. All for this week. He didn't book any; he only scanned through like he was checking prices."

"Odd selection of countries," Sue muses, scrunching her nose.

Tomer chimes in. "None of them extradite to the US, making them attractive options for someone looking to flee the country."

"Anything else?" Boss asks.

Kri responds, "This might not be anything, but I find it odd that although he's getting new identities for more than one person, the flights he was checking were only for one traveler. Does that seem odd to anyone, or is it just me?"

"He might have been only pricing or looking at high-level options, rather than actually intending to book yet," Klein suggests.

"That's likely," Sue adds. "Those search engines usually default to one person, so he could've been too lazy to change it. Maybe he only wanted ballpark pricing until he's sure when he'll be leaving."

Boss's thick sigh crackles the phone line. "Let's move on. We've got a lot to get through. Where is he now, Kri?"

"Still at his residence. Been here for about an hour now. No one coming or going. I think he's alone. Good time to take him."

"Tomer, anything to add about the tango's internet or phone activity?"

"Yeah, Boss. A few minutes ago, he sent a text message that reads as follows: *When are we meeting and where? I'm ready to do this shit. Enough dicking me around.*"

Leo asks, "Tomer, do we know who the recipient was?"

Tomer shakes his head. "Burner phone."

"Of course it is. I could've told you that," Sammy mumbles. Her nails tap mindlessly on the table. I can't tell if it's frustration, fear, or boredom. Maybe a little of each.

"Did he get a reply yet?" Boss asks.

"Not yet."

"Keep an eye on that. It's not enough to point us anywhere yet. Could be related to this or another crime. This guy is dirty, so there's no telling what all he's involved in right now."

"Copy," Tomer responds. His fingers fly across his keyboard, doing who-knows-what.

"Klein, what's the latest with the CPD detective?" Boss asks, moving us through status reports at a decent clip.

"He called me back about an hour ago," Klein begins, looking around the room to meet the eyes of everyone in attendance as he gives his update. "They're checking on the tango's alibi for the night of Sammy's abduction. He thanked us for the tip and the photo from the other night's 'little car chase' — his words, not mine — and asked us to stay out of their investigation. He offered to send a uniformed officer to Sawyer's place to take a report about the traffic incident, but it honestly didn't sound like he was all that interested in running it down. We'll need more concrete evidence to get his attention."

"Son of a bitch." Leo spins in his chair. I suspect it's so his sister doesn't see how pissed off he is. "Did he have any updates on *his investigation*?" Leo draws it out mockingly.

"Nothing he was willing to share. You guys know the police don't have the resources we have. They're bound to be behind the eight ball on this." Klein's eyes meet Sammy's, and he offers a sympathetic expression.

"Jonesy and Henderson, are you moving into position?"

"Roger, Boss. We're five minutes out from Shep and Kri's location. We'll be there to help grab him if you give the order."

"Good. Before we decide the next steps, does anyone have any other intel to share? About our primary tango or any other suspects?"

Leo eyes us one by one. Sammy and I shake our heads. Klein does too. When Leo's gaze lands on Tomer, he nods, indicating he has other details.

"Boss, I don't see any large transaction in or out of Thomas Jones's bank account. But cash is always possible, and probable, for someone like him. As for other suspects," Tomer pauses and heaves a tired breath. "Edwin Banks is still in the state. He met with another politician today. A congressman from the fourth district."

"Why is Craig's dad meeting with so many elected officials?" Leo asks.

With my peripheral vision, I see Sammy's hand move to cup her neck.

There she goes again, always taking a defensive posture whenever the ex is mentioned. *Dammit.*

On instinct, I reach over and pull her hand away, lacing my fingers with hers in the process. Leo catches the movement, his thick brows bunching and his forehead drawing tight.

I try to smooth it over by letting go of her hand and offering a more platonic shoulder squeeze. "You okay, Sammy?" I ask, trying for as friendly as possible.

Her eyes and lips are all pinched tight, but she manages a jarring nod, the movement jerky and rushed. "Mr. Banks is probably here for a business thing. I'm sure it's nothing."

Leo shakes off my folly, either believing it to be innocent or choosing not to deal with it at this point and time. "Who's tracking down that lead? We need to know what the meeting is about."

Tomer answers, "I'd love to chase it down more, but I don't have the time. I'm only one man. I need help, Boss."

"Yeah, yeah. I know." Big Al pauses. "Klein, can you take this one?"

"What kind of leeway do I have? Want me above or below the board on this?"

"Toe the line. I don't want to get us on any politician's shitlist. Poke around with Banks Software records first. See if they're filing any expansion plans or if there's any chatter about them moving operations here. Do some cold calling, see if you get a chatty secretary or legal aid to talk."

"You got it, Boss," Klein responds. "I'll deploy my charm."

"So where does all that leave us, Boss?" I ask.

"I know you guys want to go in balls to the wall and get this fucker, but I'm still not sold on that being our best play. I think we should sit on it and keep him under surveillance. See if we can get more intel first."

My teeth clench, and my pulse spikes at his words.

Leo speaks up first, beating me to the punch. "Boss, come on! We know it was him the other night on the road chasing her down. That warrants a *visit* from us — at minimum."

"Yeah, but if you don't get anything concrete from him and we have to let him go, then there's a chance he'll get spooked and run. Then what do we have? It makes more sense to give him a little rope. Just enough to hang himself. We need to make sure CPD has enough to arrest him, not only detain him."

"Boss, you're lucky you're not here right now to see everyone's reaction," Tomer says. "Any minute the speakerphone will incinerate under the heat of the death glares being shot at it from everyone at the table."

"Even my sweet little Sammy?"

"Hell yes, even me!" Sammy yells. "And I'm not sweet at all. Especially now. If you guys don't go after him, I'll fucking do it myself."

"The hell you will," I growl, unable to hold back my rage.

At the same time, Leo huffs, "Yeah, fuck no, Sammy. That ain't happening."

Sammy stands and slams her palms on the table and burns a hole in the speaker with her glare. "Big Al, it's him. He's the one who threw me in his fucking trunk and is making plans to grab me again and drag me out of the country. I refuse to live in fucking Cambodia or some shit, and I'm sick of being a prisoner to this. Now, go and freaking get him. *Tonight*. Send in your team. Let them interrogate him and get answers. I'm sick of this bullshit. I've had enough!"

She storms out of the room, slamming the door behind her. A loud scream shakes the walls a moment later.

And it's not an "oh shit, I'm startled" type of scream. Nope. It's a scream of rage and pure frustration. I feel the same fucking way.

Sue, Leo, and I all rise at the same time, ready to go after her.

"I'll go calm her down," Sue says. "You guys stay to talk some sense into him." She nods at the speakerphone and spins on her heel without waiting for permission. Gotta admire her moxie.

"Thanks, angel," Leo calls softly behind her.

Against my better judgment, I sit down and let Sue handle my girl. I take a few calming breaths to control my anger and desperation. If I don't hold some of this inside, Leo might notice that this is more than the amount of rage for a client, my best friend's little sister, or even a good friend.

Because Sammy isn't any of those things.

She's my whole world. My everything.

"Boss, I'm begging you to authorize us to go and get him tonight. I'm done watching my sister live in fear. He went after not only her but Sawyer too. We can't let him get away with going after Redleg family like that. We're all out of patience."

Leo's going hard, using Big Al's Redleg family creed to get him on our side. It's manipulative, but I don't give a deep-fried fuck. It's also justified.

Sammy's been living in fear almost all of her life.

It's not fair.

We need to fight for her. Right now.

And even if he says no, I'm going to get Thomas Jones tonight.

"Fine. You guys win. Do it."

Variations of yes, fuck yes, and hell yes echo around the room and from the team on the line.

"Just try to keep your damn hands clean. I don't need to give the police chief any more ammo against us."

Interesting.

But also not my fucking problem. *Not my monkeys. Not my circus.*

We're going after him. That's all that matters.

Chapter Forty-Four

EVERY PARTY HAS A POOPER

Sammy

My heart may possibly beat right out of my chest. The damn organ is pounding and thumping around in there so wildly it's making me wobble unsteadily.

"We're in position. Ready to breach on your signal, T." Shep's calm and cool voice comes through the speaker loud and clear.

The sound quality is so good it's like we're there with him. And with the HD footage transmitting from his chest cam, I can see everything that he can.

We're seated in the control room — a.k.a.: Tomer's office — watching the action unfold.

Sue is seated to my left. Sawyer's on my right. Leo is pacing behind me. Klein has his laptop open and is typing away.

Tomer's got seven different screens in here.

Seven.

As in one less than eight.

Some on the wall, others on desks and stands so they are positioned vertically in front of his workstation. He has four keyboards.

Four.

He only has two hands. Why the hell does he need four freaking keyboards?

Each of the four Redleg team members taking part in the op has a chest camera live streaming to our position. Tomer has them up, two per screen, taking two of the screens with just that feed. Each screen is labeled with the team member's name, so we know who is doing what. It's hard to tell since they are all dressed in head to toe black with their faces concealed in ski masks.

Big Al is on another screen, watching on his laptop from his hotel room. I can see my mother in the background munching on popcorn like she's watching a movie.

It would be comical if this weren't a terrifying scenario.

You know what? Fuck it. It's still comical.

Another screen has a wider shot — footage from a drone outside the residence that Klein's controlling on his laptop.

Another is tracking Clearwater Police Department's 911 call tracking system. No clue how they managed to get that up, but I assume it isn't legal.

A large computer terminal or some type of server takes up one half of the wall and has tons of little lights flashing and blinking in reds, greens, and blues. He's got the temperature controls set to nipple blast levels to keep the room from overheating. I wrap my arms around myself to keep from shivering; not out of fear or nerves, but because we're approaching nipple breakage at this point. My teeth are chattering so freaking hard I'm either going to chip a filling or invent a new percussion instrument.

Sawyer notices, removes his leather jacket, and tosses it over my shoulders. I try to discreetly inhale his masculine scent from the collar without anyone noticing.

But Sue does.

Because, of course, she does.

Too damn observant, that one. She winks at me, and her lip quirks, but she stays quiet.

As the recent days have progressed, she's asked more and more questions about Sawyer. It's like she's been testing me systematically to see if I'll break and confirm her suspicions.

Three times today, I almost said *fuck it* and told her we were screwing.

Tomer looks at yet another screen before answering Shep. "Heat sensors show only one tango inside. No incoming or outgoing phone calls or alarms have been raised. Good to go from my end. Mission is cleared to proceed on Shep's signal."

Each operative draws their weapon.

"Breach in five, four, three, two —" Shep doesn't say the *one*, but they all spring into action.

Everything happens in a flash. Shep and Henderson kick in the front door while Kri kicks in the back door. Jonesy is positioned by the side of the house in case he tries to escape through the window.

A loud bang causes me to recoil from the monitors as a series of three flashes temporarily blind me and the cameras, making it impossible to see what's happening.

A lot of grunting and yelling happens in a very short amount of time.

"Why can't we see?" I panic, pointing at the chest cam screens filled with grainy images and smoke.

Wait. Smoke?

"Is it on fire? Was that an explosion?" I yell.

Leo grabs my shoulder. "Not a fire. Everything is good so far. Relax."

I turn to Sawyer, and he looks equally calm.

He adds quietly, "It was just a few flash-bangs. We set those off. Smoke bombs and flashes of light to disorient the enemy so he can't fight back."

"Oh, okay. Good."

"I've got him. Tango secured."

As the smoke clears, I see Shep has a man — presumably my douchebag kidnapper — face down on the carpet and is tying his hands at his back and covering his head with a black sack.

"Zone one clear," Kri yells.

"Zone two clear," Henderson yells.

"Perimeter secure," Jonesy adds. "I'll get the SUV."

"Any 911 calls, Tomer?" Big Al asks. His broad arms are folded across his chest as he studies the screen in front of him.

"Nothing yet, Boss," Tomer answers.

Big Al nods. Behind him, my mom picks up the microwave popcorn bag to her mouth and tilts it back, emptying the contents down her throat.

Seeing that there are no casualties and everything went beautifully, I go ahead and let myself laugh at the absurdity of my mother inhaling popcorn while she watches the *show*. My laugh turns into a snort when she picks up a bottle of wine and refills her glass, emptying the bottle and shaking out every last drop.

I guess the wino didn't fall far from the fermented grape tree.

"You can't arrest me. I didn't do anything," the shithead sputters at Shep as he hefts him to his feet and parades him out of his little shack.

"Oh, you're not under arrest. Not yet, anyhow."

Thomas — the kidnapper, not the train — whips his head around inside the bag, probably trying to look around to see who's capturing him.

"You're not cops. Who the fuck are you?"

"Shut the fuck up before I knock you out." Shep shoves him into the back of the SUV Jonesy has pulled up in.

Two other team members join him in the vehicle.

Kri's camera shows her running to the other SUV to follow behind them.

The entire thing took less than five minutes.

Maybe even three minutes.

"Team is en route to HQ with the target acquired." Tomer looks from screen to screen, then adds, "Still no 911 calls. Looks like no one gives a shit about their neighbors out there."

Big Al replies, "Given the shitty neighborhood, they're likely used to gunshots, loud bangs, and other general fuckery late at night. Just get him back to base. Call me when they arrive so I can watch the interrogation. I'm taking a bio break."

"Ten-four, Boss."

Big Al's screen goes dark. Everyone in the room takes a collective breath. The drone footage screen goes blank as Klein disconnects.

"That went well, right?" I ask no one in particular, feeling optimistic.

"Textbook," Leo answers.

Sawyer uncrosses his arms and stands, giving my shoulder a squeeze as he says, "In and out without law enforcement being called. No shots fired. No injuries. Perp didn't have time to set off any alarms to alert anyone he may be working with. Couldn't have gone better."

Klein rears back, cups his hands over his mouth and hollers, "Red-leg. Red-leg." It sounds like a cheer or chant in the deep timbre of a military drill instructor.

Sawyer, Leo, and Tomer each answer his call, chanting *Red-leg* back in the same manner.

"I forgot you guys are cheerleaders as well as former military operatives," I joke.

"Just one of our many talents," Klein answers with a chuckle.

I look around the room where everyone begins to stir and inch closer to the door. "Well, what happens next?"

"They'll be back in about..." Tomer pauses to glance at the screen, then his watch. "Fourteen minutes. Is the room ready, Lionheart?"

"Yeah, but I think I should put down a tarp," Leo mutters darkly.

"For what?" Sue asks.

Oh, this innocent, sweet summer child.

Leo stammers through his reply, trying to downplay the violence he's about to administer to my assailant. "It was just a bad joke about needing to protect the floor from his..." He looks to the ceiling, searching for the word.

"Blood," I finish for him flatly.

Sue's head jerks back, and her mouth falls open. "Leo Mason, are you guys going to," she bends forward and whispers, "torture him?"

"Well, they aren't bringing him here to play cards, Susie Q," I deadpan.

Sue looks positively scandalized. If she had pearls, I think she'd clutch them in horror.

"Angel, it won't be that bad."

"Won't it, though?" I ask, happily stirring the pot. I make a fist and punch it into my other palm a few times, plastering a menacing look on my face.

With that fucker off the streets and in Redleg custody, a freeing sense of excitement runs through my veins, making me nearly giddy.

"Oh my shit biscuits! You motherfeckers!" Sue yells at a volume far louder than necessary once she finally understands the rest of the plan.

Honestly, though. What did she think they were going to do once they captured him?

Sawyer attempts to calm her down, balancing out my havoc-causing attempts. *Party pooper.* "Sue, we're only gonna rough him up a little. Not waterboard him or anything. And who knows, he might be scared enough that he'll start talking as soon as he gets here."

Her face falls. "So you're *not* planning on torturing him?"

"Not officially," Leo answers.

"Why not?" she whines, her lip sticking out in a full pout.

I'm getting whiplash from this conversation.

Klein and Sawyer snicker as they head to the door.

As they leave, Klein tosses, "We're going to go get ready. Leo, you can join us when you're done tap-dancing around this... whatever is happening here."

Leo takes Sue down the hall, effectively ending the show and leaving me with Tomer.

"Why do they call you Tomer if your name is actually Chuck?" I ask, tipping my head to the sign on his door.

"Fuck my life," he says with a groan.

I leave his office with a wide grin playing on my cheeks. I know the story behind the sign.

Rage monster, you can take a seat. Shit-disturbing Sammy is officially in charge.

As she should be.

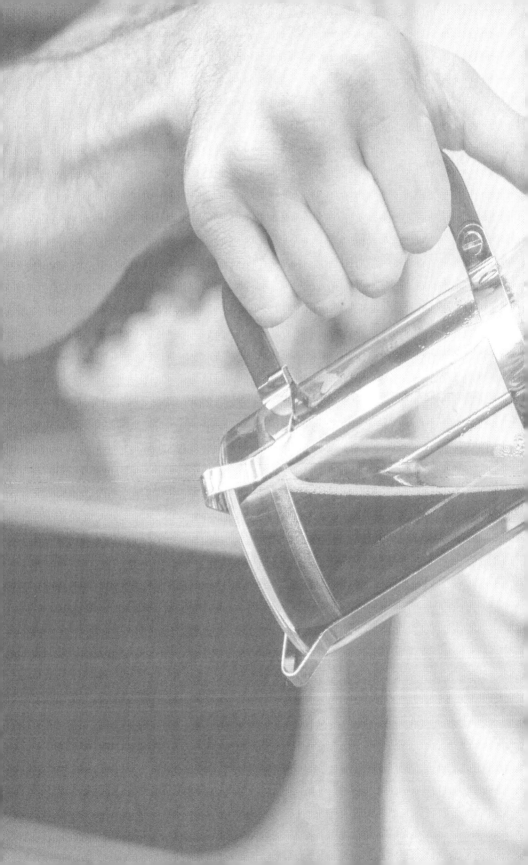

Chapter Forty-Five

IT'S NOT UNUSUAL

Sawyer

"Why are your knuckles already banged up? Isn't that supposed to happen after we have our little chin wag with *Thomas*?"

Klein keeps using the British pronunciation, making it sound something like *Tomas*.

I swear to Buddha, these fuckers need to leave the accents to the professional.

Even with his hack job of arguably the easiest accent to pull off, I manage a slight chuckle.

"You saw me going hard at the bag the other day. Gotta keep the hands in fighting shape, you know?"

He leans close, lowering his voice. "Speaking of which, what was that all about?"

"What was what all about?"

"Your rage session in the gym. I've seen you go hard before, but that was a new level." He grimaces like he's recalling something painful. "It totally cemented my decision to never spar with you again, though. I can tell you that much."

Standing on a stool, I finish adjusting the camera's angle. We placed it up in the corner of the room to make sure Big Al and whoever else is watching gets a good view of whatever is about to go down in here.

Sammy said she intends to watch from the control room. I'm not thrilled with the idea, but she's a big girl capable of making her own decisions. I expressed my concerns to her — as did her brother — but ultimately, she's the one this guy kidnapped. So she's entitled to see us pump him for information. Kri, Jonesy, and Tomer will keep her company, and I'm sure they'll get her out of there if things go wrong or she gets upset. I trust them to look out for her. Whether Sue stays to watch or hangs out in her office wasn't yet decided, the last I heard.

Once the camera is positioned to my liking, I step off the chair and put it back in the center of the room. Tomer can turn the camera on and start recording remotely once our guest of honor arrives.

We're going with the cliché solo chair in the center of the room approach. Too bad this interrogation isn't taking place in a dark, dank basement with a lone light bulb hanging down over the chair, exposed wiring and rafters, and an electric shock machine nearby. But we're at Redleg HQ, not in some shit hole.

Besides, we don't have basements in Florida.

Big Al should've built a soundproof, concrete-lined interrogation room when he had this place constructed. With a drain in the center of the floor for easy clean-up. I think I'll put that in the suggestion box. Never too late for an upgrade.

We're using an empty office and have removed any identifiable items from the room so he doesn't have anything to focus on except plain white walls. We don't want him to be able to describe anything to law enforcement that might tie back to Redleg.

I'm sure he'll know it's us — especially if he's been watching Sammy like we think he has been or done even a modicum of research on her whatsoever — but knowing and being able to prove it are two different things.

"Not sure it was all *that* intense," I lie to Klein about my session in the gym earlier this week. He's right. I unleashed the beast in there. And it felt unbelievably good.

I continue with my bullshit downplaying. "But I *am* a bit on edge about this case. I don't like it when my friends are threatened."

Friends.

Sammy — as a mere friend. *Ha.* What a joke. Hysterical.

Cue internal eye roll.

"Is that *all* that's wrong? It's okay, man. You can tell me the truth. Get it off your chest. It can't feel good to hold that in. I won't tell Leo." He taps the back of his hand against my chest, over my heart.

Swallowing a lump down my throat, I glance over my shoulder and notice that Leo isn't in here yet. He's waiting at the back door of the facility for them to arrive. The team should be getting here any minute with that sick fuck who's about to become personally acquainted with my fists.

"Tell Leo what?" I hedge.

I pull the balaclava from my back pocket and pull it over my head, leaving my face exposed for the time being. Klein does the same. Once they get here, we'll pull them down so the fucker can't identify us. We're wearing long sleeves and pants to cover our skin so he can't spot any tattoos. I don't have any visible ink, but my brothers sure do. Kri does too.

"About you and his sister. I'm not blind."

I'm so tired of lying about this. Keeping this secret is utterly exhausting.

"And what do you think you see?"

It's one last attempt to stall long enough for Leo and the guys to arrive with Tommy Boy. If they hurry the hell up, I might be able to get out of this conversation without perjuring myself.

A-fucking-gain.

"The sparks and shit. The tension. The way you look at each other. How you're always inching closer. The little touches here and there."

I'm not sure what to say without lying or admitting it, so I remain silent for another moment.

If anyone needs me, I'll be over here, praying for a sinkhole to swallow me.

He continues, "And you were hanging out in the hallway talking to her for a long time the other morning when you left the gym. I couldn't see your expression, but the look on her face said it all."

"Are we *that* obvious?"

A small weight breaks away from my chest at the near confession.

"You sure are to me. I bet Leo sees it too. You'd be better off telling him directly rather than forcing him to beat it out of you."

He checks the doorway, sticking his head into the hall and coming back to level me with the final death blow. "Even if it's not obvious to everyone else, you're going to slip up." He casts a glare at me and adds, "Again."

"Slip up?"

Shit. Shit. Shit.

While he slides on his gloves, he subtly shakes his head at me, looking a lot like a disapproving dad — or what I suppose a dad would look like. "You must have forgotten we have microphones in the elevators."

Instantly, my cheeks heat as the implications sink in. "Oh fuck."

A jolt of embarrassment zaps through my veins. Not only because we were doing inappropriate shit, but she was also talking about restraining me. *Dominating* me.

I probably should feel a little emasculated in front of my friend. The way she talked to me. The naughty shit she said and *how* she said it. That velvety tone when her dominant side comes to the surface.

I'm the man. I'm supposed to be the one in control. Right?

Nah. Fuck that. A real man will happily bend the knee for his queen. I'm man enough to realize I'm lucky to have the *privilege* of being her man. Of being inside her body. Of bringing her pleasure. Even if that pleasure is given differently from how most men may think it should be given.

Klein knowing this honestly doesn't bother me. I'm *more* troubled by the fact that he likely heard her talking about her trauma and how she's coping with it.

That's her story to tell.

The urge to protect her privacy quickly becomes the prevailing emotion bubbling up from deep inside me.

Klein must sense my rising ire. "Don't worry. I took care of it. I was popping around this evening before the op, doing some maintenance on the feeds. I purged it for you. And I didn't listen too much. Once I saw where it was going, I clicked off and deleted it. I doubt anyone else saw it either. It was too recent, and Tomer's had his hands full with everything."

"Thank you," I mutter, unable to meet his eyes.

"No sweat. I got you. Rangers for life, remember?" He holds out his fist for a bump.

As our knuckles touch through the fabric of our gloves, I glance at him and see genuine understanding reflecting at me.

He's a solid man. From good stock.

"Seriously, though. Talk to Leo," he urges, his voice laced with sincerity.

"I will. *Soon.* I want to put this case behind us first."

"Okay, be careful in the meantime. She's been through a lot. And Leo..." He trails off with a headshake.

I feel my forehead pinch. If he thinks for one moment that my intentions are less than honorable with her... "I won't hurt her." I clear my throat and add, "I'd rather die than cause her pain."

A sad smile softens his face. "That's not what I meant."

"What did you mean?"

"She and Leo. All that history. You don't want to make it worse or drive a wedge between them. Or with you and him. I'm worried about all of you. That's all I'm saying."

"I'm aware of the stakes. Let's just hope we can end this tonight so it's no longer an issue."

"Fair enough."

Before the silence stretches too long, a commotion echoes from the end of the hall. With a nod, Klein and I simultaneously pull down our masks and slip on dark sunglasses, fully shielding our heads.

Thomas Ian Jones is here, and he's not happy about it, judging by the slew of curse words flying out of his trap.

Why the hell didn't they gag him?

And does he truly think he can out-cuss this many former soldiers? Think again, cocksucker.

Klein and I step into the hallway to observe the approaching processional. No grand marshal for this parade. Just one human equivalent of weaponized diarrhea being escorted by a handful of Redleg's finest.

Even though he's also covered from head to toe to conceal his identity, I can easily tell it's Leo towering over him from behind. He's got a death grip on the fuckface while shoving him down the hall. My man's gloved hand is so freaking big it nearly encircles the scumbag's entire neck. Sadly, it's not quite large enough to conceal that pathetic excuse for a tattoo over his throat.

What a douche.

My nostrils flare, and my jaw clenches when I finally see him in the flesh. The asshole is barefoot and has pasty white skin on a lanky frame, utterly unimpressive by any stretch of the imagination. Baggy jeans hang low on his boney hips, and he's wearing a stained Pearl Jam T-shirt — which should be a crime against the band. Surprised CPD didn't arrest him on that basis alone.

Leo brushes past us and slams the perp into the chair. Shep and Henderson trail behind him, joining us in the room. When we remove the sack from his head, he'll be staring down five big-ass men dressed in head-to-toe black tactical gear. Should be intimidating as hell.

"Fuck, man! My arms!" he whines.

"Oh, sorry. Did that hurt?" Leo seethes with a menacing quality to his deep timbre. "Let me fix that for you." He reaches around the back of the chair, grabbing his arms and bending them upward, just shy of dislocating them from the shoulder. He settles his bound wrists and arms on the chair's back at an unnatural angle.

Nice.

"Ow! Ow! Fuck you, asshole!"

Shep kneels down and uses thick zip ties to secure his ankles to the chair legs, pulling his feet a few inches off the floor with toes pointed. In that position, his legs won't be able to get any purchase. It's also uncomfortable as fuck.

"Let me help you with your seat, Tommy Boy," I add, grabbing the chair and tilting it forward at an angle. With his arms wrapped around the chairback and his ankles bound to the legs, his entire body weight is now tugging on his restraints. I've been in this hold before, and it hurts like hell. Makes your shoulders and elbows feel like they're about to burst.

He whines, cussing me out for a few moments before I get bored and set the chair back down.

His breath is ragged as he settles and tries to straighten himself in the chair. "What the fuck do you assholes want? Who are you? Why are you hiding my eyes? Fucking cowards!"

Leo yanks the bag off his head, and the asshole blinks and cringes as his eyes adjust to the bright fluorescents.

He's an ugly fucker. Short, cropped hair with bleach-blond tips poking out of dark roots, like he's Eminem circa 1999. If ever a face was made for punching, it's this fucking one.

He's bleeding from his lip and cheek, but that's what happens when you get unceremoniously escorted out of your house by a special ops team after you attack their family.

Don't mess with the bull if you don't want to get the horns.

Yeah, I just quoted the asshole principal from The Breakfast Club. *What are you gonna do about it?*

He sputters and spits out a gob of blood at Shep's foot. Without hesitating, Shep smacks him across the face. Hard. An open-palm, full-face, bitch slap.

It's more demeaning than a punch.

Glad the mask is hiding my face; otherwise, everyone would see something resembling glee. A cheesy grin certainly isn't menacing, and we need to be terrifying right now.

"We just had these floors cleaned. Be respectful, asshole," Shep chides him.

Henderson can't hold back a slight chuckle. Leo gives him the stink eye. Can't see it behind his glasses, but I know it's there.

Tommy tries again to get answers from us. "You assholes have no idea who you're fucking with. What do you even want from me?"

Leo folds his six-foot-five frame in half and gets right in his face. "I suppose we could tell you, but where's the fun in that?"

"My boys are gonna come for me, and I ain't telling you shit. So you can fuck off!"

Leo stands, rising to his full height. Calmly, he looks around the room and says, "Well, you heard him, boys. He's not going to tell us anything. Guess we should let him go. Who has a knife to cut his bindings?"

"Oh, I've got a knife right here." Bending down to get down at his level, I pull out my KA-BAR and wave it in front of Tommy's ugly face, then draw the tip across his neck, right along the outline of that stupid tattoo. He gulps when I press it into his flesh, just enough for him to feel the bite of the blade.

The mind games are sometimes worse on the captive than inflicting actual pain. This is merely the tip of the iceberg, or the tip of the blade, in this case.

"You know, on second thought, let's keep him until he changes his tune," Leo says, tapping my shoulder. "He seems like a good guy. I'm sure he'll feel more talkative if we give him some time to think."

I stand and sheathe my knife.

"We'll be back later, Tommy Boy," I say as we all file out of the room, slamming the door behind us. "Enjoy the music while we're gone."

Before we're more than two steps from the door, I hear the song I asked Tomer to play blaring from the built-in speaker system. My teammates bust out with raucous laughter as Tom Jones's "It's Not Unusual" starts to wail at max volume.

For the first round, we're giving him an hour to stew. It's going to repeat until we go back in.

An hour of "It's Not Unusual" at full volume with no way to escape? That ought to do it. He'll be singing like a canary in no time.

Chapter Forty-Six

WHAT'S NEW, PUSSYCAT?

Sammy

"You didn't ask him a single question!" The second my brother strolls into the control room, I'm up in his grill. His black ski mask is pulled up so I can see his annoying face. "Why are you in here? Go ask him if he's working alone or why he did it or whatever the fuck you're going to ask him!"

What in the actual shitastrophe is happening right now?

I saw only *minimal* roughhousing and absolutely zero questioning. Hell, I was roughed up more than him. What kind of shitty excuse for an interrogation was that? I thought these Redleg guys were supposed to be badasses.

Leo puts his Sasquatch hands on my shoulders. "Easy, kid. You don't fire away right off the bat. There's a method to this. You've got to break them down and get in their heads, little by little. Extracting information is a long game. This might take a while. Just relax. Get comfortable. We might be here all night."

Patience is a virtue, but I've never claimed to be especially virtuous.

Sticking my chin out, I cross my arms over my chest. "Can I go talk to him?"

"No," Leo answers first, not even giving it a moment of thought.

I look at Sawyer, hoping he'll back me up.

Frowning, he makes a brisk slashing motion with one hand. "Absolutely not."

"So I'm just supposed to sit here while you guys torture him with shitty music?"

Klein looks offended. "Hey! Watch your mouth, young lady. Tom Jones is a music legend, and I will not allow anyone to besmirch his good name in my presence. In fact, he's been knighted. So to be more precise, *Sir* Tom Jones is a legend."

"Wait. Tom Jones? Isn't that the..."

The shitbag's name is Thomas Ian Jones. And now they're blaring *Sir* Tom Jones's music at full volume.

I face palm as a giggle I'm powerless to stop bubbles from my chest. Chuckles bounce around the room, joining me. I'm not sure if they're laughing at me because I was so slow on the uptake or if they just now realize the bad guy's name is the same as the Vegas legend. Probably the former.

Klein busts out with a top-tier Carlton from *Fresh Prince* impression, side-stepping back and forth wildly and whooshing his hands around while snapping his fingers to an imaginary beat. "It's not unusual to be loved by anyone," he sings as he dances awkwardly. "It's not unusual to have fun with anyone."

Chuckling at the spectacle, Leo gives him a playful shove, catching him off balance. Klein stumbles into an empty desk chair, knocking it to the floor and nearly falling ass-up in the process. Anyone who wasn't already laughing at the Carlton impression is now cracked up at the spectacle of Klein slipping around the room like a cat trying to bury a turd on a frozen pond.

Kri stands up beside me. She's the only one in the room who isn't even slightly amused. "Are you guys done having your fun? We have a mission."

Shep takes a step in her direction. "We're just easing the tension, Kri. Calm down." He palms her shoulder, giving it a light squeeze.

With the precision and speed of a ninja, she twists out of his hold, grabs his wrist, and bends his arm behind his back in the blink of an eye. "I warned you about that shit. Didn't I?" When he doesn't answer, she increases the intensity of her hold, making him whine a little. "What did I tell you?"

My eyes go wide, and I take a large step back, giving her space.

Half smiling, half grimacing now, he pants out his reply. "You told me not to tell you to calm down."

"That's right. Don't forget it." She gives his arm a final pulse before releasing and shoving him forward.

Yep. I'm totally attracted to her. One hundo percent.

Shep staggers for a step before straightening himself, shaking out his arm, and smoothing his shirt. "Well, that was fun."

Big Al's deep disembodied voice makes me flinch. "That's enough, assholes. Listen up."

Everyone in the room turns to face one of the screens to see their boss watching on with a look of annoyance. My mom's still in the background. No popcorn or wine this time, which is slightly disappointing.

But I do find it interesting that Big Al's letting her watch all this. I assume she's about to see her *little* boy roughing up the shitbag soon since Big Al plans to watch on his laptop. As protective as these guys are, I'm surprised she's not being sheltered more. I'd have thought she'd be more reluctant to witness this violence, but she appears to be taking it all in stride.

And hold up. Are they sharing a hotel room? I only see one bed.

Big Al starts barking orders at his team, shaking me from my rogue thoughts. Next thing I know, the guys are filing out, and it's only Kri and me up here with Tomer. Jonesy left for the night, and Sue's in her office, having opted not to watch.

Kri heaves a frustrated sigh as she props her booted foot on an empty chair.

"What's the matter?" I ask.

She shakes her head despondently but doesn't answer. From the tight set of her jaw and the crinkle of skin at the corners of her eyes, she's not just upset, she's full of bottled rage.

The rage monster inside me knows that look quite well. Game recognizing game.

"Come on. Talk to me," I encourage, giving her a little nudge with my shoulder.

"Sick and fucking tired of being treated like a flower because I have boobs."

"They seem to respect you, from what I can see."

"Oh yeah? Then why am I up here instead of down there?" She tilts her head at the screen where a few guys are entering the interrogation room.

"Did they not give you a choice?"

"Nope." She pops the *P* sound and then mashes her lips into a straight line while wobbling her chin from side to side.

"Did Big Al make that call?"

"Yes and no. Your brother proposed the game plan, and Big Al gave it the green light."

"On behalf of my brother, I'm sorry. He can be annoyingly overprotective of the women he cares about. And I think he cares about you."

Her head slants, bringing her eyes to meet mine. "Why do you say that?"

With a loose shrug, I answer, "It's just the vibe I get. He speaks fondly of you, and I've heard him brag about your background before."

She harrumphs and glances back at the screen. My attention shifts back to the unfolding action. The music has stopped, and the guys are circling Tommy, arms crossed over their broad chests.

"What's new, pussycat?" Sawyer asks while ruffling Tommy's hair mockingly.

Silent laughter at the repeated *Sir* Tom Jones references shakes my shoulders. Kri shakes her head, and when I glance at her, she's rolling her eyes.

Leo's towering over Tommy now, so he's forced to look up. *Way* up.

My brother's a big dude, and Tommy is on the smaller side. So he's got to feel seriously intimidated in there.

Leo's voice is rougher than usual when he says, "Okay, Tom, you and I are going to have a little chat. I'm going to ask you some questions, and you'll give me some answers. If you don't, my friends here will make things extremely unpleasant for you. And if you lie, it'll get even worse. You get me?"

"Fuck off!"

"Well, we're not off to a good start," Leo says, then nods at Shep.

Shep swiftly gives Tommy a quick series of punches to the gut, knocking the wind out of him. A tiny thrill spikes through me at the sight of him doubled over in pain.

When he's finally able to sit up fully, Leo asks his first questions. "Why did you take Samantha Mason? What do you want with her?"

"I don't know no bitch by that name."

Klein punches him in the face this time. Tommy's head whips back quickly, and an evil smile falls across his face.

"Why did you take Samantha Mason?" Leo asks again, his voice remaining calm and steady.

"Don't know any Samantha. Sounds like a nice piece of ass, though."

From the edge of the screen, I see Shep pull a plastic bag out of his back pocket.

"What's he going to do with that?" I ask Kri while pointing at Shep.

"Probably smother him; cut off his air supply. Works wonders for assholes who don't seem to react to getting a beating."

Instead of going right to smothering him, Shep makes sure Tommy can see the bag while Klein punches Tommy's other cheek.

This time, when his head whips back around, he has to spit out a mouthful of blood.

"Samantha Mason. The waitress at the Sassy Parrot who you couldn't take your eyes off. We have you on camera watching her. She's blond. About this tall." Leo holds his hand in front of him, indicating my approximate height. "Does that refresh your memory? What do you want with her?"

"Oh her? She looked like she'd be a good fuck is all."

Sawyer swiftly steps in and socks him repeatedly in the gut, pummeling him with punch after punch, alternating from the side of his torso to the center.

It was satisfying to see the other guys taking shots at Tommy, but watching Sawyer doing it right after the asshole insulted me fills me with an arousing sense of delight.

That's my man. Defending my honor.

Not a very feminist notion to enjoy that so much, but it's sexy as hell nonetheless.

When Sawyer stops, he pulls back and sucks in a deep breath, shakes out his arms, and paces in the corner. He looks like he's forcing himself to stay calm.

It takes a few seconds longer for Tommy to bounce back this time, but he finally does.

"That wasn't a very nice thing to say about a lady," Leo chastises him. Again, his voice has a steely calmness that's even more frightening than if he were screaming at him. "Now, we know you know who she is. Tell me why you kidnapped her."

"I didn't take any bitch."

Leo nods at Shep, who moves behind Tommy and covers his entire head with the plastic bag, cinching it below his neck. As Tommy inhales, the bag adheres to his face, and you can see the clear outline of his nose and open mouth.

After a few seconds of watching him struggle, battling helplessly for air,

I have to turn away. As much as I want to see him suffer, I don't think I can take seeing this.

When the sound of deep gasping breaths reaches my ears, I glance back at the screen to see Shep has removed the bag, and Tommy's head is slumped as he sucks in ragged breaths.

"Why did you kidnap her?" Leo asks again.

Still struggling for air, he rasps, "I don't know what you're talking about. All I did was watch her. At the bar."

"Stop fucking lying," Leo yells, for the first time losing his cool.

Shep moves back in with the bag, and I turn away.

They repeat this process over and over. He refuses to admit to kidnapping me each time. My stomach churns as the beatings and smothering continue. Tommy's moans and cries get louder and more pained with each attempt.

"This is getting hard to watch," I mutter to Kri.

"You need to step out?" she asks.

"No. I'm okay for now."

"Just remember why they're doing it. They aren't bad people for doing this. It's a necessary evil. He's not a good person. He's barely a human. More like a monster. Remember that. It might help."

Nodding, I try to control the acid bubbling in my stomach with deep breaths while I let her words sink in.

She wraps one arm around my shoulder and pulls me to her side, offering comfort.

Mmm. She smells good.

Am I a lesbian?

Wait. No, that can't be right since I love dick. Sawyer's dick in particular.

Am I bisexual? Or maybe bisexual for Kri? Is that even a thing?

I shake my head to clear the insanity and brush off my girl crush. I pull out of her hold and offer a slight smile.

I think my mind is messing with me and trying to shield me from the violence getting more intense by the second.

"Fine. Fuck! Stop with that bag, and I'll tell you." Tommy's loud breaths echo around the room. "I was taking her away to fuck her. I was gonna tie her up, put a knife to her neck, and fuck her until she was raw. Maybe even make her bleed a little for me." My eyes pop back to the screen and bulge at his crass words. "I was gonna have a few days of fun with her."

"Fun? Raping her at knifepoint would be fun?" Sawyer yells. "You sick fuck!" He backhands him, then brings him into a headlock, cutting off his airway again.

My eyes are glued to the screen. Sawyer has lost it. He's not calm or cool like the rest of the guys. Leo's body language is rigid, but he's not screaming and rage choking him.

I want to go to Sawyer. Hold him. Calm him. Reassure him that I'm okay because Tommy didn't do any of those things to me. I got away.

"Fuck," Kri mutters.

"That's not part of the plan," Tomer adds.

Tommy's face turns purple before Shep and Klein have to pull Sawyer off him.

"Get him out of here!" Leo yells, pointing toward the door.

"No, I'm fine. I'm okay," Sawyer says in a huff as he shrugs out of Klein and Shep's hold. "I'm good. I'm under control."

"If he loses it again, I want him out of there," Big Al tells Tomer over the video call. "We don't need a dead body on our hands, even if this sick fuck deserves to die."

"Well, now they have a little good cop, bad cop thing happening. It might work to our strategic advantage," Tomer muses.

"What advantage do we need? He admitted it," I say. "Didn't we get what we needed?"

Kri responds to me quietly while keeping her eyes on the screen where the interrogation has resumed. "Not yet. His story doesn't add up. If this were only an attempted abduction to rape you, he'd have moved on by now. Rapists don't like victims who fight back or have protection. But he didn't give up. He went after you again when you were with your armed body-guard. That doesn't make sense. He's still hiding something."

"Well, regardless, they got a confession from him. Isn't this video enough for CPD to have him arrested for kidnapping and attempted rape so we can put this behind us? I want my life back."

"You think a video of him confessing under duress is admissible in court? Not a chance. Plus, we can't turn this over to the authorities. We're breaking like seven laws right now."

"Then why are we even doing this? It's pointless."

A wave of dejected hostility simmers in my gut as I throw myself back into my chair, my head falling backward.

Great. I've been reduced to pouting and throwing a tantrum. Excellent.

The guys clear the room a few minutes later, having gotten nothing else out of him. The building security footage on one of Tomer's screens shows them heading to the break room to rest and regroup.

Tomer blasts the music again in the room, but he's muted it for us. We're left sitting in silence for twenty minutes. Kri alternates between pacing the floor and flipping through her phone. I try to do the same, but I can't focus on the images on my screen.

As each second ticks by, my mind wanders to darker times. Painful and sickening thoughts multiply, coming faster and faster. I press my eyes closed to try to envision something lighter, but when I do, I'm involuntarily whisked back to memories of when I was with Craig.

Not being able to leave.

Not being able to make my own decisions.

Tied and at his mercy.

Forcing my eyes open, I shake the thoughts away.

I'm safe. I'm at Redleg. I'm not a prisoner.

If that's true, then why does it feel so similar?

I fidget with the zipper on Sawyer's jacket, trying to distract myself from the harsh emotions brewing up from my gut to my throat.

I'm tied up.

I can't leave.

I'm a prisoner.

When the guys head back for round three, my jaw and teeth ache from all the clenching, and my stomach swirls. My rage monster has gone silent — even she's afraid of these feelings overcoming my senses.

I want to go home.

I want to leave.

I'm done watching this.

I need a drink and a warm bath.

What else do they expect to get from him? He's a thug who got a wild hair up his ass and a hard-on for me for some sick reason. We should be done here.

I should be free to leave. To make decisions for myself.

Enough violence. Enough engaging with a sick fuck like him. He's human filth and not worthy of another moment of our time.

Rising, I shrug off Sawyer's jacket and head for the hallway, shaking my hands at my sides. Kri glances over and sees me frantically running my hands through my hair. She strolls to my side.

"You okay?" she asks.

"No. I want to leave. *Now*. Will you take me home? I can't be here anymore."

She studies me cautiously, likely seeing the exhaustion written all over my face. "I don't think I'm supposed to."

My pulse is spiking, my chest is tight, and my stomach is about to retch. The panic inside me has far surpassed the rage, and that's a tall order. I could read my list of good things ten dozen times, fill up my rage list five times over, and still *need* to leave.

My breaths grow shallow, and I raise my hand to my neck as if I can open my windpipe. "Kri, please. I'm begging you. I can't be here anymore. I'm going to lose it."

She puts her hands on my arms and steadies me. "Just calm down and breathe. You don't have to watch what's going on in there. You can sit with Sue."

A fresh wave of anger comes over me at her words. I'm trapped. I step back and yell without even thinking about who can hear me. "Fuck that. I *need* to leave. I feel like a prisoner here! The goddamn walls are closing in on me."

"We shouldn't go alone. It's not safe. But there's no one else free to go with us right now. Wait until the guys come back out, and we'll grab one of them."

No. Now. I need to leave now. What part of feeling the walls close in isn't she getting?

I hate to do this, but I think I have to hit her with some manipulation. I'm desperate to get out of here at any cost. It's self-preservation at this point.

"My fucking admitted kidnapper is here. He can't come after me while he's being bludgeoned here, now can he? And you're a badass bodyguard. We'll be fine. I need to leave now. *Please*."

Her face morphs into concern. I can see her resolve weakening, so I go in for the kill. "It's not like you're needed here since they won't let you take part in the interrogation. Fuck them. Let's go. *Please, Kri.*"

Wordlessly, she raises her chin and marches back into the control room with a hitch of cockiness in her stride.

"Boss, I'm taking Sammy home. I'll stay with her for the night. She can't watch this anymore. It's upsetting her."

"Take another guard with you," Big Al orders.

Kri grits her teeth. "Boss, I'm perfectly capable of guarding one woman in her home. A home where all the Redleg security measures are installed. Especially when the person who's been targeting her is in our custody. We'll be fine." She adds a little dig. "It's not like you need me here for anything, anyhow."

She turns to Tomer. "I'll message when we're safe in her home so no one gets their panties in a twist."

To me, she says, "Let's go. Get your shit."

Wearing a forced neutral expression, I grab my purse and follow her from the room.

"Sexist fuckers," Kri mutters when she mashes the button repeatedly with enough force to break it.

"Thanks. I owe you," I mutter quietly while we wait for the elevator.

"When we get to your place, you can repay me by telling me what's really going on between you and Sawyer."

Oh shit. I walked right into a trap.

Chapter Forty-Seven

TOENAILS ARE OVERRATED ANYHOW

Sawyer

Closing my eyes, I visualize myself alone with Sammy as I try to channel a sense of calm into my body so this rage doesn't overtake me, leaving me benched and unable to finish the mission.

I tell myself we're safe in my bed, and her body is tucked close to mine. She's safe. Protected. Loved. Unharmed.

I've got her.

She's not hurt.

He didn't get to do those horrible things to her.

Over and again, I attempt to force these pleasant thoughts through my mind. Her laugh. Her vibrant blue eyes. Her devious grin when she's stirring the pot. The peace she brings me with her touch.

Unfortunately, it's not working.

Something tells me she's not safe. The visions start soothing but quickly turn violent. Mentally, I'm whisked back to our time in the smash place. Only this time, it's me losing my shit and *Hulk-smashing* everything in the room.

I've never wanted to kill someone as badly as I did a few minutes ago. Not even when Sammy was face to face with Craig Banks in that prison.

My regret over not killing her abusive ex when I had the chance may have clouded my vision. It's like I took all my guilt and funneled it into squeezing every last breath out of Thomas Jones for attempting to harm her in that horrific manner.

"Time for round five," Shep says, tapping his knuckles on the break room table, then rising.

The other guys join him, but I remain seated, trying to still my racing heart before I have to face him again.

"Want to sit this one out?" Leo asks.

I shift my shoulders back, stiffening my spine as I rise to my full height. "Nope. I'm good."

He studies me with a critical eye, but I press on, hoping to avoid him figuring out why I'm acting out of character.

"I thought I'd be the one going off the rails tonight," Leo mutters, mostly to himself. Louder now, he adds, "If I didn't know better..."

He lets that sit there, heavy in the air between us.

"Your sister is important." I choke on the words *to me*, stopping them before I end up incriminating myself. "Let's go finish this shit."

I march quickly ahead of him, my long strides eating up the hallway. When we enter, Shep's already got a pair of pliers in his hand, taunting the shitbag with toenail removal.

A little dark but necessary.

His little toenail is half off when he finally admits to being hired by someone to grab Sammy and hold her for him.

"A name. Give me a name!" Leo demands.

He sputters, trying to hold back the words, but breaks when Shep yanks the nail the rest of the way off.

"I didn't get his name. I swear. I'm not sure who he is. I just know he's rich and mean as hell."

Grabbing a handful of his ratty T-shirt, I yank him forward and square off right in his bloody face. "What did he look like? How did you meet him? Details! Start talking!"

"I-I-I have his phone number saved in my phone, but he never answers when I call. He got my number from a guy in my crew. He was looking for someone who could grab a girl for him. A specific girl. *Your* girl. He gave me the description and told me where I could find her."

I interject, "Did you meet him in person?"

"Yes. I met him at a hotel a few weeks ago. He gave me a down payment in cash."

"Which hotel?"

"Opal Sands. On the beach. He had a suite there. His guard was waiting for me in the lobby when I got there and brought me up."

"You didn't get his name? I find it hard to believe you didn't know who you were working for."

He pauses, not wanting to answer. Shep moves the pliers to the next toe. "No! No! Please," he begs. "I'm thinking. Just give me a second."

"Think harder. I need that name, asshole." Leo's got that steady calmness back in his voice, utterly in control.

How isn't he losing his shit right now? That's his sister. Someone paid this animal to abduct her. Why?

"His name didn't matter. He gave me the info on the girl and told me I'd get the rest of the money when I delivered the girl to him."

"What did he look like?" Leo asks.

"Like a regular old rich guy. White, shiny gray hair, wrinkly skin."

"Tattoos? Scars? Eye color? Anything that stands out?"

"No. He was just regular looking. He had seriously nice clothes, though. And a dope-ass Rolex, diamond-encrusted."

"Do you remember the room number and the night you were there?"

He tilts his head back, looking at the ceiling. "Answers aren't on the ceiling, dumbass," Shep chides, squeezing his toenail between the metal grip of the pliers.

"I'm thinking! Jesus! Fuck!"

Shep starts to tug.

"Fifteen... the fifteenth floor. Presidential suite."

"When?"

"Sunday night. Week before last."

Leo and Shep are doing an excellent job of getting intel from him. I'm sure Tomer is going gangbusters up there trying to find out who was in the suite that night. He's probably already hacked into their guest account history. We'll have his name in a matter of minutes.

"When's the last time you talked to him?" Leo asks.

"A few nights ago. When I found out she was being guarded and shit, I asked for more money and a way to escape the country afterward since it was no longer the quick grab he paid for. He agreed and said he was setting up an offshore account for me."

"Is that why you got a new identity lined up?"

He crinkles his nose and shakes his head. "That wasn't for me."

"Who is it for?"

"Her and some other guy. I don't know who he is. He's younger, though. He gave me a picture to use for the passport and shit."

"It's Craig. It's got to be," I announce to my team. A few heads nod in agreement with me.

Someone knocks at the door, distracting me from my tirade. Henderson opens it a crack, and someone slips him a piece of paper.

A picture.

Of Edwin Banks.

"Is this him?" Henderson asks, holding the printout in front of Tommy.

"Yeah, that's him." He sounds shocked that we found him that fast. "How did you find him?"

"Don't worry about it. You've been a big help. Thanks a lot," Leo says sarcastically. "Now it's time for lights out."

Klein puts the black sack back over his head, and we all turn to leave. We'll figure out what to do with this asshole later.

I need to get up to Sammy so I can comfort her. She's probably upset at all she witnessed tonight. And learning her ex-father-in-law paid for her abduction is bound to be freaking her out. She's been so certain that Craig wasn't involved, and we just proved otherwise.

As I remove my balaclava and take off my gloves, I can already picture her sitting in the control room, wrapped up in my jacket and likely cupping her hand around her neck.

I only hope she's not afraid of me for what she saw. I'm sure she knows I'd never hurt her, and everything I did in that room was to protect her. But what if her past trauma affects how she sees me now?

Too impatient to wait for the elevator, I take the stairs two at a time, rushing up to the control room. I beat the rest of the team, and when I walk in, my heart drops to the floor.

No Sammy.

No Kri.

"Where are the girls? Sue's office?" I nearly trip over my feet, turning around to head to Sue's office.

Tomer stops me dead in my tracks when he says, "They're gone. Sammy wanted to go home. Kri took her."

"What happened?"

"Sammy was having a panic attack or something. Started yelling that she felt like a captive or a prisoner. Kri tried to calm her down, but she ended up taking her home."

Oh shit. The violence must have been too much for her and triggered a flashback to when that sick fuck used to tie her up.

"Why didn't someone come and get me?"

Tomer narrows his eyes at me. "Kri tried to get her to wait, but Sammy was really freaking out."

"When did they leave?"

"Between rounds three and four. So maybe an hour or two ago."

Fear, real and raw, splits my heart open. The crushing sensation in my chest makes my knees feel weak.

Leo's voice comes from somewhere behind me. "Are they still there now? Check the security feed on the house."

"You know what? She didn't check in." Tomer pushes his chair over to another monitor. As he opens the program, he mumbles, "She said she would send a message when she got there, but I was too distracted digging into the Opal Sands hotel files. Dammit!"

The group of us gathers behind him as he clicks through the camera footage. Room by room.

"Empty. Empty. Empty," he says, scanning all the feeds. My heart drops lower into my gut with each screen he clicks on and off.

I slam my hand on the back of Tomer's chair. "Check the history. Did they ever get home?" I demand, my voice laced with panic.

"They never got there," Leo says, his phone in hand.

"You checked?" I ask, like a dumbass. Of course he'd think to check the perimeter history with the app on his phone. Glad one of us can think clearly.

Still on the video call and watching the chaos unfold, Boss cuts in. "What vehicle did they take? Tomer, find it. Could have been a traffic accident."

He wheels his chair back to another PC and clicks and clatters across the keys before answering, "They took the Dodge Charger."

"Where is it now?"

"Parked near the on-ramp to Highway 19."

Shep breaks in. "Kri's not answering her phone. Tomer, send the location of her vehicle to my phone. I'm going there now."

"Take Klein with you," Boss orders him. Klein and Shep file out in a hurry.

"Sawyer, try Sammy's phone," Boss orders. "Tomer, track their route."

I grab my phone and call Sammy. "Straight to voicemail."

Tomer answers, "So they left here, and it looks like they stopped at the

Publix on Belcher. They were there for eighteen minutes, then they headed up to Highway 19 until they stopped near the on-ramp. The Charger has been idle on the side of the road for forty-seven minutes. None of the sensors on the vehicle show an impact. But a flat tire sensor was triggered."

"Fuck, fuck, fuck! Someone could have slashed their tire, forcing them to pull over," Leo yells. "Who let them leave? They should have stayed here!" The calm timbre he had through the entire interrogation is gone, replaced with a roaring anger that rivals my own.

When Boss replies, his voice is calm and guarded. "They didn't exactly ask for permission, and for the record, I told her to take another guard with her." I bet he's trying to stay cool for Mrs. Mason's sake. She's pacing behind him on the screen and wringing her hands in front of her chest.

"Fucking shit! I can't believe this. Tomer, did the cameras on the vehicle record anything?" I thrust my hands in my hair and tug roughly at the roots. "I can't lose her again. I won't survive it twice."

"Same, brother. We *will* find her," Leo says, squeezing my shoulder. A look of confusion passes over his face, but he shakes it off, focusing on the screens.

Oh, hell. I said that out loud. And Leo reacted to comfort me before he thought better of it or realized what he was saying. But I don't give a shit right now.

"Leo, what's wrong?" A feminine voice comes from the doorway, and my hopes are raised only to be dashed when I see it's Sue.

"Oh, thank God you didn't leave with them, angel," Leo says, bringing her in his arms.

"Where's Sammy?" Sue's face morphs from confusion to concern in the blink of an eye as she studies the scene.

"She and Kri left about an hour ago to go home. They never made it there. Now, they aren't answering their phones, and the car is on the side of the road."

Boss jumps in. "Okay, I'm tracking Sammy's phone, and it looks like it's been turned off and is in the car or near it."

"What about her earrings? Tracking bracelet? What else does she have that's tracking her?" Sue asks.

Oh, thank fuck for another calm mind in here. Sue's got several trackers in her various personal items. Leave it to her to think about what we've given Sammy.

"She's on the move," Tomer answers casually.

"Where?" I demand.

"Looks like she's approaching the executive airport," he answers.

"Go!" Boss yells.

Ninety seconds later, Leo, Henderson, and I are in Henderson's SUV, locked and loaded. As we race off Redleg property to the airport, my heart pounds, and beads of sweat pepper my forehead.

I find myself pleading to a God I'm not sure I even believe in, begging and bartering for her safe return. Tremors run through my body as the adrenaline courses through my veins, but I force myself to reel it in so I'm ready for action when we get to our destination. Like other ops, staying level-headed is critical.

Only this isn't any *other* mission.

The stakes have never been higher. We have to save her. Failure is *not* an option.

Chapter Forty-Eight

RUH-ROH, SHAGGY

Ninety Minutes Earlier

Sammy

With my head slightly bowed, I hold the bottles up, one in each hand, like I'm presenting her with a holy offering. "Strawberry or regular?"

"Yes," Kri replies, a sly smile playing at the corner of her lips.

Without hesitation, I put both into the basket. "Popcorn? Chips? Candy? What else do we need?"

"Since we're having margaritas, let's go with chips and salsa."

"You're so wise."

"To be clear, mine will be virgin since I'm on duty. But I'm still looking forward to hanging out with you."

"Once we're safe at my house, you can always change your mind and have one to relax."

"Not even then, Sammy. Not until we're sure this whole mess is behind you."

I groan and roll my eyes. Kri shrugs it off, looking around the store, on high alert for even the slightest sign of trouble.

"Thanks again for getting me out of there. I already feel much better."

"I'm still not sure stopping was a good idea, but you had me at margaritas. Even if I can't have the tequila."

I take her arm as we stride to the snack aisle. It feels like we're being naughty, and I guess we are, to some extent. But not really. It's not like there is anyone out to get me since they've got my abductor in custody. And Kri's as capable as Sawyer or Leo.

She reaches for the plain tortilla chips, but I stop her with a hand on her forearm. "Wait. Have you had the ones with lime on them?"

"No. Oh, I bet those are yummy."

"I wouldn't say they're life-changing, but I'm also not *not* saying that."

We chuckle and grab two bags of lime-flavored chips. We dip into the frozen foods section for some jalapeño poppers.

"The only thing that could make this better is if we get the fresh salsa instead of this jar stuff," she says, wiggling her brows.

"To the produce section!"

We round off our impromptu shopping adventure with two containers of fresh salsa and a bunch of fresh cilantro since you can *never* have enough of that green goodness. Unless you're one of the unfortunate souls who thinks cilantro tastes like soap. *Those poor things.*

When we get to the checkout, she insists on paying. "I'll expense it back to Redleg anyway. I'll consider it a mental health expense since those fuckers pissed me off tonight."

She's careful and protective as we exit the store and stroll through the parking lot, her head on a swivel and keeping me close to her side. Just like a slightly smaller version of Sawyer. With boobs.

We're driving to my place when she looks over and says, "I like you, Sammy. You're a cool chick when you're not freaking out. Maybe we should do this again. After everything is done, and it's not a protection thing. I don't have many female friends, and I haven't had a girls' night since I was in my teens."

"Absolutely. I was thinking the same thing. Aside from Sue, I don't have any friends down here. I've gone out with a few of my coworkers, but I didn't fit in with them, so I felt like a fifth wheel. They're in their early twenties and at a different stage in their lives. Just out looking to get trashed and hook up, but that's not my speed."

"For sure. I get that. Considering your past, I'm not surprised you don't click with them. You've had a whole lifetime's worth of experiences in your thirty-plus years. Twentysomethings aren't often able to relate to that."

I'm tempted to ask about her past, but she turns the radio down as a concerned look falls across her face. Her spine stiffens, and she sits up straighter in the seat. I recognize that posture from all the protective men in my life.

Ruh-roh, Shaggy. Something is wrong.

"Do you feel that?" she asks.

"What?"

"Rumbling. A tire, maybe."

Now that she mentions it, yeah, there's a definite shuddering coming from the back of the car. "Great. That's all we need. Figures. Sorry my ever-present black cloud is attempting to derail our girls' night."

"It's okay. I can change a *flat* in five minutes *flat*." She snickers at her little joke.

She lets off the gas and puts her blinker on as the harsh vibrations increase to the point where I'm compelled to brace myself on the dash.

"Damn. It just blew out, I think," she huffs. "This isn't an ideal place to break down, but it'll have to do. We won't make it to that parking lot up there."

A loud scraping sound comes from the rear passenger side.

"Yep. That's the hubcap we're driving on now. Dammit."

Kri pulls off the road just shy of the highway on-ramp, taking up the bike lane and the small strip of pavement beside it.

"Stay here," she orders as she reaches around to the back of her pants to remove her pistol.

She checks the ammo and holds it close to her chest as she looks around the car in all the mirrors and whips her head around to search the surrounding area.

"It looks all clear. But stay in here until I check it out. You have your phone, right?"

"Yeah."

"If anything happens and you can't get to your phone, there's an emergency button under the dash. Push that, and it notifies Redleg of the emergency." She points to the button.

My heart rate spikes, and my breathing quickens. She stays calm, though, and it soothes me. She's all business.

"I'm sure it's nothing," I reassure myself. "Just a blown tire."

"Right," she says. "Here I go. Lock the door as soon as I'm out." She exits the car, and I do as she instructed.

I unlock my seatbelt while she circles the car, having pulled out a small flashlight. She peeks into the nearby brush and inspects the small ditch on the side.

"Nothing," she announces, tucking her flashlight back into her tactical pants. She pops the trunk and takes out the spare, tire iron, and other supplies.

I roll down the window a crack. "Kri, should I come and watch your back while you do that?"

"Not a bad idea. I'll be in a vulnerable position down there. Check the glove box. Should be a gun in there."

Sure enough, there's a small firearm in a leather holster under some paperwork. I retrieve the weapon and exit the vehicle.

"You know how to shoot?"

"Point and squeeze, right?" I tease. I've been to the range with Leo before.

With our backs to the car, she gives me a crash course on this gun, showing me where the safety is and so forth.

"Okay, stay right here and watch my six. Keep scanning the tree line. Gun pointed down unless you need it. I'll be quick."

She goes to work on the tire while I stand at her back, facing the trees as instructed.

"Dammit to hell!" she yells a few minutes into the tire change.

"What?" I chance a glance over my shoulder where she's got the lug nut wrench under her foot as she struggles to loosen it.

"Nut won't go."

"That's what she said," I joke.

She giggles as I move to assist her. "Here, let me try."

"No, I don't need any help," she insists. "Get back to watching the trees."

I roll my eyes but do as she says. She grunts and groans, and the wrench falls a couple of times, clinking to the ground.

"Sure you don't want help?"

"Fuck no. This damn lug nut will not best me. Nothing and no one with a nut will ever beat me!"

We giggle together at her girl power innuendo.

My mind starts to wander as she continues, eventually getting the lug nut loose and resuming the rest of the tire change. Visions of Sawyer, Shep, and Klein beating up Thomas Jones flash through my mind, but I push them away.

Focusing on looking at the same thing over and over again isn't as effortless as you'd think. It's extremely easy to let your mind and concentration falter.

"There. All fixed!" she announces.

When I spin around, she's got her hands on her hips, looking at the mounted spare like a proud mama bear watching her cub catch his first salmon.

"Good job, Kri. You're a badass."

She holds her hand out for a fist bump. "Team no nuts!"

I keep watch while she rolls the blown-out tire to the back of the vehicle and throws it in the trunk.

"You can get in the car. I'll finish cleaning up this mess."

Happy to put this delay behind me, I turn back toward the passenger door. When I spin around, I come face to face with my worst nightmare.

Edwin Banks. Craig's father.

My stomach tightens, and bile rises in the back of my throat.

With his expensive dress shirt unbuttoned at the collar and his cuffs rolled up, he points a gun right at me.

"Hello, daughter." His voice sends chills down my spine. "I told you I'd come for you."

Kri's voice comes from over my shoulder. "What the hell?"

A loud thud crackles through the night air, followed by the rustle and thump of a body hitting the ground. The sound of a heavy metal clattering to the concrete follows.

I'm too scared to turn around to see if Kri was taken out or if she did the taking out.

And I'm paralyzed with a crippling fear of who I'll see behind me if it was Kri who got knocked down.

"I'll take that. Be a good girl and hand it over." Edwin's bitter voice pierces my eardrums, causing a sickening feeling to skate across my skin.

This man.

As despicable as Craig was, and he was horrible, *this* man always made my skin crawl and terrorized my nightmares.

He's the one who was truly calling the shots.

He's the one who planted the suggestion of the faked suicide in Craig's ear.

He's the man who frightened and controlled Craig.

I saw how he treated Craig — emotionally berating him was only the beginning. The abuse he doled out went far beyond the grating insults and belittling comments. Craig's childhood was a horror movie at this man's evil hands. It made mine look like sunshine and rainbows.

This is a depraved man, capable of unspeakable horrors.

And he's pointing a gun at me.

He reaches forward with his free hand and effortlessly strips the gun out of my hand, tucking it into his pocket.

He just... took it. And I let him.

My only means of defense is gone. Because I was too scared to protect myself.

Just like all those times Craig hurt me.

Just like all the times my father beat my brothers and me.

Powerless.

That's me.

Strong hands grip me from behind, squeezing my upper arms to the point of pain. A pathetic whimper escapes my mouth.

I manage a piddly amount of courage, barely enough to glance over my shoulder to see who's got me. No one I recognize. One of his many body-guards, I suppose. Henchmen are more like it.

"Let's go before someone sees us out here," Edwin says, shooing me to the other side of the car with his gun.

My feet shuffle forward slowly as I'm manhandled to a waiting SUV pulled up on the other side of our car. Before shoving me into the car, the guard pats me down, running his slimy hands all over my body. When he finds my cell phone tucked under my bra strap, he turns it off and throws it on the side of the road.

"Get in," he commands as he shoves me inside.

"Kri!" I yell, finally starting to struggle.

If I get into this vehicle, I'm as good as dead.

Or worse.

"Kri! Help!"

"She's indisposed at the moment," the guard sneers in my ear.

While struggling to twist out of his grasp, I brace myself on the door-jamb. I place one hand and a foot on the side of the car on either side of the door, trying to prevent him from pushing me in. He grunts and shoves me from behind.

A sinister voice rings out. "Hello, darling. I've missed you."

My will to fight evaporates into thin air as I come face to face with my worst nightmare. He's sitting comfortably in the back of the SUV. Waiting for me.

This time, he's not chained to the table or wearing an orange jumpsuit. He's a free man. Come to collect me.

Craig Banks.

Chapter Forty-Nine

HOLD ON TO YOUR BUTTS

Sawyer

"Left here," Leo instructs Henderson, his voice a tad gruff but otherwise calm.

As for me, I'm not speaking. Anything I say will reveal how utterly wrecked I am about this. I already had one slip-up. I don't need another one.

This isn't how I want Leo to find out about Sammy and me.

And make no mistake, there will still be a Sammy and me after this night is over. We aren't letting those fuckers get on a plane with her.

I'll do anything and everything in my power to stop them. I'll burn down the whole fucking world before I let her go. I won't live without her again.

"She's still on the highway. Looks like they may have gotten stuck in some construction traffic. They're only moving around ten to fifteen miles per hour. We *will* catch up with them."

"Good." My voice comes out thick and wobbly, so I don't add anything else.

"You okay back there?" Henderson asks.

"Yep," I reply tautly.

I'm the furthest thing from okay.

Shuffling in my seat, I try and fail to stop my knee from bobbing up and down. I keep glancing over Leo's giant shoulder to see the tracker on his phone screen. A red dot advances down the highway, inching closer to the airport.

"Turn right up here."

Henderson makes the turn, the wheels screeching due to his speed. He's dodging in and out of cars, going full tilt through the back roads of town. He knows this isn't a typical gig. This one is personal.

Sammy.

I force my eyes closed and breathe in and out three times, trying to center myself. *Must stay calm.*

"When we catch up, we have to play it by ear," Leo says. "Not sure if they'll still be in a vehicle, how many of them there are, what weapons they might have, or what the deal is. So we have to be ready for anything."

"Ten-four," Henderson replies in a clipped tone.

"She's not getting on a fucking plane with him. Not a chance," I seethe, my voice infused with intense determination.

"Agreed. That's a mission priority. We can only assume he's got a private jet on standby to take them to who the fuck knows where."

Henderson adds, "At least he never got the fake IDs and shit from Shep's Russian guy. So he probably isn't leaving the country yet."

My head hits the back of the headrest a few times as I think through scenarios, trying to get ready for anything.

Leo responds, "Someone with the Banks's resources has more than one way to get new identification. Not sure how long they'll keep those trackers on her either. At some point, someone will probably scan her for signals."

"Fuck," I groan in frustration.

"Another left," Leo directs.

A potential scenario comes to mind, so I speak up. "We should put on our vests. And load up with more ammo. What if we end up in a shootout at the airport? He could have armed guards."

"Is there a tea case in the back?" Leo asks Henderson.

"Should be. Sawyer, check the cargo area."

I rise to my knees and twist backward, reaching over the seats into the storage compartment, looking for a tactical case.

"Jackpot!"

"Service for four?" Leo asks, barely a hint of playfulness in his tone.

There's a running joke at Redleg that these gear cases are a lot like a mobile tea set. Gear and supplies for four operatives to take into almost any operation. They're actually called tactical cases, hence the initial T, but we quickly changed it to tea like the hot beverage.

Moving swiftly, I pull out three bulletproof vests, ammo, and knives. I leave the night vision and infrared shit where it is. I don't think we need that quite yet.

I load up one vest and give it to Leo. He sets the phone down on the console and straps it on. I add the extra clips and knife into the second vest and don it myself. The third vest is geared up and ready to hand off to Henderson when we get to a stopping point. I'm sure our luck will run out soon enough, and we'll have to stop at a traffic light.

A cell phone chimes with an incoming call. Henderson taps the button on the steering wheel to answer.

"Whatcha got for us, Tomer?" Henderson asks.

"Not good news. I just got a call from my contact at Raiford Prison."

My throat grows thick, making it hard to swallow.

"Let me guess... Craig Banks is out?" Leo shakes his head and heaves a haggard sigh as Tomer answers.

"Yeah. He walked this afternoon. Got a full pardon. He's now officially a free man."

"Dammit!" Leo growls. "Un-fucking-believable."

My fist pounds the armrest beside me. "Son of a bitch."

Tomer adds, "I guess we now know the reason behind all the covert visits Edwin Banks has been making to various political officials these last few weeks."

Leo looks out the window, cursing under his breath a few times before asking, "Is it really that easy? Daddy throws money at a handful of politicians, and the next thing you know, the governor issues a pardon?"

"He's not getting away from us this time, bud," I tell him, tapping my hand against the back of his seat.

Craig Banks will *never* hurt my Sammy again. I'm going to end him myself.

"Anything else, Tomer?" Henderson asks.

"Yeah, Shep and Klein found Kri."

That doesn't sound good.

"And?" Leo's voice quivers a little.

"She's not good, guys. It's her head." He sucks in deeply. "They hit her with a tire iron. Cracked her skull." Tomer's shaky voice reverberates around the car, meeting stunned silence.

"They called an ambulance. She's still alive, but they don't know for how much longer. There's a lot of blood." He coughs, probably trying to hide his emotion.

Sure, we're all former special ops and have seen lots of bad shit in our lives. But we're out now. You don't expect one of your team to go like this. Kri's been part of Redleg for more than two years. She's family.

"Jesus, Tomer. I don't know what to say," Henderson finally speaks for us.

What can you say to news like that?

"Just find them. Make them pay. All right? Make them fucking pay."

Leo's the first to vocalize what we're all thinking. "Bet your ass we will."

"I'll call you back if we get any more intel. It looks like you're getting close to her signal, though. Be careful."

Henderson ends the call. We remain silent for the next few minutes of the ride, with the exception of Leo's navigating. If they're anything like me, their minds are probably wandering through all the ways we might be able to make them pay.

For Kri. For Sammy.

We can't take back roads the entire way there, so we reluctantly end up on the highway. In fucking traffic.

"Fuck, they made it to the airport," Leo tells us. "This isn't good."

"We need to get there. Now," I whine, stating the obvious.

Balling up my fists, I bang the tops of my thighs. The adrenaline is flowing, priming me for a fight.

"Feel like going off-roading, boys?" Henderson dives onto the shoulder of the highway, slamming down the accelerator.

"Fuck yes!"

"Sawyer, text Tomer and have him contact CPD to let them know what's happening. We need access to that airport. Right onto the tarmac."

While we're bumping along the shoulder of the highway, I make the call. Tomer says he's already called it in. Fortunately, we have a good chance of having our request granted since it's such a small airport — only one runway, a tiny terminal, and two hangars.

Leo directs Henderson to an exit, taking a series of turns to bring us to the back of the airport.

We're driving alongside the runway, going parallel to a long chain-link fence on one side of the road on our right. Leo looks through binoculars, trying to find a plane or any sign of Sammy based on her tracker's location.

"Stop or don't stop?" Henderson asks, pointing his head at the gate a couple hundred feet in front of us.

"I see them. They're boarding a plane. There!" Leo points across the airfield.

"The gate! Stop or don't stop?" Henderson asks, louder this time.

I decide for us. "Don't stop! Run it!"

If she's already getting on the plane, we're officially out of time and out of fucks to give.

"Hold on to your butts," he says, channeling Samuel L. Jackson from *Jurassic Park*.

Classic.

But now is not the time for voices.

He puts the pedal to the metal, taking us through the fence at eighty miles per hour. It feels like we're riding a bucking bronco, but we make it through and race toward the plane.

Hold on, Sammy. We're coming.

Chapter Fifty

YOU'RE NOT CLEAR FOR TAKEOFF

Sammy

"What did I tell you?"

Fuck him, yells my rage monster. *We don't owe him an answer.*

The grip Edwin Banks has on my cheeks stings as he squeezes my lips into a pucker, shaking my head back and forth in the process. When he lets go of my cheeks, freeing my mouth to fall open, he quickly rears up and backhands me for refusing to answer him.

My head snaps to the side with the force of the blow, and I leave it there, refusing to meet his eye contact.

He can beat me. Slap me. Hit me. Rape me. Fucking shoot me.

I don't care what he does to me.

He won't break me. Never again. Nor will his sniveling piece of shit offspring.

I feel the vibrations in my seat as the plane's engine roars to life beneath us.

Dammit. As the minutes tick by, the hope I once held that Sawyer or Leo would come running in and save me is dashed away. Second by second, my chances of being rescued grow slimmer.

Edwin Banks — the devil in a pressed dress shirt — grabs me under my chin, choking me as he angles my head to face him. But I keep my eyes closed because *fuck him,* that's why.

"Answer me," he demands with a sneer. "What did I tell you the last time I saw you?"

"Answer him, Sammy," Craig urges, placing his clammy hand on my leg.

A shudder runs through my body.

Craig is trying to defuse his father's rage by encouraging me to placate the old man. Only a few hours out of prison, and he's fallen right back into the same role where he's subservient to his father's wrath.

When we were married, this happened often. His dad would demand answers from me. Force me to explain what I'd done wrong to besmirch his good name or disobey him or his son. Craig would calmly urge me to answer, like he was on my side. Then, when his dad would leave, Craig would unleash all his rage on me. He couldn't stand up to his father, so he'd punish me for his own shortcomings.

It's sickening.

The grip around my neck tightens, quickly making it hard to breathe.

Growing desperate for air, I answer, "You said that you'd bring me back to Craig's side one day."

"What else? Be *very* specific, Samantha."

He increases the pressure around my neck, making me choke out the rest in a rush. "You said I belonged to you. I was property of the Banks family."

"And?"

"And you'd kill me before you ever let another man sully what belongs to your family."

"Exactly. Very good."

Craig squeezes my thigh like he's been doing since I had to sit next to him on the way here. I brush him off with my elbow. I'd punch the fucker and his father if they hadn't bound my hands.

"And did you keep yourself clean for your husband? Or have you been the disgusting tramp I always thought you were?"

"Come on, Dad," Craig whispers. "That's enough. We've got her back. It's all fine now."

Mr. Banks rises to his full height, no longer bent in front of me. With one bushy gray eyebrow raised to a point, he slowly creeps into his seat. He keeps his smarmy eye locked on Craig the entire time.

Once he's seated, he finally breaks the silence... so tense you could slice it with Sawyer's jawline.

Sawyer.

My heart pinches, and sadness overwhelms me as I realize I may never see him again.

"Well, son. It looks like Samantha isn't the only one who needs to be broken in. Apparently, while you were in prison with those animals, you started to think you were man enough to stand against me." He clicks his tongue at his son, shaking his head.

Craig slinks deeper into his seat, removing his hand the rest of the way from my leg.

Sticking out my chin, I meet Edwin's sharp glare with an indignant one of my own. "You might as well let me go and find someone else to be your little doll because I'll never be broken by you."

"Oh, we'll see about that."

Then he laughs.

An evil snicker that grows into a deep bellow emanating from his chest, shaking his shoulders and culminating with him coughing violently.

Probably has emphysema from all the damn smoke he ingests during his time in the fiery depths of hell.

"Mr. Banks," a tall, thin brunette bends over and addresses Edwin discreetly. "Your men are almost finished loading the plane. So we'll be taking off in a few minutes. Can I get you a beverage before takeoff?"

He runs his wrinkly hand over her arm and caresses her hip. I have to turn away as he gives her his drink order. It's like I can feel him touching me the same way.

Edwin never sexually assaulted me, but he sure as hell threatened it enough times to make me queasy at the sight of his advance on this poor young woman.

I catch a glimpse of her face as she leaves to get his bourbon. The disgusted expression she's trying to hold back says it all.

My eyes stare longingly at the open doorway and small staircase leading to freedom. I wonder if I could make a run for it. How far would I get before they caught me or shot me in the back? Would it be suicide to try to run?

Don't do it, I tell myself. *Just stay alive.*

My only job now is to keep my heart beating so Sawyer has a chance to find me. He won't rest until he does. Neither will Leo or Big Al. Or Shep or Kri.

Oh, poor Kri.

I caught a peek at her before we drove away. The memory of how she looked all crumpled up on the side of the road draws a shiver across my shoulders. Even in the darkness of the night, I saw the blood. So much blood.

A disembodied voice yells from outside, "We got company, boss!"

Sawyer? Leo?

The sound of tires squealing sings through the open doorway, making everyone inside the plane whip their heads in that direction.

Hope blooms in my chest.

Muffled voices are yelling words I can't decipher. Someone from Mr. Banks's security team attempts to close the plane's door from the outside. "Stay inside!" he yells before his footsteps carry him away, leaving a large crack in the door where he never finished closing it.

Suddenly, gunshots ring out, the loud pops making me flinch and fold in on myself.

It's got to be Sawyer. He came for me. He got here in time. I knew he'd come for me.

Craig jumps up. "Dad, get in the back. Hide in the restroom."

Mr. Banks rises and scurries to the back of the plane, hiding like the true coward he is.

Craig pulls a gun out of the waistband of his pants and scurries swiftly toward the door. I didn't realize he was carrying.

Good thing I didn't try to flee earlier. He might have shot me. If his sick father didn't beat him to it.

Nah. I'm not lucky enough to get out of this that easily. Besides, Craig wants me alive too badly.

Three more gunshots pop in rapid succession, and then someone cries out with a pained groan. Another two pops, and the wails stop.

How many people can Sawyer take out before they stop him? Did he bring reinforcements from Redleg?

I'm doing mental gymnastics as I try to remember how many guards there were. We had two with us in the car, plus a driver. When we got here, there were at least three more waiting.

And now Craig is *another* armed person standing between my rescuers and me.

From my seat, I can see him crouched down, still inside the plane, his gun drawn and pointed out the narrow space of the barely open door.

Another series of rapid gunshots rings out, bullets pinging off the metal of the fuselage.

"Sammy, get down," Craig yells at me.

Against my better judgment, I do as he says and slide out of my seat to the floor. Last thing I need is to get taken out by a stray bullet when I'm this close to being saved.

"Send her out, and we'll let you live."

It's Leo.

Does that mean Sawyer was one of the pained groans I heard?

Craig discharges his weapon through the crack, firing two pops before yanking the door closed and twisting the lever.

"Get this bird in the air!" he yells toward the front of the plane.

"The pilot was outside doing his final walk around," the flight attendant yells from near the cockpit.

"Dammit! Dammit!" Craig shouts, fisting his free hand in his hair.

Craig stomps over and yanks my bound hands, hauling me to my feet. "Sorry, Sammy. They've left me no choice."

Bringing me in front of him, he uses me as a human shield and marches me toward the door with his gun at my temple.

"Open the door, just a crack," he orders me, jabbing my head with the gun a little and wrapping his arm around my neck from behind.

I do as he says, slowly shifting the lever of the door lock and pressing the door outward slightly. It takes some effort, but it finally budges a few inches forward.

As soon as it's cracked open, Craig bellows, "I've got a gun to her head. If you want her to live, send the pilot up the stairs when we lower them. No one comes up but the pilot. You understand? I'll fucking kill her if you try anything."

"Don't hurt her, Craig. You don't want to do that." Leo's voice is markedly calmer this time. "Just let her go, and we'll let you fly out of here. You can start a new life as a free man. Think it over."

"The pilot. Now. Or she dies." He wraps his arm around me tighter, and my bound hands rise to wedge between his grip and my neck, but they find no purchase.

"Tell them, darling. Tell them to send up the pilot. Tell them now," he snarls in my ear, the heat of his breath making me want to retch.

"Leo, it's me. I'm okay, but please do as he says. He's got a gun to my head. Send up the pilot, please."

I hear a low rumble of male voices, but nothing I can decipher. After a few achingly long seconds, Leo finally responds, "How about a trade, Craig? We'll send up the pilot *and* your two remaining guards. You send down Sammy unharmed. It's a good deal. And no one else has to get hurt."

Instead of answering, he grabs a handful of my hair and yanks. Hard. My head goes in the direction he's tugging, but his grip around my neck tightens, holding me in place. An anguished cry escapes me.

"Better do a better job of convincing them," Craig tells me.

Crying now, from the sheer pain and fear of being choked, I somehow find my voice, shaky and quivering as it may be. "Leo, please send up the pilot."

"Okay. Just don't hurt her, Craig. We'll send up the pilot."

A bubble of disgust breaks through the pain when he presses a wet kiss at my temple, right where the gun was a second ago. "Good job, darling. You did well." He lets go of his death grip on my hair, and I whimper softly, my head throbbing and windpipe nearly cut off under his big bicep. "Push open the door the rest of the way."

"We're lowering the stairs now," I announce, a plan formulating as I place my hands on the door.

As soon as I've got the exit open fully, I lean forward to scan the scene. The pilot is standing at the base of the stairs, his empty hands over his head. I don't see Leo or the other guys, but I know they're there.

"Get up here!" Craig yells at the pilot.

This is gonna hurt. But I refuse to follow even one more instruction from this fuck nozzle.

I'm done taking orders from him. *Absolutely done.*

The second Craig tries to yank me back farther into the plane to clear a path for the pilot, I lurch forward with all my might, throwing my body down the stairs and bringing him down behind me.

Pain slices through my body, shooting from my forehead to my knees as I twist and roll down the staircase. When I've stopped toppling over, I bring myself up to my hands and knees to crawl a few feet away from Craig before I try to run for it. I curse my past-self for wearing a skirt as the ragged concrete bites against my exposed knees and shins.

The pilot must have backed out of the way because he's nowhere to be found.

A thick hand wraps around my ankle, pulling me backward. My palms and knees scrape along the tarmac as I struggle for something to hold, but there's only asphalt.

"No!" I scream while kicking backward with my other foot.

Leo's voice calls out from a few feet away, sounding deadly calm and menacing. "Let her go or die."

"Hands up, asshole!" another voice yells. It's one I'm not as familiar with. Must be one of the other Redleg guys.

Where's my Sawyer?

Craig doesn't let go. It's either his hubris or perhaps a death wish compelling him to continue pulling me back toward him. My kicking proves fruitful as I manage to connect with something hard and hear him curse in pain.

Taking advantage of his loosened grip, I shake free of him. My eyes meet Leo's as I come to my feet, preparing to run.

Unfortunately, Craig must be moving faster than me. He grabs me from behind, catching my hair and neck in one fell swoop and yanking backward. I slam into his hard chest and feel the cool bite of his pistol pressed against my temple once more.

So close. I was *so* close.

"Gun down. There's no way you win this, Craig. You won't get back to the plane. We've got you surrounded," Leo says coolly.

Craig spins me around with him wildly from side to side while using me as a shield. Now that I can see who's surrounding us, I recognize the other Redleg guy as Mom's bodyguard, Henderson.

"Back off, or I'll blow her brains out!" Craig's desperation spikes as he sees Leo pointing his gun at him from one side and Henderson on the other, blocking our path back to the plane.

Craig holds me close, wrapping himself around me, probably trying to make it so they can't get a clean shot.

A single gunshot rings out behind us. Craig and I both turn toward the source and see Henderson falling to the ground. I can't tell where he was hit, but he's down.

Edwin stands at the top of the stairs, his gun extended.

Without hesitation, Leo fires two shots, hitting the elder Mr. Banks in the dead center of his chest. He falls over backward into the jet.

Craig uses the distraction to drag me in reverse toward the plane. Leo is in front of us with his gun pointed at Craig. But he most certainly won't risk shooting him with me as his shield.

My head whips around, desperately searching for another guard to stop us from making it back into the plane.

There's no one else.

All I see are a pair of Mr. Banks's guards tied up several feet away and a few bodies littering the ground from the earlier gunfight. I don't see any other Redleg guys.

No Sawyer.

"Where's my pilot?" Craig yells as we near the plane, probably realizing we can't exactly leave without him. "Send up the pilot behind us, or the flight attendant dies."

"Dammit. Don't do this, Craig. No one else has to die. Just let her go," Leo pleads.

He advances in our direction, matching us step for step.

In my ear, Craig says, "Lift your foot up. We're going up the stairs. Together. Don't try any more bullshit." He squeezes my neck, lifting me upward with him.

One slow step at a time, we climb the steps, bringing me closer to goodbye.

Tears cloud my vision as I see the pilot following us up the stairs. Leo looks on, his gun still aimed in our direction as he angles for a clean shot. The pain on his face is gut-wrenching.

He mouths, *I'm sorry.*

I shake my head, trying to convey that he's got nothing to apologize for. I can't formulate words or do anything other than shake with sobs.

The pilot closes the door once we're all inside, and I see Leo disappear in the crack, an anguished expression on his face.

Craig shoves me to the floor of the plane, and I fall to my knees right beside a very dead Edwin Banks.

I push away from him, scurrying until my back hits the door.

"Fucking bitch!" Craig yells at me. "My father is dead because of you!"

I expect the first smack across my face, but that doesn't make it hurt any less. He put so much damn force into the hit it knocks me over to my side. Using my hands and elbows, I cover my face. Instinctively, my knees come in to protect my stomach from the kicks that will surely come.

But they don't come.

I hear clothes rustling, a pained grunt, and a crunching sound like bones snapping, then a loud thump shakes the floor where I lie. Then I hear nothing.

Nothing but haggard breaths.

Too scared to look, I stay tucked in a little ball and wait for the pain to resume.

The seconds tick by, but the blows never come.

"Sammy, it's me."

"Sawyer?" My voice is small and meek, unfamiliar to my own ears. I'm still not able to open my eyes.

I worked so hard to put that old me in the past. To no longer be a quivering shell of a woman balled up in the fetal position.

Yet here I am again.

He kneels beside me, rubs my head lovingly, and tugs at my hands to pull them away from my face.

"Open your eyes, baby. It's just me."

Through the crack of one eyelid, I see Sawyer bent over me, looking unharmed and as handsome as he's ever been. Barely a hair out of place.

"Sawyer?" I ask again as I reach for him.

A second later, I'm wrapped up in his arms, surrounded by his warmth and soothing scent. Comfort and peace seep into my soul as panic recedes.

My eyes search the small space of the cabin. "Where's Craig?" I wipe my tears with the back of my hand to see better.

"He won't hurt you ever again. He's gone, baby. For good this time."

I catch sight of Craig's crumpled body a few feet away, his neck positioned at an unnatural angle.

No feelings of shock or regret pierce me as I'd have expected. No sorrow or loss.

I only feel relief. Blessed relief.

The pilot brushes past us, exiting the plane in a hurry. A gust of wind hits my back as the door opens, but I keep my vision trained on the man holding me.

I never thought I'd see him again.

"Are you okay? Where are you hurt?" he asks, scanning over my body.

"I'm okay." With shaky hands, I cup Sawyer's cheeks. "You came for me. You came," I mutter over and over.

"I'll always come for you, princess."

Tears spill down my cheeks as I brush my lips against his before joining our mouths with a tender kiss. I squeeze him with all my might, bringing myself flush against him. I want to feel him in my soul.

I'm never letting go.

He responds eagerly, his hands roaming over my back before resting at the nape of my neck.

"I didn't think I'd ever see you again," I confess between sweet, tearful kisses.

"Get used to it, my love. Because I never want to go another day without you by my side." He seals his vow with a long, passionate kiss. I revel in the feeling of being connected once more. When he pulls back, he rubs his nose across mine.

"I love you so much," I confess, feeling a freeing sensation run over my entire body.

"You finally caught up." He beams at me, then claims my mouth again.

"Ahem," a deep voice mimics the sound of a throat clearing.

A very *familiar* deep voice.

Oh shit.

Chapter Fifty-One

TOO SOON!

Sawyer

My first instinct is to hold Sammy closer to my chest, which is a tiny bit shocking, considering I would've pushed her away if Leo had caught us like this yesterday.

But after almost losing her *again*... I wouldn't let her go right now for anything in the world.

Leo's expression is a mix of fury and confusion, and I fear he's about to rip her from my arms.

Thankfully, he doesn't.

But judging by his tense body language and the balled-up fists at his sides, he's seriously considering it.

A blade of hurt lances my chest as one of my worst fears comes true, and I'm suddenly faced with the possibility of losing my best friend because I fell in love with his sister.

I raise one hand out, palm facing him in a placating gesture. The other palm is pressed firmly against Sammy's back, holding her secure to my chest. "Leo, I swear. I was gonna tell you."

"I don't want to hear it. We've got bigger problems right now." He shakes his head, a look of disgust passing over his features. His voice echoes his expression as he says, "Once you're done sticking your tongue down my sister's throat, I could use a hand with Henderson."

Sammy spins her head toward her brother and tightens her grip on my shoulders. Together, we watch him storm off.

She whips her face back to me, tears falling again. Her voice cracks as she says, "I'm so sorry."

"Hey, it's okay. You didn't do anything wrong."

"I did. It's all my fault. I never should've —"

Pressing a fingertip to her lips, I cut off her pained words. "Princess, we can talk about it later. But I'm not mad at you. And I'll deal with your brother. For now, I need to help Henderson. Are you okay to move? I don't want you to stay up here with them." Tipping my head, I point toward the bodies littering the plane's floor.

Some of the color drains from her face as she notices the still-warm corpses of her ex and his father on either side of us.

Schooling her features, she brushes her hair from her face before standing. I study her for signs of pain and note a few winces of discomfort as she rolls her shoulders back and straightens her spine. But she doesn't let any of that stop her from heading down the stairs.

She's so damn strong.

The next few minutes are a whirlwind of chaos. After retrieving first aid supplies from our SUV, I help Leo slow Henderson's blood loss while waiting for an ambulance. Fortunately, they arrive quickly, and he's conscious when they drive him away.

He was hit in the stomach — right below his vest. He's lucky Craig's old man had such shitty aim. Either that or he wasn't smart enough to shoot for the head.

The tension between Leo and me is palpable. He doesn't speak to me other than barking out orders or relaying curt updates.

While the paramedics tend to Sammy's injuries, I give an update to Tomer and Big Al by phone. Meanwhile, Leo takes the lead with the cops. They've sent the county medical examiner to the scene, along with a shit-load of detectives — including Detective Patterson.

Tonight's fallout will be a clusterfuck, but fortunately, we've got the pilot and flight attendant to corroborate our story. The guards started the shootout, and our kills were in self-defense.

Snapping Craig's neck from behind might be the hardest to explain, but since he was brandishing a gun and beating Sammy, I don't think I'll be in hot water. Redleg has a damn good attorney who deals with this shit for us.

Paramedics tend to Sammy's injuries as I briefly recount how Craig met his demise to Detective Patterson.

"In a nutshell, I crawled into the plane through the baggage compartment while Leo was negotiating with a gun-wielding Craig Banks for Sammy's release. I was the backup plan since we figured he'd rather die than let her go again."

I was happy to grant his wish.

But I keep that part to myself.

After I run down the scene inside the plane, he tucks his notebook into his pocket and says, "We'll need you and your partner to come into the station to go over everything again for the official investigation."

"I need to go to the hospital first. We've got two of our own in serious condition." I nod my head toward Sammy. "And if she's going, then so am I."

The detective glances to where Sammy's being loaded into the back of an ambulance. He looks back at me and offers a sharp nod of understanding. "Tomorrow is fine."

I rush toward the ambulance, eager to make sure she's still okay. With the adrenaline waning, she's likely feeling more of those aches and pains.

Unfortunately, I'm not the only one anxious to be by her side.

Leo gets to the back of the ambulance a few steps ahead of me.

The paramedic glances up from her clipboard, where she's frantically filling out paperwork. "If one of you is coming with her, now's the time to get in. We're leaving." She returns to her task while another EMT tends to Sammy's injuries and a third fires up the engine.

Sammy's eyes dart between us, and I can see how torn she is. Leo and I share a brief look before our heads swivel back to face her.

No one says anything over the crackling tension.

Part of me wants to step back and let him go with his sister. But a larger and louder part says *fuck that.* Leo will have to get used to me being in her life — no better time to start than the present.

He and I start speaking at the same time.

"Look, I —" Leo says.

"I'm going to —" I start.

He mashes his lips together, lifting his hand to indicate I should continue speaking.

Before I can tell him, *I'm going, and you can deal with it,* the paramedic says, "Guys, only one of you can ride along. Make a decision already." She's either completely oblivious to our relationship drama or she doesn't care.

Probably the latter.

Leo and I both point at our chests like we're a mirror fucking image.

This is getting stupid.

Sammy groans and crosses her arms over her chest. "Fucking decide already. Grow up. I love you both, and I'm not choosing."

That's my Sammy. Always a ball buster.

Leo and I lock eyes.

With a somber look, I try for friendly and calm. "How about I go with her, and you follow in the SUV? We can talk about this shit later. Okay?"

He takes a step closer to me. "No. I'll go with her. You follow."

But I'm not backing down. I have to crane my neck to hold his eyes, but I do it. Without a hint of snark or malice, I calmly explain, "If that were Sue in there, would you let her brother go with her, or would you go?"

"That's different. Sue and I are —"

"You and Sue are what? In love?" I tilt my head to the side, hoping he catches my meaning.

He wipes his hand down his face in frustration, taking a step back. "Fine. We're not done talking about this, though."

"Good. I hope we aren't."

And I mean that. I've got boatloads to say before this issue is behind us.

He turns to Sammy, removing the growl from his voice. "I'll see you there, kiddo. I love you."

"Thank you, Leo. I love you too."

Trying to lighten the mood, I playfully toss out, "And I love you too, Leo."

As he walks away, he flips me the bird over his shoulder. "Too soon, Perry. Too soon!"

Fuck.

"Oh, that was *waaay* below the belt!" I yell at his retreating back.

He turns around, wearing a sadistic smile, and holds his arms out to each side with a shrug. "Not even close to being even."

When I spin around to face Sammy, she's got one eyebrow arched, and her eyes are wide with mirth. "Did he... did he just say what I think he said?"

Rolling my eyes, I climb into the back of the ambulance. "You didn't hear anything. You've been through a lot and are clearly traumatized."

Her jaw hangs down to her chest. "Perry? *That's* your first name?"

I press a kiss to her forehead, tip her chin closed with my thumb, then take my seat on the bench beside the stretcher.

"Like the —"

"Yes" I cut her off and close my eyes. Leaning my head back, I tap it against a glass cabinet, feeling a twinge of pain at the contact. "Just like Perry the motherfucking platypus."

Her vibrant laughter brings a smile to my somewhat annoyed face. Opening my eyes, I watch her try and fail to stop laughing four times before she finally succeeds on her fifth go.

Gently taking her hand in mine, I pepper soft pecks along her knuckles. I can't help but smile along with her. I fucking love her. She was going to find out my first name eventually. At least she already told me she loves me before she found out.

No take backs.

Chapter Fifty-Two
THE VOICE CHOOSES ME

Sawyer

"Here, Shep. You look like you need an emotional support beverage."

I hand him the coffee, which he takes appreciatively and throws back. I'd hoped my joke would make him smile or at least break the tension, but it didn't. He's far too worried about Kri.

He refuses to leave the OR waiting room until they let him see her.

We stand wordlessly together, our backs against the wall. It's killing me not to talk, but this isn't a time for idle chitchat. Kri's been in surgery for four hours and some change, and the doctors told us she only had about a thirty percent chance of making it. Occasionally, I give his shoulder a squeeze to remind him he's not alone.

Klein, Tomer, and Leo have taken turns by Shep's side. Now that Sammy's good, I came up for my turn with him.

Leo's downstairs in the emergency room, sitting with her. She shoved me away and told me to get some coffee while she talked to her brother.

He and I have yet to speak, though.

We've been too busy bouncing from room to room and taking calls from everyone who's heard about tonight's chaos. As word spread, the main hospital lobby quickly filled with concerned team members. Even Big

Al and Madeline are catching the red-eye from California to come home early.

The Redleg team is uniting for two of their own.

Like a family.

All this time, I thought I didn't have one, and I'm lucky enough to have two.

The Masons and Redleg.

Shep finally breaks the silence. "What's the latest on Henderson?"

"He's in recovery now and doing well. He'll be in here for a few days."

Nodding, he keeps his eyes fixed on the door leading to the surgical wing.

Another few seconds pass before he asks, "Sammy okay?"

"Yeah. She's good. A little banged up, but nothing broken. They're discharging her. I'll be taking her home shortly."

That gets his attention, and his head whips in my direction. "Not Leo?"

I try to hide my grin behind my coffee cup. "Nope. Me."

"And what does Lionheart say about that?"

"Nothing yet. Other than a few words, we haven't spoken about it yet. He wasn't thrilled when he caught us kissing earlier."

With wide eyes, he faces the door again and snickers to himself while shaking his head a few times. "Please tell me the whole story. It'll distract me."

At least he sounds an inch closer to his jovial norm.

"Well, I guess I can do that. Since you asked nicely."

Like a saint, I take his mind off Kri's dire situation by telling him what happened tonight between Sammy, Leo, and me.

When I finish with the story — including Leo dropping my name bombshell with his exit — Shep says, "I just thought of the perfect door sign for you."

"If you fucking so much as joke about putting my first name on that sign, I'll end you."

He furrows his brow and juts his lips in a faux pout. "You promised."

"Honestly, Shep. If you do it, I'll beat, eat, digest you, then vomit you back up and repeat the process. I hate that fucking name."

A deep chuckle emanates from his chest.

"Fine." He spreads his hands in front of his face like he's envisioning the sign. "Then I think I'll go with *Secret Sister Lover.*"

"What is this? A Jerry Springer episode?" I feign a gag. "I didn't think I could hate anything else more than I hate Perry. But it's a toss-up. However, that one doesn't work since it's no longer a secret."

"True. I'll have to come up with something even better."

"No rush."

Shep seems thoughtful, his thumb and forefinger rolling over his chin. "If Leo hadn't caught you, when would you have told him about Sammy?"

"As soon as possible," I answer definitively. "In fact, I regret not telling him sooner."

He tilts his head down, looking at me from under his brow. "Really? This coming from the guy who begged me not to tell anyone about the kiss heard 'round the bar?"

"Almost losing her again put everything in perspective. She is the most important thing in my life, and I never should have denied that."

As I hear the words out loud, I wish I could shove them back down my throat. At this point, it's pretty obvious Kri is more than Shep's coworker.

His face blanches, and he forces a tight swallow as he leans back against the wall and returns to staring at the door.

"Hey, man. I'm sure Kri will be fine. She's tough."

Blinking rapidly, he rubs the back of his neck. "Yeah. Yep. You're right. She's a fighter. The strongest woman I've ever..." He trails off when his voice cracks. He turns, pacing away from me and running his hands through his hair.

Damn. I feel like an ass. Maybe I should make my own sign that reads: *Donkey.*

A few minutes later, Klein comes in and taps me on the shoulder. "Sammy's ready to head out, man. She's asking for you. I'll hang with Shep."

"Thanks. Is Leo still with her?"

He nods and offers the three-finger *Hunger Games* salute.

After saying goodbye to Shep, I head downstairs. My hands grow clammy as I near Sammy's ER room. Knocking at her door, I rock on my heels while I wait to hear her telling me to come in.

She doesn't.

Instead, the door is opened by a somber-looking boulder of a man. He's got a beard, familiar blue eyes, and an arched brow as he stares me down, tatted arms crossed over his broad chest.

"Come on in, Sawyer."

"Where's Sammy?"

"Waiting in the lobby with Tomer and Sue." Leo closes the door behind me and shoves a chair into the center of the room at the foot of the hospital bed. "Have a seat."

Once I'm seated, he takes the other chair and spins it around so he's sitting with his arms draped over the back and facing me head-on.

"Sawyer, you and I are going to have a little chat. I'm going to ask you some questions, and you'll give me some answers. If you don't, things might get extremely unpleasant for you. And if you lie, it'll get even worse. You get me?"

Please tell me he didn't just hit me with his little interrogation opener monologue.

"Leo, come on. This is stupid. I'm not your enemy. We're friends."

He angles his head at me, leveling me with a harsh glare. "*Do. You. Get. Me?*"

I lean back in the chair, cross my arms, and prop one ankle over my knee. With a slight roll of my eyes, I answer, "I got you."

"Good. Question one. When did you first realize you had feelings for my sister?"

"You want to start there? Maybe we could ease into it."

He raises his brows at me. With more anger this time, he repeats, "Question one. When did you first —"

I throw my hands in frustration. "I think I've always had feelings for her."

"Be more specific."

"It started back when we were enlisted. From all your damn stories about her."

With a slight shrug of confusion, he turns his hands around like he's spinning a yarn around them. "Uh... romantic feelings?"

"At first, I was intrigued by her. She sounded like a crazy, hilarious, spit-fire of a girl who I wanted to know better. I'd only seen her in pictures at that point, but I still felt something spark. I know it's stupid, but that's when I first felt something for Sammy."

His posture loosens. "When did you know it was more than friendly?"

"You remember bringing me to Maine with you after we lost Bowman?"

"Yep."

"That's the first time I met her." Fuck. This is so awkward to talk about. "And she was even more beautiful than I imagined. The pictures didn't do her a damn bit of justice."

His face tenses again, and he cracks a knuckle, being intentionally threatening. "You didn't do anything then, did you?"

Through a chuckle at his dramatics, I answer truthfully, "She was a little young back then — maybe like twenty or twenty-one. And you were a *teenie-tiny-little-bit* protective of her. So I squashed it."

"Fine. So far, you're allowed to continue living."

"Jolly good, old chap," I toss out in an absolutely flawless British accent.

He fights a grin. "Question two. When did you un-squash it?"

"For the record, you've asked about five questions. But I'll allow it." I flick my wrist, tossing my hand in his direction. "Not until recently."

"How recently?"

"A few days before she was abducted was the first time I kissed her."

He mimes sticking his finger in his ear to clean it so he can hear better. "A few days before she was taken?" he echoes, his voice raised in disbelief.

I nod and squeeze the bridge of my nose.

"And you're already in love? That's a little fast, don't you think?"

"Says the guy who guarded a girl for two weeks and then obsessed over her for six freaking months. In fact, he was so consumed by her that he tracked her location several times a day. At least I've known Sammy for longer than two weeks. I've been in love with her for more than a damn decade. It took you less than two weeks. Pot, stop calling the kettle black."

It's hard not to feel a bit smug at his reaction. But I manage.

Barely.

"Fair point." He raises one hand to signal he's got something else to say. "Next question. Did you just say you've been in love with her this whole time?"

My voice thickens, and my head falls forward. "Yes. I've been in love with her for so many years. It's been killing me to keep it from you."

"Why didn't you tell me?" The sadness in his voice stops me in my tracks.

I was expecting more anger or hurt. I've lied to him for years. Hid something important from him.

As I meet his eyes, they've grown softer. "Leo, listen. You're my best friend, and you mean the world to me. I honestly don't know where I'd be without you. You know that, right?"

One side of his face raises with the smallest grin. "I know."

"You, your mom, and Sammy have been the closest thing to a family I've ever had. After we got out of the service, I had no idea where I'd go.

You took me in and welcomed me into the fold. I didn't tell you how I felt about her because I was... scared." I pause, swallowing down some of that old, familiar fear. "I was so damn scared I'd lose you. I didn't want to do anything to make you push me away. To throw me aside like..." I can't finish my sentence; the fear of another rejection chokes off the words.

"Like everyone else has," he finishes for me.

With my hand cupped to shield my reddening eyes from his view, I nod solemnly. Overwhelming sadness and shame well up from deep inside my chest, clawing up my throat to escape.

The loud scratch of Leo's chair across the linoleum floor makes me flinch. I feel rather than see his giant frame towering over me.

"Come here, brother."

Moving my hand, I look up and see him standing over me, his arms spread wide and his face solemn. As I rise to my feet, he wraps his gigantic arms around me and taps his cupped palm against my back.

I squint my eyes, holding back the tears as I lean into his embrace. For the longest time, he doesn't make a move to end the hug, and I don't either.

Alone, in a small emergency room, we hug.

I'm reminded of how Sammy said she feels love through physical touch. And dammit, if I don't feel Leo's love right now.

Not like his dick or anything. Don't make this weird.

I mean I can feel his brotherly love for me through this hug.

When he pulls back, he bends his head slightly to catch my gaze. In earnest, he tells me, "Family is forever. And you *are* my brother. Blood or not. You're my brother, Sawyer. I'll never throw you away."

Still unable to talk, I simply nod.

"Question three," he starts, pointing his fat finger in my face and making me smile. "If you were in love with her for a decade, then that means when she... when we lost her..." He steadies himself with a deep breath. "Then you lost her too. And you were mourning."

I'm no longer able to hold back the tears his words spring forth. "Yes. I was," I choke out.

"You never told me you were suffering. Not the way you must have been. You should have told me."

"It wouldn't have changed anything."

"Yes, it would have. That's part of having a family. Dammit, Sawyer, you didn't have to suffer alone."

"I didn't. You just didn't know it. But I was going through it right along with you, man. The whole time."

"Selfless son of a bitch." He coughs down the emotion.

We're both crying now. Two former Army Rangers. Crying like babies.

When we stop blubbering, I pull back and ask, "Are we good?"

He straightens and runs his hands down his shirt to smooth it out. "Yeah, man. We're good. But I have one more question."

I feign annoyance and huff, "Oh, come on! The interrogation ended when we both cried."

"Question seventy. Are you telling Big Al you slept with a client, or am I?"

"Let's have Madeline do it. Something tells me anything she says will be fine as far as Boss is concerned. Especially since they're most likely sleeping together."

He scoffs. "Don't talk about our mother like that."

My eyes and mouth all open playfully wide. "Did you just call her *our* mother?"

"Well, if you're my brother, then she's your mom." He wraps his arm over my shoulder and leads me down the hall toward the lobby. "Which means you probably shouldn't sleep with your sister. Florida isn't *that* part of the South."

Laughing, I add, "I bet there are quite a few *Florida Man* headlines out there begging to differ."

Our jokes are interrupted when Leo's phone rings.

"It's Klein," he says before answering. "Do you have news, man?"

My pulse spikes as I wait to hear the latest on Kri.

Relief quickly washes over Leo's features as his lips part, and he presses his fist to his chest. "Good. Good," he mutters. "I'll tell them. Stay with Shep." Another pause. "Thanks, man. Okay."

"She's okay?" I ask as soon as he disconnects.

He slips the phone back into his pocket and brings me in for another quick hug. "She made it out of surgery. She's not totally out of the woods, but they think she'll be okay. They're moving her to ICU."

"Halleluyerr and praise the Lort!" I yell in Madea's voice.

Well, that's a new one.

Sometimes I don't choose the voice. The voice chooses me.

As we enter the main lobby, the look on Sammy's face is priceless as she sees Leo and me walking side-by-side and acting all chummy, like nothing was ever wrong. Giant smiles beaming from ear to ear on both our faces.

Sue rises and runs into Leo's waiting arms. Instead of feeling a twinge of jealousy, I'm filled with a sense of joyful serenity when Sammy comes over to me at the same time. With no secrets to hide, she snakes her arms around my waist and burrows into my chest. I kiss her head, careful not to aggravate her injuries.

Looking up at me with those breathtaking turquoise eyes, she says, "I take it everything went all right?"

"Yeah, princess. Everything is perfect."

Epilogue

SAMMY

Hovering over him, I gaze deep into Sawyer's chocolate eyes one last time before I cover them with the blindfold. "We need to hurry," I whisper, then press a quick kiss to his full lips.

"That's all up to you, princess. It's not like I have any control in the matter." His accompanying grin is pure sin.

Once I'm finished with the blindfold, I stretch my naked body over his to secure his wrist restraints to hooks hidden in the flap of his headboard.

The bougie stud splurged on a new headboard that easily transforms from posh modern to BDSM dungeon. And we're breaking it in with a quickie before we have to leave for the ceremony.

Actually, it's *our* headboard now, isn't it?

I've lived here for two weeks — officially. Before that, I was just staying here every night and day. Once we came out to my family, Sawyer wasted no time making it known he wanted me in his bed every night. And I have zero objections to that plan.

After tugging on the hooks to ensure he's locked in place, I trail my hands over his corded forearms and down his biceps toward his chest. His veins bulge under my touch as he rolls his wrists and gets comfortable in the padded cuffs. I press my palms over his pecs, lifting myself to straddle his waist.

"This is so fucking hot," he rasps.

"Are you comfortable?"

"Yes, ma'am."

"Good."

He inhales deeply and grins. "Damn, baby. You smell good enough to eat."

Like he's speaking those words directly to my clit, my hips undulate with need, grinding my core ever-so-gently over his ripped abs. "Do you want a taste?"

"Always," he says with a little nibble of his lower lip.

"How do you ask?" I taunt, lowering my voice into that deeper register I use when I'm in charge.

"Can I please taste you, princess?"

I rock against his abs a few more times before sliding lower down his body until I'm right over his erection. "Maybe."

He tilts his head to one side. "Am I going to be inside you first?"

"So many questions, Sawyer. Are you feeling impatient?"

"No, ma'am. Just curious."

"Good. Because I'm sure you remember what happens to sexy body-guards who don't have patience."

"I'll never forget."

The other night he wouldn't stop begging to fuck me, but I wasn't done playing with him. So he had to watch while I used a vibrator on myself. I came three times before I let him claim my fourth with his dick.

When we finally climaxed together, he roared so loud I thought the neighbors were going to call animal control.

Incidentally, that was also the first time we were successful with missionary position. No one was restrained, and there was zero panic in sight. Only pleasure.

He was right about this power exchange thing. It's done wonders for helping me overcome my trauma anxiety. Even when he's in control, the old fear barely makes an appearance, and I'm learning to *love* relinquishing control to him. It's incredibly hot switching roles the way we do.

He's so perfect for me. How did I get so lucky?

Wearing nothing but a grin he can't see, I reach across him to the array of toys we picked out together. He chases my dangling breasts with his open mouth as I pass over his face. Apparently, he doesn't need to be able to see to know when my boobs are in licking vicinity.

I pause my toy-seeking mission to let him tease my breasts. A soft moan escapes me as I let him work one deep into his mouth, his devastating tongue ravishing my nipple. He groans and flexes his hips upward, driving his cock through my tender flesh as he laps at my tit eagerly.

Cradling the back of his head with my palm, I hold him in place and encourage him to continue as our bodies start rocking together. The longer we go, the closer he gets to accidentally impaling me on his fat cock.

Truthfully, it wouldn't be an accident. His dick is like a Sammy-seeking missile.

But it's not time for that yet.

I have something else I want to try first, and I'm positively giddy about it.

As I abruptly pull away, he pops off my breast and licks his lips. "Argh," he bellows in frustration and lets his head fall back onto the pillow.

"You ready to try this, babe?" I ask him.

I'm so freaking excited.

"Nervous, but ready."

I've never had this done to me, and sure as hell have never done this to anyone. It's a first for Sawyer too, but he's willing to try.

I grab the small, silicone teardrop-shaped implement and the lube. After applying a generous amount to the plug, I scoot down his body.

"Bend your knees and spread your legs," I command.

He complies immediately. "I will literally do anything you say when you use that tone with me, princess."

"I know," I tease.

His chuckle is warm and travels straight to my clit.

When I first make contact with his tight hole, he flinches backward.

"Ah-ah-ah. You have to hold still."

"Yes, ma'am."

His body is a work of art, even at this angle. I glance up at his torso and can tell from the pinch of his cheeks that he's squinting and gnashing his jaw.

"You need to relax, babe. It's not gonna hurt. From everything I've read, you're going to love it."

He nods and forces a tight exhale.

"That's better."

I run the slippery tip from the underside of his balls to his hole and swirl around the entrance a few times before pressing gently. The head slips in with less resistance than I expected. But it's the beginner size, so it's fairly small. Plus, I had already warmed him up with my finger.

His cock bobs in my face, and I can't help but lean forward and run my tongue from base to tip, using my free hand to angle it into my mouth. As I plunge my mouth down his shaft, I press the plug farther into his ass, drawing a sharp hiss from him.

I work his dick in and out of my mouth at a leisurely pace as I mirror the movement with the toy in his ass, inching a little deeper with each stroke.

"Holy fuck, baby," he rasps.

After a few more strokes, he matches my tempo with subtle thrusts.

He likes it. I knew he would.

After removing his cock from my mouth, I praise him. "You're doing so good, babe. How does it feel?"

He chuckles awkwardly. "Ah-ha-ha. Surprisingly good. Weird, but good."

"It's hot as fucking hell for me too."

"Next time, I do you."

"Deal."

Yes, yes, yes, yes.

Leaving the butt plug inside him, I give the wide base a soft tap with my fingertips, eliciting a moan from him. With one hand slowly stroking his cock, I turn my attention to his balls, drawing one, then the other, fully into my mouth.

As I increase the suction, the curses start flying from his kissable mouth. "Oh, fuck, Sammy. So good. God dammit. Fuck! *Please* don't stop."

For the next few minutes, I alternate between tapping the plug, sucking his dick, and squeezing his balls. His chest heaves, and his hips pulse with my movements.

All the while, he mumbles his obscene adoration of me. "I love you so fucking much. Oh my fucking hell. You're so damn good at that, baby."

When he's teetering on the edge of climax, I stop all my ministrations. I want him to finish inside me this time. Leaving the plug in place, I crawl up his body while he catches his breath.

"Kiss me," I say before sealing our lips.

He opens for me, tasting and teasing my mouth. As arousal shoots from the tip of my tongue straight to my clit, my hips rock over his erection again. The slip and slide of our flesh is intoxicating, as is each thrust of his tip across my sensitive clit.

A few seconds later, he glides inside me.

Oops.

I was going to sit on his face first, but this is nice too.

Breaking the kiss, I sit up and begin riding him hard, with my hands braced over his strong chest. Since he can't see me, I can stare unabashedly at the contraction of his ridged abs as he drives into me from below. He's freaking perfection.

I suspect he's concentrating on holding back his release, but I want to see the pleasure reflecting in his eyes. Those dark pools are too beautiful to leave covered this long. Reaching forward, I lift the blindfold to his forehead.

He blinks a few times before locking his gaze with mine. The sight of him writhing under me and staring so deeply into my eyes brings me seconds away from my own orgasm.

My hips buck wildly, dragging my clit over his firm pelvis as he fills me again and again. Our pace becomes frantic, and my moans and cries fill the air, mingling with his breathy groans.

"Fuck, baby. Feels so good. Can I come?" he asks, a look of desperation befalling his striking face.

The way he asks for my permission causes a tingle to start low in my stomach. I lean forward and lick his jaw.

That fucking jaw just does something to me. Something carnal.

"How. Do. You. Ask?" I pant out between thrusts as I bear down even harder on him.

"May I *please* come?" he drawls.

That does it.

This amazing, sculpted warrior of a man submitting to me and begging for permission to come is my absolute undoing every damn time. My release explodes deep within me, sending waves of pleasure all over my body.

I arch my back and feel my thighs squeeze around his middle as my orgasm shatters me. "Yes. Now, babe. Come for me."

Lights flash behind my eyes. I'm so euphoric with glorious pleasure I barely hear him roaring his release under me.

I collapse on top of him, struggling to catch my breath.

"Hottest sex of my life," he mutters into my hair a few seconds later.

Tilting my head, I meet his eyes. "I love you," I tell him.

"I know," he deadpans.

I chuckle. "I deserved that."

Before he gets uncomfortable, I unfasten his cuffs and let him take me in his arms. We cuddle together for a few minutes, soaking up the afterglow. My love well slowly fills to the brim.

After a few minutes, I break the comfortable silence. "We need to get cleaned up. Everyone is going to kill us if we're late."

He whips his head over to the bedside table to check the time. "Holy shit. We do need to hurry."

I rise from the bed and spin around to see what's taking him so long. His eyes are round with panic.

"What's the matter?" I ask.

"You forgot something. *Inside me.*"

My eyes shoot wide as a boisterous laugh springs from my chest. While I'm guffawing, Sawyer's still frozen in place.

"Does it just stay inside forever? Is it part of me now? What do we do?"

Doubled over now, I slap my hand on the side of the bed a few times before I'm finally able to speak. "Hold still," I tell him as I climb back onto the bed.

With a little work, I slowly and gently remove the plug, thus saving my love from being traumatized forever. His arms and legs flop to both sides once it's safely no longer *a part of him*. Silly fucker.

We shower and quickly get ready before heading out just five minutes late. Fortunately, my hair and makeup will be done once we get to the venue, and neither of us needs to put on our wedding clothes until later.

We're at a traffic light when Sawyer taps his phone a few times and turns up the radio. He looks over at me, wearing a playful smirk as the opening notes of Bruno Mars's "Marry You" start to play.

"Seriously?" Incredulity coats my words.

He shrugs. "Seems appropriate. Don't you think?"

Beaming back at him, I nod. He leans over the console for a quick smooch. By the time the light turns green, we're both singing along.

"You just sang an entire song," he says in astonishment. "And it was a happy song. Not an angry one."

My brows furrow. "Yeah. And?"

His Adam's apple bobs, catching my attention briefly before he explains, "I've never seen you do that before. Not since... before."

My face falls while I rack my brain. That can't be right. Is it?

Taking my hand, he gives it a squeeze. "I can see you're trying to work it out, but you should know better than to doubt me."

I know my love of music dried up at some point. Is it possible that, after all these years, I'm able to sing again? Not that I was ever that great of a singer by any stretch of the imagination. But I did enjoy belting out my favorite songs along with the radio when I was younger.

Shaking my head, I agree, "Yeah. I think you're right. I guess I'm just happy."

Finally happy.

He raises the back of my hand to his lips as I wipe away a stray tear with the other.

So damn happy.

About three hours later, he holds my gaze as I slowly glide down the aisle. He looks so gallant in his linen shirt with the single red rose pinned over his chest and a big smile stretched from ear to ear. My heart speeds up as I get closer.

Big Al, Leo, and Drew all look great too. But none as handsome as my guy.

The wedding is on the beach, and the weather is absolutely perfect.

When I get to the officiant, Sawyer gives me that sexy wink as his panty-incinerating dimple appears.

I take my place beside Millie and Fiona, Sue's other bridesmaids, and turn to face the crowd with a small bouquet covering my soon-to-be expanding stomach.

A solo violin and a Celtic harp play an ethereal-sounding tune with an unmistakably Irish lilt. Suddenly, the small crowd gasps as Sue appears at the end of the aisle, with her niece walking a few steps ahead of her to sprinkle rose petals. Their dresses match, as do their lacy headpieces with a touch of blue ribbon woven into the Irish lace.

It's precious.

Reflexively, one of my hands cradles my tummy.

I glance over at my brother and watch him wipe a tear away as his bride approaches. Sawyer claps him on the back, giving him a comforting shake.

Oh, the big lug.

I can't wait for their roles to swap for our big day, with Leo standing beside Sawyer as his best man.

However, unlike Sue, I refuse to accept a proposal uttered during sex. I already told Sawyer he better be down on one knee if he expects me to take him seriously.

Then again, he does a lot of sexual things to me on his knees. So I guess I'll need to be clearer with my instructions.

After exchanging rings, Leo and Sue promise to love each other forever while their hands are tied together with ribbon in a traditional handfasting ceremony. Once they kiss to raucous applause, the newlyweds lead the recessional behind an actual Celtic piper.

I take Sawyer's elbow as he escorts me back down the aisle. "You look absolutely breathtaking, princess."

Too choked up with emotion, I can only nod my silent thanks.

Within minutes, we're all whisked under the covered reception pavilion as the party begins.

Sue's family is huge. And very, *very* Irish.

To be more specific, drinks are passed out within minutes of the ceremony ending — Guinness and Irish whiskey to start. Her grumpiest brother Shane has one in each fist, and he isn't sharing.

Sue and Leo are getting doted on by Sue's adorable parents.

Sawyer grabs one of the thick, dark beers from Callum and hands it to me with a sweet smile.

In an Irish accent, he says, "Here ya go, lass. 'Tis an Irish wedding, so we'll be getting totally wankered tonight."

"I think I'll pass," I tell him with a slight head shake.

"I'll grab you a wine, babe," he replies with a knowing wink.

"No, thanks. Just water, please."

His head cocks to one side in confusion since I'm not known to pass up wine. Before he can question me, Mom comes up beside me and brings me in for a hug.

"I'll go get you a water," Sawyer says as he excuses himself.

Pressing a soft kiss to my cheek, Mom pulls back and beams. "You look so beautiful, Samantha."

"So do you, Mom."

"I can't believe all my babies are happily in love. I never thought I'd see the day. It's just..." She trails off as her eyes narrow over my shoulder.

I spin my head to see what's caught her eye.

Oh my gosh.

It's not a *what*... but a *who*.

"Aunt Tilly, is that you?"

She smiles the same sweet grin she's always had. The one that matches my mom's. The same gentle smile that comforted us all those times she came over to take us away from Mom and Dad's fighting.

She opens her arms wide, and I run into them without hesitation.

After exchanging pleasantries and about seventy-two more hugs, I finally bring her over to introduce her to Sawyer.

My mom looks on from the edge of the crowd while worrying her hands. Her face is a mask of concern and something else.

Sadness.

Oh, Mom. Make your peace with your sister.

If there is ever a night for a reconciliation, it's tonight. After all, weddings and babies have that magical power to bring people together, mending old wounds.

I'm in the middle of telling Aunt Tilly how I escaped from a trunk when Sawyer grabs my hand, tugging gently. "Maybe we should let them talk." He tips his chin to my right, where my mother is inching closer.

Aunt Tilly shifts her shoulders back and puts on a tight smile.

"I'll finish the story later. Don't you dare leave, okay?" I know I shouldn't be, but suddenly I'm concerned Mom is about to drive her away.

My aunt hugs me once more and whispers, "I promise I won't leave yet, Sammy."

Feeling wistful, I pull away, and Sawyer tugs me over to an empty table in the corner of the pavilion. As we sit, I notice my brothers and some Redleg guys doing whiskey shots with Sue's five brothers at the bar. They even have a silly chant that I can't understand.

Oh boy.

It's early yet, and those guys have probably already polished off their first bottle. Glad I have a built-in excuse not to drink, or else I wouldn't be able to remember any of Sawyer's upcoming best man toast. And he's worked so hard on it. He's been perfecting his Irish accent in an attempt to make Sue laugh at one of his voices.

"Talk to me," Sawyer says, capturing my attention by trailing his fingertips over my wrists.

"What do you want to talk about, babe?" I ask, innocent as a cherub.

"You're drinking water." He narrows his eyes at me. "What's wrong? Don't you feel well?"

He's not going to let this go. Sawyer is way too observant, and I know he's noticed I've been acting a little off these last few days.

I smile wide and bat my eyelashes. "Nothing is wrong."

Shaking his head, he slides back in his chair, creating a little space between him and the table. He pats his lap, beckoning me over.

I glance around to see if anyone is watching us. The reception is incredibly informal and already turning into one big party, so it's not like anyone will notice if I cuddle up on his lap. Right?

Taking my seat on his knee, I nuzzle his neck, taking a big whiff of his cologne. It smells different than it used to, probably the hormone changes. But it still smells heavenly.

He holds me close with one big hand resting against my lower back. "Are you going to talk, or do I need to tickle it out of you?"

I pull back to catch his eyes. Once I've got his full attention, I give him a quick kiss, then lean toward his ear. "Remember those odds?"

"Odds?" he asks. "Odds of what?"

The music has picked up, but I'm pretty sure he'll still be able to hear me.

"Twenty-five percent."

He squeezes my knee and draws his brows in tight. Shaking his head, he says, "I don't get it. Twenty-five percent of what?"

Moving his hand from my knee, I place it across my lower tummy and cover it with my palm. "Twenty-five percent chance," I say again, opening my eyes wide as if trying to telegraph it from my brain to his.

His gaze moves from my face to our joined hands, then back up.

"Twenty-five percent," he says. "Twenty-five percent. *Twenty-five.* Oh my God!" His head tilts to one side, and the skin at the corner of his eyes crinkles. "Babe, are you saying what I think you're saying?"

"You're going to be a daddy, Sawyer."

"Princess, don't play with me," he says, his voice shaky.

"I'm not kidding. I'm pregnant. I took a test this morning because I noticed my period was *way* late."

"Seriously?"

I nod, feeling happiness start to leak from my eyes. His answering smile is pure rapture, and his eyes fill with joyful tears.

"I love you so fucking much, Sammy," he whispers against my lips.

After claiming my mouth in a passionate kiss, he pulls back and shakes his head. "You're giving me a family."

"Don't be so sappy, stud," I jest with a playful roll of my eyes. "We played baby roulette, and it's true that the house always wins."

Wrapping both arms around me, he pulls me tight against his firm chest and peppers frantic kisses over my cheek, neck, and jawline.

"The house didn't win, Sammy. We did."

Thanks for reading Sammy and Sawyer's story

BONUS SCENE: If you'd like to read a bonus scene taking place one year in the future, scan this QR code with your phone's camera.

Acknowledgments

Dear Reader:

Thank you for reading Sawyer and Sammy's love story. A story of healing, found family, and weathering whatever life throws at you and coming out better on the other side of the storm.

I hope you loved reading it as much as I loved writing it. I'm obsessed with Sawyer and all his voices. Don't tell Cort Amos, but Sawyer might have dethroned him. What can I say? I'm a sucker for the funny hero with golden retriever energy.

Overall, it was a blast to write this story and bring these characters to life. I laughed so much along the way and fell in love with them a little more each day. Even editing it was a riot at times.

Not gonna lie, though. At times, finishing this book was a challenge. This year has been a tough one for me. Medical issues, a broken ankle, covid, family situations, and more have made me seriously question if I have it in me to keep pursuing this dream. It took me twice as long to write this one as I expected, but I kept chipping away. It's a tough business, even if you're completely devoted and working day in and day out — there is no guarantee of success. Sometimes, I feel like I'm spinning my wheels trying to get somewhere I'm not meant to be.

But nothing has ever made me happier than writing love stories filled with laughs and swoons and steam. And my loyal fans and my family have made me feel so loved and supported that I don't think I could stop writing even if I wanted to. They might riot if I quit, and I can't have that on my conscience.

I love you all. Thanks for keeping me going even when I felt like throwing in the towel.

And now for the rest of my gratitude.

Thanks to my sister Jennifer for helping with anything I need even when her own plate is overfilled. And thanks for loving the book and cheering me on. *I love you, OG muffin.*

Thanks to my amazing cover designer Kim Wilson of KiWi Cover Designs. Another beautiful job. And this photo? *Oh my gosh!* Garrett Riley is exactly how I pictured Sawyer. And best of all, he's actually a former member of the US Air Force. How hot is that? Chris of CJC Photography captured him spectacularly, and he's also a joy to work with.

My beta reading team was amazing with this release - as always. Megan and Allie, you've helped me more than you will ever know.

And now about my editor. This woman is a fearless and tireless workhorse. Wait. That doesn't sound as nice as I intended. I take it back. She's a unicorn goddess who knows my characters inside and out — often better than I know them myself. She works so hard that I often worry for her sanity. Thanks so much, Mindy. You're my ultimate BB and always will be.

Thanks to Kelsey for volunteering to help with ARCs again — goddess alert — and Debbie, Mike, and Bubba for keeping the group popping and lively. My Street and ARC teams — thanks for coming on this journey with me and helping me grow as an author. Shout out to Jodi and Bryony for being awesome fans! And a super huge thank you to the rest of my Junkies.

Cheers! Hope the rest of 2022 is a much smoother ride for us all.
Love, *Jackie*

Also by Jackie Walker

About the Author

Jackie is a new face on the romance scene destined to shake things up with her signature blend of light-hearted comedy, over-the-top characters and romantic heartwarming moments. A voracious romance reader herself, Jackie writes stories featuring the four Ss: Snark, Swoons, Steam and Sarcasm. Her heroines are badass, and her heroes are easy on the eyes and heavy on the charm.

When she is not writing funny stories about swoony heroes and the women who get to play with them, she is reading all types of romance novels or taking care of her army of cats and her teenage son (who also speaks fluent sarcasm).

Jackie
WALKER
EVERYONE GETS A HAPPY ENDING

Connect with Jackie

Website, Blog and Newsletter Sign-up: www.authorjackiewalker.com
Facebook Reader Group: Jackie's Junkies
Facebook: @AuthorJackieWalker
Instagram: @AuthorJackieWalker
Goodreads: JackieWalker
TikTok: AuthorJackieWalker

Made in the USA
Middletown, DE
06 December 2024

66300924R00288